UNDER A SUMMER SKYE

Sue Moorcroft writes award-winning contemporary fiction of life and love. *A Summer to Remember* won the Goldsboro Books Contemporary Romantic Novel award, *The Little Village Christmas* and *A Christmas Gift* were *Sunday Times* bestsellers and *The Christmas Promise* went to #1 in the Kindle chart. She also writes short stories, serials, articles, columns, courses and writing 'how to'. She is the current president of the Romantic Novelist's Association.

An army child, Sue was born in Germany then lived in Cyprus, Malta and the UK, and still loves to travel. Her other loves include writing (the best job in the world), reading, watching Formula 1 on TV, hanging out with friends, dancing, yoga, wine and chocolate.

If you're interested in being part of #TeamSueMoorcroft you can find more information at www.suemoorcroft. com by clicking on 'Street Team'. If you prefer to sign up to receive news of Sue and her books, go to www. suemoorcroft.com and click on 'Newsletter'. You can follow @SueMoorcroft on Twitter, @suemoorcroftauthor on Instagram, or Facebook.com/sue.moorcroft.3 and Facebook.com/SueMoorcroftAuthor.

Also by Sue Moorcroft:

The Christmas Promise
Just For the Holidays
The Little Village Christmas
One Summer in Italy
A Christmas Gift
A Summer to Remember
Let it Snow
Summer on a Sunny Island
Christmas Wishes
Under the Italian Sun
A Home in the Sun
Under the Mistletoe
Summer at the French Café
A White Christmas on Winter Street
An Italian Island Summer
The Christmas Love Letters

Under a Summer Skye

Sue Moorcroft

avon.

Published by AVON
A division of HarperCollins*Publishers* Ltd
1 London Bridge Street
London SE1 9GF

www.harpercollins.co.uk

HarperCollins*Publishers*
Macken House, 39/40 Mayor Street Upper,
Dublin 1, D01 C9W8
Ireland

A Paperback Original 2024
1
First published in Great Britain by HarperCollins*Publishers* 2024

A catalogue copy of this book is available from the British Library.

ISBN: 978-0-00-863681-4

This novel is entirely a work of fiction. The names, characters and
incidents portrayed in it are the work of the author's imagination.
Any resemblance to actual persons, living or
dead, events or localities is entirely coincidental.

Typeset in Sabon LT Std by
Palimpsest Book Production Limited, Falkirk, Stirlingshire

Printed and bound in UK using 100% Renewable
Electricity at CPI Group (UK) Ltd

This book contains FSC™ certified paper and other controlled
sources to ensure responsible forest management.

For more information visit: www.harpercollins.co.uk/green

Acknowledgements

Various people have kindly shared information or insight that enabled me to write *Under a Summer Skye*, but I'd like to start by thanking my editor Helen Huthwaite, whose idea it was that I should write about a whole new village on the beautiful Isle of Skye in the Inner Hebrides. Without her, I might never have travelled to that inspiring part of the world and found the perfect spot to create a pretty village between Armadale and Isleornsay on the Sleat Peninsular. Thanks also to my husband Michael Matthews for sharing the driving from Northamptonshire and trying not to talk whenever I said, 'I'm thinking'. Further heartfelt thanks to:

DS Adi Sharpe from Northamptonshire Police who advised on traffic accidents and the police's likely responsibility to investigate if fresh accusations are made years after the event.

Dr Alison Turnbull, veterinary surgeon, for all the advice on found dogs and what part a veterinary surgery might play.

Dieter Rencken, Formula 1 journalist, for our informative conversation about news agencies and the commercial opportunities of a busy website.

Karen Byrom, who I first knew as fiction editor and feature writer for *My Weekly* magazine, who helped me put together Deveron's career path, and advised on the ethics of journalism.

Gill Stewart for generously advising on Scottish matters and reading an early iteration of the manuscript.

Singer and musician Jacqueline Barron kindly advised on session musicians and how I might track them (and their obituaries) down.

My brother Trevor Moorcroft aided me with research into travel, Brittany, locating old news articles and the mechanics of adoption in England and Wales, considerably lightening my load.

Jo Mason-Lee, who introduced me to the topic of Logophobia.

Any mistakes in the subjects covered above are mine alone.

It's a constant joy to work with my publishers, Team Avon at HarperCollins UK led by wonderful Helen

Huthwaite, and reap the rewards of their expertise and friendly professionalism. My thanks to every team member.

Juliet Pickering of Blake Friedmann Literary Agency is the most awesome of awesome agents, taking the widest view of my career and going the extra mile if that's what's best for me. I'm so grateful.

A special mention to Team Sue Moorcroft, who support me so well. Some are ARC readers, or book bloggers who join my blog tours; they're all enthusiastic readers who take the time to post about my books and generally spread the word. They also answer requests for help with character or place names. And when I asked Team Sue Moorcroft if anyone would like to volunteer their dog to appear in the book as a stray who turns up in the grounds of Rothach Hall, I had an entire beauty parade of well-loved pets to choose from. I selected Daisy, so thanks to Janina Simpson for letting her appear and apologies if the personality (dogality?) I gave her is wide of the mark.

Most of all, thanks to my wonderful readers, who read and enjoy my books, chat to me on social media, share my posts, send me nice messages, post positive reviews, or just quietly read and enjoy. Every book is for you! And if you haven't found the comparatively new Sue Moorcroft Author Group yet, it's at https://www.facebook.com/groups/308079486336770. Come and join us!

To Phoebe Rey Sunshine
for aptly bringing sunshine into our lives

Prologue

Nine years ago, Suffolk, England

Thea's heart tried to claw itself out of her chest as she stooped over the motionless figure sprawled in the road. His yellow visibility vest looked jaunty in the sunlight, but his face, where not bleeding, was grey. One leg was twisted through the frame of a crumpled bicycle.

Panting as if she'd run a four-minute-mile, she gabbled into the phone in her sweating hand. 'I need an ambulance to Ingham Road, just outside Wordwell.' Her voice trembled as she blundered over whatever the operator was saying on the other end of the call. 'My car . . . well, this cyclist was stopped in the middle of the road just after the sharp bend. Nobody could have avoided him. He's breathing, but his leg's . . . twisted. He's wearing a helmet but there's blood.' Her voice caught as she glanced over her shoulder to where her silver car stood skewed across the asphalt. In the morning sun, the windscreen had transformed into a million twinkling squares that somehow hung together above her crumpled bonnet.

The voice in her ear was asking patient questions. Finally, Thea managed to tune in to answer some. 'I'm alone, apart from the cyclist . . . Yes, I'll stay till the police arrive.'

When the 999 call ended, she crouched beside the cyclist, stomach rolling at the raw flesh of his ruined leg. 'Keep breathing,' she begged him. 'Help's coming.' The strength leached from her legs, and she sank onto the scratchy road surface. *Just keep breathing.*

She'd no idea how much time passed before she heard the wailing of sirens and then the emergency services arrived, blue lights flashing. The ambulance crew checked whether Thea was hurt then ushered her aside while they focused on the unconscious cyclist. A police officer, a woman in her thirties, fair hair pulled into a knot, crouched beside Thea.

Thea barely gave her time to speak. 'He stopped in the middle of the road around the bend! There was no way to avoid him.'

The police officer gave her a keen but not unkind glance. 'And it's your car, is it? Were you driving? Did anyone else see what happened?'

'Yes, it's my car.' And, on a quavering breath: 'I was driving. I was alone. I don't think anyone else could have seen.' She glanced at the hedges either side of the lane, between the road and the fields. The first houses of the village were half a mile away.

More questions. Thea tried to concentrate and answer over the blood rushing in her ears. The police officer made notes. 'I'm going to have to take a breath sample. It's standard procedure.'

'I haven't drunk alcohol for days.' Thea's voice shook at the idea of being breathalysed, a procedure she'd only seen on TV.

The police officer smiled reassuringly. 'Then you've nothing to worry about. Just standard stuff.' She returned briefly to her vehicle, its lights still flashing, then came back with an instrument like a fat phone with a protruding tube. She held it towards Thea's mouth. 'Just blow in the mouthpiece . . . keep blowing, keeping blowing . . . that's great.' After a few moments, she turned the device towards Thea, exhibiting the green light. 'Thank you. You've provided a negative sample.'

After checking Thea was OK to be left, the officer crossed to the ambulance crew. Thea, light-headed from the blowing as well as the shock, heard her whisper, 'Did you recognise her? She stars in that garden competition show on TV.'

She shivered. She was no 'star'. *Garden Gladiators* was half gardening programme, half reality show. Though Thea enjoyed the excitement of appearing in it, to 'star', to her, would mean being paid – which she wasn't. She received only expenses and her usual salary. Her employers – Cherlington House – as location providers, were the ones who got the fees.

Being recognised right now felt uncomfortable, like the unexpected snark her appearances garnered on social media: *Bring back Charlie Dimmock* or: *Why's the camera on Thea Wynter so much? She's so ordinary.* The judgy meanness of strangers hurt, but she was on *Garden Gladiators* because she enjoyed it – and perhaps because she'd got together with Ivan, a blonde, handsome camera operator. Filming of the fourth series of *Garden Gladiators* had just been completed, and Ivan had moved in with Thea. Everything was coming up roses . . . until this.

She didn't hear whether the ambulance crew knew or cared that she was 'on the telly', but the police officer returned with a bald, stubbly paramedic who checked back in with her. 'How are you doing, duck? Feeling shocked?'

Thea looked up the road to where the other paramedic was bending over the cyclist, now in the back of the ambulance. Revulsion and guilt engulfed her. 'I'm OK. It's that poor guy who needs the care.'

The police officer took photos and measurements, then Thea called a tow service to take her vehicle to a garage. The officer regarded her assessingly. 'Why don't you hop in my car? I'll drop you at your home, seeing as Wordwell's only up the road. I need an account from you of what happened, and we may need to speak to you at a later stage.'

'Right . . . yes.' On rubbery legs, Thea rose and climbed into the back of the police car, still dazed and anxious. Her sister Ezzie was scheduled to arrive at Thea's house about now and Thea wanted a sisterly hug much more than to talk about the horror of the accident, the broken figure on the ground and the flashing lights.

Ezzie, along with their eldest sister Valentina and Valentina's son Barnaby, were Thea's everything.

What if the cyclist died? Would Thea's account of events be believed? Nightmare visions of a court case and even prison flooded her mind. Was her family about to be torn apart?

Chapter One

Thea had interrupted her lunchtime walk around the grand and sweeping grounds of Rothach Hall to say hello to Clive and Mary, the elderly donkey and pony who'd had the good luck to retire to a grassy paddock with a world-beating view of the silvery sea of the Sound of Sleat and the craggy Scottish mainland. Clive's punk-rock mane was darker than his portly body, while Mary's chestnut coat had turned grey around her eyes and above splayed old hoofs. On the gate hung a sign: 'Mary Pony and Clive Donkey' painted by the grandchildren of the owners. Between their field and the turreted grey stone hall lay first the trees and grass of the park, then the gardens, terraces and lawns closer to stately Rothach Hall, all of which Thea tended in the course of her job as head gardener.

These beautiful surroundings were her happy place, where she breathed the clear Skye air and relished the peace and serenity of the island. When a man shot across

5

the paddock towards the burn, Thea gasped in shock. 'Hey!' she cried in outrage, making poor Mary toss her bony old head. 'No visitors in with the animals!'

But, arms and legs pumping, dark curls blowing, the man fired himself across the sloping grass like an arrow beneath the puffy white clouds in the blue June sky. At the fence, he scrambled over, half falling to the ground. Thea knew both bank and burn to be thick with great leaves of gunnera, fern and even ash tree seedlings that were on her list to remove. 'Ouch,' she muttered, reaching for her phone. She'd have to inform Tavish, the manager at the hall, that a mad sprinter seemed to have missed his way to the Olympics.

She paused, finger poised without tapping Tavish's number. The man was already returning to the rail and clambering slowly over it, his bottom half drenched. His arms cradled something small and still. He knelt and placed it carefully on the grass.

Thea shoved away her phone and, not bothering to fumble with the strong gate fastening – Clive could undo simple bolts with his teeth – scaled the metal bars and began running down the slope, her work boots so familiar on her feet that they could have been running shoes.

As she approached, the man's head lifted, his jaw dark with stubble. 'Slow down, don't frighten her,' he called in a soft Scottish accent. On the ground before him, like a mop the cleaners hadn't wrung out, lay a small dog, her bedraggled fur plastered with weed. Tongue lolling, her chest heaved as she struggled for breath. 'Just got to her in time, poor wee girl. I saw her from the bridge, all tangled in the undergrowth.' He stroked the floppy ears as he nodded towards where the drive up to the hall included a stone humpbacked bridge and a steel-grey SUV.

Catching her breath, Thea revised her opinion of him as a trespassing, deranged Olympic sprinter and pigeonholed him instead as a fantastic, heroic human being. 'Well done. She only looks a few months old. And all skin and bone.'

'Aye. But she's easier now. She'll recover.' He flashed a smile as Thea knelt beside him.

As if to agree, the dog rolled onto her chest and shook her head, spattering them with cold, brackish water. She coughed, vomited, snorted, then licked her nose. Finally, she managed to wag the tip of her tail before flopping back, clearly not ready for further exertion.

'Oh, dear.' Thea bit her lip, brushing back her ponytail as the breeze teased it over her shoulder.

'It's good she's cleared her lungs,' the man observed pragmatically. Then he yanked his shirt over his head, exposing a black T-shirt with a wet hem. He wrapped the dry fabric of his shirt around the tiny canine, carefully slid his hands beneath her and cradled her again as he climbed to his feet. 'She's weak, though. Is there a vet nearby on Skye? Or must I take her to the mainland?'

Thea rose, too. 'There's a new practice in Armadale, a few miles down the peninsula. They shut at two on Saturdays, so you'd better leave soon. Shall I give you the address for your sat nav?' Her heart turned over at the poor wretch snuggling so trustingly into his arms.

He hesitated. 'It'll be difficult to drive and to hold her, and I've no travel crate, of course. I'm actually here to see someone – a Thea Wynter.' He turned to tramp up the slope towards the car abandoned on the drive, ignoring what must be the yucky feeling of sodden jeans clinging to his legs. Though it was what Thea considered a perfect

7

Isle of Skye early summer day, the breezy brightness didn't mean high temperatures.

She fell into step with him, grinning because her green ground-staff uniform with 'Rothach Hall' embroidered in red had probably already given him an idea of who she was, even if safety prevented her from wearing a pin-on 'head gardener' badge. 'I'm Thea. You must be here for the seasonal gardener's job. You're so late I'd taken my lunch hour. When you didn't answer your phone, I thought maybe you were stuck somewhere on the narrow roads, but if you were delayed by saving a drowning dog, I forgive you. You're soaked,' she added unnecessarily.

He glanced her way. His eyes were nowhere near as dark as his hair, but hazel with hints of green and ginger, like the weed-strewn rocks of Rothach Bay at low tide. 'I have dry clothes in my car, if there's somewhere to change.'

She crooked her arms in an invitation for him to pass over his burden. 'If I hold the dog, you can drive us up to the hall, then change in the studio apartment that will go with the job. Your application said that you'd like to live in, didn't it? Then we can whizz to the vet's together and I'll interview you as we go.' His application had stated his name as either Tim or Tom, but she couldn't remember which.

'Um . . . aye, OK,' he said, as if taking a second to review the idea before deciding it was workable. He transferred the slight, damp weight of the dog who, with her cute face and draggled fur, looked like a teddy bear who'd fallen on hard times. Then he fished out his keys and blotted them on a dry area of T-shirt. 'I hope the beeper still works.' He pointed it at the grey SUV, the back seat and rear compartment of which were stuffed with boxes and bags.

The beeper co-operated. Thea climbed slowly into the big vehicle, unsettled by the profusion of boxes and bags. Either he was confident of getting the job and had brought his worldly possessions, or he was living out of his car. But soon they were bowling past the car park where the sun flashed from a row of windscreens, and up the drive between the south lawns towards a pair of doors on ornate strap hinges beneath an arch. The grey granite grandeur of Rothach Hall rose above them, all windows and chimneys, its turret topped by a conical roof. From three flagpoles flew the Scottish Saltire alongside the flags of Sweden and Norway, representing the mixed heritage of the Larssons, the family who owned the hall. Members of the public strolled the lawns and gardens, admiring the hall or the towering pines and spruces. Their day would also likely include visiting the Nature Café for scones, Scottish ice cream or haggis burgers with a side opportunity to buy Rothach Hall souvenir mugs or Clive Donkey and Mary Pony cuddly toys.

In Thea's arms, the dog lay as quiet as a baby fawn its mother had hidden in the forest. 'Bear right of the house,' she directed Tim or Tom. 'The tradesmen's entrance is around the back, as the saying goes.' Then, when he'd followed the small offshoot of the drive, 'Park beside the pick-up truck by the greenhouse.' She glanced down as a small, light, warm feeling tickled her hand. 'Oh, bless. She just licked me.' Her heart turned over in her chest with a giant thunk.

'Good sign,' he answered economically, and climbed gingerly from the car, pulling wet denim from his legs, before hurrying around to open the passenger door as Thea needed both her arms for the dog.

Awkwardly, she scrambled out. 'I'll show you where

to change, then I'll find a towel for your canine rescue.' Thank goodness Tim or Tom had spotted the dog struggling in the burn. In some places the water ran fast, in a race to tumble down the steep crag to the village of Rothach and the bay below.

Tim or Tom opened his vehicle's tailgate and rustled about. When he'd slammed it closed, he clutched a pile of clothes and a pair of trainers. She led him to the building at a right-angle to the greenhouse, which housed the staff apartments. 'The keypad gets you through the outer door.' She tapped in the code and then shouldered the door open, holding it with one foot so he could edge past.

He glanced around the whitewashed passage. 'Do many people live here?'

'Four. Gwen the housekeeper has a proper apartment at the back of the hall. These studios are available to others on a first-come, first-served basis. Three are currently occupied by full-time housekeeping staff – one down here and two upstairs. Only this one's empty and as I was expecting you, I have the key.' She shifted the dog onto a forearm and searched the pocket of her dark green work trousers with her free hand. The dog didn't react, either trusting Thea or too spent to care. She unlocked room two and shoved open the door. 'There you go. Get changed, have a quick look round – there's a laundry room at the end – and I'll meet you at the pick-up.' There was something intent in Tim or Tom's eyes that – while she accepted that one person needed to drive and one to hold the dog – made her unwilling to climb into his vehicle for a trip beyond Rothach's grounds. Those bin liners could hold anything from clothes to stolen gold.

10

'OK.' Slowly, he stepped inside.

Thea retraced her steps, concerned that the dog had begun to shiver and not about to hang around while Tim or Tom changed. She hurried across the paved courtyard to the mud room, where staff members had access to lockers, coat hooks and space for boots on the cracked terracotta floor. Once she'd established that she had the place to herself, Thea began to croon. 'Did you think we'd never get here, little dog? This cupboard's full of towels for staff caught in the rain. No one will mind if I lend you one, will they?' It was highly unlikely that the dog had an opinion, but she glanced up and panted, her eyes bright.

Thea knelt on the cold floor, unwrapped the damp shirt and stood the skinny, dirty, matted dog on it while she shook out the towel and began to use it gently on the small body. 'Where are your humans? Although anyone who'd let a dog get so scrawny is barely worthy of the name "human",' she added darkly.

If the dog knew, she wasn't telling, but shook herself and wagged her tail. Her fur, which was probably a pale grey or cream when clean, crinkled like a bad perm.

'What a sweetie.' Thea gently picked debris from the fur and lavishly grabbed another clean towel for the journey to the vet.

This human, at least, would play her part in helping this little pooch.

Chapter Two

Deveron Dowie kicked free of his clammy boxers, jeans and socks. As only the edge of his T-shirt had touched the freezing water of the burn, he whipped it off and used it to dry his legs. Once dressed in dry joggers and a hoodie, he took the time to examine his surroundings. 'Studio apartment' Thea Wynter had called it and it was a bit like his old student accommodation at uni. However, the bed was a double, and the white-tiled bathroom with a shower over a compact bath was nicer than his mouldy old student wet room with its odorous, reluctant drain. Back in the main room, he inspected a kitchenette with a fridge and microwave and space for toaster and kettle. He'd had better in the comfortable Inverness home he'd shared with his now ex-wife Adaira, but he'd definitely had worse.

He pictured himself living behind gracious Rothach Hall on the Isle of Skye; spending his days doing whatever job Thea Wynter thought he was here for. Compared to surfing his mum's sofa back in Dumfries as he'd been about to do, the tiny apartment felt like a sanctuary – an opportunity, however unplanned. It seemed to say: *What would you do to live here?*

In his current circumstances, freelancing for a sensationalist, clickbait website and hating every word he wrote . . . quite a lot.

Stooping to scrape his damp, dirty clothes from the floor, he used them to give the floorboards a wipe, then he left the quiet studio apartment. A glance at the laundry room revealed two washing machines and two dryers. When he went back outside, Thea was in the driver's seat of the pick-up, her face tilted down towards the dog in her arms, its face angled up, ears twitching like floppy radar dishes.

The shirt he'd wrapped the dog in had been left on the roof of his car and he threw it and the rest of his wet things into the footwell, then jogged over to the pick-up with 'Rothach Hall' in green on the side, slid into the passenger seat and returned the apartment key.

'You look more comfortable,' Thea remarked. She was a compact woman with her dark hair in a knot atop her head, and she looked small behind the wheel of the big vehicle. 'Little dog's still not warm, so I've made her a towel toga.'

The dog made a laughing face, mouth open and ears flattened and, after securing his seatbelt, he extended his arms to receive her. 'She has a nice doggy grin.'

Thea reversed the truck, then eased the vehicle past the greenhouse. 'So,' she said, as if the word stepped her into professional mode. 'This takes us to the staff entrance into the grounds of Rothach Hall.'

'Ah,' he said. 'Not the drive I used?'

She steered slowly around a stand of fir trees. Tourists using the back drive as a footpath shifted to the edge to let her through. 'If you'd come in the back way, you wouldn't have seen the dog and been able to rescue her.'

The track cleared of people, and they passed into an avenue of sycamores. The dog snuggled into her towel, as if settling in for the ride. Then she lifted her head, looked up at him and gave a gruff little 'Arf!'

Thea smiled, though her eyes remained on the road. 'Aw. She's saying thanks for rescuing her.' She resumed her spiel. 'Rothach Hall was built in the early eighteenth century. The story goes that "Rothach" is Gaelic for "Monroe", the name of the first owner of the house. You can read the history board in reception if you want to know more.' It was cute how she said 'Rothach' in her flat English accent, so different to his own Scottish burr. 'The hall's owned by the Larsson family now. It's not a castle, like Armadale or Knock, but Rothach's been restored. We're not expecting the family to be in residence this summer, but their side of the hall and garden are strictly private unless you're working there. The grounds and a few rooms of the hall are open to the public.'

'The gardens are great,' he murmured, remembering she'd assumed he was here for a gardening job. It was a comment more likely to meet with her approval than: *I'm doorstepping you for a website called Everyday Celebs. My editor thought that as I was travelling from Inverness to Dumfries, I might as well 'call in' at Skye, even though it's doubled my journey.*

At the end of the track, tall black gates opened at her approach. 'The job's seasonal,' she continued as they accelerated between hedges of gorse and wild rhododendron onto the gravelly road between Rothach Hall and the better-kept main route down the Sleat Peninsula. 'We had someone, but they left, which is why we're recruiting in mid-June. Seasonals get basic jobs like mowing, edging, weeding, clipping, clearing up and litter picking. No

14

chainsaw or other heavy equipment . . . unless you have a CSCS card?' She took her gaze from the narrow road long enough to send him an enquiring glance.

'Afraid not.' All he knew about a CSCS card was that he didn't have one.

'OK.' She steered the truck around a curve, sending up a flurry of dead pine needles from beneath overhanging trees. 'You just need to perform the tasks I've mentioned, have a friendly attitude to colleagues and a willingness to work. And be punctual.'

'I'm usually a good timekeeper.' He watched as she slowed for the junction and turned left at the sign to Teangue, Kilmore, Kilbeg and Armadale. He'd expected Thea Wynter to look as she had when starring in *Garden Gladiators*, but her facial piercings were gone. Her hair was long and a natural nut-brown instead of short and trendy, so heavily highlighted as to be tiger-striped. The holly green uniform could have been chosen to compliment her compact shape. A part of his mind acknowledged that he was noticing a woman for the first time in a while and he turned his gaze to the scenery.

The truck joined a tail of traffic dawdling past a gap in the rocks and grassy hummocks edging the road. He caught his breath at a magnificent vista over the rocky coast of Skye, a thousand shades of green, grey and brown beside the silvery waters of the Sound of Sleat. Gulls circled above and he caught sight of a white lighthouse before a curve in the road cut off his view.

She changed down the gears as she, too, spared a second to take in the beauty. 'Your application said you'd worked in gardens before?'

'Just the summers, since I was old enough,' he said factually, but not mentioning that it was mainly in

Grandpa's garden, a corner plot the size of two allotments. 'Last summer I volunteered at Oakhill House, an assisted living facility in Dumfries. That's in south Scotland,' he added helpfully. 'Do you like living so far north?' On his lap, the dog yawned and laid her head on his forearm.

Thea's dark gaze returned to the road. 'Yes, I was brought up in Suffolk in the East of England, but I love the Isle of Skye. When I first came, I tried to pronounce "Rothach" with the *chh* sound at the end, like "loch", instead of "Roth-arsh". And I thought that "Sleat" was said "sleet", rather than "slate". I've learnt that the Sound of Sleat is an inner sea, open at both ends, whereas a sea loch is only open at one end. And some lochs are lakes, right?'

'Right,' he agreed, grinning. She didn't make a bad job of "loch", which so many English people pronounced "lock". 'How long have you been here?'

'About eight years. It's a wonderful, serene place.' She checked her mirrors, then returned to interview mode. 'The job comes with a uniform, but you need your own safety boots before you can start, boots that cover your ankles. No steel toe-cap trainers. You get a £25 allowance and there's a place in Broadford that sells work wear.'

'Great,' he answered affably. The land had fallen away towards the sound where the sun gilded the water, still and glassy apart from where a squat white ferry boat left a trail like an arrow pointing towards the far shore – what he judged to be the mainland because they weren't quite opposite the Outer Hebrides here. Islands, he thought, were mountains with their heads above the sea. On the shoreline below, a yellow rowing boat lay on its side against a jumble of rocks. Above the road, rock crags punctuated slopes green with trees, white cottages with slate roofs half hidden in their midst. A sea eagle spread its wings and soared between pearly grey sculpted clouds lit on one side. It felt unreal, like being part of a landscape painting on a wall.

As the road sank downhill, past a sign to Armadale Castle and towards a town of white buildings with grey roofs and a quay, he experienced the same feeling of serendipity and sanctuary that had struck him in the studio apartment.

This island could be his home.

Thea swung the pick-up right, jolting him from his thoughts. 'This is Armadale. There are shops and stuff here. I called ahead so the vet's expecting us.' She parked before a low, modern building with a sign saying this was Southside Veterinary Clinic. Then she paused and turned to gaze at him, arms braced on the steering wheel. Colour tinged her cheeks. 'Don't think me a terrible person, but I can't remember whether your name's Tim or Tom.'

'Deveron,' he answered. The dog shook her ears, looking around as if wondering what was happening. 'Deveron Dowie.'

Thea frowned. 'I thought your surname was McJohn.'

He stroked the matted fur of the dog's head. She hadn't tried to escape her towel or his lap but lay still, as if waiting along with Thea for his explanation. 'Well,' he began, preparing to lie his arse off. 'Maybe the applicant you were expecting was Tim or Tom McJohn, but I came on spec after seeing the job advertised online.' He switched to the truth. 'I've had some bad luck. My ex went off with my best mate – who also happened to be my business partner – which left me homeless and potless after a divorce and winding up a business. If I don't get this job, I'll have to sleep on my mum's sofa. She's not rich and

17

I'm not borrowing the deposit for my own place from her or my brother Leith. He's offered me a room, but as that would mean obliging my nieces to share, I turned it down. I've only been able to keep my car by coming to an arrangement with the finance company. Working in the beautiful surroundings of Skye with that studio apartment to come home to looks great right now.' And it would leave him time to do some freelance work, so long as . . . 'Is there an internet connection?'

Thea's gaze had shuttered. 'There's Wi-Fi in the staff accommodation.' She paused, and he wondered if she was about to tell him to get lost. Instead, she said, 'That sounds like a shitty situation.' But she sounded guarded.

Guilty heat flooded his cheeks. 'Aye, a wee bit.' His mind strayed to his previous self, standing in stunned silence while Adaira and Krisi held hands and said they were going away together, though generously leaving him the business he and Krisi had built up – which, by the way, was in its death throes.

They'd exited his life with calm decision, barely acknowledging the chaos they left behind them. The only contact since had been via solicitors, to facilitate the divorce and empower Dev to sell the house to mitigate the mortgage and other debts.

He realised she was speaking again. 'So can you do garden work?'

He nodded, not blaming her for her lukewarm response. 'Mowing, edging, weeding, digging, are all very much part of my experience. My grandpa had an enormous garden, and I spent a lot of time there after my dad died when I was eight.'

She didn't offer sympathy. 'Do you have a criminal record?'

'No.' He didn't bother with indignation because he couldn't blame her for asking.

'Can you provide references?' Her gaze had fallen to his hand stroking the dog's head, brushing the fur back from her eyes. The dog closed her eyes contentedly.

He paused, suspecting that this appearance of trust was making Thea consider his wild idea, and wondering whether the world treating him so badly justified his judicious weaving of lies and truths. He'd never been this needy before . . . 'I've been self-employed for a decade. But I did work for Oakhill House last summer. The scheme manager could confirm that I'm to be trusted around other human beings.' His stomach felt hollow. If he couldn't get freelance jobs that paid properly – unlike Everyday Celebs – then the word 'references' was going to come up again.

The silence in the vehicle grew taut. Then Thea sighed. 'Let's get that dog inside. She's been through enough.'

True. Nearly drowning was worse than even his shit life.

The veterinary surgeon was a brisk, middle-aged woman with cheeks as pink as Gala apples. She treated the dog gently, yet Thea felt horrible at handing her over, after explaining how they came to have her, still preoccupied by the confession of the man standing beside her that he was neither Tim nor Tom McJohn, but someone called Deveron Dowie.

The vet made a quick examination and ran a scanner over the small body. 'There's no microchip, so no way of establishing her owners. Illegal, but not unusual.' She sighed, stroking the dog's head. 'I'd put her at about seven or eight months old. She's undernourished and neglected but otherwise healthy. We'll keep her till we can contact the local authority.'

As Thea and Deveron left the surgery, Thea made the mistake of glancing back. The little dog gazed after them with such a look of astounded dismay that Thea's throat ached. They returned to the truck in silence, and she began the return journey. Clouds seemed to crowd in over the white buildings of Armadale as if to watch their departure.

Deveron rubbed his stubbly chin. 'I suppose I didn't think past getting the wee thing to the vet.' He sounded as dismayed as the dog had looked.

'I wonder what happens if no one claims her?' Thea felt as if someone was going over her heart with a cheese grater. Those melting brown eyes would follow her into her dreams tonight.

'I don't suppose dogs are allowed in the staff accommodation?' he ventured.

'Sorry. No pets.' She sighed.

They drove on for five minutes, the road climbing. Dusty green trees rose beside them on the landward side, some gnarled after a lifetime of clinging to pockets of soil between slices of red and grey rock. The road was a man-made ribbon interrupting the sweep down to water that both reflected the clouds and danced with sunbeams. It was ruggedly beautiful, this island she called home, and usually she loved driving through it. But now, involuntarily, her foot softened on the accelerator. The pick-up slowed.

'Are you OK?' Deveron asked, sounding alarmed.

'I'm fine,' she answered over the noise of her brain and heart locked in grim battle. She pulled over into the gateway of a white cottage with a cypress tree beside its stone wall, and a couple of cars passed. Slowly, she drew out her phone.

And called the veterinary surgery.

Chapter Three

That evening, Thea's supper was salmon and new potatoes with the last of the green beans she'd frozen at the end of last summer. She ate at the oak kitchen table that she meant to refinish when she had time, gazing through her kitchen window.

Rothach village clung to a scoop of land below Rothach Hall and whereas white or natural stone were the common colours for the buildings of Skye, here many of the cottages were painted in pastel shades. Thistledome, her cottage, stood at the top of the inaccurately named Loch View, overlooking not a loch but Rothach Bay, part of the Sound of Sleat. Thea loved the panorama over the grey roofs and green treetops of lower cottages to the crescent-shaped beach where seaweed clung to black rocks between tumbled beige pebbles and pockets of gritty sand. Rowing boats heeled drunkenly at low tide and yachts bobbed out in deeper water.

Thistledome had witnessed the tide's ebbing and flowing for a couple of hundred years longer than Thea had. She'd painted her cottage a soft thistle-purple to go with its name. The garden ran around three sides, and canopy porches front and rear provided places to leave boots. Its slate roof was bowed with age, its square window frames painted black like the doors front and back, and it was an ideal size for Thea – small.

Though she couldn't see all the village from her vantage point, she was familiar with the way Harbour View led to the old Fishermen's Cottages at the foot of the cliff where Causeway sloped into the sea at high tide. Chapel Road, lower down the slope, held no place of worship – unless you counted the pub being called Jolly Abbot Inn – and Low Road was actually quite high. The roads of Rothach village were mainly single track and edged with banks of rock, bracken and wildflowers instead of the mown verges she'd known in Suffolk.

Eight years ago, she and her middle sister, Ezzie – or Esmerelda, if you wanted her legal name – had moved into a rented place in Chapel Road. Pooling their resources after leaving Suffolk, their jobs and live-in relationships behind had allowed them to find their financial feet and decide whether the rugged, remote Isle of Skye might provide their forever home. Eldest sister Valentina and her husband Gary had moved to Edinburgh some years earlier, so the sisters were at least no further apart.

Later, Thea had felt settled enough to leave the Chapel Road cottage to Ezzie and move into Thistledome. Her landlady had been Maisie, who lived on the corner of Loch View and Portnalong Way in a lemon-yellow cottage. Jovial Maisie had inherited the cottage from her sister and lost no time in explaining to Thea that 'Thistledome' was a play on the words 'this'll do me'.

At the beginning of this year, Maisie had wanted to sell, so Thea decided Thistledome would do her, too, and it became her pride and joy. As funds would allow, she'd redecorated the lounge and kitchen, both bedrooms and the bathroom. The lounge was still a touch bare, furnished only with two rocking chairs and a low table, but sofas were expensive. So were curtains, so only her front windows boasted them. The back windows faced the garden and one of the rocky outcrops that made the village so steep. She did sometimes think about buying blinds for her bedroom as summer nights were short, but if the sun woke her at 4 a.m., the mewling of the gulls generally lulled her back to sleep.

After supper, she showered, freed her hair to blow about her shoulders, then strolled through the summer evening out of Loch View and down Balgown, waving to her neighbour Fraser, whose long silver hair hung from under a Tam O'Shanter he referred to as his tammie or his bonnet. Perched on the doorstep to his cottage – painted a no-nonsense traditional white – he shelled peas with sweeps of his thumb. 'I'm taking these to Maisie, but there'll be more in a day or two if you want some.' He and fellow octogenarian Maisie spent a lot of time together and they and Thea had a neighbourly friendship, often doing favours for each other. The village was a warm community, but Thea still spent more time with Ezz than anyone else.

'That would be great, thanks,' Thea called back. A few more minutes saw her up the steep slope of Creag an Lolaire and then into Chapel Road. A few people occupied the tables outside the Jolly Abbot and she waved to them. Everyone knew everyone in Rothach, if only by sight. Many of the live-out staff at the hall lived in the village.

Thea let herself through Ezzie's gate, her legs brushing the profusion of weeds her sister called a wildflower garden. 'I'm here,' she called as she stepped through the front door. As Ezzie liked to date, Thea had already texted to check her availability this evening, and received the laconic reply: *Will put coffee on.*

Never would Ezzie say: *Will pour wine.* Ezzie had given up alcohol because, as she'd tell people herself, she liked it too much, sometimes adding: 'Who needs it?' Not many people admitted to 'needing' alcohol.

Ezzie's voice floated back to her. 'Kitchen.'

Thea followed the sound, careful of the half-step that could send people flying into the kitchen on their knees.

Her sister waited expectantly by the coffee machine, where two mugs, a milk bottle and a sugar cannister awaited. Ezzie beamed, revealing white teeth. Tall and willowy, Ezzie wore her fine blonde hair feathered around her sharp but pretty features. She'd changed her assistant manager's uniform of black suit and white shirt in favour of a multi-coloured top and blue leggings. She ushered Thea into the lounge, where she did have a sofa – a big, squashy one, with a footstool. Thea wouldn't have chosen turquoise because she'd have to change out of her work clothes to sit in it, but in the years since Thea and Ezzie had house-shared here, Ezzie had made the place her own.

As they settled themselves, Ezzie said, 'I hope you've been working hard outdoors.' It was said jokily because head gardener and assistant manager were on a level, both reporting to Tavish, the manager. Their working days often kept them apart as Ezzie remained indoors and Thea out, and the Rothach Hall staff rota ran on a seven-day week, meaning they didn't always get the same rest days, either. 'What kind of a day have you had?' Ezzie continued.

Thea blew out her cheeks. 'I'm getting a foster dog,

24

who might become permanent, and I'm trialling the wrong man as a seasonal assistant.'

Ezzie's blonde eyebrows flew up. 'A foster dog? What the hell, Ms Soft-heart? Dogs need inoculations and food and beds and walks. You need furniture and curtains.'

'Walks are free, Ms Pragmatist,' Thea returned reasonably, not minding Ezz's hint that Thea plunged heart-first into life, whereas Ezzie's responses were usually practical. 'I already exercise Bouncer and Scotty for Maisie and Fraser sometimes.' Maisie and Fraser didn't enjoy perfect health at their age, but they did enjoy the company of their lively pets.

'Like you need exercise, with your job,' Ezzie returned drily.

Thea tipped her head onto her sister's shoulder. 'I know. But the poor little doggy nearly drowned, and she was so brave. We took her to the vet. She hasn't been microchipped and she's scrawny, so I doubt anyone will claim her. And she licked my hand.'

'Aw. You're such a softy.' Ezz rested her head on Thea's, as if they were still children snuggling up so Ezz could read a story out loud.

Thea sighed again. 'You know that a dog is on my one-day list – when the cottage is finished, the side garden's fenced off and I've got money and time. I thought *then* I'd choose a rescue dog. But this one chose me.'

Ezz was already on to the next subject. 'Who's we? "We" took her to the vet, you said. And what was that about employing the wrong man?'

'Same person. Deveron Dowie.' Thea straightened so she could sip her coffee, and regaled Ezzie with the story of how snatching five minutes with Clive Donkey and Mary Pony had ended.

'What about Tim McJohn, the applicant we expected?' Ezzie assumed her severe assistant manager look.

Thea shrugged. 'He was a no-show. And Deveron needs a job. His business failed, and his wife and business partner cleared off together. He was left with a car full of gear and an invitation to sleep on his mum's sofa.'

Ezzie took a thoughtful sip from her mug. 'But this Deveron hasn't made an application through the job agency. We don't know anything about him.'

'No, that's a worry,' Thea admitted. 'He's been self-employed, so references are tricky, too. But he's got both passport and driving licence ID and he says he's done voluntary work in the garden of the retirement home where his grandpa lives, so the manager might give him a character reference.'

'Not great employment practice,' Ezzie observed drily. 'I suppose his major reference, so far as you're concerned, is that he saved your future foster dog.'

Cheeks heating, Thea laughed. As if in an echo, she heard laughter from outside the Jolly Abbot, too.

'You've said he can have the vacant staff accommodation,' Ezzie said eventually, not even making it a question.

'Yes.' Thea winced at the resignation in her sister's voice. 'He's filled out an application form, though, and it's in the right folder on the system. He knows he's on trial, so if he does anything antisocial, we can chuck him out and change the door code so he can't get back in.' Thea made a point of emphasising that she'd completed the admin. She hated paperwork, but forced herself to deal with the small amount associated with her job. Her brainy sisters tried to be understanding about her poor relationship with the written word, even filling in forms on Thea's behalf without ever complaining, but they must feel exasperated when she shied away from writing reports. Infographics, sketches and headings were OK with Thea. Blocks of text were intimidating and impenetrable. Luckily, her gardening apprenticeship hadn't required great long essays and her assessor had understood, deftly demystifying online assessments while saying that she'd been trained to work with 'reluctant readers', a phrase that summed Thea up.

'Very reassuring to the other live-in staff, if he antisocially slits their throats tonight.' Ezzie arched her brows reprovingly.

Thea's face could get no redder. 'As head gardener, he's mine to hire or fire, but I have stipulated that you'll want to interview him too. And I haven't issued uniform.'

Ezzie drained her mug and put it down on the end table. 'It's been your day for strays, Thea.'

Thea glowed at this reminder of her foster dog and returned happily to the subject. 'So long as the dog looks OK tomorrow, the vet nurse will call me, and I'll get her after work. They have a collar, lead and a pet carrier I can borrow.'

'I suppose you're paying the vet's bill, though?' Ezzie knitted her eyebrows.

'No, smartarse,' Thea fired back. 'If the owners turn up, the vet will try to charge them, but as I'm going to foster, there won't be a bill for me. I can use my old towels to line the travel crate.'

Ezz snorted. 'You only have old towels.'

Thea giggled. 'So that's fine then. Oh, don't pooh-pooh my foster-dog experience, Ezz. I'm excited and happy. She's so sweet-natured, she won't mind being bathed and groomed and everything. I'll give her nice food and she'll be a new dog.'

'Just in time for you to give her back, I expect,' Ezzie sniffed. But she gave Thea a big hug and a kiss on the cheek, so Thea knew that even though Ezzie was efficient and academic, and Thea was more of a natural-world person, Ezz loved her.

She didn't mention that she hoped to take the dog to work with her sometimes. The gardens were her jurisdiction, not Ezzie's.

For the first time in months, Dev had slept all night – after a call to his mum to explain why his return home had been postponed indefinitely.

'Oh, Deveron, son, will you be coming in a wee while, maybe?' she'd asked.

'Sure, Mum,' he'd answered, but with no idea when. Dumfries was hours from Skye.

Still, the seasonal job he'd fallen into meant he could temporarily shelve the unpalatable fact that his agency had gone down owing contributors and everyone else money, and the name of Deveron Dowie was just as much associated with the failed company as that of Kristian Georgiev Kirov. After successful years in journalism, he and Krisi had developed a thriving news agency with a team of freelancers supplying content about ball sports and its athletes to both print and electronic media throughout Europe. Now they had nothing but a bad reputation. Worse, Krisi had made a last-ditch attempt to raise money by reselling content, blithely ignoring the fact that the agency didn't own the rights – the contributors did. 'It's piracy!' one wrathful former contributor had told Dev, amidst a welter of effs and jeffs.

Feelings against him were running high and when he'd tentatively reached out to freelance for sporting publications or sites, he'd met with nothing but rebuffs. Nobody in their erstwhile network cared that Dev had been ignorant of Krisi's dealings.

His name was tainted.

Working under a pseudonym wasn't an option, as his real name had to be on his bank account. Even if he operated under cover of a company name, reputable outlets would need to see evidence of who was behind it.

As well as now being a pariah, he was embarrassed.

He should have *seen* what was going on.

He shoved the thought away. For now, he had a comfortable bed on which to put his sheets, pillows and quilt and yesterday evening, he'd driven up the peninsula to Broadford, which was slightly larger than Armadale, for coffee and sandwiches to enjoy on a bench overlooking Broadford Bay.

Now it was morning and with no coffee to hand, he drank water and ate two cereal bars from the stash in his car, opening his laptop to email Weston, editorial director at Everyday Celebs.

For the past few months, at the same time as failing to save his home and business, Dev had stooped to supplying content for the *Where are they now?* and *You decide!* sections, though he hated the work. In the case of Thea Wynter and Fredek Kowski, Weston's intention was to start with *Where are they now?* – commonly referred to as WATN – and then follow up on *You decide!* – YD. Dev had never met Weston, but in his profile pic he looked like a junior lawyer with a trendy haircut, round glasses and a suit, and aged about twenty-seven. Dev thought any owner of a shit site like Everyday Celebs should be older and more cynical, at home in a back-to-front baseball hat.

Whatever he looked like, Weston fed contributors from the material people sent in via the *Got a news story for us??!!* button, spilling beans or dobbing in. He paid a measly £200 a piece, and never allowed any contributor more than one or two a week. New material was released when readers were on their morning bus ride or eating lunch and Weston and his digital manager were frequently rewarded by online storms and trending hashtags.

Weston, he began.
Sorry I haven't filed copy while moving house. It was a grandiose description for leaving the keys of his erstwhile home with his solicitor. *I have the material for the WATN piece on the vicar who poisoned his wife – still thinking he can clear his name, apparently.*
Ditto the YD about the guy who may have plotted to get his brother disinherited, but I'm putting the Fredek Kowski/Thea Wynter piece on the back burner as she's a dead end so far as her side of the story or a quote's concerned. Staff only offer to take messages at her place of work and won't give out her mobile number. No sign of her on socials. Have wasted too much time on this to make it worth the fee.
Will file copy on the others in the next few days.
Dev

Satisfied that his road was cleared to a summer working at Rothach Hall, he closed down, then, as requested by Thea, left to meet the assistant manager, who was Thea's sister, apparently.

After finding reception and admiring a massive staircase that swooped from a ceiling with plasterwork panels painted white and blue, he located the sister awaiting him in a tiny office, an unsmiling blonde who he wouldn't have picked out as Thea's sister in a million years. As she introduced herself as Ezzie Wynter, he mentally ran through the descriptors he'd employ if writing about her. *Blonde hair too natural to be the work of her hairdresser. Tall. Elegant. Pointed features. Cool smile. Manicured. Groomed.* Her black skirt was exactly knee-length and her heels just an inch high, her jacket and blouse immaculate. This Ms Wynter was a lot more businesslike than the other.

'Deveron Dowie,' he said, shaking her hand.

'Sit down,' she answered.

Deveron sat, his stomach suddenly cold. Ezzie Wynter didn't like him. Generally, the only people who didn't like him were those about whom the agency had put out unfavourable sporting profiles or finger-pointing match reports. And now, those clients and writers the agency had crapped on, of course.

Pulling her keyboard towards her, she clicked her mouse. 'Thank you for filling in the job application, however belatedly. Summers are busy for the grounds team and our head gardener has agreed to give you a chance.' She treated him to a frosty smile. 'As you introduced yourself by rescuing a dog.'

He cleared his throat, the chill in his stomach spreading to his chest. 'There's a problem?'

'That's what I need to find out.' Ezzie's desk phone rang. She pressed a button. 'Can it wait?' Then: 'About half an hour, probably. No, don't bother Tavish with it. Tell them I'll call back. Thanks.' She released the button and looked at him. 'We don't normally employ anyone with no recent employment *or* benefit record.'

31

'I understand, but I've been self-employed for a long time,' he cut in before she could send him to pack his things. He decided to be more transparent than he had been with Thea. 'I had a business partner in an agency. We both lived in the UK but he's Bulgarian by birth and looked after our dealings in Eastern Europe. I looked after Western Europe. A Bulgarian client successfully sued us, and my partner had cut corners with our legal liability insurance. He and my wife ran off together and I, having integrity, was left to wind up the company and conduct the divorce. "Voluntary liquidation" it's called, which seems like a misnomer, as I didn't volunteer for it.' It had been a traumatic, shitty experience, and all he wanted was to leave it in the past. 'I was about to stay with my mother when I saw the job vacancy. I prefer to work than claim benefits.'

Ezzie listened impassively. 'But Rothach Hall isn't mentioned on the recruitment site we use,' she pointed out. 'Only an applicant under consideration would receive full details.' She arched an eyebrow, as if she'd caught him out.

And she could have done, if he hadn't reverse-researched this yesterday evening, having identified the weak link in his fortuitous falling into the job. 'It's on your own website under Jobs and Volunteering. And I got to your website because Rothach Hall is listed on a blog about gardening jobs.' A journalist could usually angle a truth to give any required impression.

A frown jumped onto Ezzie's forehead, and she swung around to her computer. A few moments' clicking and tapping, then, clearly surprised, she said, 'You're quite correct. My manager deals with the web designer, and we now have a vacancies page, apparently.' She clicked and tapped again, and he imagined she was writing herself a note to talk it over with her manager.

She turned back. 'And you have literally no references other than someone at your grandfather's retirement home?'

A sigh escaped him. There was no way to slant *that* truth to make it sound better. 'A court case and a destroyed business don't create much goodwill. I had jobs before we began the agency, but none of them are still in business, or they were acquired by bigger businesses.' Regional newspapers and sports newspapers routinely suffered those fates. 'You can look up Oakhill House and see it genuinely is a retirement home and that the manager is Lena Benford. She can confirm that my grandfather, Cyril Heggarty, my mother's father, is a resident, and I joined a crew creating a scented garden there last summer. If you search Leith Dowie, my brother, you'll find he's the sales manager of a packaging company. My mother's the chair of her local Women's Institute.' But if Ezzie Wynter was going to ferret about like that, he was glad his work for Everyday Celebs had no byline and the agency website was permanently down. Even his LinkedIn profile was no more.

For the first time, her smile held some warmth. 'I'm pretty sure that if I did so, I'd be invading your privacy. HR has laws.'

Good.

'What kind of agency was it?' she went on.

He could almost see her wondering whether he'd been involved in an escort agency. 'Sports,' he said. 'Ball sports, to be precise – mainly football and tennis.'

Her brow cleared. 'Like management and events?'

He didn't nod, because that would be an outright lie as she was so obviously thinking marketing and promo rather than journalism, so just smiled, as if in admiring her mental agility.

33

She gazed at him measuringly. 'Will you stay here while I talk to my manager?' Without waiting to hear whether he would or wouldn't, she rose and tip-tapped from the room.

He had five minutes to examine the carpet pattern, as there was little else in the small room but Ezzie Wynter's desk and chair, and no window.

Then Ezzie returned with long, purposeful strides, talking as she resumed her seat. 'I think Thea explained that this is a seasonal position. So long as you're aware of that, you can start, pending a satisfactory reference from Lena Benford – will you contact her to say the request will be coming, please? It's zero hours, so if we find you unsuitable . . .'

'I understand,' he said, relieved to have got a green light, however conditional.

Ezzie, having made a decision, actioned it. 'If you have your ID with you, we can complete the formalities and I'll issue your uniform and put £25 in your bank account towards safety boots. Much of the rest of the uniform is "from stock", I'm afraid, which means that though it's been laundered, it has been used by staff that came before.'

His heart bounded at such measurable progress. 'I don't mind that.'

She nodded, her gaze on her computer monitor. Then she stopped and sent him a smile that made him aware how pretty she was. 'And do me a favour. Don't bring Thea any more half-drowned dogs. She's a sucker for a stray.'

He was almost sure she put him in the 'stray' category, as well as the dog. Oh, well. At the moment, that was what he was – though, like the rescued pup, with a temporary home.

Chapter Four

Thea couldn't believe her eyes.

It was late Sunday afternoon, and it wasn't just a foot-tall dog who waved a tentative feathery tail at her, but a clean, fluffy, pearly white small dog, floppy ears unmatted, and front paws neatly placed together. Her mouth opened in a doggy smile of welcome.

'Oh, you gorgeous thing,' Thea breathed, falling into the melting brown eyes.

The veterinary nurse beamed. 'She's a real sweetie. I'm quite in love with her.'

Thea knelt and held out her hand. The nurse dropped the lead and the dog bounced over as if powered by her wagging tail, and accepted Thea's hug. Thea handed back the second-hand – or second-paw – lead to the nurse. 'I've brought my own collar and lead for her, to make her feel welcome. I made a lunchtime run into Broadford to buy her a bed and food, too.' The collar was a cheerful tartan, and now she popped the dog into it, her heart full. Then she signed to say she'd taken the dog and agreed to the surgery sharing her details with the local authority and police in case an owner contacted them. 'Do you think her owners will turn up?'

The nurse's smile faded. 'It's been a wee while since anyone looked after this youngster properly.'

Thea stroked the puffball head and the dog's tail stepped up to double speed. 'Her fur frames her face like petals. I'm going to call her Daisy. Do you think she's a cockapoo?'

'You could call her that.' The nurse twinkled. 'There's probably some poodle in there somewhere.'

Thea didn't care if Daisy was part sheep. They headed to the pick-up with the borrowed travel crate to strap it on the back seat, little Daisy lifting her paws high like a show pony. Not having owned a dog since childhood, and that had been a brown all-sorts that had seen Thea's mum, Maxie, as the most important human in the family, Thea drove home as if on eggshells. Lifting her voice, she called, 'Daisy, you have a new home – if the shitboxes who let you get into the state you were in don't show up. You'll have your own bed, so no climbing into mine. I've got a great garden, but I need to dog-proof it before you can go out on your own.' She laughed. 'We can have a rocking chair each in front of the telly.'

Daisy barked, as if happy with all she heard.

Their route took them onto bumpy Manor Road, which led to the hall. Just as Thea prepared to indicate and turn left down Low Road to the village, she noticed a familiar grey SUV ahead. On impulse, she scooted up close behind it, and when it turned into the staff entrance of Rothach Hall, she followed.

Deveron obviously spotted her, as he looked into his rear-view mirror and raised his hand before driving up the track and parking behind the greenhouse. She hadn't seen much of him on this, his first day. Ezzie had given him to assistant head gardener Sheena to look after, Thea being in the greenhouse with Hadley, discussing the plans for the summer. Hadley had been gardener at Rothach before Thea, keeping the garden going while the property languished before Erik and Grete Larsson had come along to buy and restore it. He was white-haired now, and worked only summers, when he was invaluable for nurturing a steady supply of bedding plants.

She'd caught sight of Deveron a few hours earlier in the herb garden after lunch, clad by then in the same dark green as herself, his attention on forty-something Sheena. Her short, dark hair was cut almost boyishly, and the pockets of her cargo trousers were stuffed with jute string, plastic labels, secateurs, and the rubber bungs to go on the top of canes to prevent people from poking their eyes out. Thea had waved, and Deveron and Sheena had waved back.

Later she'd received a text from Ezzie. *His referee was effusive in praise and has known him and fam for five years. x* The next had said, *Got your eye on him?* and two smileys, a thoughtful face and a winking face. Thea had blushed. Despite an undeniable wariness of the way he'd shown up, with his sad story and his possessions filling his car, she *had* noticed Deveron's dark good looks. And those shoulders and that chest. He didn't exactly look as if he worked out every day, but she'd have no trouble in believing he was used to the outdoors. She hadn't dated for ages. When she'd first arrived on Skye, she'd gone out with local single men, but had always found something not to like. Often, it was that they expected to stay over at her house, where she liked her own space or they wanted her to stay with them, where she felt prickly and out of place. Gradually, her appetite for dating had faded but, yes, Deveron had caught her eye.

Now, she pulled up behind his car and jumped out. 'I have something to show you.' She heard anticipation in her voice and caught an answering glint of interest in his eyes as he paused to look at her. Opening the rear door of the pick-up, she released the hatch to the travel crate. As if on a spring, Daisy's head popped out.

'Whoa. Look at this pretty girl!' Deveron sounded satisfactorily pleased and impressed.

'Isn't she?' She took the lead, then helped Daisy out onto the ground. 'I thought you'd like to see her now that she's not covered in weed and muck. I've called her Daisy.'

'I'd not believe it was the same dog. Well, hello, Daisy.' He crouched and Daisy bounced up to him like a puppet dog, ears perked – as much as floppy ears could perk – and tail a blur.

'Maybe she remembers you saved her.' Thea couldn't stop beaming.

He smiled up at her. He'd shaved and his jaw was hardly stubbly today. 'Your sister has only let me stay here on the proviso that I don't bring you any more half-drowned dogs, by the way.'

She laughed, watching the breeze cause a parting in his curls like an invisible hairdresser. 'That sounds like Ezzie. I'm entitled to employ someone in the garden, but she does all the paperwork and compliance with regulations so you must have checked out OK.'

He straightened, jamming his hands into his back pockets. 'I must buy you both a drink.'

She kept her smile up with an effort. 'A doughnut would be better.' It wasn't until someone stopped drinking that it became obvious how frequently alcohol was offered in gratitude or celebration.

'Noted.' He nodded towards his car, where carrier bags pressed against the rear window. 'I've found a supermarket, so I can offer you coffee.'

Wistfully, she acknowledged that it was ages since she'd had coffee with a good-looking man, unless you counted one who'd asked to share her table outside the Nature Café recently with his wife and noisy children in tow. But she barely knew the guy, so assumed a reproving expression, trying to make her straight brows arch, like Ezzie's did. 'No pets in the staff accommodation, remember. I need to settle Daisy in at home. I have a day off tomorrow, so I can start marking out where I want a fence at the side of the house, to stop her getting on the road.'

He nodded. 'Let me know if you need help. I don't have any days off until I've worked five, but it's light so late up here in June that I could come in the evenings.' He held up his hands, as if she'd protested. 'I appreciate that you might not want to give your address to just any old dog rescuer, though.'

She answered truthfully. 'Any member of staff can find my address on the board in the gardeners' room where we keep the hand tools. But I'll have to let you know if and when I can get the materials delivered.' Lightly, she added, 'If you prove untrustworthy, I'll set Daisy on you. Or Ezzie.'

Daisy looked up and waggled her bottom, as if telling Dev not to take Thea too seriously.

'Ezzie doesn't seem the type to let anyone get away with anything.' He hesitated, before adding, 'If you don't mind me saying so, your sister looks nothing like you. I think one of you must have been switched at birth.'

Thea had heard this all her life, but never tired of watching someone's reaction when she answered sweetly, 'We're adopted – that's all.'

'Oh.' Sheepishly, he scratched his ear. 'Never thought of that. I hope I haven't offended.'

'Of course not. My parents adopted three of us – I'm the youngest, Ezzie is in the middle and Valentina is the eldest. Apart from Valentina and I both having dark hair we're obviously not from the same peapod.'

'Does Valentina live on Skye, too?' His hazel eyes gleamed with interest.

'She has a career as a lawyer in Edinburgh.' She glanced at her watch. 'Better go settle my foster dog at home.'

'Sure. See you tomorrow.' After they'd said goodbye, Dev headed towards the staff accommodation and Thea drove down into the village, noticing the tingle of awareness that fizzed through her at the idea of seeing Deveron again the next day. If Ezz hadn't been able to find a reason not to take him on, he must be OK, mustn't he?

Once at Thistledome, she focused on the excitement of showing Daisy her new home, placing her bed in the corner where the kitchen counters met, making the ideal dog cave. After Daisy had explored indoors, Thea took her outside for a sniff around the garden, at the same time telephoning Ezz. 'Come and meet my dog – Daisy.'

Ezz demurred. 'I've just flopped on the sofa.'

Thea pretended to wheedle. 'Aw, puh-le-ease.'

Ezz's giggle sounded in Thea's ear. 'Oh, OK. I'd better check her out in case she's fierce.'

When she arrived half an hour later and was met at the door by Daisy barking while performing a waggle dance of welcome, she exploded with laughter. 'That's

40

not a dog – it's a powder puff. Aw. She's adorable, Thea.'
And to Daisy: 'Oo's a wuverley wickle powder puff, den?
Oo's a pwetty girl?' Daisy, obviously recognising herself
in this description, flung herself down and presented a
tummy to be tickled.

Thea grinned. 'Who's a sucker for a stray now?'

Deveron had unpacked his shopping. The compact fridge
was full of beer, ketchup, mayonnaise, chicken, milk,
chops and veggies. The cupboard held potatoes, onions,
pasta, cook-in sauce, condiments, sugar, crackers and
coffee. As he hadn't bothered bringing kitchen equipment
from the house he'd shared with Adaira, he'd invested in
the most basic of starter sets – two saucepans, a frying
pan, plates, bowls, cutlery, a wooden spoon and a spatula.
He'd already discovered that he'd omitted a tin-opener
and a sharp knife.

After reading the instructions for the microwave oven
and the hot plate on top, he managed to cook a chicken
breast, a jacket potato and broccoli. It was so fiddly that
he foresaw a lot of ready meals in his future. Cooking
had been easier on a range.

After dinner, he collapsed onto the bed, wondering how
he could watch TV on his laptop when he'd cancelled
his subscriptions and TV licence.

Noticing he had three unread emails in his inbox, he
clicked on the icon. One email said he could check his
most recent bank statement – which wouldn't take long.
Another was a newsletter, from which he promptly
unsubscribed, no longer feeling the urge to keep an eye
on the football news. To his surprise, the third was from
Fredek Kowski, the cyclist who'd been in collision with
a car driven by Thea Wynter.

41

Just a gentle nudge to check when your piece on me
will be going live. As you know, I keep a press file to
check on my reach. My great stats have enabled me
to secure an engagement as a keynote speaker at
World Influencer Marketing Conference Glasgow in a
couple of months, which was why I approached
Everyday Celebs myself. I need to keep it going.
It would be great if you could push this up your list.

Dev read with irritation. When he'd emailed Weston to kill the piece on Fredek Kowski and Thea Wynter, he hadn't given a thought to the fact that he'd already completed a Zoom interview with Fredek. Nevertheless, he'd drawn a line under that particular *Where are they now?* piece so far as he was concerned. He didn't welcome this 'gentle nudge', but that's what you got for working for a sensationalist site that existed solely to draw paying advertisers.

Then his conscience pricked. There *was* an element of Fredek making lemonade out of lemons in using almost losing a leg as a springboard to a career as an influencer. Educating cyclists not to jink on and off pavements or nip the wrong way up one-way streets had morphed into being an expert guest on radio, TV and print media whenever a cyclist-related news item came up. He'd provided safety tips to lifestyle magazines and charged to speak in schools and even for after-dinner slots. In turn, that had led to him claiming influencer status and offering digital marketing and social media training via workshops and mentoring.

And all the time, his website and social channels were ablaze with money-spinning ads and offers of paid membership that involved motivational podcasts and training videos along with a series of what he termed 'ebooks', though Dev thought of them more as electronic pamphlets. In his interview, Fredek had boasted about members qualifying for a five per cent discount on attending conferences where he was a speaker. Drily, Dev, who knew how these things worked, had asked, 'If you give them five per cent, you must be getting ten?' Fredek had just smiled.

Nevertheless, Fredek's high-visibility influencer profile qualified him as an 'everyday celebrity'.

Now Dev knew Thea, he didn't even want to write the fairly innocuous *Where are they now?* feature. He definitely baulked at her being the victim of the follow-up *You decide!* piece where a heavily slanted story would be followed by *Your chance to vote!*

- *Is Thea Wynter as innocent as she pretends?*
- *Could Thea Wynter have avoided Fredek if she'd been paying attention?*
- *Did Fredek Kowski act like a moron?*
- *Is it Fredek Kowski who needs to apologise to Thea Wynter for putting himself on her conscience?*

The impression given was that voting was meaningful, rather than the entirely pointless exercise it was. Polls were their own form of clickbait, garnering 'return clicks', when people came back to see which option was winning. Stats showed that many of the return-clickers authored the wildly speculative comments that followed.

I'll bet she was late for a date!
I expect she was on something.
Probably plucking her eyebrows in the rear-view mirror.

Dev knew all about click stats and advertisers. Commercial deals used to be part of his role at the agency and he'd lost count of the presentations he'd given to would-be clients – but the agency content had been newsy, accurate and well written. On Everyday Celebs the keyboard warriors just wanted something on which to vent their judgy spleen and Weston wanted their clicks to tempt the advertisers. A match made in heaven.

Thea Wynter had come to public notice during several seasons of *Garden Gladiators*. The camera had loved her, probably because she'd ignored it and just been herself. He'd once watched the show with Grandpa Cyril, who'd said, 'I think she's a lovely girl, that Thea, despite her nose stud and striped hair. I like her smile.'

Deveron had seen a lot more to like, but had agreed that the smile was captivating, and so was the sparkle in her dark brown eyes as she teased a contestant who couldn't remember when laburnum flowered. Grandpa and Deveron had both said, 'May or June,' as if Thea could hear them.

The press coverage of her knocking Fredek off his bike stated that Thea was never charged and possessed an impeccable driving record. Still . . . she'd never returned to *Garden Gladiators*, and the show had ended. Weston had located her on the Isle of Skye via the electoral roll and commissioned Dev to interview her in person, as her contact details weren't public, she didn't use social media and her employer had a strict 'no personal calls' policy.

Fredek, still living in Suffolk, had been happy to connect via video call. 'Me and Thea had loads of contact, at first,' he'd told Deveron. 'She felt guilty, despite me acknowledging fault. And you know what she did? She paid for me to have a private room in hospital. Insisted, she did. She participated in some of my safety talks and was interviewed for my website.' He'd sounded wistful. 'It looked great, having someone off the telly. Then she just seemed to vanish.'

Thea might not have welcomed the publicity that Fredek evidently loved, Dev had thought. He did wonder why she should have contributed to Fredek's medical expenses, though. She didn't strike him as well-off.

Journalistic ethics, which Deveron clung to – against Weston's inclination sometimes – dictated that writing about Thea meant approaching her openly and explaining the substance of any interview. Quotes should be accurate. Oddly, it always seemed to him, these same ethics allowed him to chat to her family and friends for the supplementary stuff and contextual colour without her blessing. But that third-party material was no good on its own.

As Thea was responsible for him having this job, this respite, this escape from the toilet his life had become, he deleted Fredek's email unanswered.

And right at that moment, another email dropped. It was Weston's reply to Dev's message yesterday.

OK, re the vicar piece. Payment at usual rate. But pursue the Kowski/Wynter thing. He's got a massive social following and we'll get hits. You've already had the travel budget.

'Shit,' he said aloud, before deleting Weston's email, too. No one had said the travel budget was conditional upon success.

He noticed that while he'd been fulminating over his emails, a text message had arrived from his mother, Pammie. *Are you free to FaceTime? I'm with Grandpa in his room. Xx*

45

Spirits lifting, he clicked 'join' on the link she'd sent and was soon treated to an image of two beloved faces, each with an extra chin through looking down into his mum's phone camera. 'Hello, darling!' His mum's hand looked as big as a lobster claw when she waved.

Grandpa, what was left of his dark hair brushed straight back, showed his slightly crooked teeth when he grinned. 'Hello, lad. You okay?'

'Perfect.' Dev smiled at Grandpa wearing a thick cardigan as if it was November because, at age eighty-six, he felt the cold. 'I've already started my summer job.'

Emotions flickered in Pammie's eyes – pleasure for him but disappointment for herself. 'I'm sorry you're not coming home, though.' Dumfries was only 'home' because they'd moved there from a tiny village after his dad, Art Dowie, had died when Dev was eight and Leith ten. Pammie had been both parents to her boys. Grandpa had backed her up, listening, talking, advising, occasionally scolding. She'd scrimped to help him and Leith through uni and had been rewarded by sons with what she termed 'good jobs', the type that paid a mortgage on a comfortable house.

Until Krisi had fucked up the agency. Now she only had one son with a career, and one son with a seasonal job and not even the key money on a rental.

Shoving those thoughts aside, he answered cheerfully. 'Your sofa's safe from me for now. It's a lovely place to work. And just for the summer,' he added. Dev knew he'd been self-absorbed while he sorted out the mess Adaira and Krisi had left behind and wanted to say, 'Maybe Leith can bring you to visit,' as it was a hell of a way for Pammie to drive at her usual cautious speeds, and his brother and wife Caro could share the driving in their seven-seater that would also accommodate daughters Dee and Luce, Mum and Grandpa. But Skye was a six-hour trip from Dumfries and Leith's family had jam-packed weekends into which had to be fitted dance and drama clubs, the gym and family outings.

Casting around for an alternative way of giving them his time, he was inspired to say, 'I'll send you a video of the outside of Rothach Hall. It's a fantastic place, with dozens of rooms, gables, tall chimneys and steep roofs and even a turret. It has two storeys, except the turret, which has three with a weathervane on top. The grounds are full of trees and shrubs, with a grand view of the sea and over that to the mainland. There's a big wooden-framed greenhouse, too. I'm sure you'll be impressed when you see it on video,' he ended.

By the time the call finished the sun was behind clouds and he elected to leave the filming until the morning.

He was just settling down to read on the bed when his phone rang and Fredek Kowski's name appeared on the screen. *Damn it.* He groaned. He'd forgotten Fredek had his number. His hand hovered. He could let the call go to voicemail. He could block the number.

But . . . that wasn't really fair. Fredek had given a good, full interview, and apart from being impressed with himself, had done nothing wrong.

Deveron answered. 'Hey, Fredek, I was just going to reply to your email to say that my editor won't sanction the story, I'm afraid. Thea Wynter would have to give her side of the story for it to run and she won't speak to me, so that's it.' Fibs, fibs, fibs.

Fredek sounded astonished. 'Your editor won't . . . ?' A long, puzzled silence. But then he changed tack. 'Why won't she talk to you?'

47

'She doesn't have to give me a reason. Sorry to disappoint. Bye.' He removed the phone from his ear.

'But—' Fredek began to protest.

Dev pretended he hadn't heard and ended the call. Surely Fredek would find some other media outlet to court? But the short exchange had left him on edge, his new room now constraining. He could hear someone moving around in the next room but decided there would be plenty of time later to introduce himself to household staff, who he wouldn't even be working with, opting instead to relax outdoors. As Thea had indicated the general direction of the footpath to the village, he left his quarters and turned right, passing an area invisible to the visiting public or the family who owned the hall. It had become a dumping ground. A heap of soil and a pile of stone were studded with weeds; a broken bench lurked in overgrown grass.

Nearby, a gravelled path ran towards a stand of pines with an undergrowth of nettles and brambles. He selected some favourite music on his phone and began to jog.

It felt good to be moving and he fell into an easy rhythm, singing along beneath his breath as he wove between the tree trunks.

Soon the copse was behind him, and he jogged beside bracken and fern, and then between back gardens into a lane, close to a stone bridge. He slowed to negotiate roses tumbling over a wall into the single-track lane. When he'd passed several colourful cottages nestled into their gardens, he came to a fork in the road. Some instinct prompted him to choose the left one, and he was rewarded by what was unmistakably the sign for a pub – the Jolly Abbot Inn, its outside tables surrounded by rose bushes and populated by a number of elderly patrons who smiled and nodded. With the promise of a pay packet to come soon, he took himself inside.

He found a cosy lounge that sported a TV, a long polished bar with stools and tables with red velvet chairs. The indoor customers smiled as he settled at the bar, lodged his elbow comfortably on the brass rail and asked about local ales.

'Skye Red, Gold or Black,' the young bartender offered affably.

'Skye Gold will do me,' Dev returned. He could see from the label that it was brewed from porridge oats. 'It sounds like a true Scotsman's drink. I'll be getting out my kilt, knee socks and sporran next.' He cast an eye over the menu. 'And fish and chips to go with.'

And Dev fished his phone from his pocket and prepared to relax over his pint, feeling at home in the pub and on the Isle of Skye already.

Chapter Five

The next morning, Monday, the sun was out, and Dev rose early, dressed in the dark green polo shirt he'd been issued, trousers tucked into safety boots, cap in pocket. Life's dice had finally rolled in his favour – he'd certainly had enough against him lately – and he could hardly believe his luck at being able to work in the wonderfully fresh air in beautiful grounds on a stunning island.

Outside, the sky was an unblemished blue, ideal weather for him to shoot the promised video for Pammie and Cyril. Positioning himself in the courtyard, he zoomed in on a couple of tall windows, then zoomed out slowly, letting the imposing rows of elegant windows loom as he stepped slowly backwards. Rather than just play his camera over the grey stone, he provided a voice-over, knowing Mum and Grandpa would be entertained. 'This is the back of Rothach Hall. It was built in the eighteenth century and if you know your Gaelic, you'll know that "Rothach" means "Munroe", a name brought to Scotland in the eleventh century by the Picts.' He'd read the bit about the Picts on the history board in reception. 'The family who live here are called Larsson—'

'What the hell do you think you're doing?' a furious female voice interrupted.

Startled, Dev almost dropped the phone. He turned to find Thea storming across the courtyard, ponytail streaming. Pulling all her hair back subtly changed the shape of her face when compared to her old publicity shots, he thought.

'Stop!' she ordered. 'And I need to see you delete whatever photos or videos of the hall you've taken.'

One look at Thea's dark slanted brows and blazing eyes convinced Deveron to comply, but he felt entitled to question such unexpected anger. 'It's a no-no, then?' He stopped the video – the voice-over was spoiled by Thea's bollocking, anyway – and slanted the phone screen so she could witness him delete the video, then swiped right so she could see his last photo was of the soaring arches of Skye Bridge and Kyle of Lochalsh taken just before he drove onto the island.

'Thank you.' She looked mollified, and said more evenly, 'Didn't you realise you were filming the windows of the family part of the hall? It's private. You must respect their home. They're our employers.'

She wore uniform shorts rather than trousers and even though he was on her shitlist at this moment, he couldn't help noticing her legs. She wasn't tall but the legs were athletic with subtle muscle definition and he hadn't before realised that 'healthy' could be so sexy. Evidently, her job kept her in shape.

He tucked away his phone before she confiscated it and sent him to sit on the naughty step. Mildly, he

51

observed, 'I just wanted to show my mum and grandpa where I'm working.'

Her brows met over her fine eyes. 'I understand, but please take photos only of the public areas.' Her pupils were small in the sunlight so he could see the different shades of brown and amber that striated her irises.

'You know,' he said, 'I would follow the rules if I'd been told them.'

Thea looked nonplussed. 'Whoever did your staff induction should have explained about respecting the family's privacy.'

'What staff induction?' He shrugged in what he hoped was a disarming way.

She sighed. 'Oh. I suppose Ezz thought Sheena would do it and Sheena assumed Ezz or I had. Fair enough. Sorry.' She pointed to the left part of the building. 'The east side is the family home. It's never open to the public, and neither are the east gardens – although the grounds staff maintain them, obviously. We sometimes call it "the family side".' Her pointing arm moved right. 'The west side contains the offices and reception, and there are six rooms open to the public on the first and second storeys. A load of furniture, tartan rugs and paintings the Larssons didn't want are displayed there, and they paid someone to prepare information cards. There are some great fireplaces made of Skye marble, but most people come to see the grounds and use the café. The revenue from visitors helps with the upkeep of the hall. Also, so many old buildings are derelict that the Larssons enjoy sharing their restored one, I think. They're a very nice family. Come with me to the gardeners' room.'

He followed her diagonally across the courtyard and she opened one of a pair of duck-egg-blue doors. 'This room's generally unlocked and contains low-value gardening equipment and our noticeboard.' Forks, spades and various garden implements hung on pegs or rested in slots. The room smelled of soil and garden chemicals. A row of waterproof jackets hinted that summer showers were not unknown on the Isle of Skye. She opened a cabinet, riffled through a drawer and emerged with a glossy leaflet. Unfolded, it revealed a colourful plan of Rothach Hall's grounds, reducing the stunning land to cartoon-like illustrations and the beautiful Sound of Sleat to a few wavy lines and a drawing of a boat.

'Here's the hall from the front,' she explained, as if he couldn't see for himself a squat rendition of Rothach Hall, complete with turret. Her finger travelled across the page. 'West lawns, leading to the terraces, which lead to the Nature Café, play area and public loos. Here's the main drive, with the car park. Close to the hall is the formal area of lawns and terraces, knot garden, walled garden and herb garden. Beyond that is parkland; mainly grass and trees.'

'Cool,' he murmured, as some comment seemed to be expected. He was taller than her and could view the map over her shoulder, which meant he couldn't help noticing how well the standard fir-green polo shirt fit her.

The tip of her finger moved to a drawing of a timbered building peeking coyly from pointed green trees. 'This is the pavilion in the wood, the last part to be restored. Soon it'll be used for residential retreats. The first is in July and is for writers – the kind of people who can write a couple of thousand words a day.'

He thought he detected a note of disbelief in her voice. As a couple of thousand words a day, or even a thousand words an hour, would have been nothing for him in the days when he interviewed footballers or sat in endless press conference, he said nothing.

'So, all *this*—' she used the side of her hand to sweep from the centre of the map '—is private to the Larsson family.' She shook the leaflet into its original folds, and he caught a whiff of her herby shampoo. 'The family's main business is fish-processing plants in Sweden and Norway, and they bought Rothach Hall when it looked as if it was going to fall into disrepair. They love Skye. Mr Larsson once told me that they were looking for a holiday home here and got carried away. In fact, they were looking in the mountainous bit, the Cuillin Hills, but fell in love with the Sound of Sleat.' She laughed; a sweet, low sound. 'I expect they got it cheap and some of the staff think it's all about a tax loss, but as they've refurbished it sympathetically and given us all employment, I don't care. They got Tavish on board early on to run the place because business keeps them in Scandinavia much of the time, and Tavish has developed the visitor-attraction side of things. I get on well with Mr and Mrs Larsson senior, and their children and grandchildren, but Tavish is my manager.'

'I haven't met him yet,' Dev said. 'Is Rothach a friendly place to work?'

She shrugged. 'Pretty much. The gardeners and housekeepers form two separate teams, but we all report to Ezzie and Tavish. They're the ones who have contact with Mr and Mrs Larsson when they're away.' With a brief smile, she gave him the leaflet. 'Sorry I snapped at you about the video, but I hate invasions of privacy so I overreacted.'

'It's OK.' He willed guilty heat not to flood his cheeks. But, he reminded himself, he wasn't writing for Everyday

54

Celebs now. He was a gardener. 'During breaks or off-duty hours, am I free to wander around the grounds? Except the private gardens,' he amended hastily.

She grinned. 'You are. And the potato scones at the café are exceptional.'

Just then, Sheena entered the gardeners' room with a waif-like young woman in her wake. Sheena's ruddy face was creased in a smile, her no-nonsense dark hair neatly parted and brushed. 'There you are, Deveron. This is Nell, another summer gardener. I'd like you both to do a quick litter pick around the grounds ready for us to open at ten-thirty, OK? Unless you want him, Thea?'

Apparently, Thea didn't, as she answered, 'I'll sort out the grapevine in the walled garden.'

After watching her select secateurs and thrust her arm through the rungs of a short aluminium ladder and hoist it on her shoulder before leaving, Deveron smiled politely at the student-aged female in front of him. 'Hello, Nell. Nice to meet you.'

Nell just said, 'Bleurgh, litter picking,' in a disgruntled voice.

Sheena doled out large rings designed to keep open the necks of plastic sacks, and long litter pickers for snagging stray litter. Deveron resolved to keep earbuds in his pockets for when he was given such laborious duties and stood back to let Nell go before him and show him where they should make a start.

Thea strode across the paved courtyard and along the path between the hall and the west lawns, past the knot garden, with its many pathways and intricate geometric boxwood hedging, carefully grown in bold, Celtic knot-like patterns. Small conifers clipped into cones or neat balls added height, and red berberis created a foil for all the greenery, creating a vague impression of tartan. Thea enjoyed the precise and soothing task of trimming the hedges of the knot garden, but today her goal was the walled garden, home to espalier fruit trees, squashes and tomatoes. Once it had been a working kitchen garden, but now it was decorative, quartered by gravel paths that met at a central feature of a dozen stone dishes splashing water to dance and sparkle in the brilliant sunlight bathing Skye today.

She slowed to edge the ladder carefully through the wall arch to avoid damaging the aged bricks and mortar. The short ladder also had old boxing gloves on the ends of its arms, and she positioned it carefully near the grapevine that grew along a great fan of wires up the south-facing wall. Then she took out her phone and selected the audiobook she was currently wrapped up in, a romantic suspense novel set in New Orleans, before fishing out her secateurs. She might not find that reading came to her easily, but listening was great.

The grapevine was already ornamented by tiny green grape clusters peeping out from the shade of the vine leaves. Its major prune was a winter one, but it was good husbandry to trim and train the new growth. Thea prided herself on relying on the minimum of jute string or wire rings, instead taking the time to curl the vine's own tendrils along the wires as she pinched out wayward shoots, snipped bunches clustering too snugly with one another, and removed scruffy or overly shading leaves.

The vine had clung to this wall for as long as even Hadley could remember. Original garden records had gone astray, but Thea thought it a muscat, too leathery to eat when grown this far north, and only likely to reach the required sugar level for wine in particularly favourable summers. Dilly from the café made grape jelly out of the harvest, which Thea liked on toast. She accepted ten jars for the Larssons' kitchen each autumn, and Dilly sold the rest.

Thea thought about the Larssons as she dropped her prunings to the ground, enjoying the sun on her shoulders and the wind tickling her bare arms. Erik and Grete usually brought their sons and daughter with their spouses and a crowd of children to stay for part of the summer and Thea was sorry that this year they planned to come for Christmas instead. Grete was always interested in the gardens in summer, and the family side of the house came alive with a clamour of voices and Erik's gruff shouts of laughter. But, from their point of view, Thea supposed a Larsson family Christmas at Rothach would be great, though winter changed the Skye landscape, with heavy skies and misty horizons and the heather clothing the hills in a beautiful burnt orange. Even allowing for a dusting of snow across the mountain tops and reports of frost and mist, Erik had declared, 'We will feel warm compared to Sweden and Norway.'

The senior Larssons termed themselves retired, yet seemed still to work in their fish business. He was Swedish and she was Norwegian. Erik was a big, jovial man, given to booming jokes like: 'In our factory, we make fish balls. I bet you don't know fish have balls, ha?' Grete would give him reproving pushes with her fingertips and giggle. It was due to Grete that Mary Pony and Clive Donkey were living out their retirement in the paddock. Someone had appealed to her for help, she'd called Tavish, and suddenly a horsebox was delivering the two elderly companions.

Grete would surely approve of Thea taking in little

Daisy, presently waiting at home in Thistledome. Thea smiled as she carefully moved her ladder a couple of feet before climbing up again. Tavish had agreed Daisy could accompany her to work when her tasks meant she could take complete responsibility for her new companion, and today she intended to whizz home at lunchtime to fetch her. Apart from a tendency to bark too much, Daisy was a well-behaved young canine considering the limited home life she must have had before losing her humans.

At the end of the morning, when Thea returned the ladder and secateurs, she met Deveron on his way out of the gardeners' room. He gave her such a wary look that her conscience twanged over the way she'd ticked him off earlier. 'I'm going to fetch Daisy to give her a run. Want to come?'

A smile replaced the wariness. In the sunlight, his hazel eyes appeared green. 'That would be great.'

'I'll shoot off and get her. Meet you here in about fifteen minutes.' She jogged to the pick-up, parked near the greenhouse, and whizzed down the service drive. Cow parsley frothed white between the trees, which were showing off their summer greenery and dappling the road.

After the usual tricky navigation of the winding single-track roads of the village, she arrived at Thistledome. Daisy, having polished off the snacks Thea had left in the hopes of keeping her too busy to be lonely or destructive, was ecstatic to see her new mistress and jumped into the travel crate in the back seat as if already familiar with the routine. They bowled back to the hall and found Deveron perched on an enormous slab of granite beside the rear drive, munching a sandwich from a paper bag printed with 'The Nature Café'. He rose as he saw the car. Then smiled.

Whoa. Thea was so distracted she almost forgot to slow for an unwary tourist. It was a killer smile, crinkling the corners of his eyes and showing even teeth, all the whiter because his chin was dark with stubble.

She parked and let Daisy out. The little dog shook, wagged and panted, looked at Deveron and said, 'Arf!' as if in recognition.

Deveron crouched to greet her. 'Hi again, Daisy.' This encouraged Daisy into a waggle dance, butting her head against his legs, making snuffling noises while he ruffled the explosion of fluff about her head and body.

Then they strolled together across the park, passing the car park on one of Thea's favourite walks – to Mary and Clive's paddock. Daisy sniffed at trees but neither pulled nor baulked, so Thea extended the lead to let her range five metres in any direction. The greensward was spangled with clover and wildflowers and great stands of pine and spruce were underplanted with shrubs. The Sound of Sleat gleamed like beaten metal in the sunlight, white boats bobbing on its surface. It was always breezy up on the headland, but the sun was warm enough that Thea was comfy in her shorts.

Beside her, a sauntering Deveron was more interested in the dog than the view. 'I wonder if Daisy knows how close she is to where she almost met disaster.'

Thea watched the long fluffy tail flying and long ears blowing as Daisy broke into a cute little canter. 'If so, she's put it behind her.'

Mary Pony and Clive Donkey hung their heads over their gate to watch their approach and Daisy ran up to exchange breath, showing no anxiety over animals about twenty times her size.

Deveron laughed at the grey around Mary's eyes. 'She looks as if she's wearing specs.'

'She's old,' Thea defended her friend, patting Mary's neck. 'She needs them.'

'I'll bet she's younger than me. I'm forty-two.' Deveron pulled up a handful of grass to feed Mary from the flat of his hand. The pony lipped at it politely, not mentioning that she had plenty of grass, thanks.

'I'm forty-one.' Thea wondered about him and the wife who'd abandoned their life together. Had she taken little hazel-eyed daughters and sons with her? She didn't know him well enough to ask. Although his behaviour had been exemplary apart from his unwise video-shooting attempt, she was still wary of the way he'd turned up out of the blue and slotted into a job they happened to have open. She drew a parsnip from her pocket, snapped it in two and let Clive and Mary snuffle the halves from the palms of her hands. They crunched noisily, clearly more interested than in Deveron's grass.

Deveron patted Mary and Clive – and Daisy in case she felt left out – and then he checked the time. 'I'd better get back to work. I'm only on trial, you know.'

Thea gave an exaggerated roll of her eyes. 'And I've heard terrible things about the head gardener.'

They strolled back before parting at the courtyard. Deveron waited for Sheena and Nell while Thea collected a trug, gloves, trowel and hand fork, then she and Daisy set off for the herb garden to tackle the weeding. She hated to see groundsel or couch grass spoiling a cushion of thyme or a pretty fall of sage.

She'd just arrived, and Daisy had selected a patch of sunlight in which to sun herself, when Thea's phone sounded in her pocket. Seeing the caller was Ezz, she answered, 'Hey, sis.'

Ezz wasted no time on pleasantries. 'Fredek Kowski just rang the hall, asking for you.'

Thea dropped the trug and most of the weeds flopped out. 'What?'

'Orla on reception trotted out the usual "no personal calls" and said that she couldn't confirm who did or didn't work here. Fredek said he knew you did. Apparently, some past contestant from *Garden Gladiators* visited while on holiday. You've changed so much she couldn't think where she'd seen you at first, but remembered when she got home. Then she gossiped about it on social media.'

'*Crap*,' Thea wailed. 'Nobody's shown any sign of recognising me for years! Why do people feel compelled to spew the petty details of their stupid lives onto social media? Oh, Ezz, what the hell does Fredek want?'

'He didn't say.' Ezz sounded as anxious as Thea felt. After a moment, she added, 'We're a long way from Suffolk. I thought he was firmly in the past.'

'Yeah,' Thea agreed dubiously. 'But we can't expect him to forget an accident that changed his life.' Neither of them had much more to say apart from being glad Fredek had been baulked by whoever had been answering the phone on reception. After the call, Thea took out her phone and googled Fredek Kowski. 'Damn,' she muttered, when his name prompted pages of hits. As always, her eyes were inclined to skate over a lot of text, but she made herself concentrate hard enough to know that there was a website, a blog, a newsletter and crowdfunding campaigns. Admirably entrepreneurial, but she wished he'd leave her alone to live her peacefully offline life, free of the anxiety that had once accompanied the brief entanglement of their lives.

Chapter Six

Dev had to work three more days – the last days of June – before getting three days off. Today, Friday, all the gardeners were working in the family's private garden, even white-haired Hadley, the older seasonal gardener who spent much of his time raising bedding plants in the greenhouse or methodically trimming the topiary in the knot garden. Sheena was on the ride-on mower; Nell guided a hand mower on a patch of lawn shaped like a jigsaw piece, while Hadley trimmed around the trees.

For the first time, Dev was partnering Thea. She wielded the hedge cutter, making perfect passes over the privet, while he collected the trimmings and flung them into the greedy maw of the shredder. With two roaring machines, ear protectors and goggles, communication was minimal, but Dev couldn't help noticing a small vee that hovered between her brows.

When they took their lunch break, removing their protective gear to flop with the others on the grass, he asked, 'No Daisy today?'

She took a deep drink from her water bottle and then

wiped her face on her sleeve with an endearing lack of self-consciousness. 'It's Ezzie's day off so she's walking her. Having complained about me taking Daisy on, she's fallen in love with her herself.'

He searched for what else might be making Thea frown, if it wasn't having to leave Daisy alone all day. 'Have her owners come forward?'

'No.' She shrugged. 'The local authority called to check I was happy to look after her for now. I said I'd be happy to look after her for ever.'

He took a slug from his own water bottle and tried to think of a way to make her smile. 'Do you know the old joke about the wee dawgie?' He let his Scots accent broaden. 'There's a wee lassie with her mum, and the wee lassie says, "Aw, lookit the wee dawgie." The mum, who's a bit posh, snaps, "It's not a *wee dawgie*. It's a *little dog*." And the girl gives her mum a look and says, "Well, it looks exactly like a wee dawgie, hey?" My grandpa used to tell the story if he thought anyone was putting on airs and needed their pretensions depressing.'

Everyone chuckled, even Thea. 'I think I'd like your grandpa,' she said.

'He sounds a good man,' Hadley confirmed.

After lunch, Thea pruned a climbing hydrangea that was creeping onto the windows either side of its designated path up the wall, while Deveron alternately weeded and cleared after her. He didn't mind being given the noddy jobs. Being a seasonal worker at Rothach Hall was affording respite and removing the pressure to pursue other writing opportunities. Adaira and Krisi strolling into the metaphorical sunset had left him sick with grief and anger and yet with no alternative but to deal with the financial barbed wire they'd wrapped him in. In comparison, it felt relaxing and life-affirming to sweep hedge clippings in alternating sunlight and shade as the sun played with the clouds. His gardening co-workers were normal, straightforward folk for whom Skye was home. It was easy to forget his old stresses of frequent travel around Europe, striving for success in a pressured environment. Though he'd missed his old life at first, perhaps he was finally putting behind him some of his resentment at how it had ended.

They finished at five and gathered up their tools. Thea asked Hadley to drive the ride-on mower to its shed, which Dev assumed was because Hadley, the eldest of them, was mopping his brow and easing his back.

Deveron fell into step beside Thea, towing the garden shredder on its two wheels. 'My fencing prowess wasn't required? I meant it when I offered to help.'

She shifted the hedge trimmer in her arms and blinked, as if her thoughts had been elsewhere. 'The posts and panels were only delivered yesterday, so I'm going to start after work.'

'Happy to help. Not much on my calendar in the evenings,' he answered drily.

He felt, rather than saw her quick, assessing glance. 'I'd be glad of another pair of hands. Want to join Ezz and me for a bite to eat first? Come over when you're out of your work gear. It's a few minutes' drive, or you could walk in fifteen as it's just down in the village.' She gave him her address, which he hadn't yet noted from the noticeboard.

He nodded, not reacting to her letting him know she wouldn't be alone. 'I jogged to the Jolly Abbot the other evening. Rothach village is lovely.'

Thea paused, shooting him another look. 'Deveron.'

She hesitated and he waited for her to say she didn't need his help after all. He'd noted her slight reserve towards him sometimes, and couldn't blame her. Instead, she went on, 'Please can you not bring alcohol with you this evening? Some people automatically bring a bottle of wine, but I'd rather you didn't.' Her straight brows weren't drawn together in a frown, but neither was she smiling.

He studied her face, and read awkwardness in her expression. 'I know I said I went to the pub, but I'm safe around alcohol. I won't get embarrassing.'

Flushing, she checked that the others were ahead and couldn't overhear. 'It's not you. Ezz gave up drink. It's different at a pub, somehow, where there are loads of people, some drinking alcohol and others not, but I don't drink when it's just a small number, like at my house or hers.'

'Ah.' He was sorry he'd been defensive. 'Of course. Thanks for the heads-up.'

She smiled, looking relieved, and he was struck by how expressive her face was.

Impulsively, he asked, 'Are you OK? You've seemed a bit remote today.'

As if to play for time while she considered her reply, she wedged the hedge trimmer between her knees and pulled the tie from her ponytail, letting her hair flop down in a series of long commas on her shoulders. She smoothed its glossy length, swirled it around and caught it up again. 'I suppose we all get sunk in our thoughts.'

As if to change the subject, she glanced at the patch of ground at the side of the staff accommodation, the dumping ground he'd noticed before. 'We must get that cleared up.' She retrieved the hedge trimmer and started towards the power-tool lock-up, close to the gardeners' room.

He returned to dragging the shredder, its tyres grumbling on the courtyard paving. 'I wondered about having a go at that patch in my downtime, if it's OK. My window looks out onto it.'

She turned and smiled. 'Is it offending your gardener's soul?'

He was glad to see her lighten up. He struck a stupid pose with his eyes closed and the back of his hand against his forehead. 'Deeply.'

She chuckled as they rounded the corner. 'It's all yours. Project Deveron.'

The sun bathed Rothach village in a gorgeous evening golden glow. After collecting Daisy from Ezzie and then changing into jeans and T-shirt, Thea ate a banana while she watched the news on TV. She was surprised that Deveron had offered to help with the fence. Although she'd done plenty of hard landscaping and was equal to digging eight post holes, it would be good to share the task. Perhaps there had been no reason for the slight feeling of unease she'd experienced around him. Maybe, recovering from his divorce, he'd just come to the remote Isle of Skye to escape the past – like her. When he'd mentioned going to the Jolly Abbott alone, she'd thought it sounded lonely.

He jogged up just as she'd laid the posts close to their eventual positions. She called a greeting, and Daisy, on a long lead tied to a tree so she couldn't reach the road, bounded into his path with a challenging, 'Arf, arf, arf!'

Dev pulled a face of wounded astonishment. 'Hey, Daisy, this is me, the guy who saved your life.'

'Arf.' Daisy stood her ground, albeit with a wagging tail.

Thea shielded her eyes. 'She thinks her human needs to know when anyone arrives. That's enough, Daisy.'

Daisy stopped barking and, when Dev proffered a hand, licked it.

He straightened, his eyes smiling. 'You seem to have become fluent in Daisy already.'

'She's easy to read,' Thea returned with a grin. 'I'm off tomorrow so she's going to find herself one of a crowd, because I'm walking two other dogs, Bouncer and Scotty. Their owners are older, so I often take their mutts. Now, how are you with a pickaxe? Skye soil can be stony.'

'Awesome,' he answered modestly. He surveyed the waiting fence posts. 'I see you've made a start.'

Thea thought she read misgiving in his expression as she offered him the smooth handle of the pickaxe. 'Don't worry, I haven't forgotten the food I promised. Ezz wanted to prettify herself first. She's off on a date later.'

In the next hour, he proved his awesomeness with the pickaxe. She made a leading hole with the spade, then he sent the pickaxe soaring in arcs to loosen the packed subsoil, the late sun flashing on the metal head. Thea found her attention straying frequently to the movement of his body as he swung the pickaxe with a solid *thunk*, then jerked it free.

Daisy lay in the sun, looking baffled at their activity.

Before too long, Thea's friend Fraser arrived, attracted by the noise probably, silver hair flowing and Scotty beside him, a terrier with a square black snout and bat-like ears.

Daisy bounced instantly to her paws and shot to the end of her long lead to challenge the newcomers. 'Arf, arf!'

Scotty replied with a deep woof that made Daisy pause uncertainly and belatedly add a wag of her tail.

Fraser grinned, showing a gap in his teeth. 'Is that a wee doggie or a mop?'

Thea laughed, remembering Dev's joke about the 'wee dawgie'. 'This is Daisy. She's my foster dog, but I'm hoping her owner doesn't turn up.'

'Skinny,' Fraser observed taciturnly.

Glad to rest her spade for a moment, Thea explained Daisy's recent history, introducing Deveron along the way.

'You from the south?' Fraser demanded, upon hearing Dev's accent.

He grinned and agreed, 'Aye. I'm a "Doonhamer".' To Thea he explained, 'People from Dumfries are always going "doon hame" – down home – from Glasgow or wherever.'

Thea smiled. 'As an English person, all of Scotland feels like the north so it's funny to hear anywhere in Scotland described as "the south", or that you'd go "doon" to it.' She petted Scotty, who wagged his clipped black tail. Daisy, deciding either that her human had approved the other dog or feeling jealous, rushed in to be petted, too.

Fraser said, 'Ah well, I'm off now. I'm on my way to visit Maisie,' which made Thea grin all over again because he'd more or less walked past Maisie's to come and inspect Thea's activities.

After the elderly gent had shuffled off, Thea said to Dev, 'Fraser and another neighbour, Maisie, have gone out of their way to be nice to me since I moved to Thistledome.'

As most of Dev's breath seemed to be utilised in swinging the pickaxe, she didn't wait for an answer but moved on to Rothach Hall activities. 'On Tuesday, we've a youth group coming to learn about Scotland's native trees. No doubt the highlight for them will be a fizzy drink and snack from the café followed by an hour on the playthings.'

He laughed, then swung the pickaxe again. *Thunk.*

She took a couple of steps to her right before beginning the next leading hole. 'Dilly, the café manager, encourages groups to use it – knitting and crochet, parents and toddlers, book groups. Obviously, they buy food and drink while there. The tourists come in good weather, but she likes visitors all the time.'

Dev emitted a grunt every time he swung the pickaxe. *Grunt. Thunk. Grunt. Thunk.* It was distracting. Thea was glad to focus on Ezzie arriving, cool and pretty in a summer dress. Thea was used to her sisters outshining her in the girly-girl department, so she called, 'You don't look as if you're dressed for fencing.'

'Exactly.' Ezzie came up to inspect their line of holes, saying hi to Deveron as she stooped to fuss Daisy.

Dev joked, 'Why has she done you the great honour of not barking when you arrived?'

'Probably because I walked and fed her on my day off,' Ezzie returned.

Deveron pretended a huff. 'I saved her life, but she barked at me.'

Ezz seemed to be accepting Deveron, despite her wariness when he'd joined the team, but Thea decided that a little further ice-breaking wouldn't hurt. 'Deveron's the most recent person to say that we don't look like sisters.'

'We don't *look* like sisters, but we are,' Ezz observed, straightening from stroking Daisy. 'Adoptive families are families. Our parents couldn't have loved us more if we'd arrived in the biological way.'

Thea smiled, tears pricking at the memory of her

69

wonderful parents, and their unstinting love. 'They gave us giant names to show us how much we were wanted,' she explained to Deveron. 'I'm Altheadora, Ezzie is Esmerelda. Valentina is the only one to use her full name because she doesn't like any of the diminutives, like Val or Tina.'

'Or Vally,' Ezzie put in. 'She said it makes her sound like a place.'

Deveron listened, one hand on the handle of the pickaxe. 'Do any of you know your birth parents?' He paused. 'If that's not an intrusive question.'

Thea brushed back hair that was escaping her ponytail. 'No, none of us has searched. We were very well loved by our parents, Vince and Maxie Wynter.' She had to swallow before she could go on. 'They were backing singers and session musicians, so travelled a bit. They were in a hotel room when they died of carbon monoxide poisoning. A flue passing through a corner of their room leaked.'

Dev looked horrified as he glanced between the sisters. 'That's horrible. I'm so sorry.'

'I was just eighteen. It made me grow up,' Thea said sombrely.

Ezz threw a comforting arm around her. 'Where's that supper I've come for? Is your coffee machine on?'

Thea was glad to change subjects. 'Coming right up.' She reeled in Daisy's lead, Dev carried the tools to the shed in the corner of the back garden, and they retired to Thistledome's cosy interior.

They removed their boots to enter through the back door. 'Lovely place.' Deveron's hazel eyes roved around the flagstoned kitchen. 'But a big garden for the size of the house.'

Thea was already washing her hands at the pot sink. 'When these cottages were built, land was cheaper, and people grew veggies and kept chickens and pigs. I want a veg patch. I'll make a start in autumn; dig in compost then plant early potatoes in spring.'

'You promised me beans and peas,' Ezzie put in indignantly.

'And beans and peas,' Thea added, rolling her eyes. 'As you can't grow them in your own garden because it's a weed patch.'

'A wildflower garden, because I'm supporting the bees,' Ezzie corrected loftily, flicking water at Thea.

They sat down to chicken salad, Thea glad that her kitchen was the kind where you could wear soil on the hem of your jeans and not worry.

'Tell us about your family,' Thea suggested to Deveron. 'I think you mentioned your mum and grandfather.'

He nodded. 'And there's my brother Leith, sister-in-law Caro and nieces Dee and Luce,' he said, between bites.

Ezzie frowned. 'Aren't Deveron, Leith, Dee and Luce all . . . Scottish rivers?'

His eyes danced. 'You must've been good at geography at school. Mum and Dad started it, obviously. Leith and Caro thought it was fun to carry it on, and Luce and Dee love telling people where they got their names. If I ever have kids, maybe I'll look further afield and choose Amazon and Congo.'

Thea was registering the inference that he didn't already have children when her phone rang. She glanced at the screen. 'It's Valentina.'

Deveron made an encouraging motion with his fork that she took for, 'Don't mind me,' so she answered.

'Hey, big sis.'

71

Valentina sounded harried. 'Can I visit you this weekend? Sorry it's no-notice.'

Thea raised her eyebrows. Valentina was normally a month-in-advance person, and Edinburgh was a five-hour drive away – which was quite a trek for a weekend. 'Of course, but Ezzie and I are working tomorrow – Saturday. We're both off on Sunday, though. Are Barnaby and Gary coming, too? You'll have to stay at Ezzie's if so, as my box room only has a single bed.' The previous owner of Thistledome had wanted to move the bathroom upstairs, and half of one bedroom had been given up to it. The old bathroom had become part of the kitchen, so the configuration suited Thea well.

'Just me, so your box room will be fine,' Valentina answered. 'I need to talk to you about something. I'll aim to arrive late afternoon on Saturday and go home Monday morning. I've taken a long weekend.'

'What do you want to talk about?' Thea wondered what was going on. It was unusual both for Valentina to be so unforthcoming and to come without her husband and son.

'Got to go,' Valentina said breathlessly. 'See you tomorrow. Love to Ezz.'

Thea was left staring at her silent phone. 'Valentina sends her love,' she told Ezz slowly, and recounted the rest of the conversation.

Ezz arched a surprised eyebrow. She turned to Deveron. 'Valentina's not like us. She's a lawyer working for a big retailer, and ambitious, like Mum and Dad were. We're ordinary.'

Thea felt excitement take over from surprise. 'It'll be great to see her on her own. The forecast's good for Sunday. We could have a barbecue and laze about chatting without Gary taking over the conversation and boring the pants off us about opera and fine dining.'

Deveron listened to their discussion for a few minutes. After a while, he pushed back his chair. 'Thanks for supper, but it's time I was going. See you both at work.'

Guilt surged over Thea. 'I'm sorry. We've excluded you from the conversation, when you helped so much with the fence.'

'Not at all, it's just that I'm ready to get back,' he assured her, then went to retrieve his boots, pausing only to rub Daisy's ears. After a few moments, he passed the kitchen window, on course to round the house.

'You were noticing that man *a lot*,' Ezzie observed, arching a quizzical eyebrow.

Thea began to clear the plates. 'I wonder what Valentina wants to talk about? I hope it's not trouble between her and Gary.'

Ezz made it a dual-subject conversation. 'You don't even like Gary. I'm surprised your eyes didn't strip the shirt off Deveron to see what's underneath.'

'But Valentina likes Gary. And there's nothing wrong with noticing Deveron,' Thea observed airily, seeing she wasn't going to escape Ezzie's teasing. 'I'm a functioning woman.'

Ezz picked up the tea towel, as Thea squirted washing-up liquid into the sink. 'It's just that you haven't "functioned" with anyone lately.'

Thea snorted a laugh. 'Doesn't mean I've forgotten how.'

Then they returned to speculating why Valentina was making the journey to Rothach and left the subject of Deveron Dowie alone.

Chapter Seven

Dev was kneeling by a border in the family's garden, whipping out chick weed and grass with a hand fork, when a voice behind him snapped, 'Where's Thea?'

Glad to have a reason to straighten his back, Dev rose to see a man standing on the lawn. Wearing a dark suit, sandy hair parted at the side, Dev had to read his name badge, Tavish Macbetha, to identify him as the hall's manager, despite Dev having been at the hall for a week. Ezzie was the visible one, bustling around with an eagle-eye and a can-do attitude.

He answered politely. 'I'm afraid I don't know.'

Tavish looked exasperated. 'You're a gardener.'

'Seasonal,' Deveron amended helpfully.

Oddly, Tavish seemed reluctant to accept Deveron's lack of knowledge. 'Is she showing members of the public around the gardens?'

'I'm afraid I don't know,' Dev repeated. This guy was like a manager in a sit com, barking questions and knowing nothing. 'I'm Deveron Dowie by the way. Nice to meet you.'

Tavish lifted a hand to swat this courtesy aside. 'Thea's left you working here alone?'

The sound of the hedge trimmer hit the air. Dev raised his voice, nodding in the direction of the sound. 'Sheena and Nell are there hedging. Hadley's off. I don't know where Thea is,' he tacked on, in case Tavish was still having trouble grasping that.

Tavish puffed out his cheeks. 'Ring Thea for me, would you? I've left my phone on my desk.'

Deveron wasn't equipped with a phone at the hall's expense, and it was idiotic for Tavish to wander into the many acres around Rothach Hall and expect his eye to light on Thea. 'I don't have her number. Perhaps Sheena does.'

Tavish gave him a look he might give a child who'd cheeked his dad, turned on his heel and stalked towards the racket coming from the hedge trimmer, leaving Deveron to reflect that he'd never had to deal with management attitude when he was his own boss.

Two minutes later, Tavish stormed back past, barking into a phone. 'How much longer will you be? Meet me in my office as soon as possible.'

Deveron glanced up to see Sheena glaring after Tavish, hands on hips, and guessed she'd just had her phone appropriated. He hoped Thea wasn't in trouble. Tavish had seemed agitated.

Half an hour later, Thea sat in Tavish's office, anger and alarm making her heart thump in her throat. 'You're telling me that Fredek Kowski telephoned you directly, to talk about me? And you listened to him spill details of my private life?'

Tavish fidgeted with his pen and brushed imaginary

dust from the surface of the desk, his pale eyes guarded. 'He got my name from our website. Apparently, he'd already tried asking for you personally.' His lips were always moist and shiny, and his eyes slightly bulging. He made Thea think of a fish with hair.

Rage and fear made her defiant. 'Your policy is that staff shouldn't tie up the hall's landline with personal calls. And I don't want to speak to him. I'm entitled to my privacy.'

He changed tack. 'Why did you never tell me that you were involved in a traffic accident?'

'Why should I?' she argued, anger burning at being interrogated. 'It happened nine years ago. I wasn't to blame. It doesn't affect my work.' She knew her voice was full of attitude, but Tavish meddling in her business was uncharted territory. He always left the gardens to her, so they got along fine.

He blinked. Then, gaze dropping to the pen he twiddled between his fingers, his tone became hearty and false. 'You were on that gardening programme so you're not averse to being on camera, are you?'

A cold sweat broke over her. 'Why do you ask?'

And Tavish's answer filled her with fear.

At lunchtime, Thea trudged across the grassy park to the paddock, seeking the undemanding company of Mary and Clive, letting them blow hot breath over her and nudge her pockets. 'No treats today,' she murmured dolefully, leaning on their gate. She didn't have time to fetch Daisy for a run, as she'd opted for a half-hour lunch break to allow her to leave work early to do the food shopping ready for Valentina's visit. Fraser was going to let Daisy outside to take care of business and give her a few minutes to play with Scotty, making Thea glad she'd always been neighbourly about helping Fraser with his dog.

Since the interview with Tavish, it had been hard for Thea to recapture her bubbling excitement at the prospect of spending the weekend with her big sister, who she hadn't seen in person since she and Ezz spent a long weekend in Edinburgh in March. Above her, a seagull screeched like a squeaking wheel, as if entering her bleak mood. Watching the sun gild its sleek white beauty, she wished that her six-year-old nephew Barnaby was to visit, too, and imagined his smiling face as he played on the beach or ran around the woods at the hall. Barnaby occupied the unique position in the family of living with his blood relations.

Though curious about what Valentina wanted to say, Thea was preoccupied by the knowledge that, for the duration of her visit, Thea must pretend there was nothing on her mind. Valentina was a sharp-eyed lawyer, trained to question things, and someone who'd known Thea since she was a baby. Her default setting was to strive to understand every situation she encountered, which made it hard to gloss over things like bloody Fredek Kowski's scheming. Thea had always been glad that at the time of the accident, Valentina had been newly married and starting a different job, so, once thoroughly reassured that Thea hadn't suffered a scratch and wasn't to be prosecuted, had been distracted by her own new life.

Valentina had been unaware of Fredek Kowski falling in love with influencer culture, and it with him.

Thea and Ezz had presented their subsequent move to Skye as a wonderful adventure, rather than a welcome escape from Suffolk for Thea, and Ezz running from her own demons. Thea didn't want questions at this late stage.

At a footfall on the path behind her, she turned, hoping to see Ezzie. But it was Deveron Dowie who paused a few yards away. Mary Pony snorted as if in welcome.

'You OK?' A crease lay between his brows and unexpected concern in his eyes told Thea her expression must reflect her woeful mood.

When she couldn't reply because of a sudden lump in her throat he edged closer, voice soft. 'Anything I can do?'

She shook her head and wiped her eyes on the sleeve of her work fleece, which was stupid because her eyes immediately began to sting, her fleece being a home for all kinds of dust and chemicals. She blinked ferociously and managed, 'I'm OK.'

He stepped closer, patting Mary and Clive, one hand for each, giving her a moment to compose herself. Conversationally, he said, 'Tavish was looking for you this morning. Seems an excitable chap.'

She snorted. Clive snorted back, and then made a noise in his throat as if sniggering at his cleverness, tossing his brindled head. 'Tavish found me,' she muttered. 'He's an idiot.'

'Thought so,' he said mildly. He murmured to Clive, while Thea sniffed.

Then she sighed and leant on the gate beside Dev. 'He's left me out of a discussion I should have been a part of. He sees an opportunity for free publicity, but I won't play ball.' She scratched Clive's coarse coat. 'Tavish's not a bad bloke, but not empathetic. Usually, Ezz does all the people stuff.'

Sympathy was so clear in Deveron's face that it made her release steam from her emotional pressure cooker almost before she realised she was going to. 'Nine years

78

ago, I was involved in an accident with a cyclist. He was at fault, but he was hurt and, obviously, I was sorry,' she said gruffly. 'When he began campaigning about cyclist safety, I supported it a bit because I'd been on a reality show called *Garden Gladiators*, which was fairly popular. He said my name helped with publicity. It was fine when it was just turning up at schools or cycling clubs, or a quote for a cycling mag, but he yapped constantly on social media, bigging himself up. I don't like that crap. I fell victim to trolls over that and my *Garden Gladiators* appearances and so I deactivated my accounts. I cut contact with the cyclist, too.' She cupped her palm so Clive could snuffle into it with his velvet muzzle. 'Now he's got wind of me working at the hall and he's not only told Tavish our history, which isn't Tavish's business, but he's asked for permission to come to the hall to film a "documentary"—' she made air quotes with her fingers '—for his website. He presented it as a chance for mutual promo for himself and the hall.' Bitterly, she added, 'I think fuckwit Tavish has green-lighted it, judging by his panicked reaction when I said no. On the basis that I used to be on camera, he assumed I'd agree.'

Deveron was gazing at her. He was clean-shaven today and it made his horrified expression plain.

She heard her voice become something approaching a bleat. 'It's not fair. The accident wasn't my fault. It's a horrible burden to carry, but it's private. Ezz and me love our jobs here. I've bought a house. Fredek turning up here threatens all the peace and security I've created for myself.'

Quietly, Deveron said, 'I'm sorry.'

She felt her nose fill as tears threatened, and wished she had tissues. 'Thanks,' she muttered stuffily. 'Tavish's response was that Fredek's entitled to visit like any tourist, and that everyone films everything now.' She tried to make a joke. 'Like seasonal gardeners making vids to send to their mum.' Her laugh squeaked like a sob.

Abruptly, Deveron straightened. 'Tell Fredek you'll report him to the police as a stalker if he tries to film you. You're entitled to refuse an interview request and to go about your occupation without feeling hounded.'

Thea remembered the leg pockets on her cargo trousers and thankfully found tissues in one. When she'd blown her nose and could breathe again, she muttered, 'That would thrill Tavish.'

'Fuck him,' Deveron snapped. 'He's no right to indicate agreement without your input. Shithead.'

Touched at this support in the form of obvious anger on her behalf, Thea found it within herself to give a watery chuckle. 'I'll only tell him all that if I want to join the Jobseekers' queue.'

Fury, disbelief and guilt bubbling inside him, Dev walked Thea back up the grassy slope towards the hall, for once barely noticing its graceful lines and the sunlight glinting in its many windows. 'Do you want to use my bathroom to wash your face?' he asked, trying to be tactful about a spot of mud she'd managed to smear on her cheek.

She lifted her hand self-consciously to her face. 'I can use the staff loos. Thanks anyway.' Then, head down, she peeled off towards the door to the mud room and facilities.

Watching her go, he felt an inch tall. He was no hard-nosed paparazzo, hounding subjects with no care for their humanity, but he was complicit in this situation.

He was trudging towards an afternoon of weeding when Ezzie rounded the corner of the hall.

Her brief smile was preoccupied.

Bluntly, he said, 'Thea's had a hard time with your precious boss. He's upset her. She thinks he's given someone permission to film her without even asking her first. She's gone into the ladies' to wash her face.'

Dismay flooded Ezzie's sharp features. 'Tavish isn't good with sensitive situations.'

'He needs to refuse permission to film. Make it official, so he can call the police if the guy shows up anyway.' He tried to sound authoritative but calm.

'It's a mess.' She pressed her hand to her forehead. 'He thinks Thea's making a fuss.'

'He thinks *what*?' With an effort, Deveron modified his tone. Ezzie was stuck in the middle between her arsehole boss and her beloved sister. 'Sorry, I'm getting cross with the wrong person.'

Ezzie's gaze suddenly sharpened, a tiny smile playing about her lips. 'Are you . . . *interested* in Thea?'

His face heated. 'Is it a problem? I know she's my temporary boss but I'm single. I get the impression she is. Isn't she?'

Blue eyes thoughtful, she paused for so long he thought she wouldn't answer. Finally, she said, 'She is single. No problem from my side that she's your manager. Not that she needs my permission.'

'Oh,' he said. In seven days, he seemed to have risen from Ezzie viewing him with suspicion to her accepting that he liked her little sister.

As he said goodbye and turned to head back to the family garden, his phone beeped with a text from Fredek Kowski. *Awesome news!* it read. *I've tracked her down for you. She's working at Rothach Hall on the Isle of Skye and I've got her boss interested in me filming a documentary there,*

81

so it'll be a cinch for you to interview her, too. If not, I'll do it myself.

Deveron swore low and long as he stomped towards the family garden. Fredek was a fucking liability, thinking he could hit up people for interviews on demand. Arrogant, ignorant, idiot amateur.

But, again, he was misdirecting his anger. It should all be turned on himself: Deveron Dowie.

What would he do if Fredek turned up here? They'd 'met' on a long video conference, so Fredek was pretty certain to recognise Dev.

At least he could finally extricate himself from this situation, on a better-late-than-never basis. He opened his banking app and, with several angry stabs at his phone screen, returned the travel budget Weston had given him. It reduced his bank balance from low to almost zero, but soon he'd get his first wages from Rothach Hall. Then he sent an email to Weston, typing rapidly with his thumbs.

Weston,
I won't be supplying you with further copy. As the three-month contract you offered never materialised, I don't see a problem. Have returned travel allowance to you today.
All best,
Deveron Dowie

Resigning made him feel a smidgeon better and, as he trailed back to the weeding, he vowed that he'd work casual jobs all his life rather than write for a site like Everyday Celebs again.

Chapter Eight

When Thea was called back to Tavish's office later that afternoon, she felt like she'd regressed to teenage Thea, beginning, truculently, 'I need to leave early today. That's why I gave up half my lunch hour.'

Tavish responded to her prickliness with an indulgent smile, indicating the small chair in front of his desk. 'But you have time to sit down, I hope?'

In silence, Thea sat, thinking she'd rather have his big chair.

Tavish's smile remained pinned in place. 'I want to renew our discussion, now you've had time to calm down.'

'I'm justifiably angry, not in need of "calming",' Thea pointed out. 'I know you're not the kind of manager to think that *men* can be justifiably angry, but *women* need to control their emotions.' She let her voice rise at the end of the sentence, making it a question and not a direct challenge.

Tavish's smile vanished. 'Your sister Ezzie agrees with you that I've acted inappropriately.'

'The fact that Ezzie is my sister doesn't have any bearing

on the situation.' Thea wasn't entirely accurate there, as Ezzie would be on her side regarding everything from Fredek Kowski being knocked off his bike to who'd once dropped their dad, Vince's favourite guitar.

'Quite.' Tavish began to look uncomfortable. 'But unfortunately, I don't have any way to contact Fredek Kowski. I didn't think to note down his number and we don't have a caller ID system.'

Thea snorted. 'He's on every social media platform going. Send him a direct message. Or go to his website and fill in the contact form. And, come to think of it, isn't it an obligation to have a street address on a website? Send him a letter. In fact, do all three.'

Tavish's gaze narrowed. Quietly, he said, 'This isn't like you, Thea.'

She found herself on her feet. Maybe there were strategies for making your boss own it when he erred, but they all deserted Thea now. 'Tavish, I've done nothing to merit censure.' 'Merit censure' was a phrase she'd heard Ezzie use over staff stuff. 'You acted without consulting me in a matter concerning my private life, causing me stress and embarrassment. You said you couldn't contact Fredek Kowski, so I offered several options. What, exactly, am I being "like"?'

Scarlet flags flew in Tavish's cheeks. 'Then I will try one of the methods you suggest. I would re-emphasise, though, that the grounds of Rothach Hall are public.'

Thea whipped back at him. 'This is a *private* place that's *open* to the public.' When Tavish didn't vouchsafe a reply, she added, 'I'm off tomorrow and Monday so I'll see you on Tuesday.' She left, managing not to slam Tavish's office door in frustration at what the stupid knobhead had done and was clearly reluctant to undo.

As she was allowed to take the pick-up truck home on her own cognisance, she signed it out and gave herself a chance to cool down by driving across the moor to Broadford, letting the changing colours of the rocks and wildflowers soothe her. The landscape popped in and out of sight in a sudden sea mist and clouds gave a headscarf to the peak of Beinn na Caillich, which towered behind Broadford like a benevolent giant. Approaching the chain of villages that made up Broadford provided a view of the bay, its rippling water surrounded by lumps, bumps and peaks of land. Skye had so many crags and inlets that it was like a jigsaw piece cut by a mad, drunken giant and dropped between the west coast of Scotland and the Outer Hebrides, so even after eight years here she wasn't sure which were the islands of Pabay, Crowlin and Scalpay in the inner sea and which were knobbly bits of mainland.

After navigating the main road through Broadford, with its restaurants and craft businesses scattered amongst white cottages, she parked between the supermarket and the Skye Market Square, a colourful collection of huts selling jewellery and carvings, clothing and garden ornaments. A row of picnic tables surrounded by marshmallow-pink willowherb stood between the car park and a beach that was as much rock as sand.

Inside the cool atmosphere of the supermarket, she tried to concentrate on buying steak, fish, veggies and salad, but her thoughts strayed constantly to the spectre of Fredek Kowski popping up at Rothach Hall to film his stupid, sodding documentary.

Would it be better to contact him herself, telling him, pleasantly, 'no' to his documentary but wishing him well for the future? Or would that channel of communication be hard to shut down again?

At least her anxieties and resolutions vanished like the sea mist half an hour later when she arrived home and found Valentina outside Thistledome in her smart red convertible BMW. The sisters had keys to each other's houses but when Thea pulled up beside her, Valentina leapt out, grimacing. 'You've got a dog!' she cried accusingly. 'She won't let me in and I'm desperate for a pee. I was just about to drive down to Ezzie's.'

Despite the shitty day, Thea found herself trying not to laugh. 'Sorry – I forgot to warn you about Daisy. I should have shut her in the kitchen.'

She hurried to unlock the front door and Daisy bounded up with a delighted, 'Arf, arf!' before spotting Valentina and making a dart at her ankles, with a snappy, 'Raff, raff, raff,' as if to say, 'I thought I'd got rid of you.'

'Daisy, no!' Thea snapped. 'Sorry, Valentina. She's young and frisky.'

Daisy halted in shock at being scolded by her beloved Thea, while Valentina bounded up the stairs leading from the tiny hall, overnight bag swinging from her shoulder. Thea called after her, 'The box room's ready for you,' before hearing the bathroom door close with a thump.

She regarded Daisy severely. 'I know you're protecting our territory, but if someone comes in with me, they're OK.'

Daisy looked around as if convinced some other dog must be the target of the lecture.

Thea fetched the shopping and put away everything but the fish and vegetables she'd need for dinner. Valentina reappeared in the kitchen, changed into an oversized red T-shirt knotted at the side and denim cut-offs, looking younger than when wearing Gary-approved tailored trousers and blouse. Gary promoted formality, probably

86

because, at fifty-four, he was eight years older than Valentina, and he came from a stuffy family with older parents. He was aspirational and keen to prove himself and could be gently critical if Valentina didn't fit the image.

As they shared the preparation of the vegetables and awaited Ezz, Thea told Valentina the story of Deveron rescuing Daisy. 'I know she looks adorable now, but she was half drowned.'

Valentina took her turn with an update. 'Barnaby's doing well at school and Gary's become an assistant at Saturday morning kids' rugby because Barnaby's so keen. And how's life at Rothach Hall?' She rinsed green beans under the cold tap and then shook the colander.

'Good.' Thea deliberately overlooked the Fredek-shaped cloud hovering on the horizon. 'The pavilion opens for the first writing retreat soon. The gardens look amazing. I could take you tomorrow when I'm off, if you'd like to see, though I'd also planned a barbecue and a wander around the bay.'

'Not that Rothach Bay takes much wandering around,' Valentina joked. Then, with a quick glance under her lashes, 'Are you seeing anyone?'

'No.' Thea didn't tell her about noticing Deveron. 'Ezzie's the one who dates,' she added mischievously, as Ezz had just come in, causing Daisy to launch herself up the hall.

After exchanging long, sisterly hugs with Valentina, Ezz put up her hands as if in submission and volunteered information. 'I'm seeing a guy called Navdeep, but nothing serious. I met him on a dating app. He lives in Plockton, on the mainland. We've been out for dinner three times. We both had "no alcohol" in our profiles.'

Thea, who knew vaguely of Navdeep's existence, nodded. She'd once asked Ezz if it was hard going out with people who drank, and she'd just laughed and said she wasn't *that* fragile, but she usually waited until they were drinking coffee before allowing kissing.

Valentina smiled teasingly. 'Big change from when you were younger, Ezz.'

Ezzie lifted the lid of a casserole to inspect the sea bass reposing on a bed of onions and under a coverlet of herbs. 'We all grow up,' she answered briefly, which barely hinted at the willpower it had taken for her to halt her riotous devotion to Jägerbombs and porn-star martinis. 'Can this go in the oven yet, Thea? I'm starving.'

An hour and a half later, dinner had been disposed of. Thea shoved the plates in the sink and switched on the coffee machine. Once the first flood of news had been exchanged, she'd noticed Valentina getting quieter and quieter, so when she placed the coffee before each of her sisters on the kitchen table – black for Valentina, milky for her and Ezz – she prodded her big sister's arm. 'You said you wanted to talk. What's up?'

Ezz took Valentina's hand. 'Gary?' she asked sympathetically, her blue eyes soft.

Valentina frowned. 'Why Gary?'

'It's just that you came alone and it's usually you, Gary and Barnaby,' Ezz returned, unperturbed at her big sister's glower.

'We're not joined at the hip,' Valentina grumbled, repossessing her hand and using it to hook her dark hair back. Her expression softened. 'Sorry. I've got something on my mind.' She drew an audible breath.

A horrible apprehension filtered through Thea. 'You're not ill, are you?'

'No.' Valentina fidgeted. 'Someone told me something – about you, Thea.'

Thea's stomach did a backflip. Her gaze flew to Ezzie, whose eyes widened in reply. Surely Fredek sodding Kowski hadn't somehow followed a thread of connection to Valentina, who no longer even had the same surname as Thea? She could only imagine her big sister's wrath at being pestered about some amateur documentary. Then anxiety crawled down her spine. Just what did this documentary aim to prove . . . ? 'About *me*?' she whispered.

Valentina reached out to stroke Thea's hair. 'It's about your birth mother.'

It was so far from the road Thea's mind had been travelling that she said, 'Who?'

In the following silence, she realised both sisters were regarding her, bemused. 'I mean—' She struggled to find her way in the conversation. 'My . . . what? I'm— I don't even know what words are coming out of my mouth. What are you on about, Valentina?' She picked up her coffee cup with a shaking hand.

Valentina stroked Thea's arm. 'You remember our old neighbour, Lois Kingham? I met her in Edinburgh.'

'Why?' Thea felt as if her sister was talking in riddles.

Slowly, plainly thinking Thea was being stupid, Valentina explained, 'By coincidence. She was on holiday with her daughter, India, and they were mooching around Edinburgh Old Town with all the other tourists. I don't know if you remember India – she's a bit older than us.'

The conversation was so unexpected and Valentina's manner so odd, that Thea's heart thrummed. 'I doubt I'd recognise her, but I remember her existing.'

'Well, India did recognise me,' said Valentina. 'And Lois

was so keen for a catch-up that we went into a café. She was talking about what lovely neighbours Mum and Dad were, and then she suddenly began talking about your birth mother.'

'Nobody knows who my birth mother was,' Thea objected uneasily.

'Or do they?' Ezz inserted gently, her brow a pucker of concern.

Equally gently, Valentina said, 'Lois seems to know. She chattered on as if I knew too, and said you were adopted when you were fifteen months old.'

Ezzie clamped a hand to her mouth.

Thea looked down at Valentina's manicured fingers compared to her own square, practical ones. 'No. We were all adopted as babies. None of us knows anything about our birth families. We've never wanted to, and always felt it might be disloyal to Mum and Dad.'

'Well . . .' Valentina sighed. 'Not according to Lois. Maybe she'd been told in confidence and now she's older, that aspect's escaped her. Even when India asked if she was sure, she seemed convinced that your mother was Mum and Dad's au pair, who cared for her own baby – you – while helping look after Ezzie and me.'

Thea looked up to scan her eldest sister's dark, sympathetic eyes. 'Lois must be getting mixed up. Probably this is the plot of a book. Or a movie.'

Ezz stroked Thea's back. 'But Mum and Dad did have help for when they were away working, didn't they? We had Marsha and Ariadwen that I remember.'

Valentina nodded. 'I remember them, too.'

'I suppose so,' Thea agreed. Her throat felt almost too tight to let her words squeeze out.

'Apparently—' Valentina's voice came as if from a

distance '—and this is a bit of a shock: your mother went to prison. You stayed with us. When your mother came out, you were settled and hardly knew her. She asked Mum and Dad to adopt you because you were happy. She was French and went back to France.'

Thea found herself repeating what Valentina had just said, as if revising for a school exam – something she hadn't been good at. 'My mother got locked up? Mum and Dad adopted me. She left me. Oh!' She clamped her hands over her face, overwhelmed. 'I bet they'd got all the children they wanted with you two, but they felt sorry for me.'

'Oh, come on,' Ezz murmured. 'You're jumping to conclusions. They loved each of us equally.'

'And I'm at least half-French,' Thea stumbled on, disregarding Ezz's rationality. 'How could I not know something so fundamental? So . . . so what does my birth mother look like, then?' Thea challenged, trying to pick holes in Valentina's story.

'Small and dark-haired, Lois said,' Valentina returned, still more gently, if that were possible.

Small and dark. That's how people always described Thea. *Small and dark.* But it still couldn't be real, could it? Her mind flew to the glaring omission in the story. 'So, who's my father?'

'Lois couldn't remember ever knowing.' Valentina picked up her coffee. 'But she said that your name used to be in two parts: Althea-Dora, with a hyphen. Mum and Dad made it one name when they adopted you.'

'So that I'd have a giant name, like you two.' That detail made the story feel more real. A pain lodged itself in Thea's chest. 'Why didn't Mum and Dad tell me?'

Valentina pursed her lips. 'I've been puzzling about

91

that. Perhaps they didn't want you to feel different to Ezz and me.'

Outside the kitchen window, it was a perfect summer evening, with pink in the sky and a blackbird singing from the top of the apple tree, perhaps making its voice heard while the gulls were quiet. Thea felt as if she'd been shaken like a can of fizzy drink. And she had no idea what was going to explode out of her. 'Did Lois know my mother's name?' she asked faintly, no longer looking for ways to dispute the story.

'Ynez. Lois spelled it for me because she remembered it began with a Y. Y-n-e-z. No surname that she could remember,' Valentina added.

Small and dark. Althea-Dora. French. Prison. Ynez.

She jumped up. Her chair screeched on the kitchen flagstones and Daisy sprang to her paws with a volley of barking, looking from one sister to another as if to identify the source of any danger.

Thea's words fell over one another. 'I must take Daisy for a walk.'

Valentina and Ezz rose too. 'We'll all—'

'I want to be on my own.' Thea grabbed Daisy's lead from its hook on the wall.

'But Thea—' Valentina and Ezz said as one.

Thea stooped over Daisy, who'd given up challenging any hidden peril at the sight of her lead. 'Just me and Daisy.' This unreal, horrible feeling was like when Maxie and Vince had died. The numb, sinking feeling of disbelief was again about loss – but this time the loss of what she'd thought to be true and a loss of faith in Maxie and Vince, if they'd hidden so much from her. She all but ran from the house, jogging down Loch View with Daisy galloping beside her with an excited bark. Thea steered as straight a course as the lanes allowed, into Glen Road, then over the stone bridge to Bridge Road. Her mind spun. *Small and dark. Althea-Dora. French. Prison. Ynez.*

When she slowed, panting, Daisy seemed happy to follow suit. Flagging, they traipsed into Chapel Road and Thea's gaze fell on the Jolly Abbot, white with black trim, and wooden tables outside.

Without realising she was going to, she went inside and approached the bar, where optics tinkled. She glanced down at Daisy, who panted up at her, one ear folded rakishly back by their run through the village. Thea didn't even know if dogs were allowed in the pub.

'What can I get you?' the woman behind the traditional polished wood bar asked comfortably. Her jeans and a blue polo shirt suited her pale skin.

Thea remembered the woman's name. 'A large glass of Pinot Grigio, please, Rosamund.'

'Coming up.' Rosamund turned to reach down a glass.

'Um . . . hey,' came a man's voice. And Thea turned to see Deveron Dowie seated on a tall stool, a pint of beer and a Kindle on the bar before him. His burgundy T-shirt brought out the occasional thread of amber in his dark hair. He slid to his feet to crouch and fuss Daisy, who gave him her best greeting dance, tail a blur, snuffling and snorting.

Rosamund put down the wine and told Thea the price. Cold dismay swept over her. 'Crap,' she mumbled. 'Erm, Deveron, I've come out without my purse or phone. I'll pay you back tomorrow, but could you . . .?'

Laughter danced in his eyes as he straightened. 'Happy to stand the boss a drink.' He paid as Thea took her first slug, then glanced around. 'There's an empty table over there. Shall we grab it?'

Glad that someone was doing her thinking for her, Thea followed. When she sat on a chair, Daisy jumped up on the neighbouring one, obliging Deveron to take the bench opposite. As if Deveron had voiced the questions that she read in his eyes, Thea said, 'It's a glass of wine day. It's wrong to use alcohol as a crutch, but I'm doing it anyway.'

'OK.' Deveron sipped his amber beer.

Rosamund came over with a saucer of water for Daisy, which suggested the Jolly Abbot was jolly enough to welcome dogs, and Daisy popped off her chair to lap at it before springing back up and sitting neatly, looking from Thea to Dev.

Then a voice called, 'We don't usually see you in here, Thea.' And there was Fraser, puffing over from a corner with Maisie on his arm.

Maisie beamed, silver bun gleaming in the overhead light. 'And here's bonnie Daisy. Bouncer and Scotty really took to her.' She stooped to pet Daisy's soft fluffy head, but her wise old gaze stayed on Thea. Softly, she said, 'Dogs are our best friends. A dog will always make you feel better, hen.'

Fraser pretended a huff, scratching under his Tam O'Shanter. 'I thought I was your best pal?'

Maisie gurgled a laugh. 'After Bouncer, aye.'

'She never misses an opportunity to let people know she has no fancy for me,' Fraser said in mock sorrow. Then he looked into Thea's face, and whatever he read there made him squeeze Maisie's arm and say, 'We're away off, then.'

As she watched them shuffle out, Thea's eyes burned, and she wiped them with the side of her hand. Her birth mother! Fucksake, her mother. She wanted to identify her emotions, but they flew haphazardly, like swarming bees. Curiosity. Abandonment. Bafflement. Shock. Anger? Yes, she thought there was anger and misery and . . . well, a whole list of negatives.

Deveron cleared his throat. 'If it's more pressure from that cyclist—'

With a shimmer of shock, she realised that she'd temporarily forgotten Fredek Kowski, and that all it took to cope with bad news was to receive worse. Or at least more shocking. 'No,' she managed, and took another gulp of wine, its bite burning her throat.

To have birth parents somewhere, perhaps living, perhaps bringing up other kids, was something all adoptees must think about sometimes. For her, it had only ever been speculation on something she'd never know the answer to, like whether there was life on Mars.

But knowing that her mother had looked after Thea, Valentina and Ezz, it made her a person. Her mother had not just a name but a nationality. And a criminal record. Wow.

She only realised that her face had crumpled when Dev's voice filled with concern. 'Are you OK? Shall I get you another drink?'

'No.' It came out as a croak through drinking her first alcohol since New Year. She pushed the wine away because it hadn't improved the situation. 'No thanks. I came out to walk Daisy so I'll get going.'

He drained his beer. 'Can I come? I feel as if I have a share in the "wee dawgie".'

She didn't smile, but rose, her knees noodly with shock. 'Will you expect sensible conversation?'

Gently, he smiled. 'Of course not.'

'Then, OK.' Thea took a step and Daisy launched from

the chair, landing on the floor with her front paws together, like a dancer.

Leaving behind Thea's half-drunk wine, they went out into the breezy evening, clouds scudding across the pinkening sky that tinted the waves running into Rothach Bay. They walked in silence, except for Daisy's snuffles and an occasional bark at a shadow. Thea felt oddly as if she was floating down the steep slope of Creag an Lolaire. One foot before the other, left into Hill Rise, which she always thought a stupid name because hills fell as well as rose. A footpath took them to the quaintly named Friday Furlong, high up the scoop of land that sheltered the village. They brushed aside roses and fuchsias lolling into the road or squeezed close to walls to allow vehicles to creep past. Over cottage roofs below, they could see glimpses of the rocky beach. Further out in the sound, two white yachts skimmed along and a blue rowing boat rocked as they passed.

Ten minutes later, as they trudged up Balgown, she saw a light burning at Fraser's white cottage and heard Scotty bark. Thea realised several things as she came back to herself: the evening light had changed to lavender; Daisy was panting; they were almost home; and somewhere along the way, Deveron had taken her hand, though she'd spoken not a word to him since leaving the pub.

Ezz and Valentina tumbled out of Thistledome, wearing twin expressions of relief. 'Come indoors,' coaxed Valentina, gently taking Daisy's lead.

Deveron let go of her and hung back. Ezz spoke to him, and he politely refused something. Coffee, maybe.

'OK.' Thea felt as if they were children again and Valentina and Ezzie were looking after her. Tiredly, she said, 'I'll have to talk to Lois myself. Did you get contact details?'

'Of course.' Valentina put her arm around her and kissed her hair. 'She still lives in Suffolk, but she's moved to a flat.'

'Thanks.' Thea half turned. 'Night, Deveron. Thanks.'

He nodded and began to turn away. 'Night. Take care, Thea.'

He meant it in a friendly way, but Thea realised that the same words could be taken as a warning.

Yes.

She should take care in whatever she did next.

Chapter Nine

On Sunday, Thea barbecued as planned, though with little appetite. She was glad it was one of her rest days. In this mood, she was liable to tell Tavish to eff off if he so much as mentioned Fredek Kowski, because that blast from the past turning up was all she needed on top of the shock about her birth mother.

Not even a blue sky soaring over Rothach's pastel rainbow of cottages and the company of her beloved Ezzie and Valentina lifted her mood.

The three sisters lounged in the back garden and discussed what Thea would do about her birth mother. Thea wasn't sure, and Ezzie and Valentina didn't know what they would do in Thea's shoes.

'I suppose I'd want to know more of the story,' Valentina admitted, adjusting her expensive-looking sunglasses.

'I'd probably be scared to,' countered Ezz. 'I wish we still had our adoption certificates. Mum and Dad kept all that stuff in the little safe that was nicked when the house was broken into not long before they died.'

'I suppose the perpetrators thought it might contain

jewellery rather than paperwork,' Valentina said ruefully. 'I know I've seen my adoption certificate. It was like a birth certificate, only pink, but once you've got photo ID like a passport and driving licence nobody asks to see your birth or adoption certificate.'

'Mum did my application for my passport and driving licence,' Thea admitted. 'I thought it was because I hate form-filling, but I suppose it also handily ensured I didn't notice the date of my adoption. I'll have to look into getting a duplicate, when I can face it.'

'You know I'll help,' Ezzie began.

'Because I'm crap at that stuff,' Thea answered drearily. But then winced. 'Sorry, Ezz. That was ungracious. *Thank* you. I just don't want to worry about that this minute, OK?' She tried to keep her voice level, though her ice was swirling in her orange juice so hard one of the cubes jumped out. 'Why didn't Mum and Dad just tell me if they *knew* my mother?'

Valentina puckered her brow. 'They were so open about most things. If India can arrange for you to talk to Lois, then maybe you'll get some answers.'

Thea tried not to be grumpy or withdrawn, but there were long parts of Sunday when all she felt capable of was staring into space and puzzling over what felt like an alternative history of her early years.

On Monday, Valentina readied herself to leave for home. She hugged Thea tightly. 'Did I do the right thing in telling you?' Her eyes looked pink, as if she'd been crying. Thea hadn't been able to, which might explain her current tight, ready-to-explode feeling.

'Of course, you did the right thing. It wasn't your information to withhold.' Thea returned the hug, on tiptoes because Valentina was taller.

Valentina relaxed. 'And sisters don't have secrets.'

Thea felt her smile become fixed. Thea and Ezz *did* have a secret, not just from Valentina but from the world. She almost confessed to Valentina, but bit back the words. Instead, she said glumly, 'If my birth mother served time in prison, I'll have to hope that criminality doesn't run in the blood.' Blood that was currently feeling icy in her veins.

'Genes don't cause people to become criminals,' scoffed Valentina. Then, with one last hug, hopped into her car and drove away.

Deveron stepped into the front garden of Thistledome on Monday afternoon and hesitated, his gaze roving over the row of fence posts waiting to be concreted into the ground.

All day Sunday, the dazed Thea of Saturday evening had played on his mind while he'd occupied himself mending and painting the bench in the scruffy bit of ground near the staff accommodation that Thea had jokingly named Project Deveron. Had it been Fredek Kowski's approach that turned her into a walking ball of misery?

Slowly, he stepped into the porch and rapped the black cast-iron door knocker in the shape of a bee. When there was no reply, not even an indignant, 'Arf, arf,' from Daisy, he strode around the side of the house to the garden shed. It wasn't locked and he was soon helping himself to the pickaxe and shovel to dig out the last two post holes.

He was sweating and puffing over the second when he spotted Thea and Daisy trailing into Loch View, Daisy's pearly fur exploding around her face in the breeze, Thea's gaze trained listlessly on the ground. But Daisy barked a

100

'What are you doing in my garden?' challenge and Thea looked up and quickened her pace. He just about had time to notice the denim shorts that hit her at mid-thigh before she called, 'Sorry – did we arrange to carry on today?' A preoccupied frown furrowed her brow.

He shook his head. 'I mentioned doing a bit more, but I can stop,' he said breezily.

'Oh. Coffee?' Her words were flat and mechanical.

'That would be great.' He watched her trudging towards him up the path as if someone had poured the concrete into her shoes instead of the post holes, and she paused while he crouched to fuss Daisy, who panted and snorted and waved her fluffy-duster tail. Then woman and dog carried on in silence around to the back of the cottage. Deveron half expected the coffee to be forgotten, but he was just finishing the last hole when Thea returned with a coffee mug in each hand and Daisy on a long lead. She'd changed into jeans and work boots. 'Sorry, I didn't even thank you. That was rude.' Her mouth turned up at the corners, but her dark eyes remained dull.

'It's fine,' he said, accepting a blue coffee mug bestrewn with unlikely-looking flowers. They drank their coffee looking out over the sound, the sun painting green onto the rising crag of Knoydart over the water. Then, after hooking Daisy's lead over a nubbin on the apple tree amongst the green, half-grown apples, Thea fetched a pack of quick-setting concrete mix from the shed. They worked as a team, him checking with the spirit level that each post was vertical, and her pouring in the powder. 'This is much easier with two,' she commented, unrolling the hose so they could add the necessary water.

Then, suddenly, as if a giant hand had pressed on her shoulders, she crumpled onto her knees beside the yellow

101

length of unspooled hose and covered her face with her hands. Daisy trundled over, tail down, eyes anxious.

After a startled instant, Dev hurried to kneel beside her, surprised at how natural it felt to slip his arms around her body. 'Hey, hey,' he soothed.

She cried while he held her with one arm and used the other to fend off Daisy, who was trying to headbutt her way into the situation. Finally, Thea managed to draw enough shuddering breaths to speak. 'You know I said I'm adopted?' she gasped. 'I always thought all three of us were adopted as babies, but Valentina's just been told by our old neighbour that I wasn't adopted until I was fifteen months old. My birth mother was Mum and Dad's au pair, and she went to prison. She asked them to keep me. And she didn't stay in touch.' A sob shook her. 'And I don't have my adoption certificate to check whether it matches the story—' gasp '—and I'm just so crap at bureaucracy.'

'Wow.' He absorbed her words, aghast . . . but garnished with a shred of relief that her distress was nothing to do with Fredek Kowski. He helped her to her feet and onto a nearby bench. Daisy snorted an almost human 'Pah!' of disappointment at being left behind, still tied to the tree.

Thea wiped her cheeks with the backs of her hands. 'Ezz will help me. She knows I hate admin, or anything with too many words. I hated school. I like movies and audiobooks or podcasts. It sounds stupid, doesn't it? Because I'm not dyslexic. It's more like . . .' She groped for an analogy. 'Like asking someone who doesn't like spiders to look at a picture of a spider. They *can* look at it, but their urge is to look away. I mentally freeze up in wordy situations.'

'Fascinating,' he said slowly, trying to process this side of her, unable to imagine not having words in his own life. He searched for something soothing. 'I love reading. You hate reading. I hate peas. Lots of people love them. It is what it is.'

She sniffled and let her head rest on his shoulder as if she couldn't bother to support it. It felt warm through his T-shirt, and heavy. And nice.

His journalistic instinct was to follow the sensational lead and draw her out about the mother who'd spent time in prison, but he reminded himself this wasn't 'a story'. It was Thea's life. Something inside him responded to her need for help so instead of saying, 'Ezzie does seem a whiz with admin,' he said, 'Why don't we investigate it together?'

Her sigh was hot through his T-shirt, causing an unexpected tightening of his nipple. *Whoa. Who would have thought that would be erotic?* 'Really?' she said. 'I tried to search for info from my phone while I walked Daisy, but the signal was iffy, and I couldn't make myself focus.'

'Reading on a phone can be like working through a letterbox. Where's your laptop?' He loosened his arms when she withdrew to search her pockets for a tissue.

'Don't have one,' she responded flatly.

Don't have . . . ? His laptop felt like an extension of his hands and brain, it was so familiar. 'OK, let's go and use mine. You must have had a birth certificate before the adoption, too.'

Thea straightened and wiped her face. 'But under what surname? It can't be Wynter. Our old neighbour could only tell Valentina that my first name was once hyphenated – Althea-Dora.' She punctuated the two parts with a hyphen drawn in the air.

His heart twanged at her red eyes. 'Then let's start with the adoption certificate.'

Thea's 'Thanks, Dev' was little more than a squeak. She got Daisy and locked the cottage, and the three of them set off down to Glen Road and over the stone bridge, where they could pick up the footpath to Rothach Hall. The sun kissed their skin until they entered the copse, and then they wound between the tall pines that smelt so delicious and emerged ten minutes later close to the staff accommodation.

Thea paused before they rounded the end of the long, stone staff accommodation, her gaze lighting on the bench that he'd spruced up on Sunday. 'Wow. You've begun Project Deveron. Pretty.'

'I chose the blue paint for its availability in the gardeners' room rather than its prettiness,' he answered wryly, which at least drew a faint grin.

They entered the main door and then he unlocked his apartment and glanced around, suddenly perceiving a flaw in his plan. 'I don't have a desk, I'm afraid, and there's only one chair. Shall we sit on the bed . . . ?' Warmth tinged his cheeks. It sounded like the feeblest chat-up line ever.

Thea, however, didn't catch it or didn't care, and crawled up the bed until she could prop herself up on a pillow against the wall. He joined her, nursing his laptop while she cradled Daisy, who fell into a heavy-breathing doze. Thea had to scoot up close to him to see the screen, which was an unintended but agreeable consequence of offering to help, even if whiffs of Daisy's breath kept drowning the scent of Thea's skin.

'Where do we start?' She gazed at the fresh browser window he'd opened.

He poised his fingers, ready to type. 'I presume you don't know if your parents used an adoption agency? Or which court granted the adoption order?'

'No.' She sighed, as if they'd already met an insurmountable hurdle.

'OK, let's try the General Registry Office.' Soon he had the website on his screen. 'Look, it covers adoption in England and Wales, 1927 to the present.'

'How in the hell do you know that?' She gazed at him as if he'd just unveiled the secrets of the universe.

'I'm not an investigative journalist—' he began, then hesitated, realising he'd almost slipped up and mentioned how, when on the regional papers, such research methods were basic. He managed a verbal swerve: 'But I like puzzles and Mum's interested in genealogy. Government agencies are always a prime starting point, offering reliable, no-frills, up-to-date information.'

Her fingers smoothed Daisy's long ears and he found the movement distracting, almost as if she were stroking him. She said, 'I'm feeling panicky, as if I'm losing myself. First, I didn't know that my mother was – or is – French; and now I don't know if I used to be someone else.'

'You're always you, whatever your name was.' His eyes flew across the sentences, while she looked on. Soon he was absorbing the application process and explaining it to Thea, who sat like a warm statue beside him while he conveyed information.

Her response demonstrated how fast she caught on during verbal communication, as she said, 'Seriously? If I pay a premium for a paper, full-length certificate and expedited delivery, it could arrive in one or two days?' She fanned herself as if the idea made her anxious and Daisy roused herself enough to send her a bleary look.

'We can postpone the process until you know what you want, even if that means for the rest of your life. You're you, Thea Wynter. A name doesn't have to matter. People change them for lots of reasons – like getting married.' He closed the laptop.

Her dark gaze swept up to meet his, hunted, apprehensive. Torn. She licked her lips, and his gaze was drawn to her mouth. Even now, drowning in worries and doubts, her mouth wasn't sulky. She whispered, 'But if we stop, I'll never know.'

He nodded, and pressed his arm against hers, the one that crooked around the fluffy little dog they'd rescued between them. 'True. But it's your choice.'

Her gaze returned to the computer. Then she drew herself up and hitched Daisy higher. 'Can you get my phone out of my pocket? My credit cards are in the back of my phone case.'

As she cocked her hip towards him and hugged Daisy to her chest, he extricated the phone case with two delicate fingers, skin tingling as he brushed her hip bone through her jeans. She specified a card and, after he'd filled in the form with as much of her personal information as she knew, he used it to pay.

While she cooed at Daisy, he followed links to additional information. 'Have you registered on the Adoption Contact Register?'

She peeped at the screen. 'No, but I've heard of it. I can register my adoption wishes, can't I? Like, if my mother ever registered, I could decide whether to have contact.'

'That's about it.' He read a few more paragraphs. 'Except that even if you exercise "absolute veto" over contact, there would still be an exception in the case of genetic health issues or an inheritance.'

106

Her laugh made a welcome return. 'Inheritance sounds great. Perhaps my mother took part in a heist and will leave a letter explaining where to find the loot.'

He enjoyed seeing pain and confusion vanish from her face as she made the weak joke. 'Then there's "qualified veto", which would allow you to approach her, but not the other way around.' He followed another link and then pulled a face. 'Oh, but registration's tricky without your original name or your mother's name.' He followed her lead in calling the person who'd given birth to her "mother", reserving "mum" for the one who'd adopted her and provided love and care. 'I think you need your original birth certificate. And the easiest route to that is to wait until we can get your date of adoption from the adoption certificate. You could also use an intermediary agency.'

She buried her face in Daisy's fur. 'What's that?'

'An agency that you pay to conduct the search.' He moved from the neutral grey of a government site to a brighter, more colourful agency site to show her. 'Or we can just carry on as we are.'

'Carry on as we are, if you don't mind. Thank you . . .' Her words dried up.

He closed the laptop, disregarded the conduct he'd expect of himself when a woman he wasn't involved with trusted him enough to sit on his bed, and slipped an arm about her shoulders. 'You don't have to thank me.'

Her voice wobbled. 'But I'm grateful. It's scary and emotional.' She sucked in a wavering breath. 'Why does a mother give her child away?

His arm tightened. 'Maybe she thought it was best.'

'Why?' Scepticism rang in the single word. Even Daisy awoke to give him a disbelieving look.

107

'Maybe you'll find out,' he suggested. He concentrated on the plaintive cries of the seagulls outdoors and the distant sound of the ride-on mower, intent on suppressing his natural reaction to a hot woman in his arms. He was a red-blooded man and she had caught his eye from their first meeting. Beds and women . . . they normally went together in a way quite unconnected with research. And it had been a while.

Finally, Thea straightened, and his arm fell away naturally. 'Can I have a drink of water?' Her voice sounded scratchy.

'Sure.' He fetched them both long, cold glassfuls, then he took the armchair, leaving the bed to her.

When she finished her drink and said she ought to go, he walked her out into the sunshine. He was just congratulating himself that she looked less tightly wound up than a few minutes ago when Tavish's voice broke the air.

'Thea?' he called.

Thea turned with a wooden-looking smile. Deveron followed suit. 'It's my day off,' she said, indicating her off-duty T-shirt and jeans and Daisy wagging her tail at Thea's feet.

The sun made Tavish's fine sandy hair glow. 'I know, I know,' he said jovially. 'Got a minute?' He jerked his head and took a couple of steps backwards, inviting her into a tête-à-tête.

Thea didn't move. 'I'm on my way home.'

Tavish stepped closer again, face pink in the sunshine, holding up two hands that were presumably meant to be placatory. 'Look, I know you're not keen, but Fredek says he's coming at the weekend. I can't actually stop him, and he's coming a long way – from England.'

Dev's heart hopped. He glanced at Thea, expecting her to say that didn't give Fredek filming rights. Instead, Thea waited a beat, then answered, 'OK.'

Astonished, Dev stared at her. *OK?* No, it was not OK. Thea was entitled to her privacy.

And . . . Fredek had video-conferenced with Deveron. If he saw him at Rothach Hall, any chance of Dev distancing himself from his original purpose in coming here would be blown into the weeds.

Tavish's face lit up. 'I hoped you'd come round to the idea. It's good exposure for the hall.'

'Really?' Thea folded her arms. 'What if he tries to make it look as if I did something wrong? That would be bad exposure. I'd get in trouble with Erik and Grete Larsson and lose my job and it would all be your fault.'

She delivered these words so unemotionally that Tavish obviously assumed her to be joking, because he laughed. 'Thanks, Thea.' He turned, crossed the courtyard and entered the hall by the back door.

The moment he'd disappeared, Thea pulled out her phone and tapped the screen. 'Ezz?' she said into the handset. 'I need you to roster me off Friday, Saturday and Sunday. I'll take it as annual leave, if you like.' And she briefly recounted her recent meeting with Tavish.

Dev began to grin. He couldn't distinguish Ezzie's response, other than it being brisk and loud. Then Thea smiled a thin, wintry smile. 'Don't let Tavish know if you can avoid it without getting yourself in trouble. Thanks, sis.'

When she'd ended the call, she paused, gazing thoughtfully across the courtyard in the direction of the gardeners' room. 'I wonder if I asked the ground staff not to talk to Fredek, they'd co-operate.'

He followed her line of sight, as if they could gaze through the bricks and read the minds of everyone who used the room. 'Better to keep quiet. Then if the guy asks your colleagues what they know about this accident, the natural response will be "nothing" and a blank gaze.'

Her eyes sparkled as she glanced at him. 'Perfect. Serve him right to have driven all the way from Suffolk, if he still lives there, and go away empty-handed.'

Dev stayed silent. From what Fredek had told him during the video interview, Suffolk was exactly where he lived, which was more than ten hours away from Skye by car.

Then Thea took Dev completely by surprise. 'Are you free tonight? I know a nice restaurant just off the main road. It's a lovely walk there. Let me buy you dinner for all your help.'

Pleasure shimmered through him. 'Sounds great.' He edged closer and decided to test whether he could treat it as a date. 'Don't feel you have to pay for dinner, though. I like your company.' When she didn't respond straight away, he added with sudden misgiving, 'There's no boyfriend to rip out my gizzard, is there?' Even though Ezzie had told him there wasn't, having been cheated on, he was at pains not to inflict it on someone else. He thought of that gutting moment it had sunk in that he was losing his wife, as well as his best friend, who was also his business partner. Not to mention his livelihood.

A teasing spark entered Thea's eyes. 'You have a gizzard? I thought they were reserved for chickens.' But then understanding filtered into her pretty brown eyes, as if she'd read his mind about Adaira's duplicity. 'There's no boyfriend.'

He pushed the bad memories aside to enjoy the presence

110

of bright, sparky Thea, feeling drawn to her by the power of her gaze. However, as Rothach was their workplace, he maintained daylight between them. 'Are the men in these parts blind?' he asked softly.

She didn't pretend not to understand but wrinkled her nose. 'I date sometimes, but I've avoided serious relationships since . . .' She grimaced. 'Well, since the accident I told you about. My then-partner Ivan was behind the camera on *Garden Gladiators*. He was different once I'd left the show, and things came to a natural end when I decided to leave Suffolk.'

Though he assumed that she'd mentioned the accident to remind him that she had baggage, his inner reaction was the now-familiar wriggle of guilt at knowing more than she thought. 'Did you feel the need for a fresh start? It must be unpleasant to be involved – even when a traffic accident isn't your fault.' Faintly, he could hear voices but not see their owners as the courtyard where they stood – between the accommodation and the long, wooden-framed greenhouse – wasn't open to the public. It made him feel as if he and Thea were in a bubble while real life went on outside.

Her gaze misted. 'Horrible.' Then she hunched her shoulders, dipped her head and tears dripped onto her T-shirt. Deciding that her colleagues seeing her cry might make her feel worse, he bundled her and Daisy back inside the staff accommodation and into his room. They stood just inside the door while she quaked in his arms, her sobs muffled against his chest, Daisy whining unhappily at their feet.

Finally, she choked out, 'My mother was a criminal. Maybe it's a family trait—'

Deveron only tightened his arms. 'You're not a criminal. The accident wasn't your fault, was it?'

111

She hesitated. Then she choked, 'Sometimes . . . well, some people never believed that.'

He waved that away. 'Some people set themselves up in judgement, but the truth is a powerful thing.'

She gave a long, quivering sigh. 'True.' She stood quietly in his arms, while he reflected on his: *the truth is a powerful thing*, knowing of something that was twisting his insides. Sites like Everyday Celebs rearranged the truth all the time.

Chapter Ten

Thea arrived back at the purple prettiness of Thistledome feeling drained.

Dev had insisted on walking her home – no short distance. A hug, a quick, 'I'll come back at six-thirty,' then he said goodbye to her and Daisy, and strode back the way he'd come.

Upset and anxious after Tavish's unwelcome news, she wondered whether she'd been too open with Dev. Maybe that's what she'd been subconsciously avoiding by not getting involved with anyone here. When you liked someone, you let your guard down.

So . . . she liked Dev now?

She examined the thought, then admitted to herself that she liked him more every time they met, and now she knew him her instinct was to trust him. Like a rosebush that had been rescued from yards of bindweed, she felt freer.

Possibly her initial feelings had seesawed over him popping up when she'd expected someone else entirely, even though he'd saved Daisy.

Drawn by the sun to doze on the back lawn for half

an hour, she let Daisy curl up beside her. Thea closed her eyes and listened to the drone of bees around the hebes that were just beginning to show their tight, purple blooms, and the privet she'd left uncut because its tiny creamy flowers also drew the pollinators. The tension left her neck and shoulders, as if seeping into the warm earth beneath her, the earth that provided her way of life.

Two hours later, she awoke with a jolt, phone ringing and thoughts spinning.

Daisy had gone off to snap at flies in the shade, and Thea felt the suspicious warmth on one side of her face that told her she should have applied sunscreen. She glanced at the phone before she answered. 'Hi, Valentina.'

Valentina was in brisk mode – which she did extremely well. 'It's taken me ages to get hold of India. The call's got to be tonight while India's with Lois, because Lois's more confused than usual and if we do a WhatsApp video call on India's phone, she can make sure her mum's not overwhelmed. Then India's going on holiday, and a cousin of Lois will be staying instead.'

Thea widened her eyes and tried to process the stream of information. 'Right.' Blearily, she blinked. 'What time tonight?' A memory floated back to her of Deveron and the restaurant.

'India says seven. Her mum eats at six on the dot. I'm at the office so do you have a minute to ask Ezz if she wants to be in on it? If you want her to have the option, of course. Then I can initiate a group call at seven.'

'It's just that I have plans . . .' Thea said, flushing, though her sister couldn't see her.

Valentina made a noise as if blowing out her cheeks. 'Up to you. You can wait the two weeks, if you want.'

That took about one second to process. 'No, I can

114

probably rearrange things tonight.' Thea climbed to her feet and Daisy came waggling over for a fuss. 'What time is it now?'

'Four.' Valentina sounded amazed, as if people could survive without always knowing the time.

They said their goodbyes, then Thea spoke to Ezz, who very much did want to be included, then, with a sigh, called Deveron. 'Can we possibly put things back a bit?' She explained about the call.

His voice was rich and warm. 'Sure. How about I wait at the Jolly Abbot and you join me whenever you've finished? If it's a bit late to go to the other place by then, we can eat there.'

Relief trickled over her. How refreshing after Ivan, who'd been such a ridiculously meticulous planner that open-ended arrangements had brought him out in spots. 'Thanks for understanding.'

Deveron just laughed. 'See you later.'

Thea went to shower and then dry her hair, before applying make-up. Deveron had only seen her in uniform or shorts, face bare, so she hoped he'd appreciate the coppery, smoky treatment that made her eyes look darker and bigger than they were.

As she carefully stroked on mascara, her thoughts whirled. Had Lois become so forgetful that she'd got the wrong story altogether? Would Thea feel cheated if that proved to be the case? Or relieved?

To give her mind a rest, as she put on a summer dress and canvas flats, she listened to her latest audiobook. It was a romance, and it was keeping her guessing as to whether the hero had yet shown his true colours. She hoped he was a good guy because she'd invested a lot of listening time in him.

When her phone beeped, she found that not only had Valentina created a WhatsApp group comprising herself, Thea, Ezzie and India, but India had already posted a photo. It was in soft focus, the colour faded, but a small, dark-haired woman half smiled into the camera. Her hair was a cropped pom-pom, Eighties-style, and her eyes were fearless. An infant in a buggy frowned, while Ezz and Valentina – probably aged three and five – bestrode the woman's knees as if riding little horses. Valentina's hair was in its naturally wild curls, decades before she decided it suited her image to straighten it. Behind, Maxie posed with sunglasses atop her head, holding back her long auburn hair, and Vince's mouth was open as if caught mid-sentence. She read India's caption: *We found this in Mum's photos. It says on the back: Maxie, Vince, Ynez, Valentina, Esmerelda and Althea-Dora.*

Thea flumped into the bedroom chair, landing hard.

She stared at the group in the photo. There were her parents. Her sisters.

The small, dark-haired woman who was apparently her birth mother rested a casual hand on the baby buggy. She looked self-possessed and also comfy with Thea's family. But when the shutter had clicked, they hadn't *been* Thea's family – because the small, dark woman was.

My mother. She tried to force a sense of reality. *My French birth mother, Ynez, who did something so bad that she went to prison and then went home to France without me.* Nope. Still no feeling other than shocked disbelief, though it was dawning on her how few of her baby pictures she'd ever seen.

But Thea's sense of disconnect didn't matter. It was real. That baby was herself.

* * *

By the time seven o'clock arrived, Thea was trembling and glad that Ezz had come to Thistledome for the call. Blonde hair hanging in its usual feathery curtain, smile bright and reassuring, she stepped into the cottage five minutes early, patted Daisy then hugged Thea. 'Remember you can back out of the call or end it whenever you want. And whatever happens afterwards is completely up to you.'

Thea sank into the dear, familiar feeling of being held by a sister. 'Easy for you to say, when it's not your mother who's suddenly popped up. Do you think I should back out?'

'No,' Ezz responded frankly. 'You'll never stop wondering if you did the right thing.'

Thea and Ezz sat together at the kitchen table, Thea's phone propped against a pepper mill, while the time crawled around to seven. Punctually, the 'Boop, boop-de-dooby' incoming call alert hit the air and Thea froze.

Ezz was the one to tap 'join'. Thea watched other faces gradually forming out of pixelated murk: Valentina in one box and two faces together in another. Thea studied Lois, who was a pale, silvery version of the woman she remembered from her childhood in leafy Suffolk; her fringe swept above faded eyes, her smile sweet but vague. India was recognisably India though. A teenager when Thea was small, now she looked middle-aged and comfortably curvy, her brown hair streaked with grey.

Everyone greeted each other at once, so their voices kept cutting in and out.

Valentina was the first to attempt to chair the meeting. 'Thea and Ezzie, you remember Lois and India? Well,' she went on hurriedly before the jumble of greetings could begin anew, 'as Lois tires easily, India thinks it's a good idea to get the ball rolling straight away.'

Thea nodded jerkily, heart rate climbing, and felt Ezz take her hand and squeeze it.

India took over. 'I understand it's all been quite a shock to you, Thea. I've been talking to Mum about your mother – your birth mother – to try and help her remember. Haven't I, Mum?' She smiled at Lois.

Lois smiled back and her voice creaked with age. 'I remember Ynez. She took very good care of you girls, but she was a lively one, she was. Easily led into trouble, I suppose. I'd call her impulsive but good-hearted. And very proud of her bust, I seem to remember, which is why the boys liked her.'

Thea found herself giggling at the comment about the bust, but the candid character sketch somehow made the person in the photo more alive. It became easier to ask the question that was burning in her mind. 'Do you know what she went to prison for, Lois?'

Lois waggled her head doubtfully. 'I think it was stealing cars. She wasn't a ringleader, but she got mixed up with a bad crowd. Oh dear, I remember the dust-up when she was arrested. Luckily, your mum and dad were at home. Vince went off with the police and Ynez, his face like thunder. Very disturbed by it all, your mum and dad, but Maxie said, "Altheadora will stay with us, of course." And you did.'

A tiny part of Thea relaxed at this hint that the wonderful people she'd called Mum and Dad had chosen to keep her, rather than feeling obliged. 'Do you remember Ynez's surname?' It felt weird, effectively asking for the surname she'd once been known by.

Lois turned to India, looking troubled. 'I don't, do I?'

India slipped an arm around her mum. 'Not so far, but that's OK. Thea's interested in what you do remember.'

But Lois bit her lip. 'My memory's dodgy, these days.'

'Don't worry,' Thea broke in gently, feeling compunction as anxiety stole over Lois's face, and not wanting to increase it. 'Anything you can tell me is great.'

India tried another prompt. 'And what about Maxie's friend, Mum? You told me about her singing friend.'

'Oh, yes.' Lois's smile reappeared. 'Maxie had a friend, and they often sang as a duo. Other times Vince and Maxie were the duo, so Vince didn't like the friend, and Maxie called him "jealous bum" and said that he never complained about the money Maxie and the friend earned. But *he* said they had work coming out of their ears – which is why they had au pairs to help with the kids – and they didn't need other artists.'

Thea, Ezzie and Valentina all laughed. 'That sounds like them,' Thea agreed. 'I don't know which friend you mean, though. Did she know my birth mother?'

Lois nodded eagerly. 'Yes, she'd be able to tell you things. Vince used to grumble that Maxie and her were thick as thieves, and Maxie confided too much. He said it was embarrassing, but Maxie just laughed.' Lois's eyes twinkled. 'I think he minded that Maxie sang and played with her more than she did with him. Maxie talked about her, but she didn't come to Suffolk because of Vince.'

Thea smiled, feeling the familiar lump in her throat at the memories of her vibrant, singing, playing parents, and how their lives had been cut short when they were fifty-one – just ten years older than Thea was now. 'Dad was the emotional type, and maybe a bit possessive,' she admitted. 'I don't suppose you remember the friend's name? Musician friends often visited us. I remember an Eric, Geordie, Helga, Anna . . .'

'And one male Chris and one female Chris,' Valentina put in.

'And that drummer they called Sticky,' Ezzie added, wrinkling her brow.

Lois was already shaking her head, pressing her fingers to her temples as if she could pluck out the memories. 'A funny name. Miracle? Mule? Something like that.'

Apart from the two words sharing an initial letter, Thea didn't see too many similarities between 'miracle' and 'mule', but she smiled understandingly. 'Never mind. It's very kind of you to help me like this.' Tentatively, she added, 'I don't suppose you know anything about my birth father?'

Lois shook her head. 'I don't remember him ever being mentioned.'

Thea wasn't shocked. Her birth father could have been anything from a past relationship to a one-night stand.

Valentina began speaking again, as if she were the host of the meeting, thanking Lois and India.

Thea realised suddenly that Valentina was still in her office, a coat stand behind her bearing a single yellow jacket. Guiltily, she said, 'Yes, thank you very much, everybody. I won't keep you any longer.' When all the goodbyes had been said, she reached forward and tapped the red icon to end the call.

Beside her, Ezz sat back with a sigh. 'How do you feel now?' Her blue eyes were wide, troubled, compassionate.

Thea shoved her phone into her pocket. 'Disappointed I had a criminal mother. Frustrated Lois can't remember more – not that it's her fault,' she added. 'When I get my adoption certificate, I'll know the date my adoption was registered and then be able to get my birth certificate and find out my surname.'

Ezz sighed. 'Or you could google "Miracle Mule" and see if a musician comes up who once sang with Maxie Wynter.'

That, at least, made Thea laugh. She gave Ezz a hug, aware of her lithe form being so different to her own compact and sturdy one. 'Thanks for coming. Erm . . . did I mention I'm supposed to be meeting Deveron at the Jolly Abbot?'

Laughter entered Ezz's voice. 'You might have mentioned it once or twice. Don't worry, I won't stand in the way of your first date this year, but I will walk down with you.'

As the Jolly Abbot stood on Chapel Road almost opposite Ezz's cottage, Thea could hardly object, but said, 'It's not my first date this year.' Rising from her chair, she realised Ezz probably had a point and added defensively, 'Well, I've been busy buying Thistledome and decorating it.'

Thea checked that Daisy had water in her bowl and presented her with a chew, which Daisy took back to her bed with a snuffle of pleasure. Then Thea and Ezz stepped out of the front door and into a perfect, pink Skye summer evening, sisters who couldn't be closer if they'd shared birth parents. Their bare arms brushed comfortably as they started down Loch View, the sun's slanting rays bouncing off the sea between Rothach and the mainland outcrops of Knoydart and North Morar.

At the corner of Portnalong Way, they saw Fraser and Maisie stepping through Maisie's green-painted gate. 'Hello now, girls,' said Maisie in her rich Hebridean accent. 'We're just away to the pub.' Maisie patted her silver bun. Her pink lipstick followed the lines around her lips in an elegant tracery.

121

Bouncer, on a lead that dangled negligently from Maisie's knobbly hand, lived up to his name and tried to helicopter into the air, while Scotty stayed firmly on the ground, tail beating.

Thea laughed, patting the doggie heads, one brown and one black. 'Hello, everybody.'

'We're heading towards the Jolly Abbot too,' Ezz said helpfully.

So Thea found herself going to meet her date accompanied not just by her sister but by two elderly neighbours and their dogs, who slowed progress as they sniffed stone walls or tangled their leads in drooping willows. Fraser's grey hair blew back over his shoulders from beneath his tammie and the sequins on Maisie's cheerful red trainers twinkled in the evening sun. 'We'll take Glen Road, to avoid Creag an Lolaire,' Fraser decided for them all. 'Aye, it's steep, that one.' That meant crossing the bridge, and Maisie and Fraser pausing to admire the burn that splashed down the hillside from the grounds of Rothach Hall, far above and out of sight from their vantage point.

'The burn's the colour of weak tea,' Maisie observed.

Fraser grinned at her. 'More like whisky. I tried to tell an American tourist once that it came straight from the Torabhaig distillery, but he did'nae believe a word.'

Finally, they crossed into Chapel Road and Thea spotted Deveron at one of the chunky wooden tables outside, where he had a grandstand view of the company's snail's pace progress, the dogs stopping to examine every blade of grass.

Ezz sent Dev a wave, then peeled off for home. Maisie and Fraser headed towards the table furthest from where Dev waited, relieving Thea of the worry that the two

122

genial octogenarians might not realise they were on a date and simply join them. Thea approached Dev alone.

He rose and smiled. 'You didn't need so many chaperones.'

She grinned. 'Maisie and Fraser are friends and neighbours and we all happened to set out at the same time.'

He smiled at the elderly couple, who gazed back in blatant interest. He said, 'It's nearly eight-thirty and apparently the kitchen closes at nine.'

She hovered by the bench opposite his. 'No restaurant seems to stay open late on Skye. Sorry. The call—'

'—was important,' he ended for her. He seated himself and passed her a menu. 'It's no bother to eat here.'

Thea felt herself warm to him. Maybe if all men were as kind and willing to adapt to her needs, she wouldn't have been single for so long. She sat on the sun-warmed bench and transferred her attention to the menu. Once their decisions were made, Dev went inside to order mussels for himself and fish and chips for Thea.

He returned with a frothing pint of beer, gleaming copper in the evening sun, and the glass of white wine Thea had requested. Rosamund from behind the bar followed him out with cutlery wrapped in blue napkins and a pot of condiments in sachets. 'I've put extra ketchup in the pot, as well as tartare. It's a fine night for the beer garden.'

'Thanks.' Thea thought that 'beer garden' was a grand description for the three outside tables with lolling pink roses and the occasional thistle growing through the crazy paving, but she enjoyed the community aspect of the Jolly Abbot even if, because she was so often with Ezz, she didn't frequent the pub much. Thea liked Thistledome and its garden or walking Bouncer and Scotty – and now

123

Daisy – along Friday Furlong. She didn't go off-island much either, but left that to Ezz, who often drove over the bridge to the mainland on dates.

Thea took two sips of wine, then relaxed with a sigh.

Dev twinkled at her. Behind him, the front of the pub was shaded. 'I hope your call went well.'

'Lois tried to help me, but she's elderly. She gave me just enough information to be tantalising.' She managed a smile, experiencing a mixture of frustration and disappointment as she recounted the gist of what Lois had managed to recall. 'Ezz suggested we try and find this friend of Mum's by googling "Miracle Mule".'

'You don't remember her yourself?' Dev's brow furrowed.

She shook her head. 'None of us do. Our parents were hospitable with other musician friends, though I suppose most of them stayed living in London or other cities when Mum and Dad moved out into the countryside and decided to adopt.' She frowned. 'Lois said Dad was a bit jealous of this particular friend of Mum's.'

Their meal arrived, and Deveron unwound his napkin from around the cutlery. 'Did you ever see your parents perform?'

'Of course.' Thea reached for the ketchup. 'But I was a typically self-absorbed teen, and it was just the norm that they travelled to London for Dad to play guitar and Mum provide backing vocals, which she used to call "doing the oohs and ahs". They were like other commuting parents, but instead of commuting to an office, it was to a stage or a studio.'

Thea concentrated on pouring a pool of ketchup and shaking the perfect amount of salt on her chips. Wistfully, she added, 'Till I was fifteen, everything was great. I was no bookworm or academic, but I hadn't developed my aversion to reading. It was then I began to struggle at school with assignments and exam pressure. Mum and Dad were disappointed, especially when I left school the same year as Ezz, though she's two years older. She got three A levels, and I left with a few low-grade GCSEs. She went on to do business, and I had a couple of unambitious jobs. I refused to see a problem but I'm happy that I'd begun my horticulture apprenticeship before Mum and Dad died. Maybe I wasn't such a disappointment to them by then.'

'Maybe they were exasperated by common teenage issues rather than disappointed. They sound like great parents.' His eyes widened and he straightened, dropping his knife and fork. Excitement lit his eyes. 'If you know the date of your parents' death then friends might be mentioned in any obituaries – your local paper, for example. They were . . .' But then he tailed off uncertainly.

'They were . . . ?' she prompted.

He reached over to touch her hand. 'I can't think of a sensitive way to say it, but their deaths were newsworthy. I could imagine a provincial paper running a story about local musicians dying unexpectedly and tragically.'

'Oh.' Her appetite waned, despite the aroma of deliciously battered fish. She looked down at his hand touching hers. His skin was slightly darker, but both were working hands, firm and capable. Though she rubbed coconut oil into her hands every night, they'd never be soft and girly while she was a gardener.

She closed her eyes in concentration. 'It *was* on the front of the local paper. The headline was something like "Local songbirds in tragic death". It was horrible. Journalists don't worry about how the family might feel when they see screaming headlines.' Noting his suddenly uncertain expression, she tried to smile. 'Thanks for those brilliant ideas, though. Maybe Valentina kept the obituaries. I'm afraid I didn't. I was too young and distraught – difficult and truculent too. Let me quickly text her to ask, then we'll change the subject.' Message to Valentina sent, she determined not to waste the rest of the evening.

As the conversation moved on, she tried to enjoy her crispy, golden battered fish and salty chips, while Deveron spoke of his family in Dumfriesshire. 'Mum's a doting grandma. Luce and Dee love her to bits, and she's always taking them shopping or for a snack. I didn't get that with Grandpa. He'd say, "I'll show you how to trim a hedge," and that would be my afternoon taken care of.' His eyes crinkled, obviously not holding the memory against his grandfather.

She laughed. 'He sounds a character.' The long summer day was preparing for dusk, as if someone had washed the sky with violet watercolours. Moths fluttered around the outdoor lights that were slowly coming to life. Thea caught Rosamund as she passed to order coffee and allowed herself to be tempted by the dessert menu. 'I didn't really mean to order that,' she said ruefully, when her meringue and cream layered with red berries and strawberry puree arrived.

Deveron had opted for a huge slice of gateau, which looked as if it had been rolled in nuts and he just managed, 'Mm,' as he tucked in.

Finally, he blew out his cheeks. 'I need to walk that lot down. Do you fancy giving me a tour of the village? I've lived on the edge of it for more than a week but so far have only found my way to the pub and your house.'

His words reminded Thea that, despite the unsettling video call, this was a date. 'Sounds great, though we did cover a lot when we walked Daisy on Saturday night.' He was good company, and his kindness and compassion about the birth-mother bombshell had impressed her as much as him racing across Clive and Mary's paddock to fling himself into the burn and rescue Daisy.

As they paid for their meal and left the pub garden, he took her hand. 'So,' she said, assuming an instructional air. 'This is Chapel Road and the Jolly Abbot Inn. Ezzie's cottage is over there, second from the right.'

He peered over Ezz's wooden fence. A giant fuchsia spilled its magenta petals onto the narrow road and a small yellow hatchback was parked at the side. Light streamed through Ezzie's upstairs windows illuminating dandelions, daisies and yarrow on what Thea had once called a lawn. Wild sweet peas scrambled up a trellis and couch grass vied for space with cow parsley. 'The wrong cottage is called "Thistledome",' Deveron observed, indicating a patch of purple-headed thistles with spiky collars.

'True. It wasn't like that when I lived there.' Thea guided him to the junction with Bridge Road, and they hung over the parapet of the bridge in the last of the light, watching the water splashing over the rocks. 'This burn comes down from the hall – the one you saved Daisy from.' She turned and backtracked down Creag an Lolaire. A single car crept up behind them and they pressed into a patch of irises to let it through, then resumed in the lurching gait demanded by a steep hill. 'The village is like half a bowl, curving up from the sea. You probably can't see in this light but there are cliffs and scree at the end, above the old fishermen's cottages.'

They meandered through the balmy evening, Thea pointing out her favourite bijou cottages, one painted tangerine and another twilight blue, where front gardens were natural rockeries because of the gradient and the sparse soil. 'Rothach and Portree are the only places in Skye that I know of that have colourful cottages, rather than white or natural stone,' she commented as they turned into Harbour View, the lane called Beach Road forking off left. 'Most people who keep a car in the village make it a small one as the roads are single track. Only what the villagers call "the road above", Manor Road, between Rothach Hall and the main road, has lanes in both directions.'

Streetlights lit Harbour View, making a rocky patch gleam as the tide ebbed. They stepped from the road to crunch over the beach on a mix of rock, pebbles, grit and sand, the wavelets whispering as they quietly withdrew.

'It's so quiet,' Dev marvelled. 'Is the sea here always so still?'

She let the breeze brush her hair back. 'Rothach Bay and the Sound of Sleat are sheltered, but in winter or during storms, they still get dramatic.' When the rocks became too slippery, they returned to the road, along the curve to Old Fishermen's Cottages. A rowing boat listed near the foot of Causeway, as the water left it behind. Thea pointed above the cottages. 'If you could go straight up like Spider-Man, you'd be at the hall. You can't see it from down here, of course, with the cliffs and the copse in the way.' His hand was warm around hers and she began to relax and enjoy it. They turned their backs on Fishermen's Cottages and retraced their steps to where Portnalong Way forked off Harbour View, climbing steeply.

'Maisie lives on the corner here, the yellow cottage,' she panted. She paused to give her aching calves a break and pointed down the next opening. 'And Fraser lives there in Balgown, in one of the white ones.'

'They don't live together?' His breathing was laboured too. 'I wasn't sure if they were a couple.'

'I don't think they know,' Thea said frankly. 'Their spouses died before I came to the village. I see them as more than companions but less than a couple. And now, I think you must have seen all the village.'

Thistledome came into view, dreaming in the moonlight behind its hedge, windows cosily reflecting the streetlight outside as if welcoming Thea home. 'Back to work tomorrow,' she said. 'I have a youth group visiting in the morning.' She paused. With all the tension around Fredek Kowski and the real-mother-went-to-prison bombshell, she hadn't given much thought to what came next for them. She turned to face him. 'I've never dated anyone I've worked with at the hall. It was different with Ivan because we only worked together for short blocks of time, for the filming of *Garden Gladiators*.'

He settled his hands on her waist, not quite an embrace but definitely more than friendly. 'Well, you're my boss. Why don't you set the parameters?' he teased.

It was harder to concentrate with his hands on her, however lightly, and she was aware of his body heat bridging the small gap between them. 'How about we don't advertise the situation at work but don't lie if anyone asks? It's only been one date and I don't think it's anyone else's business.'

'Suits me.' He edged closer so he could drop a kiss on her forehead. 'But as you've raised this subject, I take it a second date wouldn't be out of the question?'

A smile tugged at her lips. 'I wouldn't rule it out. How about you?'

'It would be great.' Then he slowly closed the remaining distance between them, giving her plenty of opportunity to retreat if she wanted. But Thea met him halfway, heart rate rocketing as their bodies brushed once, then melted together. Warm. Firm. He felt right. His lips met her cheekbone, then hovered over her lips. She closed her eyes and touched his mouth with hers, giving herself up to the sensation of discovery, of the heat of his mouth, the *zing* that shimmered through her at the silken touch of his tongue. Her thoughts spun. *Wow.* His mouth literally made love to hers, caressing, stroking. She looped her arms around his neck, as if her body didn't want him to escape. Each time she edged harder against him, he edged harder against her . . . oh, yeah. *That* kind of harder. Every inch of her skin tingled. Her focus narrowed to his mouth, his body, his heat.

Then slowly, gently, he ended the kiss, breathing hard. Dazed, she came back to herself and the evening around her – a rustle in the hedge and the sound of a car rumbling up Loch View. 'Wow,' she breathed.

He gave a grunt of laughter. 'Yeah. Wow, Thea.'

She gazed up at his half-hooded eyes that glinted as the car's headlights swept over them. He looked stunned. She liked feeling that she could do that to him and lifted her face, wanting his mouth again.

Then, finally, after several minutes, she gently withdrew, knowing it was time to call a halt. They weren't going to bed together tonight. Dating a colleague could be managed, but having what might turn out to be a one-night stand with one was idiocy. 'I'd better go. See you at work tomorrow?'

He nodded, still looking dazed. 'Tomorrow, aye.' Then he waited while she made it up her front path on rubbery legs, aware of his eyes upon her at every step.

It wasn't until she was upstairs in her white bedroom with the gold carpet, getting ready for bed, that Valentina's text arrived. *Here's a pic of the obituary in the local paper. It doesn't mention anyone apart from family. I didn't keep a copy of that horrible article from the front page. Didn't want to remember them as a tragic news story. X*

The obituary, when Thea enlarged the photo to read it, was standard and dry. *Vincent Wynter and Maxine Elaine Wynter née Alders . . . suddenly . . . much missed . . . daughters Valentina, Esmerelda and Altheadora . . .* Both sets of parents had been described as 'late' and Thea had only vague memories of them. Shame. If her grandparents had been around today, she could have asked them for answers.

Rereading the obituary of the parents she'd adored, Thea wished Valentina hadn't happened upon Lois and discovered the truth about her adoption. Then she would have carried on with her life without revisiting her loss and grief, and feeling hurt that Mum and Dad had kept her in the dark.

She'd never tried to find her birth mother, but everyone in her situation probably wondered about their origins at some point. In not a single one of those fleeting thoughts had Thea ever anticipated the complications and undercurrents she'd encountered today.

Chapter Eleven

Deveron couldn't say he floated home, as the steepness of the footpath through the trees to Rothach Hall made it feel more of a toil, but his heart felt floaty, at least.

Using his phone torch to light his way between the trunks and over gravel, enjoying the smell of dewy pine needles, he relived those goodnight kisses. The memory of Thea's shapely body in his arms was enough to ensure his groin felt pumped full and tingling pleasurably all the way home, a heat that the summer evening air couldn't cool.

All was quiet when he emerged from the trees. Lights showed in the apartment above his own and on the ground-floor rear of the hall, which he knew to be the housekeeper's apartment. The young women in the apartment above his were Peony and Georgia, and he'd seen them holding hands as they ran downstairs. He was twice their age and they made him feel it, barely seeming to see him as they passed. The guy in the apartment next to him was also around their age – Dev couldn't remember his name. He'd had little to do with the housekeeping staff apart from an occasional passing 'Hello' around the accommodation. He'd have trouble recognising most of them out of context.

He entered his cosy studio. Too restless to sleep, he fired up his laptop. He could check whether the Suffolk papers had online archives, or if the British Library's digitisation services could supply copies of regional newspapers from 2001. He held a reader pass for the British Library and wanted to help Thea in her search, not just because she was hot and they were now officially dating, but because of the constantly nagging guilt about having once colluded with Everyday Celebs.

Now he knew her, it was obvious that she'd never have granted him an interview in a million years, even if he hadn't disclosed what type of site it was to appear on.

The *You decide!* page could be pretty brutal and he was finding good, honest gardening more rewarding than writing for the modern-day equivalent of a scandal sheet. The open air was cleansing his mind and soul. Summer's end would be time enough to look around for something more in line with his writing skill and experience.

Unfortunately . . . the first thing to pop onto his screen was his inbox.

And the top message, in bold to indicate it hadn't been read, was from <u>Weston@EverydayCelebs.com</u>.

Dev, it read.
Sorry to hear that you don't wish to write for Everyday Celebs anymore, but you agreed to provide a piece on Fredek Kowski and Thea Wynter. Just returning the travel fee to the Everyday Celebs account doesn't absolve you of the obligation to file that commissioned copy.

133

'I think it does,' Dev murmured. 'I've opted out, buddy.'

The email continued. *Fredek Kowski is pushing for the piece to be completed. You are the contracted journalist and he is an influencer with the kind of following I can make use of.*

'The contract that never arrived?' he snorted.

This piece is overdue, but I'm extending the deadline. Shall we say 6 p.m. on Wednesday? Thanks.
Weston

Deveron stared at the email, his mind ticking. Why was Weston pushing? Dev had killed pieces before when something wasn't working. Weston didn't care so long as pieces on his shit website would create revenue. A chill crept over him. Did Weston somehow know that Dev had never left Rothach Hall, and suspect him of sitting on an exposé in the hopes of securing a bigger fee from a print daily?

No, that sounded far-fetched.

So, probably, it was simply that Fredek was pestering Weston, just as he'd tried to pressure Dev. And Weston, as his email suggested, looked at Fredek's shoals of followers and saw pound signs.

Dev clicked 'reply'.

Weston,
There's no story without Thea Wynter's co-operation and she's not going to give it. There's nothing special about the story. I suggest you move on, as I have.
And let's be clear – there's no contract. We did agree one piece a week for three months, but you neglected to send a contract to that effect.
Deveron

134

He went to bed missing the light-as-air and hot-as-hell feelings he'd enjoyed earlier. Bloody Weston. Bloody Fredek. They'd completely soured his mood.

He returned to searching out the news article in a Suffolk newspaper issued in August 2001 concerning the deaths of musicians called Maxie and Vince Wynter. Without too much trouble, he discovered that the British Library held it on microfilm, and he could request a copy electronically, which he did.

But he still went to bed feeling uneasy.

He slept badly and was up early on Tuesday, changing his bedding and using the laundry room. Then, washing twirling in the machine, the sunlight at the windows drew him outside with his first cup of coffee. He meandered around the staff accommodation building to perch on the blue bench in the neglected patch of garden. He sipped and considered. That pile of rocks just begged to be made into something. And that large, broken terracotta pot.

His phone buzzed in his pocket. He cursed as he saw the screen notification of an email from Weston.

Reluctantly, he opened it. Weston had highlighted in yellow one line from Deveron's last communication. *We agreed one piece a week for three months.*

Underneath he'd typed: *If we agreed it, that constitutes a contract. I have the original email thread too.*

Shit. Deveron had the sinking feeling that Weston was right and it only took him a minute on Google to discover that, very roughly, the conditions constituting a contract could be said to have been met – intent and agreement on both sides and rewards stated. Terms and conditions often ran to pages of boring small print to comply with increasingly restrictive legislation and attempts to cover one's own arse, but that didn't mean *You give me X and I'll reward you with* Y wouldn't hold up.

He called Weston.

'Hello, Deveron. This is an unexpected pleasure,' came Weston's smooth, English voice through Deveron's phone sounding, as always, slightly amused and snotty.

'What's going on?' Deveron demanded. 'Why are you so fixated on this one small story? It's bullshit, Weston.'

'It's not bullshit,' Weston corrected him affably. 'Fredek Kowski has become an influencer. If Everyday Celebs doesn't work with him, all those lovely clicks will go to some other site.'

'It's about revenue,' Deveron stated flatly. 'Your site's all about the clicks.'

'It's *always* about revenue; *all* about the clicks,' Weston agreed gently, as if breaking bad news sympathetically. 'Everyday Celebs allows me to make money from content. That's not news, Dev.'

'No,' Deveron agreed hollowly, leaning back on the bench.

Weston sounded pleased that Dev had grasped it. 'Fredek Kowski's lovely army of followers will flood to Everyday Celebs, clicking away, voting in the poll and commenting. Commenting on comments . . . I just need the "Where are they now?" piece to start the whole lovely ball of revenue rolling and there's no time to start again with another writer. Fredek's speaking at a big influencer conference in August, a speech he wants to base on this campaign. He'll be an influencer with an audience of influencers – you see the possible halo effect, and how Everyday Celebs could be caught up in something that goes viral? And it all feeds from his original road safety campaign, which began when he was knocked off his bike. It's a great story.'

136

Dev's coffee churned in his stomach. 'And that's a good enough reason to hang Thea Wynter out to dry?'

Weston sounded surprised. 'Why should the narrative change after all these years? She's innocent. Fredek was foolish. Depict her as an angel, if you like. The slant of the story isn't as important as its ability to spread like wildfire. Tell you what,' he added with enormous generosity. 'Because I need this copy like yesterday, you write it for me and I'll end the contract thereafter.'

Dev tucked that detail away to think about. 'I've never known you so fixed on something.'

'But you've only written for the site for a few months, Dev. Sometimes I sense outstanding potential to encourage a flood of visitors to the site, and I focus on it. This is one of those cases.'

Could he write the story? Deveron hunched forward on the bench while he struggled with himself. Of course he *could*, ensuring Thea came out of it an angel, as Weston had termed it. *Physically* he could. Ethically, he couldn't. Thea had not supplied information in the knowledge that she was being interviewed. If she'd thought that, she'd have sewn her lips together rather than talk to him.

He considered the scenario. Fredek wanted exposure; Weston wanted money; Thea wanted Fredek to leave her alone – which he should do, once he got the coverage he wanted on Everyday Celebs. Thea would never co-operate in Fredek's documentary and had already side-stepped his intention to come to Rothach Hall at the weekend. With a fudging of his usual standards, Dev held it in his power to give everybody what they wanted.

'Well . . .' he hedged. The problem would be quotes.

137

His code was still strong enough to prevent him from utilising anything Thea had told him as a friend and colleague. And they were dating, for fuck's sake. Maybe he could use quotes from old news already out in the public domain. It would be lazy journalism, but it got him out of this hole, did Thea no harm as she had nothing to do with social media these days and didn't read much at all. This could draw a line under everything.

Weston spoke again, slowly and emphatically, all affability gone. 'I could always let Fredek write it.'

Dev jerked upright. 'That's not ethical. He hasn't met Thea Wynter for years and he's no journalist.'

Weston laughed. 'He doesn't have to be a journalist. You should remember that the editor may not always be right, but he is always the editor.'

Trapped, loathing Weston, Deveron snapped, 'Send me an email releasing me from our previous agreement if I write the piece. Then I'll send it over.'

'Good man,' Weston began, but Deveron was already ending the call, dropping his phone on the bench. He felt like slime.

And if ever Thea found out . . . well, he could only imagine the hurt expression that would crumple her lovely face. He'd hate himself for being the cause of her pain much more than he'd hate waving goodbye to Rothach Hall and his studio-apartment home, before resuming his journey to his mum's sofa.

He dragged himself to his feet and trailed back into his studio, where he reached for his laptop and opened the document containing his interview notes on Fredek Kowski, and links he'd amassed to previously published news and features. He read through a couple of local press pieces written at the time of the accident and interviews Thea had later given in support of Fredek's cyclist safety awareness campaign in a cycling magazine and a lifestyle regional glossy.

He started typing, steeling himself to fudge his way around the quotes he lifted with: *Thea Wynter told media* or *anonymous sources.*

At least this way he could make things look as good as possible for Thea, including a heavily slanted poll.

- *Has Thea Wynter been unfairly traumatised by an accident not of her making?*
- *Is it time for Thea Wynter to forget the past and move on?*
- *Should Fredek Kowski have been prosecuted for causing the collision?*
- *Is Fredek Kowski really the right person to advise and train others?*

By the time he'd finished the feature, stabbing bad-temperedly at his keyboard, Weston had sent the requested email agreeing that upon timely submission of the Wynter-Kowski *Where are they now?* feature, Everyday Celebs would release Deveron from the expectation of further material.

After a final read-through and a muttered string of expletives, he replied, attaching the feature and adding a paragraph that he accepted the terms. Pointedly, he added, *I will not be writing for Everyday Celebs again in this lifetime.*

After a moment's thought he sent a follow-up. *Who will write the second part – for the You decide! page?*

Weston replied laconically. *I'll find someone.*

* * *

On Tuesday morning, Thea ran the planned workshop about Scottish native trees for a group of summer camp kids, smiling happily as she helped them identify oak, beech, ash and elder leaves for their worksheets. At lunchtime, she fetched Daisy from Thistledome to enjoy a visit to Mary Pony and Clive Donkey. When Mary blew down her nose at Daisy, the little dog almost fell over wagging her fluffy-duster tail, and sneezed in reply, making Thea laugh.

She'd messaged Dev to see if he wanted to join them but had received no reply. Visions of yesterday evening rose in her mind. Those kisses . . . his body against hers . . . she shivered, wondering where the relationship would go.

After a few minutes with Clive and Mary, Thea and Daisy were sauntering back up towards the hall when Thea's phone rang and Ezz's name appeared on the screen. To make up for wishing it was Dev, she answered with a welcoming 'Hiya, sis.'

Ezzie was in brisk and breathless work mode. 'The Larssons are arriving on Thursday. Do the family gardens need attention?'

Thea halted and Daisy looked back enquiringly. 'In two days? *All* the Larssons?' She pictured who the staff sometimes referred to as 'the parent Larssons': big, bluff Erik with a thatch of brown hair, a ruddy face and a big smile; Grete – pronounced 'Gretta' – with silver hair and twinkling eyes that almost vanished when she smiled. Son Mats was fair-haired, and his brother Jonas and sister Maja both dark. Mats, Jonas and Maja each had a spouse and children, though Thea had lost count of how many children. It seemed like dozens, but in truth was probably six or seven altogether.

'Just the parents,' Ezzie answered. 'Gwen's put the housekeeping staff on changing linens.' Linens would have been changed when the family last left of course, but Gwen would want everything smelling fresh. The family might live in Norway and Sweden for months, but everything had to be spot on when they descended. Erik and Grete were kindly but used to running a successful business and being listened to.

Thea passed the family garden under mental review. 'We'll put stripes on the lawns and weed borders. Hedges have been trimmed recently, but we'll tidy them up. If there are no kids coming, presumably we don't have to get the treehouse and playthings checked over.' Her mind switched to staff. 'Everyone's rostered on today apart from Deveron, and everyone tomorrow apart from Hadley. We need to get paths mowed around the pavilion as well, though, because the ladies running the writing retreats – Nita and Fiona – are coming to make up beds and stuff tomorrow and Thursday. The paths are what I'd planned most of us would be doing this afternoon.' She gnawed her lip. It all added up to a lot of work over a short period for her small team. 'If Dev's around now, it would help if he'd come back to work and tack on a half-day to his next rest days.'

'Great. I'll leave that with you.' Ezz sounded ready to move on to the next job on her list. She was at her best when she was busy and would fly about checking everybody was doing his or her part until the second the Larssons arrived, when she'd switch to instant calm to welcome the family back.

Thea sped up, calling Dev as she hurried, Daisy breaking into a trot to keep up. When he once again failed to answer, she rang Sheena. 'Change of plans,' she said, by way of introduction, and explained as she rounded the knot garden.

Sheena responded cheerfully, 'OK. Me, Nell and Hadley are just finishing lunch. Deveron's having a busman's holiday, I think, because he asked if it was OK to use a strimmer on that scruffy bit by the staff accommodation.'

'Then he probably can't hear his phone.' Thea whizzed past the west lawns and armed with this new information, swerved across the courtyard in the direction of the shriek of a strimmer she now heard filtering through the summer air. 'I'll call you back when I've talked to him.'

As soon as she rounded the staff quarters, she spied Deveron's tall figure arcing a green strimmer through the knee-deep grass, yellow ear defenders clamped over his head. Her heart gave a skip at the way his shoulders moved beneath his T-shirt. Mindful of power-tool safety, she picked up Daisy and chose a circumspect route to enter his field of vision.

Still, he jumped, and the strimmer halted with an indignant *fnuf*.

As he dragged off his ear defenders, his smile was warm. 'Sheena said I could use the strimmer, boss.' He reached out and fussed Daisy's ears, and Daisy beat her tail against Thea's ribs.

Thea grinned, took a swift look around to check they were unobserved, then reached up to brush a kiss on his lips. 'She told me about your busman's holiday, cleaning this patch up.' She glanced about, noticing a heap of rock had been moved, breathing in the scent of fresh-cut grass and working man. 'Is there any chance of you working this afternoon?' She explained the Larsson situation. 'Sheena could take Nell and Hadley to work in the family garden, while you and I mow the paths around the pavilion. Daisy can stay with us.'

'Give me ten minutes to change.' He turned, then halted and turned back. 'And tell me where the pavilion is.'

She found herself laughing into his smiling eyes like a besotted teen. 'It's between the kids' play area and the back drive. But I'll meet you in the gardeners' room. Bring the strimmer.' She set Daisy back on her paws and called after him as he headed for his apartment, 'Wear trousers, not shorts, in case of nettles.' She waited until he was out of sight to fan herself. *Whoo.* She wasn't sure any man had ever had such an instant combustion effect on her. Wow. He made her good parts feel alive.

At the shed, Thea perched the strimmer and a black, businesslike mower in the four-wheeled garden cart, along with their batteries. Grete Larsson preferred equipment that didn't rely on petrol or diesel. Secateurs, gloves, string, jumbo garden waste bags and a hedge trimmer also went into the cart. She filled a water bottle from the tap, put on her sunglasses and ball cap and was ready when Deveron arrived, curls blowing back from his forehead, uniform neat.

'Dog or cart?' she asked, offering Daisy's lead with one hand and the handle of the cart with the other.

He took the cart with a quirk of his eyebrows that suggested, *I know we don't differentiate between men and women, but this is clearly my job.*

She didn't mind. The cart was heavy and as steerable as a dented shopping trolley, so she swung along happily as he fought the cart, greeting a group of meandering tourists enjoying the summer breeze and the sunlight painting a neatly trimmed stand of specimen trees with shades of gold and green. Daisy panted, her fluffy fur almost silver in the sun.

Past the play area, which was scattered with bark from the nearby shrubbery, they eventually turned off the service drive onto a path that carried them through the woods and into dappled shade, where lichen grew in shady places and last autumn's leaves had been trodden into the beaten path. They came upon the back of the pavilion suddenly, which meant Deveron got the full effect of the timbered building with its veranda running around.

'Whoa.' He halted.

Thea paused to drink in the gracious wooden building, too, cedar shingles covering its steeply gabled roof. The veranda railing had a rustic air, adding to the building's pretty appeal. 'I'm glad they left it natural wood rather than painting it,' she said. 'It was refurbished last year. We cleared up the mess the builders had made and seeded the surrounding to make a wildflower meadow. Pretty, isn't it?' The waving meadow grass in which they stood was spangled with red poppies, purple cornflowers and borage, white daisies and yellow cowslips.

'Seriously,' he agreed admiringly.

She brushed back the tendrils of hair the wind had teased from her bun. 'Apparently, in the past, the pavilion was for family guests. Judging by the distance from the hall, they must have saved it for people they didn't want to see much of. Leave the cart and let's go around to the front.'

Their work boots made tracks in the long grass and wildflowers. When they rounded the pavilion, Dev halted. Between them and the sea was a cliff, falling away in a series of shelves but impossible to climb without mountaineering gear. It looked out not over the village

144

but directly off the headland to the Sound of Sleat. As it was a clear day, they could see right down the sound and the ferry trundling across the surface from Armadale on Skye to Mallaig on the mainland. A yacht with red sails carved a wake into the glittering water. The knobbly coastline opposite rose in greens, browns, and a slate grey that seemed almost blue.

After she'd allowed him a minute to absorb it all, she turned and pointed to two groups of picnic tables. 'We need to cut the grass around them, those loungers and benches, then mow footpaths between them, the pavilion, and the woods. A single width of the mower should be enough. If you can start on that, I'll cut back the wild roses climbing like Jack's Beanstalk onto the veranda.'

He blinked as if emerging from a dream. 'I'd love to live here.'

She smiled, but his words increased her pulse rate. He probably meant he'd love to live somewhere with a view like that, but for the tiniest instant she'd thought he meant he'd like to stay on Skye. She knew there wasn't enough work for another gardener on the winter-time staff but people did relocate here. Look at her and Ezz . . .

For the rest of the afternoon, they each attacked their own tasks. Thea had brought her earbuds and listened to a book about a woman searching for her mother, and wondered why the woman was so certain that finding her mother would be a positive experience. Maybe the author was slanting things that way to achieve the most impact when it turned out that the mother was toxic or just embarrassing. It was hitting too close to home, so she switched to a podcast about the gardens of Versailles. They didn't sound much like the gardens of Rothach, but she'd like to see them. The thought of visiting France gave her a twirly feeling. Was her mother Ynez in France still? Was Thea more likely to visit her mother or Versailles?

Bees buzzed peaceably as she clip-clip-clipped with her secateurs, her heavy-duty gloves protecting her from thorns. The clippings would be shredded later, probably by Hadley, who seemed to gain satisfaction out of feeding the screaming machine.

They took their break at a picnic table amidst the scent of freshly mown grass, passing a water bottle between them. Daisy sat on the bench next to Thea as if expecting a dish to be put before her at any moment. Thea was about to share her thoughts on the book about a lost mother when Deveron brought up the parallel subject.

He linked fingers with her across the table. 'I found the article about your parents.' His eyes looked almost green in the sun. 'Unfortunately, it provided no leads to friends, musical or otherwise. Maybe the Musicians' Union or Equity might have info.'

Her ears pricked up. 'Oh? Mum and Dad were both members of the Musicians' Union and I think I remember them talking about Equity cards, too. Thanks for working that out. Shall we look tonight? I could cook.' When Thea saw him hesitate, she rushed on. 'Sorry. We only saw each other last night and you probably have things to do. Maybe Ezz would help. Or Valentina.' Her cheeks flamed as she heard herself babbling. 'Or I should force myself to do it.'

But Dev grinned and stretched over the table to kiss her. 'I don't have things to do. It's my good luck to spend another evening with you. I'll bring my laptop and my best research skills.'

'Oh, thanks,' breathed Thea, awash with relief. And

146

then, when she realised that she was gazing soppily into his eyes, 'I suppose we'd better get back to work.'

Deveron Dowie, rather than her birth mother, took centre stage in her thoughts for the rest of the afternoon.

Opting for an easy supper, Thea had chicken and jacket potatoes in the oven already when Dev arrived, and was chopping salad, enjoying the traffic-light colours of yellow peppers, green cucumber and red tomato.

Daisy, who'd posted herself at Thea's feet, demonstrating an unexpected partiality to dropped slices of cucumber, turned and skittered to the front door in a rush of clicking claws. A second later the door knocker sounded, and she turned with a swish of her floppy ears to summon Thea. 'Arf.'

Thea wiped her hands. 'I think you're forgetting who's in charge here.' She hastened to let Dev in.

When she opened the door, she found him holding a cake box, his black T-shirt making his hair look darker. 'I brought cupcakes from the cake shop near Duisdealmor for dessert.'

'Yum, they do amazing cakes.' Thea took the box and kissed his cheek.

'That wasn't much of a kiss in exchange for amazing cupcakes,' he observed gravely, though with a teasing light in his eyes. 'They're iced to look like flowers – perfect when the lady you're visiting is a gardener.'

Laughing, she planted a big, jokey, 'Mwah!' on his lips.

With an elaborately reproachful look, he took back the box.

Laughing and blushing, Thea melted against him and slipped her arms around his neck, sinking slowly into a hot, deep kiss, the kind that involved stroking tongues

147

and no hurry. Then she snatched the cakes while he was distracted and skipped off to the kitchen, Daisy panting at her side as if laughing at the joke.

'No fair,' he pretended to grouse as he followed, hanging his laptop bag on the back of a chair. The table was laid with red woven placemats, a pot of rosemary ornamenting the centre. He sniffed approvingly. 'Something smells good.'

As he'd dipped his head to nuzzle the back of her neck, she wasn't sure if he meant her or roasting chicken, but the brush of a cleanly shaven chin on such a sensitive area made her shiver. Her caution over sleeping with a recent co-worker was fading. It felt as if she'd known him longer than the ten days since he'd come to Rothach, especially when he showed understanding of how she hated grappling with word-based tasks. Breathlessly, she said, 'Dinner's just about ready.'

With a last kiss on her spine, he stepped back to carry the salad and dressing to the table while she took things out of the oven, waiting until she'd taken her place before seating himself.

'No sign of the adoption certificate yet.' She nudged the salad bowl his way. It was a favourite, a beautiful Mediterranean blue.

He glanced up from adding salad to his plate. 'We only ordered it on Monday evening, so it might be too optimistic to expect it by Wednesday, especially as we're away up here in Skye. Are you feeling impatient?'

She shrugged, cutting open her jacket potato to slather it with butter. 'Impatient. Curious. Apprehensive. Doubtful. Generally mixed up.'

'Understandable.' He sent her one of the warm smiles that seemed to light his eyes before it found his mouth.

As they ate, they talked about the Larsson family, who Dev had yet to meet.

'Everybody likes Erik and Grete,' she told him. 'Despite the money they've made, they're ordinary, nice people.'

Dev looked interested. 'What do they do?'

'Fish products, with factories in Norway and Sweden. Erik has a favourite joke about fish balls, but his jolly exterior hides a strong personality. Apparently, he and Grete saw Rothach Hall about twenty years ago, when it was on its way to becoming derelict, like Armadale Castle. He decided it needed to be not only restored but also lived in, and didn't care that it took a decade to complete the purchase, get the necessary permissions and finally embark on the work. Then came the palaver of opening to the public – including recruiting staff. That's when Ezz and me came here. Hadley had been keeping the grounds from returning to the wild with minimal help, once the old owners decided the place was too expensive and lost interest in it. Tavish came from a big house near Edinburgh – it was much more commercial there and I think he chafes at Erik and Grete seeing the tourist trade as a helping with costs of the hall, rather than the be-all and end-all.'

He tilted his head. 'Was coming to Skye a big change for you?'

Her mind flashed back to the flatter, greener landscape of the English county in which she'd been brought up, the farm fields and occasional windmill or vineyard. 'Suffolk's lush and Skye's wild and craggy, but gardening's gardening. I wasn't as happy there as I had been . . . after everything that happened. I can't have caught the performance bug from Mum and Dad because I didn't want to continue *Garden Gladiators*. Unfortunately, my bosses at my old place, Cherlington House, wanted the TV money, so that was tricky, especially when *Garden Gladiators* didn't go on without me. I started looking around and Rothach Hall was recruiting. Ezz applied for a job too. It was a complete change of pace for us both, but also a relief, and a chance to start afresh. Hardly anyone recognises me now. I used to have short streaky hair and a nose and lip stud.' She touched a fingertip to each of the two barely visible imprints that were all that remained of her old piercings. 'And it's almost a decade since I recorded the last show.'

He dropped his gaze to his plate. 'I'm glad you're happy here,' he said. 'I like it fine. It's a lot wilder than Dumfries, too.'

Welcoming the change of subject, she asked, 'I'm confused about Dumfriesshire versus Dumfries and Galloway.'

His Scots burr thickened briefly. 'Aye, well, Dumfries is a town in Dumfriesshire; Dumfriesshire is the eastern part of Dumfries and Galloway. Kirkcudbrightshire and Wigtownshire make up Galloway, the western part.'

'Nothing to be confused about there, then,' she said ironically. 'And you're from Dumfries?'

'Nearby.' He wiped his fingers on the kitchen towel she'd put out to serve as napkins. 'When Dad was alive, we lived in a village called Hightae. Mum moved us to Dumfries after, because it was easier for schools and for her work, and close to Grandpa. My brother Leith and his family live in Lockerbie, about twenty minutes from Dumfries.'

She screwed up her forehead. 'Were you living in Dumfries before you came here, then? It seems a long way to come for a seasonal job.'

He shook his head. 'I lived in Inverness with Adaira. It was where she was from and it has a regional airport, so I could link to international flights OK. I was on my way back to Dumfries from there.'

The geography of Scotland wasn't a strong point with Thea, but she thought Inverness was on the east coast, which made the Isle of Skye on the west by no means on the route to Dumfries in the south.

He must have read her thoughtful frown because he added, 'Like you, I was attracted here because I fancied a change, after a tricky time.'

'Funny that we both ended up in Skye,' she said lightly, and let the topic drop because he didn't look comfortable. Probably he didn't enjoy reminders of his wife leaving.

After supper, Deveron insisted on washing up, so Thea picked scraps of chicken off the bones for Daisy, who snuffled them up as if she hadn't been fed all day. She was filling out nicely but obviously didn't intend to let undernourishment return.

Thea made coffee, then opened the cake box he'd brought. 'These are works of art,' she marvelled, setting the cupcakes carefully on plates and admiring the petals constructed from icing. One cake was a dark red rose, the other – appropriately for what had brought them together – a white daisy with a yellow centre. She arranged plates and mugs on a tray. 'We'll take these into the lounge, shall we? I haven't exactly fully furnished it, but the rocking chairs are comfortable.'

Soon they were settled on her wooden rocking chairs with green velvet cushions, chair-arm-to-chair-arm so Thea could see Deveron's laptop screen. He'd hooked the laptop up to his phone's data. Luckily, the village got a good signal if you weren't too low down. They munched their cakes while Deveron manipulated the keyboard and scratchpad to search the Musicians' Union website. 'Not a searchable database, unfortunately,' he observed, frowning.

Thea had chosen the daisy cake, and enjoyed the rich chocolatey sponge under the white icing as much as watching his tanned fingers flicking over the computer keys. The colourful site's photos of musicians at pianos or holding guitars made her nostalgic for her parents, for everything from their hours of practice in their home studio, to catching a glimpse of one of them backing a band at Glastonbury, to leading singsongs for their daughters in the garden.

He munched his way absently through the rose-decorated cake as he browsed pages. One of the links made him pause. 'The union has a journal, *The Musician*, which might cover something as significant as the death of its members. Some copies are available as PDFs.' He ferreted about some more, but grunted with disappointment. 'Nowhere near as far back as 2001. I might have to enquire at the British Library. I wonder what's on eBay, though?' Another few minutes of research, another grunt, this time more hopeful. '"Musicians' Union National Directory of Members, for sale". It's old enough that I'd expect your parents to be listed, but a directory suggests only contact details.' He scrolled and searched, scrolled and searched. Ah!' He tilted the screen towards her. 'Here's a bundle of five copies of *The Musician* dated 1999 to 2001. Twenty pounds the lot.'

A surge of excitement lifted her heart. 'Shall I buy them?'

He waggled his head. 'Maybe. But what if there's nothing useful about your mum or who she sang with?

You've wasted twenty quid.' He typed again, muttering, 'Musicians' Union Obituaries.' His eyes tracked across the lines of text. 'Nope. Nothing about your parents.' He paused to sip his coffee. 'I'll check if the British Library holds copies. But to search through several would mean a trip to London or Boston Spa.'

Dismay sank her stomach to her boots. 'On the off chance that there's an obituary or something about this Miracle Mule woman? That would be a massive undertaking on thin hope. From here it's four or five hours to Glasgow to access the airport or the sleeper train. Or London's about a twelve-hour drive.' Dubiously, she added, 'Valentina goes to London occasionally on business. She might be able to do it for me at some point.'

'She'd need a readers' pass organised ahead of time and arrange for editions to be made available. You can't just wander in and rummage around.' He drained his coffee and leant forward to deposit the empty mug on her small table, then frowned at the screen and began to type again.

Computer screens rarely held Thea's attention, and her focus drifted to him. His bare elbow was close to hers, and she was conscious of a wave of heat. By moving only millimetres, she could brush his elbow with hers. Huh. Who'd have thought an elbow could feel that good? She liked skin-on-skin . . .

'Result,' he said suddenly, jerking her from her reverie. He propped the laptop on the chair arm, closer to her. 'I googled "Maxie Wynter obituary" and it's come up on a blog.'

'Really?' Battling her usual feeling of revulsion for a page of text, she glanced mistrustfully at the screen. 'Oh, there's Mum's photo!' A youngish Maxie, her auburn hair

153

piled up above her slender face, shared a microphone with a woman with frizzy blonde curls. Both wore headphones, eyes closed as they sang. It wasn't an image Thea had seen before. It gave her a new layer of loss and she wished she'd paid more attention to her parents' careers when she had the chance. 'Mum and Dad are musicians,' had tripped off her tongue often enough, but they'd seemed like any other parents. Sometimes they worked long hours and other times they were away for days. Then might come a compensating period when they were at home, attending to bookings and what Vince termed 'the biz side of things', as well as their endless practising. Valentina still had one of Vince's guitars, but they'd had to sell Maxie's baby grand piano.

Dev leant so close that his hair brushed hers. 'The site's about session musicians and backing singers.' He glanced into her face. 'Do you want to read it? Or shall I?'

The text didn't look too dense. The paragraphs were widely spaced, with photos in between.

It felt like a test. Swallowing, she began to read. '*Maxie Wynter, 1950–2001. Great friend, great vocalist. Also played piano and guitar. Provided stage-side vocals for* Phantom of the Opera *and other large productions and worked countless sessions at studios, mainly in London, Birmingham and Norwich. Born in Suffolk, spent many years in London before basing herself in her home county once again with husband Vince Wynter and their family. Tragically lost her life aged 51 to carbon monoxide poisoning emitted from a faulty appliance in a B&B.*' The text began to blur as her eyes filled with tears. Had she even known her mum had sung in *Phantom of the Opera*? Shame crept over her that she hadn't done more to keep her parents' memories alive. What *did* stick was the three years of friction before she lost them, when Thea knew she'd been a truculent teen, falling behind at school, frustrating her parents who'd had a relatively easy ride with super-bright Valentina and industrious Ezzie.

Her mum's voice floated back to her, fond but anxious. *Oh, Thea, you're going through a strange stage. It's as if your skin doesn't fit. What's wrong, darling?* Thea would vehemently deny there was a problem other than longing for the day she could leave school.

When she'd got her wish, she'd had no idea what to do next, until a seasonal job, not unlike Deveron's at Rothach Hall, had led to the offer of a horticultural apprenticeship. Thea hoped her parents somehow knew that she'd found a skin to fit her in the end . . .

Deveron's voice intruded on her thoughts. 'Have you seen who wrote the obituary?' He spoke the words softly, as if drawing her attention to one of the island stags that might gallop off if he caught words on the air.

She sniffed, wiping her eyes with her forearm. 'Um . . .' She focused on the page again. Found the place at the foot of the text. And gasped. 'Meryl Muller! Do you think that's the other woman in the photo? And who Lois meant when she came up with "Miracle" and "Mule"?' She tried to laugh, but it caught in her throat like a sob. And then his arms were around her and she snuggled into him as well as she could with two wooden chair arms between them. It was comforting to close her eyes against his shoulder for a few moments, while she thought about her mum and the unknown Meryl Muller, someone who described Maxie Wynter as a 'great friend' and had known her well enough to ensure her obituary made it onto the internet, possibly years after appearing somewhere in print. Yet Meryl Muller wasn't known to Thea *at all*.

Against her hair, Deveron murmured, 'If Meryl Muller is still working, we can probably find her online. On social media, at least.'

Urgh. Social media. But Thea shook herself. It couldn't hurt her to look at *someone else's* channels. 'Good idea,' she croaked, and sat up to leave Deveron free to enter 'Meryl Muller' in a search box. Top of the results was merylmuller.com. He clicked again and a website sprang into multicoloured life. *Meryl Muller, musician,* with turquoise headings like *recording work* and *stage and concert work.* A couple of pictures caught the same frizzy blonde woman singing soulfully into a mic and, less naturally, smiling from a professional headshot. Thea craned closer to the small screen. 'Can you click on the gallery? Maybe there are photos of her when she was younger. She looks to be in her seventies now, which is what Mum and Dad would have been.'

Opening the gallery produced additional photos of Meryl Muller, sometimes blonde and sometimes not, usually singing with two or three others in the traditional backing-singer spot, rear of stage. '*There!*' Thea almost shouted, as her eyes fell on one of the larger photos. 'There she is again with Mum.' Maxie and Meryl shared a mic, dressed in matching shimmery black, Maxie in a dress and Meryl in a jumpsuit. Maxie's reddish hair was smooth and straight, Meryl's a frizzy halo. Both women beamed, eyes shining as they seemed to look past whoever was taking the picture. In Thea's imagination, they were looking into the audience, accepting applause, flushed and excited at a rapturous reception.

'Contact,' Deveron murmured, and clicked a button that made the gallery vanish.

And there was an email address: *Meryl@MerylMuller. com.*

'Wow,' Thea whispered. 'Click it, before I lose my nerve. Please,' she added, as she found herself clutching Deveron's upper arm, his skin warm, her heart thrumming as she stared at a contact form inviting her to send a message to Meryl, including an option to sign up for Meryl's free e-newsletter or follow her on social media.

Deveron, showing no sign of discomfort at Thea affixing herself to his arm, asked, 'Any idea what you want to say?'

'Erm . . . "Dear Meryl",' she began haltingly.

Deveron's typing fingers paused. 'Maybe . . . you introduce yourself?'

Thea tried to force her brain to work. 'Of course. Erm . . . "I hope you don't mind this message. I'm Thea Wynter, the youngest daughter of Maxie and Vince Wynter."' She paused, watching him type apparently without even looking at the keys. Then, gaining confidence, she went on to ask if Meryl would be kind enough to talk to Thea about her parents. He filled in her email address in the appropriate box and added her phone number and street address in the message box.

Dev read it through, his chin propped on his fist. 'Just wondering . . . is mentioning your dad the best approach? Thinking about persuasive language, you know.'

Thea didn't know, and had never heard of persuasive language, but got his drift. 'Because Lois said Dad didn't like Meryl?'

He flipped back to the obituary. 'And he's not mentioned at all in the obit Meryl wrote. Maybe she'd be more tempted to just talk about Maxie.'

'You're right.' Struck by this insight, Thea watched as

Deveron deleted both allusions to Vince. He turned the computer towards her so she could click ceremoniously on *send*.

She relaxed into the rocking chair. 'Thanks,' she said simply. 'I suppose you just think I'm dim.' Plenty of people raised their eyebrows when she avoided the written word.

'Not at all,' he said. 'I did a bit of research after you mentioned your feelings. There's a condition called logophobia – a fear of the written word. It's not talked about enough.'

She twisted in her seat to regard him sceptically, though her pulse picked up. 'Seriously? It's a thing? Other people feel the same?'

His eyes smiled. 'It's definitely a thing. It can spring from a traumatic event but, like any anxiety or phobia, might be more complex. Or the source simply may not be obvious.'

She blew out her cheeks. 'For me, it just developed. As my GCSE coursework pressure grew, my ability to deal with it shrank. Even practical subjects were spoilt by endless coursework.'

She paused to remember her sense of overwhelm as frustrated teachers demanded assignments and homework. The last chances, letters home and detentions. 'It caused conflict with Mum and Dad so I'm glad they lived long enough to see me started on my apprenticeship. I tried extra hard to finish it after they'd gone, to make things up to them. I'd never have got through my apprenticeship without a sympathetic assessor, though. She read questions aloud to me to get me going, and some of it was multiple choice. I used to like producing drawings of planting schemes and stuff, so that was OK. I scrambled through.' Then, feeling her eyes burning again, she grabbed her phone. 'I can't wait to tell Ezzie and Valentina that you've found Meryl Muller.'

Abruptly, he withdrew his attention from his screen, picked up his laptop and closed it. 'Aye. I'll leave you to have that conversation in private.'

'Oh,' she said as he rose, remembering that only a couple of hours earlier she'd been thinking the evening might end quite differently. 'I was going to suggest we walk Daisy. But I understand if you'd rather go now.'

His gaze slid away from hers. The room was full of the pearly pink of the last of the summer daylight and he looked through the window, as if deliberating. 'How about I walk with you and Daisy down to Ezzie's house? You must be bursting to discuss things. Then I'll get off.'

She smiled widely. 'Sounds great. Daisy? Walkies!' But his words had sounded hollow to her. Maybe he had plans for later. It wasn't even ten yet. For all she knew, he could have another woman patiently awaiting him at the Jolly Abbot, ready to be whisked off elsewhere. 'Dating' didn't equal 'exclusive'. Her experience of men told her that they were a lot more into physical contact than commitment.

Dismayed that she might have misinterpreted his level of interest in her, she went to the kitchen to find Daisy's lead. Deveron waited at the open front door, gazing out at where a gauzy layer of cloud veiled the setting sun, lending a luminous quality to the waves in the bay below.

Then they strode down Loch View, pausing to let Daisy sniff and snuffle, wafting away the evening patrol of dive-bombing midges. When Thea noticed that she was doing all the talking, she stopped, and let Deveron walk her silently to Ezzie's cottage, where lights shone in downstairs windows. There, he brushed several kisses on her lips and cheeks before stepping back. 'See you tomorrow?'

Thea nodded. 'Thanks again.'

And though unsettled by the unexpected sobering of his mood, she was glad to watch him turn and set off back up Bridge Road, rather than going on to the Jolly Abbot.

Deveron didn't wait to get home. The second he'd crossed the bridge and was out of sight of Chapel Road, he opened his email on his phone. Just before he'd closed his laptop at Thea's, he'd spotted an email notification at the top right of his screen.

Weston@Everydaycelebs.com
Subject: *WTF?*

Dev needed to discover what the pithy subject line meant, a greasy feeling of apprehension coursing through his stomach. He clicked to open.

Ha fucking ha, Dev. I know I said you could make her out to be an angel, but I need something more balanced than this, mate, or the follow-up You decide! piece won't work.
Weston

Deveron lost no time in replying, typing with one fingertip:

I slanted the piece precisely as you invited me to. If our earlier emails constituted a contract, then so did that. You gave me a brief. I stuck to it.

160

He tucked his phone in his pocket, heart lightening at the news that Weston mightn't be able to see a second piece on Thea and Fredek working and strode towards the footpath. Weston was like the horrible elf in a book he used to read his nieces Dee and Luce. The elf loved to make people believe he was leaving, only to pop up again with a twisting of words and misrepresentation of events. For some reason the girls had loved the book.

Dev had hated it and had told Leith so. Leith had rolled his eyes and said that the girls might as well learn that there were manipulative people about.

His big brother. The person who'd always been in Deveron's corner and also on the other end of the phone line while Deveron had waded through the sewage of winding up a business and a marriage. Guiltily, it struck him that they hadn't been in touch since he'd first announced his temporary job, so when he got back to his apartment and dropped onto the bed, he called. It was only just after ten and Leith was more of an owl than a lark.

Sure enough, the ringtone sounded only once before Leith's deep voice, boomed, 'Hi, stranger. How ya doing, working at that swanky pad? I looked it up online.' He whistled.

'I'm a gardener, not a guest of the owners,' Deveron retorted. But his shoulders relaxed just to hear Leith again. Then somehow, though he hadn't meant to, Dev found himself pouring out the whole story of how he'd ended up at Rothach Hall. 'Now Weston's being a shit and I feel guilty. Having met Thea Wynter, I like her. She's no longer a name on a brief but a living, breathing, hurting human being.' Woman. Hot woman.

Reassuringly, Leith just snorted. 'Oh, tell this Weston

161

creep to screw himself. You're well out of that situation. When are you coming down to see us? I know it's a fair drive, but we could put the girls in one room to give you a bed.'

'Soon,' Deveron promised, feeling a tug at his heart. He hadn't seen his family since Hogmanay. 'Maybe when I can get three days off together.' Being provided with a bed by the girls going in together for a couple of nights wouldn't be too much of an imposition.

Later, once the call was over, he got ready for bed, his mind on Thea. She must have thought he was bonkers tonight, rushing off home, but knowing Weston's email had been waiting had worried him. He got between the sheets and stared at the ceiling.

All evening his head had been full of Thea, admiring her smile and her compact, athletic body. The way she looked at him sometimes with an expression that shouted 'sexy' but whispered 'vulnerable'. He'd indulged in several quick hook-ups via dating apps in the immediate aftermath of being made a fool of by Adaira and Krisi. He hadn't broken anybody's heart because none of his partners had been looking for love, though one – Pippa – had said it would be nice if she could call on him to be 'her plus-one' sometimes. Envisaging family parties or weddings, he'd thought 'not freaking likely' and politely explained that he was not the right man.

It had made him take down his dating profile and it was now six months since he'd had sex.

And he wanted Thea. Wow, he wanted Thea. Her face had fallen when he'd made it plain that he wasn't going to hang around this evening. But it wasn't in him to get closer to her, perhaps even make love to her, blithely ignoring Weston's email with its aggressive subject line, knowing that so far as Weston was concerned, Thea's past trauma was just a vehicle to make him money.

Absolutely. No. Way.

But now that he'd dealt with Weston with what he hoped was finality, he felt better about himself. Leith's contempt for Weston had also calmed him.

Tomorrow was another day, when he would meet Thea with an easier conscience.

Chapter Twelve

The adoption certificate arrived on Thursday.

It was delivered while Thea was taking Daisy for a brisk turn around the sloping village, munching her lunchtime sandwich as she admired a row of three cottages that went pink-mauve-sage, and enjoyed the trees in their summer finery. It hadn't been possible to take Daisy to work because of the imminent arrival of the Larssons, and Thea had told Tavish – before *he* could tell *her* – that she'd keep Daisy away until she could check with Erik or Grete to see whether they minded Thea sometimes having a canine companion. The atmosphere between Thea and Tavish was so chilly since she'd refused to be in Fredek's stupid documentary that he'd merely nodded.

'We'll have a longer walk this evening, Daisy,' she promised as she stepped back into the cottage. Almost treading on the large stiff envelope on the doormat, she knew at once what it must be. Her hands trembled as she freed Daisy from her lead and dropped a few snacks into her bowl. 'That'll do you till I get home,' she murmured. Daisy wagged her tail and inhaled the beefy bites.

Trying to pretend it was nothing *too* momentous, Thea picked up the envelope on her way out, and then threw it on the passenger seat as she got into the pick-up. Shakily, she drove back to work, wincing at the scrape of a hedge on the vehicle's paintwork as she navigated the lanes. She parked in the courtyard and hurried inside the hall on shaky legs. To her relief, Ezzie was seated in her office-cum-cubicle, head bent over her keyboard, suit jacket on a hook on the wall. Thea smiled at Orla on reception as she rounded the desk, arriving in front of Ezzie in a rush.

'I think this is it,' she said opaquely, dropping the envelope on the desk.

Ezzie regarded it with wide eyes. 'The certificate?' she whispered. 'What does it say?'

Thea collapsed into the other chair, a blue one on wheels. 'I haven't opened it.'

'Right.' Ezzie gazed at Thea. 'Are you scared?'

Thea nodded. 'Not the same kind of scared as being faced with thousands of words. Just . . . scared.'

Thoughtfully, Ezzie picked up the envelope and read the address, as if to check it was genuinely addressed to Altheadora Wynter, Thistledome, 9 Loch View, Rothach, Isle of Skye. 'Do you want me to open it?'

'I don't know. I don't know if I still want to know.' Aware that wasn't the clearest of remarks, Thea clutched her chest, her heart chugging like the pick-up truck on a steep hill.

Ezzie, being so lovely a sister, didn't judge or advise. 'Do you want me to keep it for you until you decide?'

'Would you?' Thea asked gratefully.

'Sure.' Ezzie opened a desk drawer.

'No!' Thea blurted. 'I want to open it. We can do it together.'

Ezzie laughed, blue eyes twinkling as if she'd known it would happen, and Thea dragged the chair around the desk and gingerly took the envelope back. Last night she'd sat next to Deveron like that while he researched her mum's obituary, until he'd abruptly headed home. Maybe her weakness with words had disappointed him? This time, she forced herself to be strong, the one to slit open the envelope and extract the certificate.

Gingerly, she laid it on the desktop. On the pale pink background, some printing was darker pink and some black. '"Certified copy of an entry",' she read aloud, forcing herself not to stumble, though of all the things she didn't want to read, this was definitely one. '"Name and surname of child: Altheadora Wynter".'

'So far, so good,' Ezzie joked, slipping an arm about Thea's quaking shoulders.

Thea heaved in a breath. '"Female." No shocks there.' She skimmed over the names and occupations of the adoptive parents. '"Vincent Wynter, Maxine Wynter, musician, musician. Date of adoption order—"' her voice rose on a squeak '"—13th May 1984". It's true! I was fifteen months old.' She wiped damp palms down her uniform trousers. 'Then the rest is probably true, too, about my mother going to prison.'

Ezzie's arm tightened protectively, and she peeped round into Thea's face, her straight blonde hair shifting like a curtain. 'Were you hoping Lois was wrong?' Though the question was direct, it was delivered with such love and care that it made Thea feel safe.

'Yes. No. I don't know.' She wiped her palms again, forcing herself to read to the foot of the page. The certificate said little more, just mentioning the family court, the date of the registration which was a couple of weeks after the order, and the name of the signing officer. 'I feel funny. You know when you discover something about someone, and you realise you never knew them at all? I feel like that about myself.' The sound of tyres on the drive reached them across reception and through the open front doors.

'Really?' Ezzie sounded shocked. 'But you haven't changed.'

Thea struggled to find the right words. 'My history has. And my history is part of who I am. I wonder what I thought when my mother disappeared off to prison.'

Ezz propped an elbow on the desk. 'If you were fifteen months when Mum and Dad adopted you, you were tiny when your mother went . . . away. Everything else would have stayed the same.'

'I suppose so.' Thea looked up as a deep, loud voice sounded outside. 'Whoops, it sounds as if the Larssons are here. I can hear Erik.'

Ezzie was already reaching for her jacket. 'Let's talk later. Come round tonight . . . unless you're seeing Deveron.'

'No plans,' Thea said briefly. She'd seen him today, but never alone. First, he'd been finishing the last hedge in the family garden with Nell clearing, while she and Sheena had joined Hadley in the greenhouse to finalise the planting plan for the rest of July. Next, she'd gone to the pavilion to check Nita and Fiona – the two pleasant, energetic women in their fifties who were putting on retreats – were happy with the mown paths.

'It's such a gorgeous venue,' said Nita. 'I love the wildflowers.'

Later, Thea and Deveron had happened on each other in the gardeners' room, but then Nell had burst in with, 'Anyone want a little brother? You can have mine. He's "borrowed" my phone and taken it to his mate's to play games on. I wish I was back at uni already.'

Deveron had grinned his usual easy grin. 'I talked to my big brother last night and he happened to mention that little brothers are perfect. He even invited me to stay.'

Nell had rolled her eyes while they'd all laughed, but Thea had had no opportunity to gauge whether he might be over yesterday evening's sudden remoteness.

Now, she picked up the adoption certificate and slid it back into its envelope. 'I'd love to come tonight.' She followed her sister out into the vaulted reception. Tavish had beaten them there, of course, and was already shaking hands with Erik and Grete.

Ezzie was next in the round of greetings, and then Thea, who was genuinely glad to see twinkle-eyed Greta and big, ruddy Erik. Once she'd said, 'Lovely to see you back at Rothach Hall,' she slipped off to her own duties, leaving Ezzie to discuss the luggage and Gwen being available to cook for them this evening, should they wish. Usually, they availed themselves of Gwen's culinary services on the first night, then looked after themselves.

Thea was pretty sure that if she ever had as much money as the Larsson family appeared to, she'd want someone else to cook every night. But she'd always want to plan her own garden, even if there were gardeners to do most of the grunt work. She tucked the adoption certificate in her backpack in the mud room, still not sure how glad she was to have it. Then she hurried off to her afternoon's work with Hadley, measuring and marking out the flowerbeds either side of the south lawns ready to change the bedding plants.

As she approached, Hadley straightened stiffly, extending one end of the tape measure to her. 'Can I have Deveron with me tomorrow when I plant out? I could do with a strapping lad for the heavy work.'

Thea nodded, moving up the drive to mark out the first set of bedding. Although much of the grounds were grass and trees and shrubs, Grete liked the area immediately around the hall to be more manicured. 'Check with Sheena, though, because I'll be on annual leave from Friday to Sunday. Maybe Sheena will put you all on flowerbeds, so they'll be redone quickly while the Larssons are here.'

'Bet she'll want Deveron for herself and give me Nell, because he's the handiest seasonal worker we've had for ages,' he grumbled.

'Aside from yourself,' Thea replied gravely, knowing that Hadley, having worked at Rothach every summer since he'd retired from full-time work at age sixty, considered himself above the usual parade of seasonal workers.

Hadley winked. 'Glad you know it, lass.' Then he scowled as he looked past her. 'Who's this lot tramping across the lawn as if they own the place?'

Thea swung around. Marching across the south lawns came four men hung about with small items of black equipment. Three of them were in their twenties but one was about fifty.

And he walked with a stick, his leg held stiff and straight.

'Oh, no,' she breathed.

'Hello, Thea,' cried the one she regarded with such

horror. 'We've come to make the video. You can talk while you work, don't worry.' When Thea stood frozen, he assumed an amazed-you-don't-remember-me voice. 'Thea, I'm Fredek Kowski. It's ages since we spoke, but I recognise you.' He smiled genially at Hadley. 'Are you her boss, sir? We'd love to interview you about Thea's work in these magnificent gardens. It'll be like *Garden Gladiators* all over again, won't it, Thea?'

'She's *my* boss.' Hadley looked sideways at Thea, brows beetling.

'Oh.' Fredek dismissed Hadley and focused again on Thea. 'These lads are smartphone filmmakers. So, the plan is, you and I will chat while these three film from various angles, and then we'll edit it all together later.'

The tallest of the young men lumbered towards Thea importantly. 'You need a lapel mic. I'll clip it on. It's wired to record to this phone—' he brandished a smartphone '—which you can stick in your pocket. Fredek's got the same rig, and we can sync the tracks together in the edit.' With no ceremony, he reached for the lapel of Thea's polo shirt.

And Thea sprang to life.

'Get off!' she snapped, taking a sharp step backwards into the freshly dug soil of the flowerbed. 'I've no intention of taking part in any filming.'

Fredek's smile didn't falter. His hair was brindled with grey now, and he wore silver-framed glasses that looked chosen to match. 'Tavish has OK'd it,' he cajoled, as if Thea was being tiresome.

The man with the microphone, who'd stepped back with an air of injury when Thea snapped at him, began consulting his oppos in a low voice about push shots and crane shots, frames per second and shutter speeds.

'I don't care if Tavish OK'd you filming the premises,' she said coldly. 'You're not filming *me*.'

Fredek puffed out his cheeks. 'Sorry,' he said sympathetically, though with a glint in his eye that said he wasn't. 'But Tavish is the manager at Rothach Hall. And we've got nice soft afternoon light. It's taken us two days to get here, but we dropped everything and came as you're not going to be here at the weekend.' He looked triumphant at possessing this knowledge.

'Please leave me alone,' Thea snapped, wondering whether she could hide in the gardeners' room or if the men would pursue her. The idea made her feel anxious.

'But Thea,' Fredek entreated, stepping forward every time she stepped back. 'You're used to cameras. I've developed my career since my road safety campaign. And don't you think you owe it to me to co-operate . . . as you were the one driving?'

A cold sweat swept over Thea and the scent of freshly turned earth suddenly made her feel sick. The friendly outdoor broadcasts of *Garden Gladiators*, with proper cameras and overhead mics and an agreed running order were a long way from this ambush.

'Why have those lads put their phones on those frames?' Hadley demanded mistrustfully.

'They're called gimbals,' Thea answered automatically. 'They smooth out motion and make object tracking easier. You can attach filler lights to them.'

'See?' Fredek cried. 'You're a seasoned pro. Mic her up, Grant. Thea, I'll have to stand up to interview you because of my leg—'

Thea's control snapped. '*Leave me alone*,' she thundered, perilously close to tears and hoping no members of the public were nearby.

Another voice hit the air. 'Thea, who is these peoples?'

To her horror, Thea saw not visitors but owner Erik Larsson stalking down the drive between the lawns, his weathered face puckered in a scowl.

Realising that she'd been raising her voice, she said more quietly, 'They have the impression that I want to be in their video. I do not.'

Erik marched up to them. 'Who is in charge here?'

Fredek looked less sure of himself in the face of Erik's thunderous frown. 'Tavish, the manager, said we were OK to film Thea, and we could come today because she'd be off work at the weekend.'

Erik's already ruddy complexion went redder as he glared at Fredek. 'Tavish is *my* manager, because I own this property. I meant who is in charge of these men?' His wave encompassed the three now standing uneasily aside.

'Well . . .' Fredek shifted his injured leg. 'I'm the front man.'

Erik looked at Thea. 'What is this thing, a front man?'

'He means he's the one in front of the camera rather than behind it,' she said numbly. 'I'm so sorry, Mr Larsson. I didn't agree to them coming here.' Her throat constricted. Not only her peace at Rothach was under threat but perhaps even her job if Erik Larsson held her responsible for the situation.

Erik Larsson turned back to Fredek. 'You are in my garden, and I do not like you. Get out or I call the police. Understand?'

Fredek jutted his chin. 'Now, listen—'

'Go.' Erik turned to Hadley. 'Please, escort these men from my land. Call the police if necessary.'

'Aye, sir,' said Hadley importantly.

172

Erik glanced at Thea. 'Please, come with me.'

Heart sinking, Thea followed Erik's rigid back like a child being taken indoors in disgrace. Up the imposing flight of stone steps, they passed through the double doors and then turned right into the private quarters.

Thea had hardly ever had occasion to enter the family preserve and followed Erik down a hall to a small room. Judging from the laptop on the desk, it was Erik's Rothach office. Its window had a clear view of the drive and the south lawns, now empty. 'Sit, sit,' he said testily, as if she'd said she'd rather stand. He plumped into a large black chair and bent his forbidding frown on her. 'You will tell me why the men wished to film you.'

Deciding that nothing but transparency would be acceptable to her employer in this mood, she spooled out the story of the accident. At his expression of surprise, she hurried on. 'I used to be on a gardening show on TV. He found it useful to his campaign to highlight the fact that I was the driver involved. He uses social media a lot and some—' she paused, thinking that 'trolls' might have a different meaning to someone of Swedish ancestry '—of his followers said bad things about me. When I was offered the job at Rothach I took the opportunity to break contact with him.'

'But here he is today,' Erik observed.

'Yes.' She stifled a groan. 'A visitor recognised me from *Garden Gladiators* and put it on social media, so he found out where I work. He contacted Tavish to ask to interview me in a documentary for his website. I refused. Tavish said he couldn't stop Fredek coming when we're open to the public. I arranged to have the weekend off because I thought that was when he'd be here. But he turned up today.'

For several seconds, Erik considered, eyes narrowed. 'But,' he said slowly, 'Fredek, he said Tavish had *allowed* filming today.'

Thea nodded. It threw Tavish under the bus, but it was his hard luck that Erik had involved himself instead of instructing Tavish or Ezzie to sort things out.

'You did not agree to filming,' Erik emphasised.

Thea shook her head. This was going to lead to a shitty relationship with her boss. While she'd never precisely liked Tavish, until lately he'd never done more to antagonise her than make sure everyone knew he was the boss, especially to Ezz, setting up Thea's protective hackles. 'He thought it would be good publicity for Rothach Hall,' she ventured.

Erik only lifted one thick eyebrow. After a silence, he said, 'I am sorry that these men bothered you. You are well to return to work, yes? Or you go home?'

Thea rose, relieved. 'I'm fine to return to work, thank you.'

Courteously, Erik showed her back into reception.

When Thea heard the door close behind her, she let out a breath and hurried off to rejoin Hadley. Stepping back into the fresh air to concentrate on a beautiful floral display was just the thing to overlie the memory of the recent unpleasant interlude.

Late in the afternoon, Deveron had been set to digging out June's bedding plants from the flowerbeds against the front wall of the house. Sheena and Nell were mowing and edging the lawns, and Thea and Hadley were doing something with string at the beds beside the drive. Though Deveron had his back turned, he had only to glance over his shoulder to see that Thea's hair was in a tight topknot today, and that her bare, tanned arms protruding from her polo shirt were distracting even from a distance.

Hadley's creaking laugh floated on the breeze, and Dev wondered what Thea had said to amuse him. He moved on to the next area of flowerbed, a narrower area beneath a bay of sliding sash windows. As it was more suited to his trowel than the border fork, he pulled the wheelbarrow closer and knelt to dig out past-it petunias and leggy lobelia. Around him bees droned, as if disapproving of his removing flowers, however bedraggled.

It was only when he heard voices that he realised the window above him was open.

'Come in and close the door.' From the accent, it must be Mr Larsson, who Dev knew had taken up residence today. He would have moved to another flowerbed if he hadn't immediately heard, 'Thea told you she did not wish to be filmed. Is this true?' He froze.

The other speaker was easily recognisable as Tavish. 'I used my judgement on that one, sir.' He spoke quietly, overly courteously, as if to let Mr Larsson know that Tavish was the manager, the professional.

'Yes or no?' barked Mr Larsson.

A short silence. Then Tavish answered stiffly. 'The video was to be competently made and the good publicity—'

Dev found he was clutching the trowel with suppressed anger. And the word 'filmed' meant Fredek. He'd been here, at Rothach?

'Yes? Or no?' Mr Larsson persisted.

A longer silence. 'Yes,' Tavish conceded sulkily.

'Also, Thea arranged holiday to avoid the filming. Yes?' English might not be Mr Larsson's first language, but he could certainly put his point across.

'Yes.' Tavish's assent was quieter this time.

175

'So why did you allow? Encourage?' The Scandinavian voice was lightly curious, but cold.

Deveron didn't think he could stop listening now if his right arm depended on it, his story radar and inner alarm pinging with equal force. Tavish stammered, 'The – the publicity—'

Mr Larsson cut him off. 'I never ask for such publicity. Neither Grete. The visitor income helps with upkeep of our home. With this, you are good – the pavilion, the café, the garden. But now Thea can complain against you. She is allowed to work without men bothering her. Yes?'

Tavish stopped justifying. 'Yes.'

'Good.' Mr Larsson's voice was more clipped than ever. 'Return to work, please. Send in Ezzie.'

With the sound of a door opening and closing, Dev imagined Tavish trailing from the room like a naughty boy. Stealthily, head down, Dev crept away from the window, unwilling to indulge in further eavesdropping, especially if Ezzie was to get a rocket as Tavish just had. At a safe distance, he straightened and glanced down the drive. Thea was clearing up whatever she and Hadley had been doing, prompting him to check the time. It was past five. He whistled as he returned to his tools to alert those inside the room to his presence, threw the trowel and fork on top of the discarded bedding in the barrow, and wheeled it in the direction of Thea and Hadley.

When she looked up and saw him, she smiled. The sunlight bounced off her gleaming nut-brown hair and wisps escaped her bun to blow around her face as if the elements were caressing her. His voice emerged more huskily than he'd expected. 'Do you have a moment, Thea?'

Hadley tucked a large tape measure beneath his arm

and began to move off. 'I'll leave you to it. See you in a few days, Thea.'

Although Dev remained a step distant, he gazed into her face. 'I heard some guys bothered you today. Are you OK?'

Her smile vanished. 'News travels fast. It was bloody Fredek – you know, the cyclist in the accident. He turned up with some guys to make the video I absolutely, categorically said they couldn't make. I couldn't believe it. Then Erik Larsson barrelled out of the hall and chucked them out. That part was great,' she added with a wicked grin. 'But then he wanted to know what was going on, asking me direct questions about Tavish's involvement. It was uncomfortable.'

'I think I might have just overheard Erik giving Tavish a bollocking.' He explained his inadvertent eavesdropping. As he talked, he absorbed what might have happened if Sheena had sent Deveron to clear those flowerbeds a couple of hours earlier and Fredek had seen and recognised him. Suddenly he was sweating more than the bright July afternoon warranted.

But, unaware of the pangs of his conscience, she awarded him her cheerful, beautiful smile. 'It's over. I doubt Fredek will dare come back because I believe Erik would call the police and not care if they had to come all the way from Portree.' She looked at her watch. 'I'd better go. I'm eating at Ezz's tonight.'

'Have a great time.' He hefted the handles of the wheelbarrow. Funny how the evening ahead felt empty now he knew Thea already had plans.

After he'd dumped the bedding on the compost and stowed the tools, he went to relax on the blue bench behind the staff accommodation. Project Deveron made

177

a great hidey-hole. Via his phone, he located a shop in Armadale that sold a few plants alongside their general goods and then collected his car keys from his accommodation and drove off to investigate. He arrived just as the shop was closing but they were happy to let him buy some of his favourite alpine plants – dianthus, Lewisia, saxifrage and creeping thyme.

Back at Rothach Hall, he grabbed a quick meal then began work on Project Deveron. First, he dug out the grass and weeds from a section in a corner, then began the building of the rockery, lugging stone from various points in the plot.

There was nothing to hear but birdsong and the sighing of the breeze.

But his mind was nowhere near as peaceful. Should he come clean to Thea about his past involvement with Everyday Celebs and that its owner Weston declared himself to be working with Fredek?

His conscience screamed, 'Yes!'

Rather than give in to it, he tried to use logic. What good would it do to confess? He couldn't change history. He'd tried to bail on the project and had been backed into a corner until the best option had been to write the piece after all, but slant it in Thea's favour. As she hated both social media and reading, she'd probably never know about the crap on Everyday Celebs. And if she ever did? Well, he had, as Weston so bitterly complained, depicted her as an angel.

He hadn't anticipated bloody Fredek turning up ahead of schedule, but Erik Larsson had thrown him out and Deveron had been out of sight, by lucky chance, so surely nothing else could go wrong?

Gradually, his conscience calmed as he tucked plants

between rocks and packed soil around their roots. Eventually, he placed the big, broken pot at the top of the mound, arranging it to look as if it had been dashed to the ground, and planted thyme spilling artistically from it.

Then he stood back and examined his creation. It reminded him of life. Things that weren't perfect could still be beautiful.

Chapter Thirteen

It was a perfect summer evening. Thea drank in the clear blue sky and the sun slanting on cottage rooftops and twinkling in windows. When she saw Fraser and Maisie sitting in Maisie's garden sipping hot drinks, she stopped at the gate to greet them. Bouncer and Scotty raced up to whimper to Daisy through the garden gate.

Fraser and Maisie looked so comfy, silver-haired and possibly holding hands between their chairs, that Thea offered to take their dogs on her walk. 'I'm going around Friday Furlong, to end up at Ezz's. I'll be back before your bedtime.' She knew they wouldn't go to bed before ten-thirty, which was when the daylight faded on Skye at the beginning of July. Her elderly friends would be much less visible in winter, when daylight hours shrank to six a day.

As both dogs woofed at the sound of the word 'walk', Thea was soon in possession of their leads and being towed towards Glen Road, until a dog paused to sniff an enticing lamppost, whereupon the other two joined in. It was a full-time job keeping the leads straight, and when a car wanted to creep past, she had to drag them into someone's drive. After the bridge she was able to gain the comparative quiet of Friday Furlong. Sparsely populated as it was, she met no vehicles as she ambled along, admiring the pink willowherb fringing her view of the bay at high tide with even the rowing boats afloat. From this spot at the top the village she could see tiny figures on the slim crescent of beach left by the tide. As Rothach was so small, there weren't many children, but those there were had an eternal fascination with slipping and sliding among the rocks and pebbles. Valentina's Barnaby spent hours doing the same when he visited and had once cried because the tide had returned to swamp a rockpool he'd tried to claim as his own.

Finally, Low Road descended into Chapel Road. Thea and her doggy friends passed the Jolly Abbot and Thea let them all into Ezzie's house.

'Arf!' called Daisy, announcing their arrival. Bouncer and Scotty added their deeper woofs, Bouncer knocking Daisy clean off her paws in his hurry to follow the smell of cooking towards the kitchen.

Ezzie appeared, clutching a wooden spoon. 'Good grief. Have you taken over a dogs' home?' But she gave each dog a fuss before letting them through the kitchen to the back door. The dogs, being dogs, immediately stormed through it as if they hadn't been outside in weeks.

'I thought we'd eat in the garden, as it's so lovely.' Ezz gave Thea a hug. 'I've been dying for you to come. You won't believe what happened late this afternoon.'

Thea washed her hands then made herself useful collecting cutlery and the wipeable cloth Ezz kept for her patio set. 'What happened?'

'Wait till dinner's on the table,' Ezz commanded, so Thea

poured the dogs some water while Ezz strained spaghetti and ladled carbonara sauce. Once seated, Ezz didn't even take a mouthful before she began. 'Tavish came and found me, all red in the face, and snapped that Erik wanted me in his office. I thought I was in trouble.' She swirled spaghetti on her fork and popped it into her mouth.

'And were you?' Thea prompted.

Ezzie shook her head as she chewed, hair dancing about her face. 'No,' she managed when she'd swallowed. 'But Tavish is.'

'Oh.' Thea dropped her own fork. 'About Fredek and his half-arsed camera crew turning up? Erik threw them out. He was awesome. He already knew Tavish was involved, so I couldn't cover for him. I expect he'll hate me now.' Her stomach twisted, her imagination conjuring up a scenario where Tavish found fault with her work until he either drove her out or could sack her. 'If I lose this job I'll be screwed. There are other gardens around the island, of course, at Armadale Castle or Dunvegan, but I don't have a car and stretching to one will—'

Ezz held up a hand. 'Stop catastrophising! Obviously, I'm not supposed to be telling you this, but Erik said Tavish had no reason for ignoring your refusal to participate apart from self-importance. Then he quizzed me on employment law and he's going to give Tavish a formal written warning for gross misconduct. Can you imagine, me having to write a warning for Erik to hand to *my boss*? Tomorrow's going to be interesting.'

'Oh.' Thea felt sheepish about getting so wound up. She gazed across the sunny garden – or mini meadow, really. Bouncer and Scotty had sprawled on the warm flagstones of the patio, but Daisy had curled up in the long grass, flattening out a nest for herself. Butterflies danced above the dandelions that had yet to close their petals for the night. Ezz's wildflower garden fitted well with the general wildness of the Isle of Skye. 'I never thought it would go that far. I'm glad I've taken a few days of leave. It'll give Tavish time to cool down.'

'With your annual leave and rest days, you won't have to meet him again till Thursday, a week from today.' Ezz scooped up more spaghetti. 'Grete says she and Erik are likely to be here for a couple of weeks, so Tavish will be keeping his head down for at least that long.'

Thea pressed a hand to her chest. 'What's happened to our peaceful life, Ezz? Fredek with his stupid video, Tavish behaving like a moron and my birth mother becoming a real person.'

'No answer from Meryl yet?' Ezzie asked sympathetically, pausing to sip water.

'None. But at least now I've got details from my adoption certificate, I can request my original birth certificate.' Thea's pleasure in the peaceful, wild garden and the lovely home-cooked meal faded a degree at the reminder of things she had yet to face.

Ezzie's blue eyes softened into pools of sympathy. 'It's one of the odd things about being an adoptee – knowing your now-name but that your birth name was probably something totally different. You at least know now that you were Althea-hyphen-Dora, if not a surname. I don't know whether my birth name was anything like Esmerelda.'

'Are you thinking of finding out?' Thea paused, her glass halfway to her mouth.

Ezzie looked thoughtful. 'I never felt the urge before because we had such wonderful adoptive parents. But I have felt some curiosity since you've known more about your history.'

183

They cleared their plates in silence. Thea sat back with a big sigh, and Daisy popped her head above the grass as if to check Thea was OK. Now awake, she rose, shook herself, and trotted over to sniff Bouncer, who lived up to his name by springing up, his long tail whipping side to side in a plain invitation to play.

'So, you'd want to know more, if you were me?' Thea asked, watching Daisy and Bouncer absently as they danced around while Scotty sat up to watch, black ears twitching.

Ezz arched an eyebrow, but managed to frown at the same time, making her look quizzical. 'I think I'd want to hear what Meryl Muller had to say. And I'd want to find the original surname, just because it will probably be French, and French names sound amazing.'

Thea laughed and felt suddenly decisive. 'I can't force Meryl to reply to me, but I'll at least apply for the birth certificate.'

Ezz flashed her a knowing look. 'Shall I fetch my laptop so we can do it now?'

Pleased at being so easily understood, Thea said, 'Yes, please.'

Within minutes, they were filling out the online form together, although Ezzie was more of the you-do-it-while-I-supervise-and-encourage school. Probably, she was right to support Thea by reading out the instructions while Thea laboured over filling in the little boxes herself, but it made Thea feel anxious and on edge, as though someone was poised to tell her off for being slow or uncooperative. Ezz didn't of course, only waiting patiently while Thea tapped slowly, but, when Dev had helped her, it had been nice to watch his strong, capable hands flying over the keyboard without having to make the effort herself.

184

Later, after she'd hugged Ezzie goodnight and walked the dogs home, it was nice to receive a text from Deveron. *Hope you had a good evening. Do you fancy dinner Saturday or Sunday evening? X*

Replying instantly wasn't cool, so she waited until she'd settled Daisy, showered in her slope-ceilinged bathroom and slipped into pink-striped cami pyjamas, brushed her hair and cleaned her teeth. Then she responded: *Good, thanks. Saturday evening would be lovely. X*

Deveron obviously didn't know or didn't bother about being cool as his reply pinged straight back. *Great! X*

She tapped out her reply. *It's usually worth booking a restaurant in Skye. We could go to the Stag Inn, where I meant to take you before. X*

Two minutes later, she'd slipped beneath the sheets and was wiggling her bare toes against their coolness, when she received: *Leave it with me. Goodnight. X*

She returned: *Goodnight. X* Then she lay awake thinking about Dev. They had lots in common. They both liked gardens. He talked about his family with affection, as she talked about hers – setting aside the birth mother, who Thea didn't know, so couldn't like or dislike.

Her phone buzzed on its charging stand as another message arrived from Deveron. *I'm in bed.*

A smile curled one side of her mouth, and she wondered about his nightwear. Tee and boxers? He didn't seem a pyjamas-type guy. Maybe nothing? *Me, too. X*

A short pause, then: *Thinking of you. X*

Heat trickled through her. *Me, too,* she repeated. Then, for clarity: *Thinking of you.*

A longer pause, before: *Good. Xx*

When sleep still eluded her, she set her phone playing a podcast about a woman who travelled around France restoring frescoes in churches. Thea had never visited France but tried to conjure up a mental map. Provence was in the south-east, Normandy in the north, which she vaguely thought close to Picardy and the Loire Valley. Maybe she ought to visit the country just over the English Channel as it seemed French blood at least half filled her veins. She took up her phone again and opened a browser page, searching for a map of French regions. She had to scroll about the map to read the names. Alsace. Lorraine. Champagne-Ardenne. The area around Paris was called Île-de-France. She remembered her dad, Vince, singing a song called 'These Foolish Things' that mentioned the Île-de-France, but he'd told her it was a posh ocean liner.

She closed her eyes and let some of the things that reminded her of him wash over her: his kind face, his shaggy hair, his tattoos when they weren't even fashionable, the way he'd curled himself around a guitar to play. Maxie singing along to the line about lovers walking like dreamers, her auburn hair swinging and fingers clicking.

And once there had been a small, dark figure living with them, a Frenchwoman who'd brought to them a little girl called Althea-Dora.

And left her behind.

She finally drifted off to sleep dreaming about strolling around vineyards or breakfasting on croissants and coffee. It was easier than thinking too deeply about the Frenchwoman.

On Saturday morning, Thea lay in bed, watching the shifting branches of her birch tree outside the window while she took stock. This was the first of five days off and she hadn't planned much beyond avoiding Fredek Kowski.

Except, of course, she had a date with Deveron tonight. Her pulse speeded up.

But she also had a fence to finish, with two panels to affix and the gate to be hung before Daisy could be allowed in the back garden alone. After breakfast, she went out to begin. It wasn't easy on her own, but with the use of props to hold one end steady while she fixed the other, she managed the panels. The gate was trickier, and she was struggling with wedges and props when Fraser arrived.

'Need a hand?' he called in his soft Hebridean accent, as he strolled up the path, Scotty panting at his heels.

Gladly, Thea straightened. 'That would be great. It's hard to mark the hinge holes accurately on my own. Hello, Scotty!' Scotty wagged his straight black tail. With a bit of steadying from Fraser, whose foot turned out to be perfect to act as a wedge, Thea soon had the gate swinging and latching.

'Awesome,' she said, straightening for the last time. 'Fancy a cuppa?'

'Oh, aye,' said Fraser, as if surprised she needed to ask. Thea freed Daisy from the kitchen, who was overjoyed to find Scotty in her garden – though he showed a lack of manners by cocking his leg up the new – firmly closed – gate.

Later, after Fraser had gone, Thea rang Valentina to see if she was accepting visitors because Thea hadn't seen Barnaby for months except on FaceTime. Valentina groaned. 'Wish I'd known a few weeks ago. We're going away for the weekend.'

'It's short notice,' Thea acknowledged. 'I just decided to take a few days' leave.' She didn't elaborate as to why.

After the call, she decided she'd just about saved enough

187

to augment the sparse furnishings in her lounge. She went online and found a lovely faux-leather grey two-seater sofa within her budget in a store in Balmaqueen, further up the island. It was in stock and delivery for her area was Wednesday, so it would arrive just before she returned to work.

Finally, she and Daisy enjoyed a hike out of the village and into the woods behind Friday Furlong, where Daisy proved herself to be responsible enough not to run away when let off the lead, though she did wade into the burn and lie in two inches of water. Then she leapt up, zoomed across the stream sending a shower of water into the warm air, screeched to a halt beside Thea and decided it was the perfect spot in which to shake her long, fluffy coat.

'Charming,' said Thea wryly, wiping droplets from her face.

Daisy panted and wagged, looking pleased.

In revenge, Thea took her home, trimmed her coat, then washed her in the bathtub, which reduced a small fluffy dog to something perilously close to a sad, wet rat. Then Thea laughed to watch Daisy whizzing all over the house, drying herself on the carpet as if it was the best game *in the world*.

Seven o'clock saw Thea ready for a leisurely summer evening stroll to the Stag Inn, dressed in a flowery summer top and cream-coloured jeans, her hair loose. She'd suggested meeting Deveron at Manor Road to save him extra walking, but he'd insisted that a proper date should begin with him presenting himself at her door.

He arrived, freshly shaved, a sage-coloured shirt making his eyes look closer to green than hazel. His curls bounced in the wind and his smile was warm. So was the glint in his eye when he saw her. 'You look gorgeous.'

It seemed ages since Thea had experienced the half-shy, half-excited nervousness that came with early dates. 'You look great too.' She accepted a kiss, and then let him take her hand as she stepped out into the sweet, perfumed evening, ignoring Daisy's huffy bark from the kitchen.

'I thought we'd go down to Harbour View then out of the village via Blackrock Road,' she told him, as they strolled downhill, and the bay spread itself out below them in a sheet of glassy water punctured by craggy rocks. 'How was your day? I rang Valentina, but she and her family have plans for the weekend, so I can't visit. It's a long way on public transport but I was going to get Ezz to let me borrow her car.'

'I've had an easy day at work with the boss absent.' He winked.

'Ratbag,' she answered affably. 'Watch out when she comes back. She'll have it in for you.'

He laughed and slipped an arm around her. He smelled of shaving gel. When they reached the bridge, where the cow parsley was taller than Thea and the bracken lolled into the road as if too tired to stand, he steered her towards the footpath through the copse.

She hung back. 'This isn't the way to the Stag Inn. Or, at least, not a direct way.'

He dropped a kiss on her hair. 'I arranged something different.'

'What?' Thea demanded, joining him on the path, though wary of the brambles that were growing like spiny Triffids in the undergrowth.

'Surprise.' His slow smile sent tingles all the way to her toes.

She didn't have long to wait to discover what the surprise was. Emerging from the trees fifteen minutes later, he steered her left to what had been the scruffy patch out of sight behind the staff accommodation, which she'd christened Project Deveron. There, she found a small table painted the same blue as the bench he'd refurbished, cutlery and glasses set out upon it. 'How pretty,' she breathed, touched that the date consisted of something that had cost him effort. 'You've been busy. Project Deveron looks great.' The ground was still uneven, but the grass was trimmed so it didn't show too much.

He gazed around with an air of satisfaction. 'Glad you like it.'

Her gaze moved to a rock garden that had been a heap of discarded rock in a different spot, last time she'd seen it. 'Did you go buying alpines? You could have asked Hadley what bedding he could spare from the greenhouse.'

He slid an arm about her waist. 'Bedding is annual. I wanted perennials. Something that would be here next year.'

Was he saying, *'Even if I'm not'*? She regarded him. 'That's nice, to want to have a lasting effect on the landscape. Where did the table come from?'

'A skip. It was scratched so I painted it,' he said laconically. 'Sit down. Everything's ready.'

He strode off, leaving her to perch on the bench and wait. The scratches on the table showed through the paint, but she quite liked the idea of furniture bearing the scars of its life, just as humans did. The table was a slightly odd height for the bench, but that was OK. Her height didn't match perfectly with Deveron's, but she could adapt to that, too. She realised that, by positioning the table close to a wall, he'd managed to pick a spot out of sight of anyone in the staff accommodation – her colleagues would have to come out and walk behind the building to spot them on their date. Evidently, he had thought of everything.

Then he was back with wine in a cooler, a bottle of water and a cardboard box, all balanced precariously in his arms. 'Sorry I don't have a coolbox.' He set out plates, then a big plastic platter of sausages, salad, chicken breasts, and cheese and crackers. He seated himself beside her, surveyed the picnic and asked, almost bashfully, 'Will it be OK? Maybe I should have just booked the restaurant.'

'It's *gorgeous*,' she assured him, and kissed his cheek, touched that he'd created this for her.

He turned to catch the second kiss on his lips, and there followed an interval where neither of them used their mouths for eating. 'Now, that's better than saying grace before a meal,' he said irreverently when they came up for air, and poured her wine.

'Absolutely,' Thea said, her heart thudding. Inelegantly, she added, 'Phew,' which made him laugh. She liked his readiness to laugh and smile, as if there was so much goodness inside him it had to bubble to the surface.

They began to help themselves to food. Deveron said, 'I met the ladies running retreats at the pavilion. As they're going to be there on and off all summer, Sheena asked Hadley to make up a pot of fresh herbs as a welcome present, and Hadley asked me to take it over on the garden cart.'

She grinned. 'He likes you because you're big and strong.' Then, giddy with the loveliness of the summer evening, the sound of birdsong and a handsome man sitting beside her, she added, 'I feel much the same.'

He lifted his wine in a toast. '*Slàinte mhath*. I like *you* because you're gorgeous and fun.'

'Oh. Thank you.' With his gaze so heavy upon her she felt exposed, yet safe at the same time as she clinked her glass with his. '*Slàinte mhath*.' When it came to Gaelic, it was an advantage not to want to see written words as she knew to English eyes that the toast pronounced, 'Slanja va,' looked like 'slanty muhath'.

He turned to his food. 'I met the Larssons as well. Lovely people. What are you going to do with your time off, if you're not visiting your sister Valentina?' Deveron asked, his knee against hers under the table.

Thea liked the feel of it. 'Laze about. Work on my garden. Maybe do something with Ezz when she has time off. Long walks with Daisy.' Then she sighed. 'Mum's friend Meryl hasn't answered me and trying to get in touch with her has made me miss Mum and Dad all over again. And no sign of my birth certificate yet, so a decision about whether to try and track down my birth mother is on hold.'

'Getting impatient?' His eyes were fixed on hers as he took a cracker for his cheese.

She considered. 'To be honest, I haven't decided whether to look for her. But even if I decide not to, I might still visit France. It's odd to not even have seen the country that gave me at least half my heritage.'

He munched his cracker before answering. 'It's a great country. I did French at school, and it came in useful when I travelled in Europe.'

'You travelled on business?' He seemed so at home in the gardens of Rothach Hall that until he mentioned driving in Europe, she'd almost forgotten about the agency that his business partner had steered badly.

'Quite a bit. Scotland's more distant from continental Europe than England is, so I often flew to France, picked up a car and then drove.' He turned a distant gaze on the rockery, as if looking into his past.

Perhaps because he'd described the rockery as leaving his mark on the landscape, she reminded herself again how temporary his stay on Skye was likely to be. 'It's a huge change to be stuck out on the Isle of Skye mowing lawns. What comes next?' A small, empty place opened inside her at the thought of him leaving Skye, but she supposed that at least it meant there wouldn't be time for what was between them to go wrong – even if, in other circumstances, she might be wondering whether they were at the start of something.

'I'm no nearer knowing than when I arrived. I do love it here, though.' He turned back to his meal. 'I want to see my family soon. I think maybe I'll do that on my next days off. I try and talk to Mum and Grandpa every week. Though they're happy that I've found a summer job I like, they're also disappointed I didn't go home for a while. And I like to see my wee nieces reasonably often, so we're not strangers.'

'I feel the same about my nephew Barnaby. You didn't have any children of your own?' She remembered him joking that if he ever had kids he'd name them Amazon and Congo, but it didn't hurt to be sure when you were dating someone.

He didn't seem to take her question amiss. 'Whether we were both too busy to change our lives, or too selfish, I'm not sure. But the time didn't come.'

'It's never come for me, either. I haven't been in that kind of relationship for ages.' She changed the subject. Talking about children was too much of a 'looking to a future with you' conversation when they'd only known each other a couple of weeks and she'd had so many thoughts about the temporary nature of his stay. 'What did your wife do? Was that something high-powered, too?'

He snorted. 'She did the admin and finance for the agency.'

A clammy feeling slid over Thea. 'So,' she said slowly, 'she understood the agency's situation? She ran away with your business partner, knowing that it was failing?'

He nodded, his eyebrows dipping into a frown.

'What a pair of shits,' Thea said quietly.

His eyes glinted. 'I've called them much worse – and to their faces. It doesn't change much.'

'I suppose not.' She put down her fork in favour of taking his hand, feeling the hairs overlaying his warm skin. 'How was winding everything up?'

He winced. 'I thought I was going to go mad with the mess. It was a big complicator that the trouble originated in Bulgaria, and I don't speak Bulgarian. But once it became obvious that there was no money to pay people off, it came down to paperwork in the end.'

With Thea's hatred of admin, the truly horrible, hurtful time he'd stoically recounted would have been torture. She kept her gaze steady. 'Do you still have feelings for your wife?'

His eyes turned flinty. 'Only bad ones.'

'Good,' she said. 'If you'd had good feelings for such a two-faced, conniving bitch, I would have lost respect for you.'

He laughed, flinging back his head, showing his white teeth. 'You are so uncomplicated and honest.' Then he kissed her in a way that suggested he'd put his marriage behind him and he was very happy to be here with Thea.

* * *

194

They remained in the seclusion of Project Deveron, lingering over the wine as they talked about gardens, childhood pets, family, music, films and all the other getting-to-know-you stuff. Thea even kept her end up in a conversation about books, because audiobooks were books, right? They both enjoyed crime fiction and biographies, though she preferred biographies of musicians or public figures and he liked sports personalities.

And all the time, Thea felt herself falling under his spell. It wasn't a loud *kerchunk* or a flash of light, just a growing feeling of rightness, and of knowing that things could develop . . . *if* he stayed.

Finally, she said, 'I'd better go home to let Daisy out.'

They cleared the table then walked the mile or so back to Thistledome. Thea didn't bother pausing at the door to ask if he'd like to come in, but simply led the way to the kitchen where Daisy blinked in the light, wagging her tail and giving welcoming woofs, sniffs and snorts before gambolling out of the back door. When she returned, bouncing over the doorsteps like a puppet dog on strings, she let them both fuss her, then climbed back into her bed, curled round like a doughnut – if doughnuts were ever covered in pearly fur – and closed her eyes.

Thea made tea and they took their mugs into the lounge, switching off the kitchen light as Daisy had plainly indicated that it was night-time. They each took a rocking chair. Thea stroked a chair arm. 'I do love these two beauties, but I've bought a sofa. It'll be delivered on Wednesday.'

His eyes gleamed above the steam rising from his mug. 'Easier to snuggle up on a sofa than a rocking chair.'

She giggled and flushed, as that was pretty much why she'd bought the sofa. 'Then you've no imagination.'

195

In a moment he was on his feet, stowing his tea mug on the floor and taking hers to stand beside it. He swung her out of her rocking chair and in an instant had taken her seat, settling her crosswise on his lap, his arm behind her to guard her from the hard wood. 'It's a fine place to cuddle,' he said smugly.

'That's OK,' she allowed. Daringly, she turned and settled so she bestrode him, her thighs snug beneath the wooden armrests, and dropped a kiss on his face. 'This is better.'

'You're right.' His voice was low and husky. He pulled her forward so he could nuzzle her neck, letting his mouth travel over her collarbone and awakening delicious tingles, as if sprinkling magic dust over her skin.

And though she had a king-sized bed upstairs, she was unwilling to break the spell. Somehow, slowly, they struggled him out of his shirt and her out of her top, touching, stroking, exploring, kissing, both of their bodies firm with exercise yet soft with wanting.

She groaned, letting her head tip back as he kissed and sucked her breasts, cupping her bottom to ensure she didn't roll backwards off his lap.

He paused only long enough to say roughly, 'If you want to send me home, now's the time.'

She laughed at the raw longing in his voice. 'Do you want to go?'

'No.' He tugged gently on her nipple with his teeth. 'But we're going to have to move, or my jeans are going to do me damage.'

'OK,' she said regretfully, beginning to edge backwards, freeing her thighs from the armrests. 'Shall we go upstairs?' The magic would follow them as they made their way to her bedroom beneath the eaves, she was sure, but it was a shame to hit pause just when she felt so ready.

He leant forward to unbutton her jeans, dotting kisses on the bare flesh he exposed. 'We could. But I did read a scene about rocking-chair sex, once. I've always had a hankering to try it. I have a condom.'

She pulled back to study his face, her pulse leaping at the lust in his eyes. 'Rocking-chair sex is a thing? Then we must try it.' And they found that once they were both naked and he was inside her, there was more than one way to start that chair rocking.

Chapter Fourteen

That Sunday evening, Deveron arrived at Thea's little purple house with the ingredients for a barbecue. Apart from the promise of grilled steak with salad and then a nice saunter with Daisy, his mind was also much on the hot, hot sex of the evening before.

Having shopped at the Broadford supermarket, he'd driven straight to Thea's cottage, mind wandering from the roadside chunks of rock that were the bones of Skye to memories of Thea's naked body. Though he had the bruises to show for their rocking-chair sex, her throwing back her head like a cute she-wolf baying at the moon was going to stay with him a long time.

Afterwards, dragging themselves up her narrow, uneven stairs had tested their shaking legs, but there he'd remained until five this morning, when he'd woken her briefly with a farewell kiss before strolling through a lemon-yellow early morning to his own quarters. He would have loved to stay beside her, but knew that being seen leaving in the morning might give rise to village gossip. She deserved respect.

As he stood on her doorstep now, he gave a jaunty rat-a-tat of the bee-shaped door knocker and Thea opened the door. But rather than the brilliant – or maybe sexy or knowing – smile he'd anticipated, she held a phone pressed to her ear and a deep groove had dug itself between her brows. At least Daisy greeted him with a wide doggy grin, though she changed course when she scented the food in his carrier bag. Fearing for the steak, he swung it into his arms. Daisy gave him a disgruntled look.

Into the phone, Thea said, 'Ezz, I'm going to kill him.'

He found himself making a 'Who? Me?' face.

Impatiently, she shook her head and beckoned him in, continuing with her conversation. 'Does Erik know? Can't he? Why not? Oh, *Tavish*.' She snorted contemptuously. 'OK. Thanks for letting me know. I'll have to think about how to play Thursday. Thanks, Ezz.'

She ended the call with a hard jab on the phone screen.

Pushing the door shut with himself on the inside, he slipped his non-carrier-bag arm around her and kissed the top of her head. 'What's up?'

She returned his embrace. 'Just before Ezz left work today, she glanced through the guests listed for the writing retreat at the pavilion. She needed to know for fire drills or insurance or something. Anyway, one of them is Fredek Kowski. Nita and Fiona, the retreat ladies, say he was a last-minute booking late on Friday, via the website. Sly little shit.'

His stomach tumbled. Fredek at the pavilion?

She led the way into the kitchen and flumped into a chair. 'Apparently, retreat guests have freedom of the public areas and there's no mechanism to allow the hall to veto a retreat guest. Erik's unhappy, apparently. And so am I.'

So was Deveron. If retreat guests could wander the grounds, then he was going to be on pins in case he stumbled on Fredek and was recognised. Once again, he cursed the situation he'd been a part of creating. 'Thea,' he said tentatively, not even sure what he was going to say next but feeling he should say *something*.

Thea cut across him. '*And*, Ezz says, a link to some stupid article on a nasty, dodgy news site has been posted on the hall's Facebook page by some random visitor. It's about me and the accident.' She mimed pulling out her hair.

'Oh,' he said hollowly. The confession that had hovered on the tip of his tongue refused to be spoken. Judging from the fire in Thea's eyes, it would end their relationship. And for what? His writing the piece she was presumably referring to had at least safeguarded her from it being given to someone less sympathetic – including Fredek himself.

'Have you read it?' he asked, his voice tight.

She shook her head, her hair dancing about her shoulders. 'Ezz sent me the link but the last thing I'd ever want to read is meddlesome, uninformed crap.'

Deveron felt a ripple of relief for her logophobia; then a crashing wave of guilt for having such a selfish thought. But surely there was nothing more to come? Thea wouldn't see because she didn't do social media. The subject would die.

Weston's last email suggested he'd been cornered into letting Dev out of writing anything else for Everyday Celebs and had said himself that he'd been left with little scope for the opportunity of a follow-up *You decide!* piece.

Still, Dev had no more appetite for the barbecue than Thea exhibited, and Daisy did very nicely out of leftovers.

*   *   *

Thea was shocked to receive a 10 a.m. phone call from Erik Larsson on Monday morning.

'Hello, Mr Larsson,' she murmured, caught off guard, lying on her back lawn watching clouds bobbing like boats across the blue sky above the rocky outcrop that marked the end of her garden. Daisy, zonked on the grass beside her, was using Thea's left boob as a pillow.

'You are on your holidays,' Erik observed punctiliously. 'But it is possible that Grete and I arrive at your house to drink coffee this morning?'

'Erm . . . of course.' She sat up, dislodging Daisy, who snuffled reproachfully.

'Ten-thirty,' Mr Larsson said politely. 'And you please remember to call us Erik and Grete. Goodbye.'

The phone screen went blank. Thea looked at Daisy, who looked back, as if hoping for clues as to what was going on. As Thea didn't know, she hurried indoors to change into a clean T-shirt.

By the time Erik and Grete arrived, she'd started her coffee machine and wiped the outdoor chairs, having realised that her seating options amounted to those, gathering around the kitchen table or three people sharing two rocking chairs. And those rocking chairs made her blush to look at them after the use she and Deveron had put one to on Saturday night.

Erik and Grete arrived punctually, and it took a few minutes to exchange greetings and settle around the patio table with mugs of coffee and chocolate-chip cookies. To Thea's fascination, Erik put two cookies together and ate them as one. 'Good,' he pronounced thickly.

It took him two more bites to dispose of the snack and get down to business. 'Ezzie has told you of Fredek at the pavilion?'

Thea nodded. As if sensing a spike in her anxiety, Daisy jumped onto her lap, then waffled her nose in the direction of the cookies, which Thea pushed out of her reach. 'It's unfortunate,' she replied diplomatically, giving Daisy a consolatory pat.

Grete, who was usually quieter than Erik, spoke up. Her English was more flowing than her husband's and her eyes were kind behind her glasses, crinkling to slits when she smiled, which was often. 'We are distressed that a man is making you uncomfortable at Rothach Hall. As your employers, we feel responsible.'

Erik nodded earnestly and took two more cookies. Daisy followed his movements with her eyes.

'We think it would be good if you remain away from the hall until this man has left the pavilion.' Grete gave a nod, as if agreeing with herself.

Thea had been thinking along the same lines, though reluctantly, because there were a lot of flowerbeds to be replanted before the fresh influx of visitors that normally marked the start of the English and Welsh school holidays. Also, in some small corner of her mind, she was thinking about going to France, and didn't want Fredek making her use up annual leave. But she sighed. 'I'll talk to Ezz about taking more holiday. Maybe I can tack next week's rest days on, so I don't use it all.'

Erik finished his cookies. 'No,' he said immediately. 'We give you . . .' He turned to Grete and said something to her, presumably in Swedish. Or Norwegian.

Grete nodded. 'Additional paid leave. Ezzie says four days, Thursday to Sunday.'

Spirits lifting, Thea found herself smiling. 'Really? That would be incredibly generous.'

'Ha.' Erik took another two cookies. 'This man is not

your fault. And a member of our staff did a contribution to your problem.'

Realising he meant Tavish, Thea maintained a discreet silence.

It seemed the discussion was at an end. Grete asked Thea about Thistledome, and Thea cheered up enough to eat a cookie, Daisy vacuuming up crumbs.

Her employers stayed only as long as it took to drink their coffee and Erik to polish off the last of the cookies, then they told her they'd see her on Monday, and returned to the smart Volvo they kept at Rothach Hall, which looked oversized in the narrowness of Loch View.

Thea waved them off, relieved and grateful for such wonderful employers.

Four additional days of paid leave! *Ha, Fredek. You've unintentionally done me a good turn.*

When Sheena said someone needed to weed around the knot garden's ornamental box hedging today, Deveron volunteered. 'I'll do that.' It was a tiresome task involving delving about with a hand fork, but crouching at the base of a hedge was an excellent way to hide if Fredek came stooging about.

'Great.' Sheena looked surprised at getting rid of the crap job. 'Nell and I will take mowing and edging while Hadley plants out.'

Hadley pulled a face. 'Thea had said I could have Deveron with me.'

Sheena patted his shoulder. 'He'll carry the plant trays over for you, but we had some rain in the night, and I want the knot garden weeded while the ground's soft.' Hadley grimaced, but didn't argue.

After a back-breaking morning winkling out knots of

weeds, at lunchtime Deveron opted to spend his break in his studio apartment. As he crossed the stable courtyard, he met Ezz, wearing a face like a wet Monday. 'OK?' he asked, pausing. Like Thea, Ezz usually had a ready smile.

Glumly, she shrugged. 'Thea says you know about this guy Fredek making a nuisance of himself? He has me on edge.' She sighed. 'Erik Larsson had a chat with Fredek, but Fredek just said that it's hard to get accommodation at short notice on Skye, so he was delighted to find the retreat had a space. He wants to use the retreat to write posts for his blog.'

Dev rasped the stubble on his chin. For obvious reasons, he didn't like Fredek lurking, but he wasn't ultra-keen on Erik Larsson issuing probing questions either. If Fredek gave him chapter and verse, the name Deveron Dowie might come up. 'So he's staying?'

Ezzie turned down the corners of her mouth. 'I suppose so. Erik explained the situation to Fiona and Nita, and they agreed to take no further bookings from Fredek.'

Feeling his way, Dev asked, 'What is it about this Fredek character that has you bothered?'

Ezzie's gaze slid away. She contemplated the back of the hall for several seconds before saying offhandedly, 'I've not met him, but if he bothers Thea, he bothers me. Following her all the way to the Inner Hebrides is hardly normal behaviour.'

Before Dev could comment, his phone rang, and he glanced at the screen. 'This is Thea now.' He answered the call.

'I'm in the copse,' she said, sounding out of breath. 'I want to speak to Ezzie but she's not answering her phone, and I'm worried Fredek might spot me if I go looking for her.'

Instinctively, he glanced around. 'I'm in the courtyard and he's nowhere to be seen. Ezzie's with me, so I can put you on. I was just going to my room for lunch.'

Eagerly, Thea suggested, 'Can we all meet there? Ezz too?'

'Sure,' he agreed, and a few minutes later was letting Thea into his room, Daisy trotting happily at her side. He didn't remind her of the 'no pets' rule for the live-in staff. Maybe it didn't count when the pet was just visiting.

'Meryl's answered my email,' Thea gasped as she half fell through the door, brandishing her phone.

Ezzie's hands flew to her cheeks like Minnie Mouse and, appropriately, she squeaked. 'Really? Have you read it?'

'Yes.' Thea sounded surprised at herself. She trained her gaze on her screen. '"*Dear Thea,*"' she read. '"*Sorry to take a while to reply. I was working in London, and wanted to give myself a chance to think.*"'

'About . . . ?' Ezz prompted.

Thea shrugged. 'She doesn't say. Probably whether she wanted to talk to me.'

'Your message might have come as a surprise, if you never remember interacting with her,' Deveron put in.

'True.' Thea read on. '"*Your mum was a fantastic friend to me, and so, yes, I'd be happy to talk. Do you prefer phone, video call or in person? I'm semi-retired now and live in the Lake District.*"'

Ezzie's blue eyes grew enormous as she gazed at her sister. 'What do you think?'

'I'd like to meet her.' Thea's gaze was earnest. 'I have so many unanswered questions. It's a fair drive, though. I could hire a car, I suppose. Or take the bus to Glasgow and see if I can reach her by bus or train from there. I don't want to borrow your car to put hundreds of miles on the clock, Ezz.'

'Don't worry about that,' Ezz said instantly. 'I'd love to come with you, but Tavish isn't about to do me any favours by swapping days off with me. He must know I wrote his formal warning, and he's been growling at me like an angry bear.' She grimaced. 'It's *your* birth mother you want to talk about, Thea. And I wouldn't want to listen to Meryl slagging Dad off, if they didn't like each other,' she ended frankly.

Thea's brown eyes danced. 'You were always Daddy's girl, reading the same books as him and learning the guitar.'

Ezz gave her a tiny shove. 'I liked those things. Don't make me sound like a suck-up.' But both sisters were grinning, and Deveron could see that the friendly insults were a sign of sibling love.

And as Ezz had opted out, he could step in with the perfect solution. 'My family live in southern Scotland, conveniently close to the lakes in northern England. I've been wanting to visit my folks. We could go in my car, Thea. I could wait somewhere while you see Meryl, and then we could stay overnight with my brother, Leith. He lives in Lockerbie, right close to the motorway.' It would also mean he didn't have to leave Thea here with Fredek about while he went to visit family.

Ezzie's eyebrows rose in Thea's direction. They could have said, 'What do you think?' Or, 'You know him well enough to spend the night?'

But all Thea's attention was on Dev. 'That would be amazing if you honestly don't mind.'

'I don't.' He sent Ezz a deliberately speculative look. 'But I have to see the assistant manager to get my next rest days to coincide with yours.'

Thea's smile only broadened. 'Erik and Grete visited me this morning and they're giving me paid leave, so I won't have to work while Fredek's at the writing retreat. That gives us a bigger window to work with.'

Ezz was already nodding. 'We'll work it out.' She checked her watch. 'I must get back to the office. Thea, find out when Meryl will be available, and then Dev can tell me what days to roster him off.'

'Aye, aye.' Thea snapped a salute and Ezz made a much ruder gesture in reply.

Deveron was left alone in his bedroom with Thea, which was an agreeable way to spend what was left of lunch hour, even chaperoned by a panting Daisy, who wriggled into the tiny space between their legs when he tried to kiss Thea. 'Spoilsport,' he told her severely, then made himself and Thea cheese salad sandwiches. He did give Daisy the cheese crumbs, though, because she sat and looked so hopeful that it melted his heart.

When it was time for him to return to work, he checked the coast was clear of a skulking Fredek, and then Thea and Daisy scurried out. Once safely behind the staff quarters, Thea paused and glanced back to blow a kiss before she disappeared among the trees as the ground fell away towards the village. It seemed to slip into his chest and deliver itself directly to his heart.

Later in the afternoon, he was once again hard at work in the knot garden when Thea texted him. *Meryl can meet Thurs 11th or Fri 12th. X* She added a wide-eyed emoticon, suggesting apprehension.

He returned: *I'll talk to Ezz. X* and a smiley.

After straightening cautiously, partly to check Fredek wasn't around amongst the few visitors drifting around in the afternoon sun and partly because his back and legs felt like concrete after crouching for much of the day, he went to Ezz's tiny office off reception, a poor relation after the ornate ceiling and stairs in the lobby. When she looked up from her computer, he showed her Thea's text.

After some clicking and scrolling while gazing at her computer screen, she asked, 'Would you be OK to take Friday and Saturday? Obviously, the garden team's depleted and Sheena's already off Wednesday and Thursday to take her children somewhere.'

'Sure. I'll tell Thea.' He annotated his phone calendar.

When he looked up, Ezz was regarding him quizzically. 'What?' Disquiet wriggled through him. Had Ezz somehow discovered his connection to Everyday Celebs?

'It's interesting that my sister's apparently placing trust in you,' she said. When he made no reply, she continued, 'Thea told you about the recent online thing about her? This hashtag-where-are-they-now crap?'

'Yes,' he agreed cautiously.

She bit her lip. 'It happened just as Fredek came out of the woodwork. We've had no contact with him for eight years.'

'That's what Thea gave me to understand,' he answered truthfully.

She pursed her lips. 'I don't usually feel that women need men to look after them. But this time I'm glad someone will be with her. It sounds as if you and my sis are a thing.'

'Aye,' he agreed still more cautiously.

She cocked an eyebrow. 'What kind of a thing?'

Uneasily, he shifted from foot to foot. Family could be very suspicious when you were sleeping with one of their own. 'We haven't hung a wee label on it.'

Her mobile brows drew down. 'It's been a bit like a

meet-cute romance novel, hasn't it? With you turning up to save Daisy and then infiltrating Thea's life.'

She seemed on pins, and he knew the feeling. '"Infiltrating" doesn't belong in a romance. It sounds more like crime and thriller.'

Ezz snorted a sudden laugh. 'Do I sound like the mad, overprotective sister? It's just that Thea and Valentina are the people I love most in the world.'

Involuntarily, he felt his face soften into a smile. 'I'm pretty keen on Thea, too.' And getting keener by the day. If this *were* romantic fiction, there would one day be a happy-ever-after ending. For an instant, he allowed himself to imagine them walking off into a sunset over Rothach Hall.

But it was real life, so he returned to work, uncertain whether to feel wary of Fredek stumbling over him, or excited at the prospect of having Thea to himself for a couple of days.

He texted her the news about his rest days and then returned to winkling out thistles and sticky weed. His conscience was not quiet, even when he tried to reason with it that his involvement with Everyday Celebs had been a matter of taking work he despised when he was in a bad way and had been nursing a bad attitude in reaction to the shit that life had sent him.

His conscience didn't award him a get-out-of-jail-free card and shame followed him right along the hedge. He wondered what would happen if curiosity ever made Ezzie google him – though she'd find only sports reportage with his byline. She might be surprised, given that he'd deliberately never told anyone here that 'the agency' was a news agency and in fact let Ezz assume it was involved in promotions. But he'd never said it *wasn't* a news agency.

His mind wandered to past summers. Before the agency folded, he would have spent July setting up commercial deals relating to the coming football season, as well as chasing down off-season transfer news and managing journalists covering other ball sports. Now, he felt as if all his former passion for footie had been scraped off his soul.

He paused to savour the warmth of the sun on his back. It dawned on him that, apart from the spectres of Fredek and Everyday Celebs – and despite a nagging feeling that he should have stayed away from Thea, having come here to cynically make money out of her story – he was happy.

They were bloody big, black spectres though.

His phone vibrated. What he saw on the screen whipped any tentative vestige of happiness away. It was a bank account notification that a sum had been deposited with the reference 'Everyday Celebs'. It was the fee for the *Where are they now?* piece about Thea, along with the travel allowance he'd returned in an attempt to cut ties with Weston.

He knew exactly how Judas felt when he'd received the thirty pieces of silver, and considered returning the fee. But the bloody piece was out there now, so it would be an empty protest that would probably make Weston laugh.

Savagely, he stabbed at the soil, vowing to do what he could to help Thea from now on. If ever there was a case of 'bad things happen to good people', it was hers. She was indubitably 'good people' and all he wanted in the world was not to be one of the 'bad things'.

Chapter Fifteen

Thea's days off dragged, as her mind kept returning to Meryl Muller like the butterflies flitting around the roses. What would Meryl have to say about Thea's beloved adoptive mum Maxie and Thea's birth mother Ynez?

She tried to distract herself with evenings with Dev or Ezzie, walking Daisy with Bouncer and Scotty, and once joining Maisie and Fraser for lunch in the beer garden of the Jolly Abbot, where she found herself the only one who hadn't retired years ago.

Her lovely new grey sofa arrived as promised on Wednesday, and she and Deveron road-tested it in the evening. Maybe it wasn't as titillating as the rocking chair, but it was certainly less bruising.

Finally, finally, Friday arrived. Thea left Daisy with Fraser, who'd kindly entered into a dog-share with Ezzie while Thea was away – Fraser daytime and Ezzie evening and night. Daisy gambolled over to Bouncer and barely spared Thea a backward glance as she unpacked the dog's bed and bowls.

Meryl had suggested that Thea arrive at 3 p.m., and

as it was a more-than six-hour journey, they were driving over the glorious length of Skye Bridge by 8 a.m., admiring the sea glittering like a field of blue diamonds below and the white cottages of Kyleakin as they crossed to Kyle of Lochalsh. Thea drove the first stint along the A87, on a shelf above Loch Alsh, Loch Duich and later Loch Cluanie. The hills and mountains rose green, grey and brown above them, burns tumbling down like streams of molten glass.

At the pretty, bustling town of Invergarry, Dev took the wheel for the journey beside Loch Linnhe before a sharp left turn through the Grampian mountains, where every other vehicle was a campervan and tourists milled at viewing spots with their camera phones. Thea took over again for the twisty road beside Loch Lomond, edged with small stone walls that seemed to be lying in wait to scratch Deveron's car, and then they swapped back for the stretch from Glasgow to Penrith, passing the 'Welcome to England' sign that made Thea realise, with a shock, that she'd hardly been back to the country of her birth in the past eight years. Dev hadn't said a word about passing signs to Dumfries and Lockerbie, so she asked, 'It's very nice of your brother to say I could stay with you at his house. Are you looking forward to seeing your family?'

He said drily, 'Aye, a wee bit,' but the blinding grin he flashed at her told her it was a whole lot.

They arrived at the small place just outside Penrith where Meryl Muller lived, in time for lunch at a coffee shop. Without the long drive to focus on and with the meeting with Meryl Muller staring her in the face, Thea found herself unable to swallow anything but a mug of coffee while Deveron munched a sandwich and attempted a conversation.

'Sorry,' she said ruefully when he'd repeated himself

twice. 'I'm rubbish company and in danger of sticking to my chair with nervous sweat.'

He slipped a hand over hers, warm and gentle. 'It'll probably be better once you're there. It's like an exam – you're fine once you get in the exam hall.'

Thea tried to laugh. 'I was a petrified lump in exam halls, so that's not much comfort.' Impetuously, she added, 'I know you said you'd wait somewhere, but would you come in with me, instead? I'm scared I'll forget every word she says.'

Deveron didn't hesitate. 'Of course I will.' He abandoned his empty plate and pushed his chair closer to hers, pulling her into a hug, letting her draw comfort from the feeling of his body next to hers – a body she was getting to know.

Then suddenly there were only ten minutes before three o'clock. Thea visited the ladies' room, peered at her pale reflection and wondered for the hundredth time what Meryl would say and what she'd think of her. Then she took a few deep breaths and went out to where Dev waited, concern lurking in his eyes, despite his boyish smile.

'Still up for it?' was all he said, and when she nodded, he used his map app to guide them from the café and up a couple of residential streets where sunflowers grew tall enough to peep over stone garden walls. Thea clutched Dev's hand. 'I feel as if the pavement's rocking beneath my feet.'

Finally, they stopped before 20 Eden Street, a grey-stone three-storey terrace with a glossy black door and spiky purple-leaved berberis growing beneath the bay window.

'Ready?' Deveron squeezed her hand.

'Ready.' But her voice quavered, and she wanted to squeak, *No! Let's go to your family now. I don't want to meet a stranger who knew both my mothers and might tell me things I don't want to know.*

213

But she didn't. She squared her shoulders instead.

She couldn't remember afterwards whether she or Deveron had rung the bell, but suddenly the black door was open and a woman in her sixties stood gazing at them through deep blue eyes.

A wild mop of blonde hair hung onto the shoulders of her black T-shirt, and she looked older than any of the photos on her website. 'Thea?' she asked, and the slightest wobble in her voice somehow made Thea feel less afraid.

'Yes, hello, Meryl.' Thea summoned an uncertain smile. 'And this is Deveron. I hope you don't mind another guest.'

'Not in the least.' Meryl ushered them in and then turned to lead the way down a short passage that smelled of coffee into a garden room at the rear of the narrow house, with blinds keeping it shady, but leaving the view of a garden of lawn and rambling red roses. A tray containing water, fruit juice, a coffee carafe and biscuits sat on the low table and soon they were seated around it.

'Well,' she said, slapping both of her knees as if bringing the room to order. 'Your message took me by surprise, Thea. I haven't seen you since you were a baby, but your mum was my greatest friend. We did sessions together all the time. Someone would say, "Get Maxie and Meryl".' Her accent suggested London to Thea's ears.

Thea licked her lips. 'When you say you saw me as a baby, was I with my birth mother – Ynez? Or with Maxie? Do you know why you and I don't know each other, if you were so close to Mum – Maxie, I mean?'

Thoughtfully, Meryl pursed her lips. 'The last time I saw you, you were with them both, because I drove Ynez and you to Maxie's house in Suffolk.' She dropped her gaze. 'Me and your dad, Vince, we didn't really get on.'

Thea frowned, settling into the cushions of her bamboo-framed chair. 'Dad didn't make many enemies.'

Meryl smiled, creases forming at the corners of her eyes. 'If Vince was here, he'd tell you that I was possessive of Maxie and was in love with her. As she and I were friends before she met him, I was a bit jealous of him.' A pensive look crossed her face.

'Were you in love with Mum?' In her surprise, the words came out of Thea's mouth before she considered them.

'More of a crush,' Meryl said stiffly. 'But we never discussed it. She was straight and had your dad.' She picked up the plate of biscuits and offered them around. Deveron took one, but Thea shook her head. Meryl sipped from her glass of juice and then sat back, waiting.

Thea felt as if her stomach had solidified. 'Do you know Ynez's surname?'

Forehead puckering, Meryl shook her head. 'I used to, but I've forgotten.' A black cat padded into the room. It paused to gaze at Deveron then Thea with green eyes, before jumping silently onto Meryl's lap. Meryl ran her hand over the cat's head and shoulders as it settled itself. 'Ynez had been left high and dry with her baby,' she said reminiscently. 'She'd got a bit of work babysitting with someone I knew in London but by the time you were a few months old, she was running out of money. Maxie and Vince had moved out of London to Suffolk to a family home. They were finding it hard to manage your sisters and their careers and I suggested to Maxie that they give a live-in au pair a try and told her about Ynez. It worked brilliantly at first. Ynez was there when they were both working. She got a nice room and her food, as well as a small wage, and when they were having an evening at home, they didn't mind her going out and leaving you with them, Esmerelda and Valentina.' She hesitated, eyeing Thea. Delicately, she went on. 'I expect they wanted her to be happy and have friends, never dreaming that she was doing anything to get in trouble with the law. Vince was upset when Ynez was arrested. He told Maxie it was only good luck that he and Maxie were home when the police turned up and that if Ynez had been alone with you kids, you could have been put into care. I told Maxie that was bullshit. The lady next door would have had you. They were all buddies, living in the country like that.'

'The lady next door was Lois,' Thea supplied.

Meryl looked pleased. 'That's it.' She stared at Thea, a small smile playing on her lips. 'You have the same colouring as Ynez. Poor kid. Her worst sin was falling for the wrong blokes. She had backbone over most things but was a fool for her boyfriends.'

'Do you mean my birth father? Lois didn't think he was ever spoken of.' Thea was feeling steadier now. Meryl's calm recitation of events was easier to listen to than she'd feared, and Deveron was sitting silently by her side, their legs touching.

'He was the first loser she fell for,' Meryl acknowledged. 'I don't remember his name, but he was some English boy at uni. He got her pregnant and then went on his merry way.'

'Oh, so he wasn't French,' Thea said faintly, recoiling from such callousness from the man who'd given her life. She surfed an unexpected wave of hurt.

Meryl flushed. 'Sorry if that was a bit blunt, but it was harder to prove paternity than maternity, wasn't it? No DNA tests in those days, I don't suppose. I got the impression he just left poor Ynez to it.' She sighed. 'Then, once Ynez was nicely settled in Suffolk with Maxie and your family, damned if she didn't risk it all by taking up with this bloke who sent her delivering things to his dodgy cronies. She was a good kid, really, but just seemed to attract the wrong type.'

'Delivering things?' Thea repeated hollowly.

'Stolen cars. Banned substances,' Meryl elucidated briefly. 'The boyfriend vanished and she took all the blame and got caught with the keys to a stolen car full of drugs – *a lot* apparently. The police had been closing in for a while. Even though she was a young mum, the judge said he could only show so much leniency and she went to prison for several months.'

'And I stayed with Mum and Dad?' Thea already knew this, but the landscape of her past had shifted so much recently that she needed to cross-check.

Meryl smiled proudly. 'Maxie wouldn't have it any other way. They got a new au pair, and you were part of the family. Maxie was a fantastic person.'

Thea's throat ached with tears, and she had to stop to drink her water to ease it. 'But Dad didn't want me?'

Meryl looked alarmed, and even the cat raised its head to look at Thea as if in surprise. 'I never said that.' She shifted uncomfortably. 'Look, I call a spade a spade. I was no fan of Vince, but I never heard that he didn't want you. Did he ever treat you differently to your sisters?'

'No,' Thea allowed, feeling a bit better.

Meryl regarded Thea, then said in a rush, 'Vince was a natural dad, from what your mum said. He loved kids and would have loved his own, but he was the one who couldn't.'

'Oh.' Thea felt worse again, imagining her dad yearning for his own biological kids and knowing they'd never arrive.

'Am I making a balls of this?' Meryl demanded, her forehead furrowing. 'I'm not trying to upset you. Vince loved you. Maxie loved you.'

The tears filled Thea's throat again. 'And what about Ynez?'

'She loved you too.' Meryl shook her head, as if Thea was exasperating her. 'Maxie visited her in prison, and one day Ynez asked her to adopt you. You were settled, see. You were beginning to talk and calling Maxie and Vince Mum and Dad, like your sisters did. Another au pair was living with the family. What were they to do? Sack her to have Ynez back? I don't think Vince would have done because he'd gone right off Ynez. He really minded about the prison. Scandalised. Even soft-hearted Maxie wouldn't have wanted someone around her kids who'd been mixed up in drug dealing. If Ynez had taken you away, you would have been lost without those you thought were your family and she would have had to look for work – tricky when she had a record.' Meryl's eyes were troubled when her gaze rested on Thea. 'I can see by your woebegone face that this isn't what you wanted to hear. I'm sorry it's not a cheerier story.'

With a gigantic effort, Thea smiled. 'Kids aren't adopted out of happy homes, are they?' To give herself a moment, she leant forward and took a biscuit. It was a Jammie Dodger, something Maxie had liked, too. It was a connection, however tenuous.

Meryl curled her feet beneath herself in the chair. 'The adoption happened before Ynez even finished her sentence. It was just coming up to the end of when privately arranged adoptions were lawful and after that, it would have had to go through an adoption agency.' She shrugged. 'It would still have happened eventually, I suppose, but your sisters

218

had been adopted through an agency and Maxie already knew it was a palaver. And with Ynez being inside, and not knowing if the British authorities might even send her back to France . . . though you were British, of course, being born here, which could have made a difference. Maxie said Ynez didn't get on with her family in France so they wouldn't have made you welcome.'

Thea nibbled a biscuit while she thought. 'Do you know why Maxie and Vince never told me about my mother?'

Meryl looked pleased. 'I do. Maxie talked to me about it. She and Vince had agreed that they'd co-operate if any of you girls showed an interest in your birth parents, but your story was different to the others, so it would be more peaceful if the past stayed in the past. Vince, particularly, thought it would be bad for you to know your mother had done time and didn't want you to feel ashamed over something that wasn't your fault. He said you were more impetuous than the other two and he worried how you'd react. And you were a bit of a rebel in your teens, so Maxie hoped you wouldn't ask then, because she didn't think you were mature enough to cope.'

'They always promoted the idea of us being a family, fine as we were, and none of us suspected Mum and Dad knew anything about our birth parents. People often don't know the history of a baby they adopt, do they? They might have once had our original birth certificates, I suppose, but we never saw them,' Thea murmured. But it gave her a prickle of pain to know Mum had thought her a rebel, when Thea had actually been feeling misunderstood and overwhelmed. Her sisters had sailed through coursework and exams, whereas for Thea it had piled up until she thought it would smother her. As Maxie and Vince had died when Thea was eighteen, she'd never had the opportunity to look back with a more experienced head and discuss it with them.

'I expect Vince was protective of you girls, as he was of Maxie,' Meryl added. 'Some adopted children are disappointed or hurt by what they find if they meet their birth parents. He might even have worried he'd become second best.' She gave a rueful smile. 'Vince was the emotional one, wasn't he? Your mum had the cool head.'

Thea smiled at the memory of her dad, bouncing around, unruly hair fairly dancing around his head when he was getting wound up. 'He was a bit, but also very loving.'

Meryl laughed. 'Yes, from what Maxie said, he was mad about you all.' Her laughter faded. 'I miss Maxie so much. Through not trying to get on with Vince, I was left out of your home life. I've often thought of that, since him and poor Maxie died. I should have cleared the air with Vince and been a sort of aunt to you girls, but I felt hard done by instead. I was young and stupid.'

'I miss them both,' Thea said, with a fresh sense of loss.

In the silence, the cat yawned and wriggled until it lay upside down between Meryl and the chair arm, eyes closed. Dev took Thea's hand and stroked her fingers. She glanced at him, taking in the concern in his kind eyes. He'd been incredibly patient, sitting silent during this emotional interview, but she had a couple more questions to ask, so squeezed his hand in silent apology and turned back to her mum's best – but hidden – friend.

'Do you think Ynez ever wanted to keep in touch?' She tried to keep any trace of tremor from her voice.

Meryl frowned. 'I don't know,' she said slowly. 'But I could imagine everybody thinking a clean break would be best. How could you be Maxie and Vince's daughter if you were Ynez's too?'

Thea wrinkled her nose. 'Or could Ynez have been glad to abdicate responsibility for me and go back to France unencumbered . . . like rehoming a pet?'

Meryl exploded with laughter, startling the sleek black cat into jumping down and stalking into another room. '"Rehoming a pet." Maxie's sense of humour must have rubbed off on you.' She sobered and said more gently, 'I couldn't guess what Ynez thought, but she looked after you very well until she got in a mess. Does anyone want a glass of wine?'

Thea was about to refuse but then thought that alcohol might relax Meryl and she'd remember more. And if they refused the wine, Meryl might wind the interview up. 'A small one would be lovely, thank you. Do you have red?'

'I do.' Meryl rose and returned with three glasses and a bottle, shoving aside the water and juice to make room on the tray.

Deveron had only half a glass, probably because he'd seen the size of the 'small' glass Meryl poured Thea. 'Driving,' he said, by way of explanation. 'We're staying with my family tonight. I haven't seen them for months.'

He talked about Dumfries for a minute, then they both told Meryl about the Isle of Skye, and Thea filled Meryl in on what Ezzie and Valentina had done with their lives. Meryl recounted a few anecdotes of gigs with Maxie, turning up at sessions to find the artists they were backing still drunk from the night before or session singers waiting for things to blow over while arguments raged between artists and producers or sound engineers.

Then, unexpectedly, Meryl slapped her leg and exclaimed, 'Brittany! That's where Ynez came from, towards the west coast. She worked in a pottery or something but left her apprenticeship when she came to England.'

Thea was silenced by the new information, as she wrestled with her mental map of France and located Brittany in the top-left corner. 'Nice region,' Deveron said, and he and Meryl chatted about France, as Meryl had often sung in Europe, especially at Christmas.

Eventually, the conversation petered out. Thea rose, thanking Meryl for seeing her. 'You've filled in a lot of blanks.'

Meryl gave Thea an unexpectedly warm hug. 'It's lovely to see one of Maxie's daughters. I'm glad I could help.'

After another round of farewells, Thea and Deveron strolled back to his car, as home-time traffic filled the roads and people hurried along the pavements. Thoughtfully, Thea said, 'I think she did love Mum. As more than a friend, I mean.'

'Yeah.' He slipped an arm around her. 'I thought the same. I didn't get the feeling it came to anything, though.'

'No. But it makes it understandable if she wasn't Dad's biggest fan.' They paused to cross the road. 'It would have been good to have her as the kind of family friends that the kids call "auntie". We were a small unit, with grandparents dying when we were young.' She caught his hand, feeling lighter than she'd felt all week, even if what she'd heard today had been uncomfortable at times. 'And speaking of family, now I'm going to meet yours. I hope they'll like me.' The meeting with Meryl uppermost in her thoughts, she'd barely considered this until now.

He smiled reassuringly. 'They will. After Adaira, they thought I'd grow into a grumpy, woman-hating old git.' He beeped his car unlocked as they approached it, parked

222

near the café where they'd had lunch – or Deveron had, because Thea had been too nervous to eat.

She climbed into the passenger seat. 'Adaira's a beautiful name.' He hadn't talked much about his ex, aside from her leaving him in a sinking ship of a business and she couldn't help being curious.

'She was beautiful . . . on the outside,' he explained briefly.

It seemed a pointed indicator that she hadn't been as lovely on the inside. When he said no more, she changed the subject. 'As it's nearly an hour to your brother's house, will it put you off if I call Ezzie and Valentina as you drive? They'll be dying to hear about Meryl.'

'Of course not.' He started the car.

She went to the Siblings WhatsApp group and initiated a video call.

Dev drove silently, concentrating on the busy traffic apart from a joking little cheer when they crossed the border near Gretna Green and saw the Saltire and the sign welcoming them to Scotland. Thea outlined to Ezz and Valentina the meeting with Meryl. Deveron was so easy to be with, she chattered to her sisters without feeling self-conscious or that she was boring him. She trusted him.

It was a nice feeling. Discovering so much about her birth mother had rocked her, and Fredek Kowski's machinations were making her anxious. But Dev? He just made her happy.

Chapter Sixteen

Dev had expected a warm welcome from his family but hadn't anticipated finding his nieces perched on the garden wall built, like the house, of the local red sandstone. Seven-year-old Luce crooked a sisterly arm around five-year-old Dee, and Dev's mum, Pammie, was visible at the window. Probably, she was ostensibly watching over the girls but also couldn't wait to see him.

His conscience twanged that he hadn't made more effort to come home to Dumfriesshire and reassure her that he was OK, after Adaira left. He'd even dissuaded her from visiting once he was alone in Inverness. *You hate driving long journeys. The parking here's terrible. I've sold the bed for the spare room.* He'd wanted to be alone to grieve his losses while simultaneously fighting a tide of bureaucracy and disappointment.

He focused on the present as he parked on the capacious drive then switched off the engine. Dee and Luce abandoned the wall in favour of dancing and waving from the lawn. 'Uncle Dev! Uncle Dev!'

'What a lovely house,' Thea said, gazing at the russet-coloured blocks and the dormers in the roof. 'I love the colour of the stone.'

He let his seatbelt whizz back onto its reel. 'There's a lot of sandstone houses in Lockerbie. I should think they could afford a bigger house if they hadn't wanted a stone one.'

The front door to the house opened, and a beaming Pammie stepped out, a cardigan around her shoulders. 'Did you have a good journey?'

His brother Leith's face hove into view above her head, grinning a welcome.

'Ready?' Deveron asked, keen to join his loved ones.

'Judging from this welcome committee, I'm not sure anyone will notice I'm here,' Thea joked.

In that, she was wrong. No sooner had she climbed from the passenger seat when Luce scampered around the car. 'Are you Thea? Are you Uncle Dev's new girlfriend?'

Dev interrupted. 'Hey, Luce. We stopped at the supermarket to buy you chocolate, but I need a hug first.'

'Hugs, hugs,' she shouted without actually hugging him, sprinting back to grab the bag from his hand. 'Can me and Dee give the presents out?'

'Hug,' he persisted, and she dropped the bag – luckily the bottles of craft beer for his brother and grandpa weren't in that one – and threw open her arms. Dee copied her big sister, and soon Dev was almost overbalancing as he hugged their small bodies. He rose from a crouch with a giggling niece under each arm and stooped to kiss his beaming mother. 'Hi, Mum. Good to see you.'

She cupped his face in her hands and pinched his cheeks, as if he was Dee and Luce's age. 'Lovely to see you, son.' And she smoothed his hair as she had done all his life.

Luce began to kick. 'Can I get the bags?'

He popped both children down. They were getting too heavy to be carried like paniers. 'I don't think you said hello to Thea. She's English, so you must make her welcome.'

'Hello, Thea,' Luce and Dee chorused. Dee was shyer than Luce and hung behind.

Thea grinned. 'Shall I show you which bag your chocolates are in?'

'Yeah!' The girls clapped.

'Please,' Pammie and Leith corrected simultaneously.

Chocolate satisfactorily distributed, Deveron took Thea's hand. 'Thea, this is my mum Pammie and brother Leith. Mum, Leith, this is Thea. Are Caro and Grandpa here?' Then, to Thea: 'Caro is Leith's lovely wife.'

'Caro got a work call and Grandpa's stirring something in the kitchen,' Leith explained, giving Thea's hand a hearty shake.

Dee bounced on the spot, her pretty face alight. 'Thea, Thea, we're having cocker van with tatties. Can we open our chocolate?' Then, belatedly: 'Please.'

A new voice came from the hall. 'After dinner. Hey, Deveron.' And Caro was there, giving Dev a big hug, brown hair whisked up behind her head. 'I presume you're responsible for filling our wee girls up with sugar?' Her twinkling eyes belied her severe tone.

'I am. But I brought you and Mum some too,' he replied easily.

'Then you're forgiven.' She turned to Thea, an interested light in her eyes. 'Hello! Welcome. It's great to meet you.'

Soon Caro had herded everyone inside, sending the girls to wash their hands, and Leith to open wine and lemonade, while she explained to Thea, 'Sorry that we're eating straight away, but the girls get hungry.'

'Smells delicious.' Thea didn't look the least overwhelmed by his noisy family.

Grandpa emerged from the kitchen with a tea towel over one shoulder. 'Hello, lad, found your way doon hame eventually?' He hugged Deveron hard.

Dev hugged him back, conscious of how far he had to stoop, and how awkwardly his grandfather held his arms because he suffered with arthritis – understandable at the age of eighty-six. 'This is Thea, Grandpa Cyril.'

Cyril abandoned Deveron and took Thea's hands. 'You're so welcome, lass. Pammie's shown me the Rothach Hall website and the photos of your bonnie gardens.'

'I don't look after them on my own,' Thea demurred, but the family had fallen into the usual hurly-burly of everyone speaking at once, chairs scraping as they gathered around the table at one end of the kitchen, both girls clamouring to sit next to Thea. From their expressions, Deveron surmised that Pammie, Caro and Cyril had each hoped for the same. His mother and sister-in-law would be curious about the woman he was seeing, and Cyril would want to talk to her about roses, honeysuckle or his old garden.

Luce and Dee won the contest and were soon pointing out the tiny onions Grandpa had put in the coq au vin specifically so Dee and Luce could easily avoid them. 'We hate onions,' Dee said.

'We do.' Luce took a mouthful of her lemonade, burped, then said, 'Auntie Adaira was a teeny bit prettier than you, but you're nicer.'

'*Luce!*' cried every adult at the table, apart from Thea, who giggled.

'What?' asked Luce innocently. 'Oh, sorry I burped. Pardon me.'

Dev sent Thea an apologetic look, but she just said to

Luce, 'I think you'd like my nephew Barnaby. He tells me I look like Dora the Explorer but with longer hair, and she's better because she's a cartoon.'

Dee joined in. 'We like Dora the Explorer.' Then, as if thinking she might have been remiss: 'We like you too, though.'

'Girls, eat more and talk less, please,' Leith said equably. He, Dev and Cyril were seated together at one end of the table. 'We want to hear what Uncle Dev's been doing.'

'You know I took a summer job as a gardener at Rothach Hall on the Isle of Skye,' Deveron began obligingly. 'Thea's my boss. Her sister Ezzie is the assistant manager. We're "doon hame" because Thea wanted to see a friend of her late mother's in northern England.'

Dee screwed up her forehead. 'Late for what?'

Pammie murmured, 'Oh, dear.'

Thea didn't seem fazed by the childish question. 'Uncle Dev meant my mother's dead. She was my adoptive mother. Do you know what that means?' When the girls shook their heads, she explained, 'If a mum can't look after her baby, other parents take it, and the baby becomes part of their family.'

Two pairs of big eyes gazed at her. 'Do you mean some children change families?' Luce breathed. They glanced at their parents as if worried that fate might befall them.

Thea hurried to reassure her. 'Not very often, and only for very good reasons My birth mother couldn't look after me, and she didn't know where my father was, so I got a new mum and dad. And they were awesome. They were musicians called Maxie and Vince Wynter. Dad played the guitar and the lady I went to see today used to sing with Mum.'

Thea didn't mention Ynez going to prison. Dev couldn't

blame her for that omission. Perhaps her dad Vince had hit the nail on the head when he'd said she'd feel ashamed. He was glad his family appeared so open to Thea, and she to them. Adaira hadn't been particularly family-minded and, though his crowd had tried to welcome her, the relationship had never seemed more than lukewarm. Since she'd left, he'd often wondered whether he'd once been too loved up to see that she was basically self-absorbed, or whether she'd gradually shown her true colours as she'd tired of Dev. He'd read that happy people didn't have affairs, which must mean she hadn't been happy. He knew how that felt because their relationship had become tetchy, which made him unhappy too.

Now he was in a place where he could be glad it was over, leaving him free to explore what was happening with the warm, uncomplicated, pretty woman who was Thea, presently explaining to his nieces that her full name was Altheadora and had once been Althea-hyphen-Dora.

Instantly, the girls wanted to marry up their own first names.

'That makes me Lucealison,' proclaimed Luce.

'And I'm Deeanika,' piped up Dee, trying to speak over Luce. 'Deeanika Dowie.'

Presently, after dinner, Caro said, 'Well, Deeanika and Lucealison, it's your bath time.' And the party broke up. The girls said goodnight and vanished upstairs with Caro and Leith while Cyril took Thea to the lounge to talk gardens.

Dev and his mum loaded the dishwasher. The instant they were alone, Pammie said, 'She's a nice girl, Deveron.'

Dev wasn't certain about calling women in their early forties 'girls' but was happy to hear eager warmth in his mum's voice. 'She is.'

'I watched you during dinner. You're looking the most relaxed you have for years.' Swiftly, she upended glasses in the rack. 'Is it your new job? Or Thea?' She sent him a knowing smile.

Dev sidestepped the question. 'I'm glad to have all the other rubbish done with.' He'd only known Thea a few weeks and if things came to a natural end when summer was over, he didn't want an inquisition about 'what went wrong' or 'what happened'. What he and Thea had was . . . what he and Thea had. As he'd told Ezzie, it was a *thing*. A good thing.

Pammie and Cyril went home before nine, as Cyril grew tired. 'We'll see you tomorrow, before we head back,' Dev told them, kissing Pammie and hugging Grandpa before waving them off in Pammie's little car.

Dev and Thea settled down to enjoy a glass of wine with Leith and Caro. As soon as he'd poured the drinks, Leith said, 'Sorry the wee girls brought up Adaira's name.'

'Doesn't matter.' Dev gazed at the contemporary lounge in his brother and sister-in-law's house, and remembered when he and Adaira had had an even bigger, more expensive house – even if mortgaged to the hilt. It seemed unreal now, as if it had belonged to other people.

Mock-mournfully, Thea said, 'But they said she's prettier than me. I may not sleep tonight.'

Caro sniffed. 'Fantastic make-up and hours at the gym.'

Thea laughed, her twinkling eyes inviting everyone to join in. 'Was that supposed to make me feel *better*?'

As everyone laughed, Dev hugged her to him, glad that it hadn't occurred to Thea's merry heart to take offence, and firmly changed the subject from old-wife, old-life.

He'd say something romantic about Thea's natural prettiness when they were alone later.

But when they finally went up to the room Luce usually occupied and Thea saw the single bed with a truckle that rolled out from underneath, she got the giggles. 'Neither bed's long enough for you!' She took the smallest, the truckle bed, and he squeezed himself into the single, his feet overhanging the end.

Perhaps giving her something to laugh at after her difficult meeting with Meryl was more helpful to Thea than a few honeyed words, anyway.

In the morning, Thea was sorry to say goodbye to Leith, Caro, Luce and Dee. They were such a loving family, in their pretty sandstone house. Seated in Dev's passenger seat, she waved them goodbye, saying to Dev, 'It'll be nice to see Dumfries, where you grew up.'

He waved too, before reversing from the drive. 'We only moved there after Dad died, when I was eight,' he reminded her. 'I thought we'd take the scenic route, via Hightae where we lived at first. We've plenty of time to pick up Grandpa for lunch and then meet Mum at the coffee shop in that garden centre she likes.'

'Great.' Thea sat back to enjoy the journey through the lanes, passing a sign to Lochmaben Castle which Deveron stigmatised as 'a heap of stones'.

Finally, Dev pulled up at a small, triangular village green. 'Here we are. Hightae's lovely, but small.'

'Not at all like Lockerbie with all the sandstone buildings. The cottages are white, like on Skye,' she commented, climbing out. 'How pretty.'

Their tour of Hightae showed them a few streets of cottages, a primary school, dog walkers who called hello, and a little girl on a bike who rode past staring. Dev halted before a yellow door with a brass knocker, a golden

Labrador watching them through a window. 'This was our cottage.' He sounded nostalgic. 'Mum didn't want us bussing to secondary school from here, so away we went to live in Dumfries, where we could walk everywhere.'

'How far are they apart? Did you resent the move?' she asked, seeing the ghost of a small, bereaved and bewildered boy standing beside the tall, stubbly, confident man.

He turned away from the little house. 'A twenty-minute drive, I suppose. What could Mum do? Dad was gone. Grandma was still alive then and she and Grandpa lived in Dumfries and could help with us, allowing Mum to work longer hours. I didn't want to leave Hightae and start a new school, but that was how life had turned out.'

She took his hand as they strolled back to the car. Dev said suddenly, 'I have such a soft spot for my grandpa. I was adrift, without Dad. He died of an infection, and I felt angry that someone should have been able to stop it. Everyone gets infections. You dab on antiseptic or get antibiotics. You don't get septic shock and *die*. Grandpa seemed to understand my feeling of powerlessness. It seemed as if he gave me lots of jobs, but really, he gave me lots of reasons for us to spend time together. In his gruff way, he showed me love every day, and he must have been hurting to see us distraught over losing Dad – especially Mum, his only child. Leith dealt with Dad's death better – maybe changing to secondary school gave him other things to think of. Without Grandpa, I'm not sure Mum or I would have got through.'

Thea listened in silence, her heart going out to the little boy he'd been, and how he'd felt abandoned by his dad – however unfairly. She thought about his ex-wife, Adaira, and his ex-business partner, Krisi, abandoning him, too, and her eyes burned. Rather than let him know she felt sorry for him, she squeezed his hand. 'I liked your grandpa a lot. All your family's lovely.'

'Aye, they are,' he agreed seriously as they reached his big grey car.

Bowling to Dumfries, their road threaded through a patchwork of green fields until they entered the town, with more stone buildings, stately churches and – like anywhere – roadworks that made Dev swear because they stopped him taking the route he'd planned. 'I thought I'd show you Mum's building,' he said, slowing and pointing out a modern low-rise block. 'Her flat's at the top. She likes it fine because it's affordable and easy to keep.' He drove on, taking another few turnings to an area of wide streets of sandstone houses around a golf course and a park. 'This is the Crichtons, a great spot for Grandpa's assisted living place, with all the green space.'

When they pulled up, they found Cyril waiting on a bench outside a big building with a long, low side extension, smart in a tweed jacket, his hands resting on a stick. 'Hello, Deveron and Thea, stay where y'are,' he called, as Deveron began to get out of the car to help him.

'Stubborn old goat,' Dev muttered, and got out anyway. 'I just want to be sure you make the slope OK.'

'Bossy wee lad,' Cyril grumbled as he secured his seatbelt. Thea hid her smile at their gentle bickering.

Ten minutes later they arrived at the garden centre, with greenhouses on one side and a green and white canopy on the other. When they'd parked, Cyril unbent from the back seat with difficulty, confiding to Thea, 'I like it here. Even if I don't have my own garden now, I like to look at the plants.'

She slowed her pace to match his. 'We're lucky at the

hall, having our own greenhouse, but there's nothing like a garden centre. We'd have to drive over an hour to Portree or onto the mainland to get a big one.'

Pammie appeared, breathless and beaming, in time to hear this. 'You'd walk round for hours, given the chance, Dad.' She gave him a wink. 'But I'm in my own car, so we could stay a wee while to browse when Thea and Deveron leave. They have a long drive.'

Inside the coffee shop, decorated with pretty items from the garden centre shop, they managed to find a corner table and perused the menu cards. When Dev chose bacon rolls and potato scone, Thea said, 'I once made "tattie scones" and when I tried to make the mixture the traditional thin, flat circle, it disintegrated.'

Cyril roared with laughter. 'I'll bet you used a rolling pin instead of the side of your fist. I think I'll have a nice morning roll for lunch today.'

When morning roll proved to be potato scone in a bread roll, Thea thought it too carb-heavy for her tastes. 'I'll have salad.'

'I'll join you,' said Pammie, closing the menu, eyes crinkling through her gold-rimmed glasses.

After a while their drinks arrived, and it seemed as if the sight of them made Cyril want to visit the gents. Deveron went along, and Pammie sighed fondly. 'Deveron's a good lad to go with his grandpa. He looks so much better. The horrible lines of strain have gone. I was a teeny bit disappointed when he didn't come home, but I see that working outdoors is good for him. I don't know if he'll ever go back to journalism,' she added reflectively.

Thea paused, her coffee cup halfway to her mouth. 'Journalism? I thought he had an agency of some sort?'

'Yes, a news agency. European ball sports.' Pammie

beamed and waved across the busy tables to someone she must know.

Frowning, Thea tried to remember if Deveron had ever used the word 'journalist'. 'He said something about providing content for clients, I think.'

Pammie nodded, upending her red teapot over her mug. '"Providing content" is the modern way of saying "writing", isn't it? He went to university for journalism, then on to regional papers, and then sports press. Then he and Krisi began the news agency.' She scowled so hard her eyebrows met. 'If Krisi hadn't buggered everything up, they'd probably still—' She halted, perhaps realising that if Deveron had still been working with Krisi, he might still be with Adaira, and it wouldn't be diplomatic to say so.

'Well,' said Thea, to fill the silence. 'As you say, he seems happy as he is for now.' And there were times, in bed, when he seemed *ecstatic* . . . She drank deeply from her white china mug to hide the sudden heat in her cheeks.

Later, after they'd said their goodbyes and left Cyril and Pammie to amble around the plants, Thea took the driving seat for the first stint of the long journey back to the Isle of Skye while Dev pointed out places he knew. She kept her attention on the road, but the conversation with Pammie kept returning to her.

She'd obviously misunderstood something. When he paused in his list of familiar sights, she jumped in. 'Your mum talked about your agency. You never said you're a journalist.'

'Didn't I?' His gaze remained on the scene beyond the window. 'Originally, yes. But at the agency, most of the content was written by others. I was managing them and networking, funnelling stories their way. Doing deals for the website ads and sponsorship. You know how it is –

235

all roads eventually lead to management. Like, you don't spend all day gardening. You manage people, supplies – even if some are grown on site – and create planting schemes. Sheena's your deputy. You're a department head.'

'I don't feel like a department head. I'm a gardener.' She slowed for a wildflower-covered roundabout.

'So am I, now.' He slouched comfortably in his seat. 'If I'd known how much I'd enjoy it I might have done horticulture from the start, like you.'

The miles passed quickly on the motorway over the Southern Uplands towards Glasgow. As they progressed north, wide roads turned into narrower, twistier roads. Hills turned to timber-clad mountains with their heads in the clouds. They passed glassy lochs and lonely houses, road signs in both English and Gaelic and many place names that began with 'inver' or 'dun'.

Then they pulled into a lay-by to change drivers and it was Thea's turn to watch the scenery. The craggy, rugged landscape reminded her of Skye. She thought of the island as home now. Suffolk was just a memory.

With a quick break to eat at the village of Spean Bridge, they arrived back in Rothach at nearly nine. They parked at Thea's, yawning and stretching, then strolled across to Fraser's white cottage to reclaim Daisy. The little dog flew out to greet them, circling and bouncing, giving snorting little 'arfs' of joy, her pale fur fluffing out like a dandelion clock.

Then they collected Thea's things from the car and opened the door of Thistledome. Dev paused to scoop up the mail from the doormat and hand it to her. 'I'll go straight off. Work tomorrow.'

But Thea's eyes had locked on a brown official-looking envelope. Fumbling, she took it from him and slowly slit it open. Dev, obviously realising that it was something

236

significant, waited silently. A letter fluttered to the floor, and she was left with a sheet of stiff paper headed *This is a certified copy* and, underneath *BIRTH*. Her heart put in a giant thump.

She forced herself to concentrate on each line.

Registration district: Islington. Date and place of birth: Thirteenth January 1983, City of London Maternity Hospital, Hanley Road, Islington . . .

Name and surname: Althéa-Dora BOURGAULT. Female. Father: not known. Mother: Ynez Laura BOURGAULT. Ynez's birthplace was given as Quimper, France, and her occupation as 'domestic', her address as Hoxton, London.

'Bourgault,' Thea tested the name on her tongue. 'Althéa-Dora Bourgault. I'm not even sure how to pronounce it, but for the first year or so of my life, it was my name.'

Deveron slipped his arm around her and studied the certificate that trembled in her hand, his voice low and soft. 'Does it feel unreal?'

'Very.' She had to clear her throat. 'First a French mother, then a hyphen, now an accent and a last name. It's disorientating.'

She turned her face against his T-shirt, and he stroked her hair. Daisy sat on Thea's foot and whined. But if she'd been able to speak human and asked why Thea was crying, Thea wouldn't have been able to tell her – except that after the relaxing interlude with Dev's family, this brought her back to reality.

Since Lois had let slip Thea's beginnings, she'd felt as if she didn't know herself at all.

Chapter Seventeen

Thea returned to work on Monday, glad to get back to normality after life's rollercoaster shaking her up recently. Ezz had already reported that Fredek, thank goodness, had left when the retreat ended after lunch on Sunday. Hadley and Nell were off, having worked while Thea and Deveron were away but Sheena was waiting for Thea in the gardeners' room when she arrived.

'This bloke with a walking stick asked about you, when I was doing some edging on Saturday.' She grabbed a rake and a hoe. 'He said he used to know you, but didn't want to give his name, so I pretended I didn't know you.' She gave Thea the kind of long look she probably gave her teenage children. 'I hope I did the right thing.'

Thea had to moisten her lips before she could answer. 'Absolutely, thank you. Can't even think who he was,' she added as airily as she could, though instantly identifying the man as Fredek. Thank goodness Sheena had natural discretion. If she'd been the gossipy type, she could have told him Thea's sister Ezz worked at Rothach, and he'd probably have badgered her, too.

Sweat broke over Thea at the thought of Ezz's likely horror.

On Monday evening, Thea and Daisy trotted down to Ezzie's cottage to video-call with Valentina on Ezzie's laptop, so Thea could enlarge on her meeting with Meryl, after providing the highlights in the call from Deveron's car.

First on-screen was a small boy in green pyjamas with 'Always hungry' printed above a toothy dinosaur. 'Hello, Auntie Thea. Hello, Auntie Ezzie!'

'Hi, Barnaby,' they chorused, craning closer to the screen to beam at their nephew.

'You look great. Tell us what you've been doing,' Thea suggested.

Barnaby considered. 'I've been playing Crazy Gears on my iPad. We had sports day at school and I got two seconds and a third.'

'Great day,' Ezzie said admiringly. 'And does Mummy know you're FaceTiming?' Her voice was conspiratorial, as if not knowing that Valentina would employ suitable parental control filters.

Barnaby laughed, a liquid, joyful sound, more beautiful than any orchestra. 'Yeah. I'm on her laptop.'

Valentina poked her head into shot. 'Barnaby's on first, then Daddy will put Barnaby to bed while I take a turn.'

A frown curling his brows, Barnaby objected, 'But not yet. I've hardly talked.'

So, Thea, Barnaby and Ezzie discussed Spider-Man, who was Barnaby's latest craze, and Daisy – who was lifted to wave a paw and pant doggily all over the screen.

'Wow, a dog,' Barnaby breathed, eyes enormous. 'Can I have her?'

'I'm afraid she lives with me,' Thea said gently, covering

up a tiny jealous shock at the thought of Daisy being Barnaby's. 'But you can help me walk her next time you visit.'

'Time for bed, now Barns,' came Gary's voice, hitherto unheard. He appeared on-screen as he urged Barnaby off the chair. 'Hi, girls. Time for this one to go to bed.'

'Night, Barnaby,' they chorused.

'It's too early,' Barnaby groused, but nevertheless saying goodnight and leaving with his dad.

Valentina flopped into the armchair he'd vacated. 'Phew. Sorry Gary called you "girls".' She rolled her eyes.

'That's OK,' Thea and Ezzie said in unison, although Thea knew neither of them enjoyed Gary's condescension. At fifty-four to Valentina's forty-six, he sometimes assumed an annoyingly fatherly air towards her younger sisters.

Valentina looked tired and creased, in what looked like a work skirt and blouse, but she summoned a smile. 'So, Thea, Meryl was really OK?'

'Tentative at first, maybe, but we warmed to each other. She's a strong character and tells it as she sees it.' Thea recounted everything she could remember, even what she'd already been over.

Then she turned to the question of her birth certificate. She'd already WhatsApped photos of it to them. 'And now I have to decide what to do about my birth mother – if anything,' she concluded. But then added, 'Ynez,' feeling that the woman who'd carried her warranted a name.

Valentina tilted her head, dark hair unusually rumpled. 'Did Meryl think she was nice? Or horrible?'

Thea sighed. 'I think she liked her and felt she'd had a raw deal with men, which Lois touched on, too. Whether that's from naivety, stupidity or natural inclination to walk on the wild side, I don't know.'

Valentina frowned from her side of the screen. 'Nobody would blame you if you were put off by her prison sentence. You're so law-abiding.'

Thea went hot, because she absolutely wasn't, mumbling, 'I'm no saint.'

Valentina smiled suddenly. She was so often serious, with her career and her parental responsibilities, that when she did smile, it felt worth waiting for. 'How about instructing one of those agencies that trace people? Knowing if she's alive and where, maybe whether she's married again and has kids, might give you a picture of the person she is now.'

Thea considered this, possibilities flitting through her mind like flashing images: a funeral for a mother she'd never known versus her still living, and/or there being a collection of half-siblings and cousins who Thea had never known. 'That makes sense.'

Ezzie hugged her. Her arms were slender and led to a shoulder that was always there for Thea to lean on. 'I can't decide what I'd do myself, but I see what Valentina means,' Ezz said. 'If Ynez has passed away, you might spend every day wondering, and all for nothing.'

'And if you spent a year wondering, *then* checked her out, you might have found she'd died in that very year.' Valentina pointed out. 'How would you feel?'

'I don't know,' Thea said faintly. Her mind was beginning to feel like it was a washing machine on 'spin'. 'In that photo from Lois she wasn't much younger than Mum and Dad, so will be in her early sixties if she's alive.'

Valentina leant closer to the screen and her arms seemed to lead into it as she began typing. After a second she said, 'Google gives me two good options straight away – a UK agency that traces worldwide, and a French agency who offers to *recherché des personnes* . . . search for people.'

Valentina and Ezzie had both taken French at school, but Thea had dropped it as soon as permitted. If only she'd known that she was half-French . . . She found herself smiling at the mere idea that it would have made any difference to her fidgety, non-academic younger self. But Valentina was right: information would help with decisions. 'Could you send me the link?'

'We can just google Ynez Bourgault of Quimper.' Ezz set her fingers to her own keyboard and began to type, making Valentina's image minimise into a corner of the screen.

Thea's mouth went dry as she watched. *Was it going to be so simple . . . ?*

Ezz frowned at the results for several seconds. 'Plenty of Bourgaults, but no Ynez.' *So, no.*

Valentina shrugged. 'We wouldn't know if it was the right Ynez Bourgault, anyway. An agency would be more reliable.'

The rest of the call was taken up with catching up on news and Thea was glad that her beloved sisters were showing just the perfect amount of support and curiosity over her birth mother. She'd hate for them to feel hurt that she was cautiously tracing a blood connection when the three sisters, though so close, shared no DNA.

By the next day, Thea had decided to try the agency that traced people. If her birth mother was dead or untraceable then the lurking questions in her mind would fade.

She spent the morning on the ride-on mower, cutting the south lawns while Deveron whizzed along the edges with a strimmer. Sheena was working out of sight in the shrubbery.

As it approached break time, Thea drew up noisily beside Deveron and let the mower's engine note fall. The strimmer paused and, automatically, they each pushed back one ear defender to converse. She asked, 'Is there any chance I could use your laptop? Valentina's convinced me that if I trace my birth mother it will make it easier to make decisions. She sent me a link to an agency.'

He nodded, dark curls bobbing. 'Of course. Lunchtime? Or this evening?'

Lunchtime would be sooner, but this evening would mean longer with him . . .

He seemed to read her thoughts. 'How about we begin at lunchtime? That gives us the evening if we need it.'

'Perfect.' She beamed, a flutter of butterflies in her stomach – possibly because she'd made a decision about Ynez, partly because she would again be with Deveron.

At lunchtime, they gathered outside the gardener's room in the sun, Sheena on the doorstep, Thea on a coil of hose and Deveron on the floor with his back to the stone wall.

Sheena glanced between them. 'What did you two do with your time off?'

No one at work knew they were seeing each other apart from Ezz. Thea shied from putting her personal life on show, and said evasively, 'I visited an old friend of Mum's.'

Deveron took his face out of his coffee cup. 'I went to my family in Dumfries.'

Thea smiled at him. 'How were they?'

'Good. I stayed with my brother and family, and Mum and Grandpa visited.' He smiled back. 'How was your family friend?'

'Meryl? Fine, thanks. It was lovely to hear about my mum's life as a musician and vocalist. How's your family, Sheena?' Thea knew that if she and Dev kept seeing one another it would soon become public knowledge, but it was early days yet. She didn't like being talked about. Much better that Sheena share the latest anecdotes about her teenage kids.

Thea and Dev met at Thistledome at lunchtime to provide Daisy with company – though after, 'Arf, arf!' a greeting dance and a snack, Daisy sunbathed on the back lawn and ignored them. At the patio table, in the shade so they could view the screen, Thea pulled the laptop towards her. 'I feel as if I ought to make myself fill in this form. Could you just help if I get stuck?'

'Sure.' He folded his arms comfortably behind his head. The only sound apart from her uneven clicking of the keyboard keys was the rush of the wind and gulls bickering 'yow, yow, yow'.

Thea concentrated. Gradually, she gained confidence and stopped saying, 'Is that right?' or 'The cursor has a mind of its own.' Finally, she sat back, putting away the credit card after paying the fee. 'Phew.'

He hugged her against his firm, warm body. 'That was awesome.'

When they returned to the hall, Erik Larsson was standing with his hands in his pockets peering into the greenhouse through the glass. When he waved, Thea crossed to join him, while Deveron went on to the gardeners' room. 'Very good,' Erik said approvingly, gesturing at the neat trays on the greenhouse benches.

Then he sent her a keen look. 'So, soon we will return home. You are OK with this Fredek acting silly sod?'

Thea didn't let any amusement show at his pithy

phrasing. 'Hopefully, he's stopped.' Behind her back, she crossed her fingers, wondering whether she believed it herself.

He frowned. 'Grete, she says two more pony. For the grandchildren to ride when we come at Christmas.'

She nodded along to the change of subject. 'To live with Mary and Clive? We'll need a bigger field shelter. And younger ponies would need exercising when your grandchildren aren't here.'

He smiled. 'I talk to Ezz. She says she will find someone.' Then, perhaps voicing a connected thought, 'Tavish, he takes a new job soon, I think. I receive . . .' He frowned, pinching the bridge of his nose in thought. 'Reference,' he brought out triumphantly. 'And I give him reference quick. Ezz helped me. Get rid.' He made a *phut* noise.

'Wow.' Thea tried to imagine Rothach without Tavish. He'd been there longer than Thea and Ezzie and had created a cushy number for himself, sitting in his office and working at his own pace. 'So, we'll get a new manager?'

'Yes, yes.' He waved this tiresome detail away. 'Thea, if Fredek annoys, you tell to Ezz and she tells to police. OK?'

'OK,' she said, her heart warming anew to this bluff, direct man. 'Thanks.'

He laughed suddenly, a huge, startling bellow. 'Or I give him my fist to smell.' He shook his fist in demonstration.

Thea laughed too. 'Then the police will also arrest you.' She was pretty sure Erik's fist would be effective, it being a great ham of a thing, but hoped he wouldn't use it.

'OK, OK,' he said, moving away. 'I will work now.'

'Me, too.' She hurried after Deveron. They'd planned

245

to tie up the rampaging wisteria on the west side of the house this afternoon.

She wasn't totally shocked when Ezz appeared out of the back door and crossed to intercept her, her pretty face alight, blonde hair blowing. 'Tavish is going,' she whispered.

'Erik just told me,' Thea whispered back. 'Isn't it amazing? And the family are leaving again soon.'

Ezz pouted. 'Aw, Erik's given you the news.'

Thea laughed at her crestfallen expression.

It was evening when Thea saw her sister again, when Ezzie turned up beaming at Thea's door. 'Ta-dah!' she trumpeted, waving a box of chocolates and a bottle of fizzy apple juice. 'Erik and Grete have offered me Tavish's job – and I've accepted.'

'Oh, whoa, you superstar.' Thea dragged Ezzie's slender body into a massive hug, heart swelling with gladness for her sister. 'You so deserve it. You'll be brilliant.'

Ezzie simpered. 'I know.' Then they both laughed and did a happy dance, with Daisy dancing with them, contributing the occasional 'Arf!'

Working at Rothach Hall could only get better, with Ezz at the helm. And with Deveron working alongside her – for however long that lasted – it was Thea's sanctuary.

Chapter Eighteen

'I don't know how to tell her,' Sheena was saying to Ezz next morning at the foot of the stone steps up to the hall's majestic front doors. Neither woman seemed to notice Thea's approach as they pored over their phones.

Ezz's lips were set and her voice was sharp. 'I'll find her and let her know.'

'What's up?' Thea demanded, feeling tension that wasn't due to the overcast sky that threatened a summer storm. Shame, when Saturdays in July were good for visitor numbers.

Ezz glanced up, dismay in her eyes. 'Oh, you're here, Thea. Um . . . let's go into the office.'

She ascended the steps so rapidly that Thea, with her shorter legs, had to hurry, sending Sheena a quizzical look as they left her behind. Ezz bypassed her own cubicle and marched straight into Tavish's office. 'Shut the door – it's his day off.' She dropped into Tavish's chair, half flung her phone over the desk in Thea's direction, slapped her hands over her eyes and burst into tears.

Thea gaped. 'What's happened? Aren't you getting the job after all?'

Ezzie wiped her eyes on her sleeve. 'Not that. Read it. Thea, I'm so sorry.'

Gingerly, Thea picked up the phone and stared at the screen. Using one finger, she scrolled up and saw the heading: *Everyday Celebs*. Her eyes slid away from the text. 'That horrible site's published something else? What does it say?'

When Ezz just continued to hide her eyes, Thea made herself look again. To her horror, she caught her own name and her reluctant gaze homed in on the headline: *Thea Wynter v Fredek Kowski – the truth at last? You decide!*

As if someone had removed her leg muscles, she half fell into the nearest chair, skimming a paragraph, which reminded readers of the bullet points of the story of Fredek's accident.

After Everyday Celebs dug back into this case – the underscoring suggested a link to an earlier piece – *Fredek Kowski has experienced something extraordinary. Was his memory just waiting to be jogged? Or is some power we don't understand at work?*

Thea's rising panic made the words blur. 'Read it to me, Ezz,' she implored, palms sweating.

Ezz wiped her eyes, took back the phone, sniffed, and began to read. 'Fredek says, "*I must have blocked it out before, but I now remember that as I lay in the road, broken and bleeding, Thea Wynter was urging someone to run away, saying that she'd pretend to be the driver who hit me and caused my present life-changing injuries.*" Then he goes on in loving detail about having no romantic relationships or work and everything else he can dredge up to elicit sympathy,' Ezz finished bitterly.

248

Thea's blood froze.

'He's remembered,' she said numbly, her voice echoing distantly in her ears. Then her blood unfroze and raced around her body until her head spun. 'Ezz, he's remembered the truth. What are we going to do?'

Deveron was startled when Sheena told the gardening staff that Thea and Ezz had gone home this morning. He checked the time and saw there was now just half an hour until the working day ended. With the Larssons gone, he, Hadley and Nell had been assigned to the family garden to catch up with trimming shrubs and weeding. 'Are they OK?' he asked, surprised Thea hadn't texted him.

Sheena shrugged. 'Maybe they both ate something.'

The moment five o'clock came and Deveron was free to return to his accommodation, he tried Thea's phone. Straight to voicemail.

She'd been bouncing with health when they'd arrived at work at nine, yet had apparently been ill enough to return home before twelve? 'Don't think so.' He grabbed his car keys.

Minutes later he was rapping the knocker on Thea's door. No reply, not even from Daisy.

He jumped back into his car and trundled down Glen Road and over the bridge to park outside Ezzie's place. A few strides carried him up her path, long grass brushing his ankles. He knocked, and heard Daisy's raspy little bark. Bingo.

It was several moments before the door half opened and Daisy scampered out, tail whirring like a fluffy propellor. Thea stood before him, sporting red eyes. Ezz crowded in beside her, saying, 'We've had an upset. I'm sure you understand—'

But Thea stopped her. 'I told you: he was once some kind of journalist. He might have ideas about what we ought to do.'

His stomach plummeted at the anguish etched into her usually sunny face. 'What's happened?'

Miserably, Thea led him into Ezzie's lounge and indicated an open laptop. He stooped over it, stroking Daisy's fluffy head as he read. He froze to see the masthead of Everyday Celebs above the headline: *Thea Wynter v Fredek Kowski – the truth at last? You decide!*

Nausea rolling in his belly, he sank down to read on. A sentence leapt out. *Thea Wynter was urging someone to run away, saying that she'd pretend to be the driver who hit me.* 'What?' he asked blankly, his gaze lifting to Thea's.

She and Ezzie had huddled together on the sofa. Thea's voice emerged as fragile as spun glass. 'It's true. I wasn't driving. Ezz was.'

'Oh, crap.' In shock, he looked from one face to the other. Wretched tears slid down Thea's reddened cheeks. Ezz's expression was wooden, her pallor stark.

Thea drew in a quavering breath. 'The day before, Ezz had taken my car in for its MOT because she worked in town, and I didn't. She left the car at her house that night and took a taxi to and from a party. But she drank enough that she shouldn't have driven the morning after – alcohol was her refuge after losing Mum and Dad. But she'd promised to bring my car back, so she did. When the accident happened, we didn't *know* that she was over the drink-drive limit . . . but we knew it was possible. Probable, even.'

Ezz's haunted gaze fell to the carpet.

Thea pulled out a tissue and blew her nose. 'Thing is, she'd been banned for drink-driving once. And if you've been done before and then cause someone a life-changing injury and blow over the limit . . . well, a prison sentence is usually automatic. *Prison!* What good would that have done? He stopped astride his bike in the middle of the road around a blind bend and texted someone. She had no chance of avoiding him.' She swiped at her eyes with her now-sodden tissue. 'She called me in a panic. As it was just outside my village, I ran to the scene. There were no houses nearby, so I made her get behind the hedge and hurry back to my place while I rang the emergency services.'

Numbly, he stared at the two women, half expecting them to burst into giggles and tell him it was a black joke. But both faces remained tear-stained and etched with fear. 'You've kept this a secret all this time?'

Wearily, Thea nodded. 'We had to. Covering up a crime is a crime – however reasonable you think your motives. Valentina's a lawyer, so we couldn't tell her.' She stared at her hands in her lap. 'We felt guilty, so we helped Fredek with medical expenses. It took most of our savings. But then when he was well enough, he began posting all over the place about his cyclist safety campaign, and this shitty witch-hunt against me began on social media, just because I was on TV. What turned out to be the last season was airing at the same time. Amazing, how being in the public eye even in a small way makes you a target for hate. His responsibility for the accident didn't seem to come into it because trolls are like foxes, attacking for the joy of it. Ezz and I left our jobs and came up here to live. She stopped drinking and I stayed off social media, and we put it behind us . . . we thought.'

Stunned, Dev returned his gaze to the laptop. The poll at the foot of the piece was as biased at the rest.

251

- *Is Thea Wynter covering for a lover?*
- *Should Thea Wynter be brought to answer for her deeds?*
- *Does Thea Wynter owe Fredek Kowski compensation?*
- *Should the police investigate?*

The scores indicated that nobody much cared who Thea was covering for, but opinion was equally divided as to whether she should pay compensation or be investigated by the police. He flicked through some of the comments.

Knew there was more to it . . .

Never liked her on Garden Gladiators. Bet they'll start playing repeats now and she'll be smarming all over the screen.

And a rare voice of reason. *Doesn't change the fact he was being a dick, texting in the middle of the road.*

He reread again from the beginning to give himself time to ride the enormous wave of shock. Then fury.

Close behind came shame and guilt. His Thea-friendly *Where are they now?* article had been used to provide contrast to this shitty piece of finger-pointing. It didn't matter that he hadn't foreseen this when he wrote it. He *had* written it. He licked his lips and met two desolate gazes. 'Ignore it,' he said. 'Or deny it if you're directly challenged.'

Thea's voice emerged as a croak. 'Challenged by the police, you mean?'

His stomach knotted at what he thought a distinct possibility, but he produced a smile. 'Would the police read crap like this? If Fredek goes to the police, I suggest you involve Valentina after all.'

The women exchanged horrified glances. 'Never,' Thea gasped. 'We can't compromise her.'

Ezz looked as if she were about to pass out.

'Right.' He gnawed this over. 'Does anyone else know? Like Sheena?'

'No,' they chorused, clearly horrified by the idea.

He closed the laptop, revolted by the familiar Everyday Celebs masthead. 'Don't admit the truth. Be astonished. Dismiss it. Nobody will be surprised that you're upset, Thea, but Ezz . . . ? If you look as ghostly white as you do now, you'll give the game away.'

'Shit.' She covered her face and he thought how wretched she must feel, as Thea skated towards ever-thinning ice, all through trying to help her beloved sister.

For a while they went over and over the same information as if a fresh answer would miraculously appear. No one came up with a plan better than Deveron's 'deny everything' strategy.

Ezzie did say, tragically, 'Maybe I ought to just give myself up, Thea.'

Dev couldn't help a curt: 'That will *definitely* get Thea in trouble.'

Eventually, Thea yawned, her eyes pink and desolate. 'Time for me to go home.' When she rose, Daisy woke blearily from a nap, then jumped to her paws, shook her ears and was ready to go.

Deveron picked up his keys from Ezz's coffee table. 'I'll run you home.'

Thea's gave him a small smile, a single sunray in her storm-ravaged face. 'Thanks. I'm wrung out.'

When he pulled up outside Thistledome a few minutes later, Daisy panting from the passenger footwell, Thea turned to him, her beautiful brown eyes still red and swollen. 'Do you mind if I just go in? I'm not feeling very . . .'

He leant in to kiss her forehead. 'Of course. I'll see you tomorrow.'

After she'd closed her front door behind her and Daisy, he drove away, not sorry to be alone with the murderous swell of rage he'd had to hide from her.

Once home, he slammed the door to his room so loudly he heard one of the young women on the floor above, exclaim, 'Whoa! What was that?'

Prowling like a bear in a cage, he ripped his phone from his pocket, unblocked Weston's number and dialled it. And though it was past eleven, it rang only once before Weston answered. 'Deveron. I've kinda been expecting your call.' His young voice was rich with schadenfreude.

'You prick.' Deveron's words crackled with rage. 'You wanted a positive piece from me – to make this shit you've posted more sensational. Readers will feel they were tricked into liking Thea. Now that crap Fredek's spouting is supposed to be *the truth*, they'll react badly. Who wrote this bilge today?'

Weston chuckled. 'Fredek,' he admitted. 'But you know how this game goes, Deveron. You slant the article this way, he slants it that. He wrote it while he was at that place where Thea Wynter works, sticking it to her because she refused to co-operate.'

Though that was infuriating, Deveron recognised an opportunity to gather information. 'The accident happened years ago. This is a laughably convenient return of memory, isn't it?'

'He swears it's true,' Weston answered, sounding as if he didn't care much either way. 'Seeing and hearing Thea Wynter again jogged something loose in his brain, he reckons.'

'Oh, fucksake.' Deveron made sure his voice oozed disbelief.

'Convenient return of memory or not, ten thousand clicks already,' Weston gloated. 'Fredek had his social media networks all primed and ready to share. The keyboard warriors have joined the feeding frenzy. The poll's going nuts.'

Dev felt sick, and glad Thea said she'd come off all social media channels years ago. What she didn't know couldn't hurt her. 'Amazing,' he said, letting reluctant admiration colour his voice this time, as if coming around to applauding Weston and Fredek's cleverness. 'Though I still don't understand why you've put so much effort behind such a small story. And an old one at that. Isn't there a puking actor or ranting singer who you can make more mileage from?' Deliberately patronising, he hoped Weston would rush to fill in the blank.

Weston did. 'He's getting big in the influencer world, on the edge of getting speaking gigs on a cruise ship.'

Dev automatically went for the hole he spotted in this story. 'Bullshit. Last time you said it was some influencer conference. At least get your lies straight.'

'No lies,' said Weston silkily. 'The conference comes in August and he plans for it be a roaring success because there'll be a scout there from an agency that supplies speakers to cruise lines. And they even have those influencer conferences on ships – who knew? It's a full-on campaign, Dev, my friend. A *campaign*.'

And he ended the call.

Deveron sank onto the bed, flopping down to glare at the ceiling.

That little bastard Weston had made Deveron complicit in something he'd have turned down even if he'd never met Thea . . . but Dev had never dug deeply into Weston's set-up. He'd justified his lack of due diligence in pursuit of keeping the wolf from the door. At the same time, by freelancing for Everyday Celebs, he'd stepped into a different wolf's lair – a young, shameless wolf called Weston. He could scarcely breathe.

As Ezz had done earlier, he considered confessing his sins, but there would be no winners from that. Thea would shove him away in disgust. Not only would he lose a woman he cared for, but she'd lose what support he might be able to offer.

He wasn't yet sure what form his support would take, but he was going to try and come up with something. He had to.

Chapter Nineteen

Thea read today's date on the planner on the gardeners' room wall: *Monday 21 July.* To her relief, Sheena had today and Tuesday off, so she wouldn't be around to give Thea updates on Fredek's sweat-inducing claim – which Thea did not want, thank you very much. But Sheena probably wasn't the only one frequenting that crappy Everyday Celebs site, judging by the odd looks Thea had received this morning. Either that or it was word of mouth. One of the housekeeping staff had even whisked away from a window when Thea glanced up and caught her staring.

Tavish called Thea's phone just before ten o'clock. 'Got a second, Thea? Come to my office.'

'Sure,' she agreed glumly. As she entered the hall via the mud room, she felt none of her usual enthusiasm for the beautiful building. She trailed to Tavish's office and knocked on the open door. Soon, Ezz would be seated in his chair and that, at least, would be something in this shitty, horrible summer that had gone right.

That and getting Daisy.

And being with Deveron, of course, but only till

summer's end . . . if he stuck around that long now he knew the truth.

'Ah, Thea.' Tavish made a show of dragging his eyes away from his computer to notice her. 'Close the door. Sit down.' He barely waited for her bum to touch the seat of the blue chair. 'I hear you have a problem with someone posting about you online.'

She stiffened. As Tavish had colluded with Fredek in the attempt to video her, that 'someone' was insultingly disingenuous. 'I hear there's some rubbish, yeah.'

His eyes narrowed. 'Will it affect your work?'

She wanted to ask, *Has effectively being given the boot affected you doing yours?* But she just shook her head. 'I don't let sites like that affect anything.'

'Good,' he said. 'Well, I felt I ought to check.' He returned to his computer.

It took a moment to dawn on her that what had just taken place must have been Tavish's idea of a staff welfare interview. 'Thanks for your concern.' She left, not caring if he detected the sarcasm in her voice.

She worked mechanically and alone, sweeping up pinecones, feeling conspicuous and gossiped about. When Deveron's duties briefly put him nearby, his concerned glances made her want to hold out her arms for a hug. But she resisted giving Rothach staff more to talk about.

After lunch, she and Hadley stepped into the humid, earthy atmosphere of the greenhouse to check the bedding plants. The most mature would be planted out at the beginning of August and the final batch nearer the end. First the Scottish school holidays would be over, then those further afield, and then summer itself. The gardeners would ready the grounds for winter and clean out and shut up the greenhouse.

And the seasonal contracts would end.

She blinked away hot pinpricks in her eyes, wondering what Deveron would do then. She hadn't asked him recently whether he was applying for jobs, or even working on a plan to start a new business.

She tried to concentrate on what Hadley was saying. 'There's something off in the wee water butt,' he told her. 'I'm wondering if maybe Deveron could drain it and clean it out. The good summer rain will soon refill it.'

'Fine,' she said vaguely. Her phone pinged in her pocket, making her jump.

As Hadley had just taken out his own phone to call Deveron, she glanced at the screen and saw a notification. *JG People Tracing.* Her heart skipped. She hadn't really believed the 'information within two–three working days claim' from the company she'd engaged to find her birth mother, but here it was, bang on time. Fumbling, she opened the email, her eyes sliding and skidding over the lines.

A deep breath. She clenched her eyes and then reopened them before forcing herself to read each word separately.

Your mother is believed to be Ynez Laura BOURGAULT, born in Quimper on 4 April 1963 to Phillipe BOURGAULT (1 July 1940 to 1 January 1992) and Sylvie-Marie BOURGAULT (née SEZNEC) (12 December 1941 to 4 May 2008).
Ynez Laura BOURGAULT currently resides: Appartement 116, Place Terre au Duc, Quimper. Registered as a business owner at: Côté Rivière, Place Terre au Duc, Quimper. Quimper is in the department of Finistère and the region of Brittany, north-west France.

We are not able, on this occasion, to establish personal email or telephone details but contact details for Côté Rivière are of public record and an internet search reveals social media references too numerous to list.

Thea's vision seemed to swing around. She put out a hand to grab the edge of a bench.

'Are you OK, Thea?' Hadley's voice was sharp with anxiety.

Shakily, she laughed. 'Whoo. I went giddy for an instant. I hope you're not growing anything in here that you shouldn't, Hadley.'

Though laughing at the idea, Hadley pulled a stool from under a bench and shoved her onto it. Then Deveron appeared. When he saw her, he lengthened the stride carrying him between the benches, forehead puckered in concern. 'What's up?'

She licked her lips. 'It's hot and humid in here.'

Hadley shambled off to fetch a glass of water, and Deveron crouched beside her. 'Really? That's all?' His keen hazel eyes searched hers.

She shook her head, and shakily showed him the email. His brows flipped up, and he squeezed her hand, but then Hadley returned. Thea took the water and sipped it. 'Thanks. That's better. I'll go out for some air.'

She left Hadley to buttonhole Deveron about the offensive water butt, but felt his eyes follow her, her heart stuttering at the knowledge that she'd taken a giant stride towards contacting her birth mother . . . if she wanted to.

If. If. *If.*

* * *

Deveron, a little to her surprise, hadn't sought Thea out after he'd left the greenhouse, but had continued to throw glances from a distance, as if hesitating over what best to do. She couldn't blame him for not knowing, as she didn't know herself, but took his lack of approach as a sign that she should make Daisy's after-dinner outing the route to Ezz's cottage. Daisy scampered up the correct pathway without even a glance to check with Thea, giving a sweet little 'Arf!' to notify Ezz of their arrival.

Ezz met them in the tiny hall with a dispirited 'Hey.'

'Is now a good time?' Thea hugged her, then withdrew, trying to read Ezz's blue eyes. 'I texted but you didn't answer. I'm not interrupting something with your latest date?'

Ezz turned and drifted into the kitchen, reaching mechanically for the kettle. 'Angus? He's moved on. I just haven't been looking at my phone. Sorry.'

While she unclipped Daisy's lead, Thea studied her sister's back view, knowing it wasn't the latest date worrying Ezz. Generally, Ezz's dates moved on because Ezz suggested it. She'd been subdued since the 'Fredek suddenly remembers the truth' post. When Ezz handed her a mug of tea, Thea said, 'Thanks,' and followed on into the lounge. Summer storms were forecast, and a gusting breeze made it a good evening to sit indoors.

'So,' Thea began tentatively. 'If you haven't read my texts, you won't know that the agent's sent details of my birth mother. Seems she's alive.'

At that, Ezz showed signs of life. '*Really?* Wow. How do you feel?'

'I don't know.' Thea took an armchair. 'One minute seeking her out seems the obvious thing to do. The next it feels preposterous. You know what I'm like – even the

261

idea of researching how to travel from the Isle of Skye to Brittany is enough to send me into a panic. I love the isolation here but we're hours away from major airports and trainlines.'

For once, Ezz didn't leap in with an offer of help but just gave an absent 'Yeah.'

Daisy approached Thea's feet and executed the bunny hops that were Daisy-speak for 'I want up on your lap'. Thea obligingly patted her leg, and an instant later Daisy was curling up and closing her eyes almost in one movement.

'I should never have agreed to it,' Ezz burst out, raking her fingers into her hair so that it stood up as much as her flat, fine hair ever did.

'What?' Thea almost spilt her tea in surprise and even Daisy opened her eyes before closing them again.

'The *accident*,' Ezzie snapped, as if Thea were being dense. 'I shouldn't have let you pretend you were driving, and then all this horrible stuff with that nasty website wouldn't have happened.'

Thea struggled for calm, stroking Daisy reassuringly. 'Even with twenty-twenty hindsight, I don't agree. If I hadn't covered for you, *you would have gone to prison*. We looked it up. A past offence for you and life-changing injuries for him meant you'd probably have got out after two years, with good behaviour. Ezz, you'd have been *destroyed* by then.'

Ezz covered her eyes. 'But perhaps I deserved it. You're paying for my mistake. I'm not sure I can keep up the pretence.'

'So . . . WHAT?' Thea spoke so loudly that Daisy jumped. 'Who do you confess to? The police? Then we'll both be in trouble. Real trouble, with the law, not just some half-arsed, troll-attracting website. I've no idea what the punishment would be. Have you? But perverting the course of justice is serious stuff.' Her heart took up a rolling, sickening beat.

Ezz's hair clung to her tear-streaked cheeks. She whispered, 'I can't bear it.'

Thea started to say, 'But you're only making things harder for me,' then halted with it half spoken. They were *arguing*, something she and her sisters never did. And Ezz was in bits, which she never was.

'Tell you what,' she said, when the urge to have a strop had faded. 'Let's have a birth-mother summit with Valentina. Barnaby should be in bed by now.'

''Kay,' Ezz sniffled, blowing her nose.

'When you've washed your face with cold water, so Valentina doesn't demand to know why your skin looks like sausage meat,' Thea added candidly.

Ezz managed a smile before going to do as she was bid.

A half-hour later, the three of them had convened on FaceTime, Thea having forwarded the agent's email for Valentina to read and learnt that 'Quimper' wasn't pronounced to rhyme with 'simper', as she'd assumed, but 'kan-*pare*'. Now they were pondering the wider subject of how being adopted felt. 'We were a minority at school but a majority at home,' Valentina offered from the screen. She'd shoved her hair up on her head and removed her make-up, which made her look softer. Barnaby was in bed and Gary playing backgammon at some buddy's house. Backgammon sounded very Gary.

'Day to day, we weren't different to our friends,' Ezz said. Her fair skin was pale now, instead of sausage-meat pink, and she'd regained her usual composure. 'I suppose it's always there at the back of your mind though, those feelings of disassociation, of wondering about things that didn't affect others – like whether, somewhere, there's just one photo of you in another family's album.'

'Whoo.' Valentina visibly shuddered. 'Thanks for planting that idea, Ezzie. I won't sleep tonight now.'

'You two are still not inclined to trace your birth parents?' Thea queried.

On-screen, Valentina shook her head. 'Despite Ezz's slightly creepy thought about the photo album, I've never needed to know. Our family made me happy, and I assume I would have been less so with whoever put me up for adoption, who either couldn't look after me or didn't want to. Ezz and I are likely brushed-under-the-carpet babies. Unwanted pregnancies. Mistakes.'

Ezz rubbed her head, which was probably aching after her earlier tears. 'Thea's made me think about it more now than I ever have, though. I'm more curious, but my adoption still seems—' she wafted her hand '—unreal. Your birth family *is* real, Thea. From the agent's information, we know your grandfather died when he was fifty-one and your grandmother died when she was sixty-six. Your birth mother runs a restaurant – one we could walk into and order a meal.'

'Eek,' Thea said faintly. 'Goosebumps.'

Her sisters responded by moving the conversation on to Ezz's impending new job, and Barnaby moping over leaving last year's teacher and deciding in advance not to like next year's.

Neither Thea nor Ezzie mentioned Fredek Kowski's revelations on Everyday Celebs. Luckily, Thea couldn't imagine her legal-eagle, grown-up, sophisticated sister reading clickbait.

It was after ten when Thea walked Daisy home through the luminous Skye twilight, troubled over Ezz and hoping her sister wouldn't feel the need for the relaxing power of wine. For Thea's part, she wouldn't have minded the relaxing power of a hug from Dev.

In the distance, thunder rumbled, and Daisy growled back, her fur sticking out from her head as if bristling with static electricity.

'Whoops, better hurry,' Thea said, quickening her steps, because Skye's summer storms could be exhilarating when viewed from behind glass, but not much fun to be out in.

She paused on Loch View to look out into Rothach Bay and the Sound of Sleat, where the sea was as grey as the sky and filled with white horses. Fraser and Scotty popped out of Maisie's cottage, hurrying as fast as Fraser's elderly legs would allow. 'It's fair goin' ta pish!' he shouted as he passed her, clapping his Tam O'Shanter to his head.

But the thunder seemed to pass north of the island, and, before it was even properly dark, Skye was restored to tranquillity.

In fact, it wasn't until Saturday that the storm broke. And then it wasn't borne on a capricious wind.

It was brought directly to Rothach Hall by a bunch of forty-something women who behaved as if they'd spent lunchtime in the pub. In their heels and heavy make-up, they looked more done up for a Friday-night escape from husbands and kids than a Saturday afternoon ramble around public gardens, and perhaps coffee and scones at the Nature Café. They were not Rothach Hall's typical visitors.

Thea, returning from a lunchtime walk with Daisy, saw them from a distance, and frowned as one pushed another into a flowerbed. The victim emerged howling and giggling, uncaring of the slew of broken salvias she left behind. They used their phones to take selfies, wide-mouthed in expressions of exaggerated joy. They swore loudly. They jostled quieter visitors.

They pissed Thea off.

Judging that a jovial suggestion that they visit the café for black coffee might be all it took to calm their high spirits, she set off down the drive, Daisy trotting alongside with her ears blowing. Her pale fur was glossy now she was being looked after properly.

Then one of the women glanced Thea's way and emitted an ear-splitting 'It's her!'

The others took up the cry. 'It's her, it's her from *Garden Gladiators*! But isn't her hair different?' As Thea stood stock-still in shock and confusion, they flew towards her as if it was the mums' race at school sports day, boobs thrusting, knees wobbling. And cameras waving.

The one in the forefront panted, 'Yoohooh, Theeeee-yar! Can we have a pic, honey? Angie, you get in there with Thea, and I'll take the photo. You too, Binda.'

Too late, Thea spun on her heel. But her way was blocked by more visitors pausing to see what the noise was about, scrabbling for phones, obeying the instinct to photograph first and post later. '*Who* is it? Oh, *is* it?'

Diving to one side, Thea dashed across the south lawn, while Daisy, much in favour of running, gave a joyful 'Arf!'

'Aw, Thea, wait a minute!' The women's disappointed cries made Thea risk a glance over her shoulder, gasping to find the gang in hot pursuit. And she hated to think what those heels were doing to the lawns.

As she rounded the hall, she put on a spurt, racing across the courtyard to the staff accommodation door. Gasping, she stabbed out the entry code and half fell into the foyer, closing the door as she heard the approach of the first of the running feet. She gathered Daisy up, whispering, 'Sh, good girl, don't bark.'

Daisy gave Thea's face a reassuring lick.

'Aw,' panted a voice from outside. 'Where did she go? In the back door of the house?'

Someone else puffed, 'Or in the greenhouse? There are lots of frickin' doors off this yard.'

The hubbub rose. Thea crouched against the wall. A new voice crowed, 'I got her. Look at her gobsmacked expression in this pic. I'm going to upload it. What's the hashtag? Is it #WynterLiar? And the tags are @EverydayCelebs and @FredKowskiCyclist. He'll share it all over social. Hope I'm first. The competition only went up on the Everyday Celebs site this morning.'

'You're not first,' someone else chimed with enormous satisfaction. 'While you've been blethering, I've uploaded it. I got one of her sprinting across the lawn with her furball dog, looking over her shoulder.'

Thea closed her eyes. Social media vultures, uncaring that they were disrupting the life of another human being.

'Squee!' the satisfied voice went on. 'Fredek Kowski's already replied. "You're the most awesome of awesome, lovely. Sharing now." And he's got squillions of followers. The post with the most shares by midnight third of August wins the gold necklace – and it's gonna be me-eee!'

'No, me!' shouted another. 'I got her, too.'

'Ach, shit,' said the first voice.

Competition? For a gold *necklace*? Thea couldn't believe her ears. Was Fredek mad?

Another voice broke the air, this one male, and so familiar that Thea almost collapsed with relief. 'Hello there, ladies. Are we lost? Are you looking for the café, maybe? This area's not for visitors, I'm afraid.' *Deveron*. Daisy wriggled, trying to free herself, but Thea cuddled her tighter. 'Sh, *sh*.' Miraculously, Daisy shushed.

A pause. Thea imagined the women looking Deveron up and down. Then one said, 'We *were* looking for Thea Wynter.'

Deveron laughed. 'Thea? She shot around the building and into her car a few minutes ago.'

'Awwwww.' Thea could almost hear the women deflating. 'Her car? Expect she's miles away by now so we might as well go to the caff.'

'Particularly if this lovely man's going to *show us the way*.' The next voice sounded positively flirtatious.

Deveron laughed. 'Just follow me, ladies.' Voices and footsteps faded. Thea remained on the cold tiled floor, stroking Daisy. Her breathing calmed but her heart flailed wildly. This was her worst, worst nightmare. Pictures of her at Rothach were going to go viral under Fredek's orchestration.

She was still sitting on the floor ten minutes later in ice-like misery when Deveron let himself in and crouched beside her. 'They're stuffing their faces with cake. Are you OK?'

Belatedly, she realised tears were trickling down her cheeks. 'Not really.' She let him help her up and into his room. He made instant coffee while she told him about the competition and a proper *prize* for the post that got the most shares. 'And if the competition ends on 3rd

August then there's a whole week of this to come,' she finished despairingly.

Deveron cursed and checked the Everyday Celebs website on his phone. 'Afraid they're right,' he confirmed gloomily. 'The competition launched this morning; Everyday Celebs in association with Fredek Kowski. The prize is a nine-carat-gold necklace. Even supposing they bought it second-hand, a lot of effort's going into this.'

Perched on the edge of his bed, Thea felt dismal. 'I need to get away. I hadn't decided whether to search for my birth mother, but a trip to France is suddenly looking attractive. I'll have to plan the journey. It'll be a pain, because travelling anywhere is when you live on Skye.' She accepted a mug of coffee, while Daisy stuffed her whiskery face into a bowl of water.

Dev sat beside her. 'Sorry if this is overstepping, but I researched it the day you got the email from the people tracer, just in case. And . . .' he hesitated, obviously unsure, '. . . I thought I could come with you, if you want. I speak enough French to get by.'

Such a hot wave of relief engulfed her that she didn't stop to think. 'Oh, *yes please*. I don't know what I did to deserve you.' She buried her face in his shirt. Then, when she thought she felt him stiffen, she added a strangled laugh. 'To deserve you on my side, I meant.' Obviously, it was too early to speak possessively. They only had another two or three months, and then he'd be gone.

She sat up and plastered on a smile. 'We'd better chat up Ezz to get the time off.'

He winked. 'I'll leave her to you.' Then he sobered. 'Unless you'd rather she was the one to go with you?'

'I'll check, because it would get her out of the line of

fire, too,' she said, realising that Ezz might very well want that.

He drew her into his arms and hugged her tightly, and she let the rest of the world drift away. All she wanted for now was this.

Chapter Twenty

As they descended towards Quimper Airport, Thea looked down and thought it must be a Breton law that five trees should exist for every dwelling, there were so many between the houses. Like Skye, but without the rocky moors and the red and black Cuillin Hills.

As the less-seasoned traveller, she let Deveron take the lead through passport control and baggage reclaim, and to locate the shuttle bus. For flexibility, they'd arranged a maximum of eleven days off but he'd only booked travel to Quimper and two nights in a hotel opposite the train station, leaving stay length and return travel open. The Isle of Skye being central to nowhere, there had been a bewildering array of combinations of flying, driving or rail travel. Thea had opted for what seemed the easiest and so on Monday they'd driven to Glasgow Airport and then flown to London City Airport, to overnight at a budget hotel. London City to Quimper had then been an easy flight on the Tuesday afternoon British Airways service.

Ezz had not wanted to accompany her sister, even

though Thea worried that more 'Thea-spotters' would descend on Rothach. Despite Skye's remoteness it was a popular destination, so there might be a wave of visitors interested in the online competition, but there had been no budging Ezzie in her resolve to stay behind. 'I'll take off my name badge, so nobody sees "Wynter" and stay in the office as much as is practical,' was her concession. 'Tavish leaving means I must recruit to fill my role. And you need someone to look after Daisy while you're gone. I don't want to spoil things for you and Dev . . . and I think you will think more clearly about Ynez without either of your sisters there.'

So here she and Deveron were, on an orange bus, looking out at green fields and woods. Thea felt Deveron's hand cover hers and realised she'd hardly spoken since they landed. She squeezed his strong fingers. 'You're great at travelling on a budget. Thanks again for giving me some of your air miles.'

His face lit on his slow, sexy smile. 'I've picked up a few tricks – looking on TripAdvisor for cheap but clean hotels. Buying salads from supermarkets or quick meals from street vendors rather than eating out. And those air miles were just lying around.'

Thea tried to return the favour by being considerate, despite her butterflies whenever she thought about Ynez Bourgault. 'I feel bad that you hadn't accrued enough leave for this trip.'

He pressed a kiss on her temple, his lips soft and hot. 'You know that Ezz says I can catch up when I get back. I'm not worried.'

The bus dropped them off outside the station, its brickwork a soft russet and '*Gare de Quimper*' in white above the doors. A turquoise train stood waiting. They crossed the road to their hotel opposite, and booked in, Deveron utilising a mix of French and English to say they might want to stay longer than their booking and the member of staff saying it should be easy to arrange.

Their room was at the rear on the second floor, in a separate building. It boasted a king-sized bed, a table, a hanging rail, a stand for the suitcase and a clean shower room. The view was of a lightwell and the building next door. Deveron seemed satisfied. 'Everything we need. Now—' he checked his watch '—what would you like to do? We're a five-minute walk from the historic centre. Do you want to wander around? Or go straight to Place Terre au Duc to see your mother's restaurant?'

Panic flamed through Thea. 'I can't go straight there. Shit.'

She must have looked aghast, because he grinned. 'Then, shit, we won't go straight there. And you'll need to say *merde*, now you're in France.'

'*Merde*, then. Let's have a look around. I'm antsy.' She couldn't even muster a proper smile at his teasing.

'OK.' Back in reception, Deveron picked up a visitor map provided by the Office de Tourisme, and they turned left out of the hotel. 'Let's head for that amazing cathedral we saw from the bus,' he suggested, tapping his finger on a drawing of a cathedral on the map. They set off, dawdling beside the River Odet, which ran between the carriageways of the main road, with bridges for traffic and footbridges – called *passerelle* – every few metres.

Thea felt more relaxed as soon as she saw each was edged with flower boxes in full bloom. 'How pretty,' she marvelled, standing on a passerelle to admire the dozens of bridges crossing the river, frothing with colourful plants.

273

A couple of turns took them to the impressive Gothic twin-towered Cathedral of Saint Corentin. 'Wow.' Thea had been impressed with the flowery bridges, but this was a work of art. They sat at a nearby café to drink coffee and admire the arches and elegant spires, and the craftsmanship that had somehow made the stone look lacey.

Afterwards, they wandered down a cobbled street designed for feet rather than vehicles, pausing at shop windows to gaze at macarons and chocolate, handmade soap on strings or pretty watercolours. The shops were painted in jolly combinations such as blue for the timber and lemon for the rendering between. Some had window boxes and others sported carved and painted figures of angels or men and women in Breton dress, with wrought iron here, and shutters there. 'It's beautiful,' Thea marvelled. 'So gorgeous. Look at the colours. Look at that fountain glistening in the sun.' And: 'Phew, it's hot here.'

Eventually, they found themselves standing on a bridge over a smaller river, and Deveron took out the map. 'This is the River Steir near where it joins the River Odet . . . and that means we're close to Place Terre au Duc.'

Thea's heart kicked into a sudden gallop as she stared at the map. If they turned left and took maybe fifty strides, they would, indeed, be in Place Terre au Duc, where they would find the restaurant Côté Rivière. And Ynez Bourgault. Sweat beaded at her hairline.

Deveron's hand ran down her spine, gentle and comforting. 'We can go back or walk the other way through a park.'

Trying for a weak joke, she said, '*Merde*,' to prove she'd retained the fact that it was French for 'shit'. 'Let's—'

274

she swallowed hard '—peep at the restaurant . . . from the outside.'

They found Place Terre au Duc, broader at one end than the other, ringed with narrow buildings and paved with cobbles. In the centre was a seating area, with umbrellas and a dried-up fountain. The seat that ringed the fountain was topped with colourful ceramic tile.

Each building boasted its own colour scheme: terracotta timbers and cream render, brown and peach, grey and lemon, blue and white. The roofs were steep and would look like witches' hats if witches had square heads.

Only one building was stone, a soft grey, with a green canopy. Its upper windows were door-sized with wrought iron across them. French doors. She wondered, inconsequentially, whether the French called them English doors. Between the first set of windows and the canopy was a sign in gold script: *Côté Rivière*.

When she saw that the restaurant was shut, colourful chairs and tables stacked and chained together outside, Thea sighed, 'Oh,' not knowing whether to be disappointed or relieved.

Deveron slipped an arm along her shoulders. 'In some parts of France, the main meal is at midday, so not all restaurants open in the evening.'

She stepped back to gaze at the building's gracious façade. It had at least one apartment above, maybe several. Did one belong to Ynez? A shadow passed over a window. *Did that belong to her too?*

'I feel strange.' Her breath wouldn't behave, but leapt and fluttered in her throat, making her heart leap and flutter too.

He steered her gently away. 'Then let's go.'

Their route took them to where the Steir flowed into the larger River Odet, water surging gently where the two courses collided. Thea found herself babbling, as if that would quiet the butterflies doing backflips in her stomach. 'I wouldn't have thought to put yellow dahlias in the flower boxes with orange nasturtiums, but it works, doesn't it? The flowers are bright, but the colours of the buildings are muted.'

Deveron ambled by her side, answering, nodding, just being there, holding her hand and being calmly Deveron. It calmed Thea, too, and she fell silent to absorb what she'd seen and felt.

Eventually, she'd steadied enough for them to buy kebabs from a street vendor and sit on a bench to eat them. Thea slipped her arms around Dev's firm body. 'We haven't made love for a while.' She kissed the stubbly skin on the side of his neck.

Deveron's return embrace enveloped her. 'I won't put up a fight.' She laughed and they returned entwined to their hotel. There, his touch was particularly tender, as if realising that she felt as fragile as glass.

Afterwards, she whispered, 'I don't know what to do about her.'

He kissed her hair. 'I know. It's incredibly difficult for you.'

It was comforting to know that it *was* difficult, and therefore, it was understandable if she felt confused and anxious, and was dithering even now she was in the same place as her mother. But there was one point she hadn't brought up with him; not when she'd confessed the truth about the accident, not even during the planning for this sudden trip.

His heartbeat was steady beneath her cheek, whereas

hers put in an extra beat as she asked, 'Do you think criminal tendencies run in families?'

He stilled. 'No.' Then, carefully, he added, 'I think people make mistakes under pressure. There's no blood tie involved.'

Chapter Twenty-One

A night's sleep steadied Thea's nerves. It was delicious to wake up beside Dev and hear the French language spoken outside and see sunlight on the blinds.

Hard on the heels of this positivity came the realisation that it would be mad to come this far for nothing. 'I'd like to go to Côté Rivière for lunch,' she said, as soon as he awoke, as if launching the words onto the air would make the resolution stick.

Deveron blinked sleepily and kissed her naked shoulder. 'Aye, OK.'

They filled the morning wandering around the shops in the old quarter. Thea was too keyed up to take much in, apart from the fact that some of the ceramic art bore price tags of thousands of euros. Unsurprisingly, such pieces were behind glass.

Finally, Deveron glanced at his watch and cocked an eyebrow. 'It's almost one o'clock.'

It's time. Thea knew that if she chickened out then he'd understand and her heart did flutter as if she'd been drinking triple espresso, but bravely, she said, 'Right.

Which way?' She could have checked the map, but it was as if all her energy had focused on staying upright and in control. He took her sweating hand and led her up a cobbled street and over the correct bridge, while her heart beat out: *Birth mother, birth mother, birth mother. PANIC! Birth mother!* And the ghosts of Maxie and Vince walked by her side. She wished she could read their expressions and know what they thought of her quest.

In contrast to yesterday evening, Place Terre au Duc was in a bustle, with every eatery busy. Thea stopped and clutched her stomach, which jumped like a panicked frog.

Deveron took charge and beat another couple to the last vacant table, which was painted red with yellow hollyhocks and improbable purple leaves. In a few minutes, a young man appeared, dark-haired and with heavy stubble. '*Bonjour.*'

'*Bonjour,*' they chorused. Thea glanced at Deveron, the few phrases of French she'd mastered curling up in her memory like dried leaves.

Deveron smiled. 'Madame Ynez Bourgault, *s'il vous plaît.*'

The young man nodded, '*Oui, oui,*' and gestured to the interior of the restaurant. Then he paused, plainly expecting some explanation before he'd bother the business owner.

Dev looked at Thea.

Thea knew a panicked moment when her impulse was to jump up and flee across the cobbled square. Instead, she fumbled in her bag for a pen. Shakily she wrote on the back of a discarded receipt:

Altheadora Wynter
Althéa-Dora Bourgault

She offered the waiter the scrap of paper, mumbling, '*Je m'appelle . . .*' and hoping he got the gist.

The waiter's eyebrows leapt at the sight of the name Bourgault and he shot her a curious look. '*Un moment.*' He whisked away.

Belatedly, Thea wished they'd ordered drinks. Her lips felt coated in sand and her throat blocked by hopes and fears. The July sun beat on her arm, despite the table's parasol.

A minute dragged by. Thea stared at the hollyhocks painted on the table and mentally corrected the appearance of the buds. Then Deveron whispered, 'Thea!' She looked up and saw a wide-eyed woman slowly heading their way.

Paralysed, Thea watched. She was petite, like Thea, but heavier and more bosomy, probably in her early sixties, her short dark hair shot with silver. 'Althéa-Dora?' she whispered, pronouncing it *Al-TAY-uh Dorr-uh*.

Swallowing, Thea nodded. Shakily, the woman pulled out the vacant seat at the table and sank into it, her eyes never leaving Thea. Dark eyes, familiar from Thea's mirror – eyes that held an expression of wonder. 'I never thought to see you again. I am . . . Ynez Bourgault.'

Despite the clatter and chatter of the restaurant and nearby shops, Thea felt enclosed in the moment. At her silence, Ynez called to the hovering waiter, who nodded, and in a moment hurried back with a carafe of water and three glasses. Both Thea and Ynez sipped.

Finally, Thea found her voice. 'I only discovered my story recently. I didn't know Mum and Dad had known you.'

Ynez's expression became guarded. 'They are well?'

Thea shook her head. 'No. They died when I was eighteen.'

'Ah.' Ynez's shoulders drooped. 'I wondered. We agreed that, once a year, Maxie would write to tell me you were well and happy. It stopped when you were eighteen and I thought she had decided you were an adult, and it was time.' Her English was fluent – not surprising when England had once been her home.

The knowledge that Maxie had reported on her made Thea feel odd. She was about to ask whether Ynez had tried writing to Maxie when the letters stopped, but realised the answer must be 'no' or the letter would have been redirected to Valentina, who'd dealt with that kind of stuff.

Then Ynez reached out one fingertip and touched Thea's bare forearm, as if to check she was real. The touch ricocheted through Thea, hot, as if creating static electricity. She stared at the spot her mother had touched and tears formed a ball in her throat as she realised it must be forty years since they'd last touched.

Ynez drew in her breath with a whoosh, as if she'd been forgetting to breathe. 'I cannot . . .' She stopped to sip her water before starting again. 'Are you passing through Quimper, or will you come to my apartment this evening? At the moment, the restaurant is hellish busy and my manager, Virginie, is away.'

Thea found a smile curving her mouth. 'Hellish' had been one of Maxie's words. Somehow, it made it more real that once the two women had lived together . . . decades ago, when Thea's life had just begun. 'We could come,' she managed huskily, glancing at Dev for confirmation.

Ynez spared a glance for Deveron too, as if just realising he was there. 'Forgive me.' She extended her hand. 'Ynez Bourgault.'

Dimly, Thea was aware of Deveron introducing himself.

Then he once again laced his fingers with Thea's, and he was the only thing that felt real.

The waiter ran back to say something in Ynez's ear in a rush of French and anxiety, and she rose. 'There is a kitchen problem. You *will* return?' she asked Thea intently.

Shakily, Thea nodded.

Ynez glanced behind herself into the depths of the restaurant, her brows meeting anxiously. 'Please, give your order to Émile.' She indicated the waiter, who smiled and nodded.

But now the first moment of meeting had passed, it would feel uncomfortable to sit here knowing Ynez would catch glimpses of her as she ran around her 'hellish' restaurant. 'Thank you, but we'll see you later,' she said politely, rising. People were waiting nearby as if ready to pounce on any free table.

Ynez wrung her hands, eyes panicky. 'Wait.' She hurried inside, returning in moments with two business cards. On one she wrote a telephone number, prefixing it with +33 for France and crossing her sevens in the French way. 'Please, write yours,' she begged, giving Thea the other card.

Thea's mind went as blank as the rectangle of white and Deveron had to pull her number up in his contact list for her to copy out.

She didn't cross her sevens. It seemed like a comment on the difference between herself and the woman who'd given her life.

Before finally letting her go, Ynez escorted her to a wooden door to the left of the glass front of the restaurant and showed her the entry system. 'At seven, perhaps?' she asked breathlessly, clutching the card bearing Thea's number.

'Yes. Fine.' Thea nodded. They stared at each other with odd, unnatural smiles, then Thea turned away, the cobbles feeling spongey beneath her feet.

Dev steered her to a café a few minutes away. Thea ordered salad she didn't want, but sipping a cup of coffee made her feel more herself. Finally, she looked at Deveron. 'That was—' she searched for a word that would encompass her sensation of floating in a sea of disbelief, populated by sharp rocks of fear '—discombobulating. When she touched me, it was like a force field. But I don't know if it was a good force or a bad one.'

He dropped his fork and grasped her hands, almost too hard. 'I am so fucking proud of you. I can only guess how disorientating and destabilising it felt. You were so brave. If I ever buy a lion, I'll call it Thea.'

She found herself half laughing and half crying. 'Why would you buy a lion? A *lion*? You're crazy.' But a little Scottish craziness seemed to ground her because she was able to pick at her salad.

Afterwards, they found a place on the map called Jardin de la Paix, or garden of peace, which sounded exactly what Thea needed. A couple of steep streets took them there, and they wandered the gritty pathways and stone arches, admiring hydrangeas and orange crocosmia, palm trees and banana plants, until Thea sank onto a bench in the shade of a fig tree. 'I'd better see if my sisters want to hear how it went.'

Deveron grinned, laughter lines fanning out from the corners of his eyes. 'I predict that they will.'

It was two minutes past seven. Côté Rivière's colourful chairs and tables were stacked nearby and Place Terre au

283

Duc was wrapped in evening quiet when Thea tentatively pressed the button on Ynez's entry system. The line opened immediately as if Ynez had been standing beside it. 'Althéa-Dora?'

'Yes.' Thea licked her lips. A buzzer sounded and Dev pushed open the door.

A flight of tiled stairs led up to a landing, where Ynez waited at the banister. 'Dear God,' she groaned, clutching her chest. 'All afternoon I feared you would not return.'

Thea gasped a laugh. 'And I thought you'd be out when I got here.' She glanced around. A further flight of stairs led to another storey. A pink chandelier dangled from a high, ornate ceiling.

'This is my apartment,' Ynez said, wafting her hands. 'Once I shared it with my parents, but now it is just for me.' She showed them into a large room overlooking the furled parasols and dry fountain of the square below. On a table, bottles of red and white wine waited with a carafe of water and glasses. No sooner had they settled into gold brocade armchairs when Ynez leapt up again. 'I have snacks.' She began to trot back and forth with small, gold-edged plates, waving away Thea's offer of help.

Eyes smiling, Deveron leant towards Thea to whisper, 'She's nervous.'

Weakly, she smiled back. 'Me, too. I'm not sure I want to face the truths that must be coming.'

Then Ynez was back, evidently in time to hear Thea's murmured comment. She pulled an agonised face as she perched on the edge of a chair. 'Yes! Now I must explain how I was, as a young woman. And I was a little twat.'

It surprised a laugh out of Thea to hear Ynez speak like the young adult she must have been when she learnt English. 'I always thought I was adopted as a baby, like

Valentina and Ezz – Esmerelda. Valentina uses her full name, but Esmerelda is usually Ezzie and I'm Thea,' she tacked on.

Slowly, Ynez nodded. 'You choose your name. But this sound, *th*, does not come easy to the French. May I call you Althéa?'

Thea found she liked Al-TAY-uh. 'Of course. And I—' her breath caught '—I'd prefer to call you Ynez. "Mum" was Maxie.'

Ynez's gaze fell. She occupied herself with choosing a tiny savoury pastry. 'Of course.' Eyes still downcast, she continued with her story. 'My parents were older parents. I am an only child. Papa was a *sacristain* at the church. Not the church of Locmaria, near here, but where we lived then, a little out of the centre.'

'*Sacristain*,' Thea repeated, testing the word.

Deveron was already on a translation app. 'Sexton, apparently. An assistant at the church.'

'Truly?' Ynez raised both her eyebrows wryly. '"Sex" is in the English word? My father would not have approved.'

Thea smiled at the small joke. 'I used an agency to find you, so I know your parents were Phillipe and Sylvie-Marie.'

Ynez nodded. 'When I became pregnant, to them it was a catastrophe.'

Thea's heart squeezed. 'Mum's friend Meryl said my father was an English boy at university.'

Ynez smiled brilliantly. 'You know Meryl? She helped me.' Her brows descended. 'Your father's name was Bobby White. He came to Quimper as a language student.'

'You didn't meet him in England?' Thea frowned.

Ynez shook her head. 'No, he was here.' She turned

her pastry around on her plate. 'Althéa . . . I was a very, very stupid girl.'

Thea glugged half her wine and braced herself for what came next.

'I liked bad boys,' Ynez confessed sombrely. 'I believed their big talk. Their—' a hand wave as she conjured up the appropriate English '—bullshit. I liked attention. I attached myself to anyone who seemed to like me, like a puppy. I am much stronger now. I no longer welcome bad boys. I have a good man, my Jean-Jacques. He is my lover.'

Thea wondered if she should have introduced Deveron as her lover. She quite liked the no-frills term.

Ynez went on. 'Bobby didn't answer my letters when he was back in England and I thought I must have noted down his address incorrectly.' Sadly, she shook her head. 'See? Stupid. When I confessed to Maman and Papa that I was pregnant, they were horrified. My father – the *sacristain*! They – the respectable owners of the local café! They were good people, but their attitude was "What will people think of us?" rather than "What does Ynez need?" So they gave me money to catch the train and live with Maman's friend in Nantes, who would help me find parents for the baby.' Her eyes twinkled unexpectedly. 'I was rebellious. I had savings, so went instead on the trains and ferry to England. I arrived at Bobby's address in Blackheath in London.' All humour faded from her face. 'His parents said he was at university – though it was not term time. Eventually, Bobby's father gave me money to go away. I suppose Bobby was hiding.'

'That's shitty,' murmured Thea, trying to imagine how a twenty-year-old pregnant woman alone in a strange country had felt. And Thea felt queasy that Bobby, her *father*, had hidden from the woman carrying her baby. And the man paying Ynez off had been Thea's grandfather. *Not in any real meaning of the word*, she thought, remembering how loving Erik and Grete Larsson were with their grandkids. 'Did you speak much English then?'

Ynez nodded. 'English was my good subject at school, and I learnt from the months Bobby was my boyfriend. I could work in England, but it seemed problems would come when I could no longer work and did not have private health insurance.' She dropped her pastry untasted on her plate. 'It was a very horrible time,' she said, gaze distant. 'But I had enough money for a week or two in a room in a house. A girl there was like me – but English – and she explained London was a good place to work unofficially. "Don't ask for money from the government," she said. "And don't give them any."' She paused to pour more wine. The sound of children's voices floated up from the square outside.

Gently, Deveron asked. 'You didn't want to return to Quimper?'

Ynez puffed her lips. '*Non*. My parents did not want me to be pregnant and would not accept a baby. I worked for people who wanted help in their houses. But after I gave birth, everything became difficult.'

'Of course. It must have been horrible, living in one room with a baby and no job or benefits. It was a wonder you didn't give me up for adoption then.' There had been no accusation in Thea's words, but Ynez looked pained.

'I did not want that,' she said firmly. 'A lady I worked for before you were born, she knew Meryl, who introduced me to Maxie. I felt *so* fortunate. Lovely children to look after, a clean room, nice food.'

287

Silence fell. A clock ticked. Thea reached out for Dev's hand. If this were a horror movie, they were coming to the scary bit.

Ynez whispered, 'But I was so stupid that I found another bad boy. An even worse boy, though I did not realise. When he asked me to deliver a car or a package to someone, I felt important.' She stopped and wiped her eyes, smearing her mascara. 'Then the police came to the house. The boy had run away. The court . . . it did not believe me that I had been used by another person and sentenced me to prison and called me a drug dealer and a menace. I could not believe it! I had a baby to look after. I was so frightened. Maxie said, of course, you would remain with them. She was kind. Vince was upset with me but he, too, said you must stay.' The grief in her eyes was replaced by something emptier. 'By the time my sentence was over . . . you were their child, not mine.' Then, tautly: 'I realised that my parents had not been wrong to be virtuous. I came home.'

Thea lifted the fine crystal wineglass and swallowed a mouthful. It was as if her adoption by Maxie and Vince had been pragmatic rather than emotional. The brisk conclusion to the story of her long-ago abandonment stung. 'So, you left me.'

Ynez's gaze fixed on the silvery pattern on the wallpaper. 'You had a good life. With no baby in my arms, my parents welcomed me. We gave each other second chances. My English was good, so I joined a course on business. After some years, we put together our money and borrowing power, sold their café and bought Côté Rivière.'

The room seemed to hold its breath. At the start of Ynez's confession, Thea had felt compassion for a wronged young woman clinging to her baby. But then the mood had changed. The story became chillier and harder for Thea to hear.

She drank the rest of the wine, knowing Deveron's eyes were on her and not wanting to meet them, because if she read sympathy there, she'd begin to sob. She tried to sound as brisk and pragmatic as Ynez. 'Did you have more kids?'

'None. I was too old by the time I met Jean-Jacques,' Ynez said softly. She refilled the wineglasses. The food had remained largely untouched.

'Didn't you even want to visit me?' Thea felt more wine would make her sick.

Ynez's eyes flashed. 'It was impossible! Who would you think I was? A friend of the family? Or should I have taken you away from your home, parents, sisters? Give you one room, not enough heat, with me, a stranger now? And no father?'

And Thea saw the past in a harsh, clear light. Herself as a burden, a mistake. Out of charity and expediency, she'd been tagged onto the nuclear family that had been Maxie, Vince, Valentina and Ezzie. And now she'd come to France bleating for affection and received cold, hard truths instead. 'Thanks for seeing me,' she heard herself say, voice artificially bright as she stumbled to her feet. 'Goodbye.'

Ynez jumped up, wide-eyed and stricken. 'Althéa—'

But Thea was running from the gracious room and down the tiled steps and out into the square. In seconds, Deveron was by her side as she raced past closed shops and cafés, trying to outdistance her emotions, until she reached the broad road that was Rue du Parc with the River Odet running down the centre, wide and serene, its decorative bridges one behind the other. Breathing hard, she found a bench and she half fell into it.

Deveron, only a second behind, hugged her. Cautiously, he said, 'I'm sorry if that didn't go as you wanted.'

She dropped her head onto his firm, broad shoulder. 'Not really.'

He stroked her hair. 'Was it . . . what hurt you? I'm not judging,' he added quickly. 'And don't talk about it if you'd rather not. But she really did seem shocked in a good way, at first, didn't she? Then she got defensive.'

She twisted to look at him, frowning. 'But I didn't accuse her of anything.'

'No,' he agreed, but dubiously. Then he dropped several kisses on her face.

She nestled into him again and they watched the water slipping by, the traffic in constant motion on either side. 'It's no wonder adopted kids can have attachment issues. Question the life they got . . . wonder about the life they never had. If she'd brought me here, I would have grown up French, in this picturesque city. Different mother. No father. Strict grandparents. No siblings.'

He continued to stroke her hair.

She sighed. Grudgingly, she admitted, 'Or brought up dirt-poor in England with no family apart from her. Can we leave tomorrow?'

His hand paused. 'I'll have to work out how. There's no plane until Tuesday so it would mean the train to Paris. We'd need a hotel there, then take the Eurostar to London, overnight train to Glasgow, and then the bus to the airport to pick up my car.'

'Followed by a four- or five-hour drive home,' Thea finished, on a chilly wave of shame. How self-absorbed she'd been, dragging him all this way, letting him take unpaid leave and spending money and air miles, only to turn around and embark on an even more tortuous return journey, just because *she* was rocked by the turbulent mess of this summer and longed for the peace of the Isle of Skye. 'Or,' she said, sounding upbeat with an effort, 'let's have a lovely holiday here in Quimper and fly back on Tuesday.'

He pulled back to look into her eyes. 'We *could* leave tomorrow, if you want to—'

She jumped up and pulled at him to rise with her. 'No, let's stay,' she insisted. 'The sun's out, there are lovely gardens and a beautiful old city. We haven't been inside the amazing Gothic cathedral or the theatre or anything. I haven't had a holiday for ages.' Deveron didn't deserve to suffer for her misery and overwhelm. He was, after all, her lover.

'OK,' he said slowly, as if wrong-footed by her sudden swerve, the wind blowing his hair into his eyes. 'If that's what you want.'

'Definitely,' she lied. 'We'll have a fantastic week together, with no work and no worries. I met my birth mother. It wasn't great, but at least I'm no longer curious.'

It sounded good, delivered with a big smile as she slid her arms around him and rained kisses on his throat, but in her heart, she knew that the past wasn't always that easy to escape.

Just look at Fredek Kowski.

After the meeting with Ynez Bourgault, followed by a FaceTime session so Thea could recount it to Ezz and Valentina, Dev found joy in the succeeding sunshine-soaked days.

He loved travelling again, but not like the old days, when he'd juggle writers and clients while trying to keep up with football news. He needn't care whether Stade Brestois 29 had their summer football training camp in nearby Brest. He was with Thea, and work was not on the agenda.

But a lot of lovemaking was. When Thea had been upset about Fredek Kowski's weirdness and Deveron had felt guilty as hell, afraid she'd discover his involvement and hate him, initiating intimacy had felt wrong. But here, with Fredek out of the picture and Thea needing or wanting to lose herself in bed, it wasn't in him to resist.

He adored her naked body.

It was more than being aroused by a pretty woman. He was fascinated by the sexy way she moved and the firmness of her limbs. Her curves drove rational thought from his head. It was bliss to learn what made her gasp and clutch at him, or to watch her face as she rode him. He loved to see her hair tumbling around her face when she smiled sleepily at him in the mornings.

They filled their days taking picnic lunches to eat on the warm grass of Jardin du Théâtre, behind Théâtre Max Jacob; or climbing the dappled footpaths of the steep park that gave Rue du Parc its name, the city below glimpsed between the trees.

Once they visited the Breton Museum, close to the cathedral. Thea wandered among the exhibitions of folk art and everyday objects of past Brittany, and he guessed she was trying to absorb how this was a part of her, yet she was not a part of it. She studied gorgeous Quimper pottery, perhaps thinking that Ynez had once trained in the art.

'Hey,' he said, reading the cards under the exhibits.

'Breton has a rich Celtic history. Just right to make a Scotsman feel at home.'

Her smile was pensive. 'That's more than I do.'

He caressed her hair, which ran like silk through his fingers, and thought the week couldn't last long enough for him. On Skye . . . he didn't know what waited. When Thea had been showering that morning, he'd checked out Everyday Celebs and the competition-prize necklace had been awarded, with a lot of fanfare and no mention made that only a few people could possibly have secured a photo because Thea had escaped.

It at least put to rest his dread that when Fredek and Weston at Everyday Celebs realised Thea had vanished, they'd simply extend the deadline until she reappeared. Hopefully their hands had been forced by the approach of Fredek's conference, when his precious 'campaign' must be complete.

Another cloud on their horizon was that every day, Thea's phone rang, and *Ynez* flashed on the screen. Thea would decline the call and tuck away her phone with a pensive smile. 'My parents were Maxie and Vince, who loved me and looked after me. I understand that Ynez had a hard time and why she let them adopt me. I'm glad she did. Better to draw a line under the situation.'

Deveron booked their long homeward journey to Skye, Rothach and the glassy calm of the Sound of Sleat. On Monday, the day before catching the bus to the airport, they spent the evening at a pavement café, drank several glasses of wine and then meandered hand in hand to their hotel. As they strolled through the hotel reception, Deveron was looking forward to another night in bed together when the clerk called, 'Ms Altheadora Wynter, I have a note for you.' She pronounced Thea's full first name with French pizzazz.

'Oh?' Frowning, Thea released Deveron's hand and reached for the fold of paper.

Simultaneously, a smartly dressed man rose from a chair in the corner. In his sixties, his thin silver hair was brushed back behind his ears. 'Althéa,' he said.

Clearly confused, Thea looked from him to the message in her hand.

Deveron angled his head to read the note in black, slanting handwriting. *Althéa, please allow Jean-Jacques to speak.*

The man didn't wait for Thea to make a choice. 'I'm sorry to ambush you. I am Jean-Jacques Bolloré. Ynez spoke to you of me, perhaps.' His English was excellent, his smile warm. In his hands was a parcel, rectangular, wrapped in flowered paper and tied with red string. 'She understands why you do not want to speak with her, but this is something she wishes you to have. Please, will you accept?' He extended the parcel towards Thea.

She treated him to an unwinking stare.

Jean-Jacques' eyes twinkled. 'I assure you I'm no threat to you. I'm a respectable businessman from here in Quimper. You are much like Ynez, I think. I wish I had been here when you met your . . . Ynez. She is dear to me, which is why I agreed to bring this gift.'

Dev was bursting with curiosity, but it wasn't his parcel, or his mother. It wasn't his heart that was struggling to cope with the shocks and surprises this trip had thrown at it.

Finally, Thea spoke. 'How did Ynez know where I'm staying?'

Jean-Jacques looked unabashed. 'I have an app. I typed

294

in your telephone number, and it showed us the location. We checked several times and always it came at night to this hotel.'

'What?' Thea said faintly. 'Is that even legal?'

'So far as I know,' he answered, shrugging, still proffering the parcel.

Finally, Thea put out her hands and took it, staring at the packet as if it might bite.

Sounding wistful and hopeful, Jean-Jacques asked, 'You wish to send a message to Ynez, perhaps?'

Thea blinked. 'Um . . . say thanks.'

The three of them stood under the lights of reception, the woman behind the counter discreetly tapping at her computer. Traffic rumbled outside and Dev heard the hiss of a train leaving the station.

'Thank you for coming,' Thea continued formally. 'Goodnight.'

Jean-Jacques muttered gruffly, 'Ynez has a good heart.' Then he smiled sadly and left via the glass doors to the street.

In their room, Thea crawled onto the bed and regarded the parcel. Slowly, she pulled the ends of the red string and the paper fell away from the contents – a fat, worn, flowered notebook.

Gingerly, she flipped the pages. It was filled with handwriting. Pages and pages of handwriting, not particularly neat. There were a few drawings, mainly of flowers and one of what looked like a child's dress. Further in, a newspaper clipping was stuck in with yellowing tape. Thea squinted at it. 'I think it's the obituary of my . . . of Ynez's father, Phillipe.' Later came the matching clipping that spoke of the death of her grandmother Sylvie-Marie. She closed the book and rose to stow it in her suitcase, face shuttered.

With an inner sigh, Dev thought that there were few gifts Thea was less likely to engage with than a book. He considered offering to read it to her.

But instead he opened his arms, and she snuggled into him. What she wanted was a hug. And, feeling her in his arms, he realised that it was all he wanted, too.

Chapter Twenty-Two

By the time Thea and Dev returned to work on Thursday, the first week of August was over. Sheena was on annual leave. Nell told Thea she would be giving up her job at the end of the month because she wanted time to tackle work her university tutors would expect completed before her final year began. Hadley was busy in the greenhouse, probably because it was raining, so Thea and Dev put on their waterproofs and dug over the flowerbeds for the final time before summer's end.

Thea was happy to be back at Rothach Hall until she popped indoors to find Ezz in Tavish's office – Ezz's office now, really, as Tavish wouldn't be back – staring morosely through the window. Alarmed by her sister's dismal expression, Thea closed the door. 'What's up?'

Slowly, Ezz turned, her sigh louder than the rain on the glass. 'I didn't want to spoil your holiday, but while you were away Fredek Kowski called on the hall's landline and I decided I'd better take it. He says that if he gives the police a new statement then they'll start asking us questions.'

Thea's good mood drained into a sinkhole of fear. 'Shit,' she breathed, plummeting into a chair and staring at Ezz's white face. 'Fredek Kowski *stopped his bike in the middle of the road.*'

Ezz's lip trembled. 'That's not the only thing the law's interested in if a driver who hits him fails the breathalyser.'

Thea's heart felt as if was playing the bass line of heavy metal in her ears. 'We don't know you were over the limit.'

'But that's no longer the issue, is it? We gave false information to the police. According to what I've been reading, we could go to prison,' Ezz reminded her.

Stoutly, Thea declared, 'Fredek can't prove a thing. There were no witnesses. You weren't even there when the police turned up.'

'But what if I can't lie convincingly to the police if they interview me now? They'd only be doing their job to keep on at me.' Ezz heaved another sigh. 'I should have served my time, because this fear's an unending sentence.'

As it had always done, the thought of Ezz in prison made Thea feel sick. Dimly, she wondered whether she should have given Ynez more credit for vowing to lead a better life once she'd left prison behind. But it was different, wasn't it? Ynez's guilt hadn't been in doubt.

The silence in the room grew. Finally, Ezz summoned a ghost of a smile. 'Obviously, I'd do my best not to confess because I know it would rebound on you. And imagine the office gossip for poor Valentina if it came out now.'

Thea groaned. 'It was my idea to say I was driving. You do things for people you love, even when you know they're not the right things.' Like . . . Ynez? Had it been love that had led her to let that 'bad boy' use her to help in his crimes?

Ezz fidgeted with a notepad. 'Fredek says he won't go to the police if you'll appear with him at some influencer conference.'

Thea didn't realise she'd jumped to her feet until she felt herself swaying. 'That bastard,' she hissed. 'I hate him.'

The twist to Ezz's lips suggested she felt much the same.

Slowly, Thea sank back into her chair and watched the rain make rivulets down the window. Finally, heavily, she said, 'Well, I suppose I ought to go back to work. Nell's leaving at the end of August and Hadley's going on holiday with his wife in September and isn't sure whether he'll want to return to the hall for October. Maybe his summer stints will get shorter as he gets older. This year, Deveron might be the only seasonal remaining into October.'

Ezz cocked an eyebrow. 'Has he dropped any hints about future plans?'

'Not really.' Thea's cheeks heated, getting the inference that Deveron's plans would be about more than the staff roster. They could include – or not include – Thea. 'He hasn't talked to me about staying. Loads of jobs on the Isle of Skye are seasonal, like here or Dunvegan Castle, or in hospitality at the hotels.' Thea knew she sounded pessimistic.

'Would you want him to stay?' Ezz's voice was soft.

Thea looked at her sister's dear face, pointed and pixie-like but full of love. 'Yes. But though Skye's been a healing place for him after what his wife and partner did, I'm not sure he loves it enough to make a life here, like I have. He's used to a high-powered job and his own business.'

'Why don't you ask him? I think you're great together,' Ezz argued.

'Not until I see if Fredek's able to cause trouble for me. I wouldn't drag Dev into that.' Thea felt tears scald her eyes.

When she reached home that evening, Ezz's questions remained in her head.

As usual, Daisy stationed herself between the kitchen units and Thea's legs, hoping for scraps to fall as Thea made her meal. She even placed her neat paws atop Thea's feet. 'Idiot,' Thea said affectionately, distracted enough from her gloomy reflections to 'accidentally' drop shreds of cooked chicken, just to watch Daisy pounce, gulp, then look up at Thea with a wagging tail and shining eyes.

The smell of cooking had filled the kitchen when Deveron called, his voice warm down the phone. 'What did the wee dawgie say to her owner?'

Thea smiled, heart lifting. 'I don't know. What did the wee dawgie say to her owner?'

He chuckled. 'She said, "Just follow my lead." And I think Daisy would like me to be there because I'm missing her owner something fierce.'

Warmth blossomed inside Thea. 'I miss you, too,' she admitted. Her bed had felt empty last night. 'And the wee dawgie says she'd love you to join in our evening walk to the beach, now the rain's cleared.'

She ate, feeling more cheerful, able to shelve the spectre of Fredek Kowski alongside her disappointment in Ynez. She had yet to open Ynez's notebook again, and had left it in her empty suitcase after unpacking the rest of her things.

By the time Deveron arrived, the village was enjoying a clear, warm evening, the rainbow colours of the Rothach cottages refreshed by the rain.

'Brought my swim things,' he reported.

'What a great idea.' She wriggled into her swimsuit and threw a dress over it. They strolled down to the beach, where the waves were skipping to shore and the clouds had retired to hover over the mainland, leaving the island its own sunlight to bask in. Thea and Deveron threw off their top clothes and paddled out, hand in hand, amongst the rocks poking their heads from the water like enormous seals, scuffing through seaweed and gritty sand.

'The water feels great.' Deveron scooped handfuls of clear seawater and let it dribble through his fingers.

'Arf,' complained Daisy from the sand, staring after them.

Thea laughed at her. 'Come on then. Your coat won't shrink.'

Daisy plunged in, paddling energetically, her ears blowing back in the evening breeze as gulls swooped to look at her. 'Hope they don't think she looks good to eat,' Thea joked. 'She's not big enough to fight them off.'

Dev, his good-humoured face creased in laughter, scooped Daisy up and sank into the water, managing an odd sidestroke with her on his shoulder.

'This is gorgeous,' Thea said contentedly, floating on her back and staring up at a sky assuming its evening streaks of pink and lavender.

Dev floated up beside her and nuzzled her naked shoulder. 'Paradise.'

They became chilly after a few minutes, so headed back to the beach to dry themselves while Daisy shook vigorously then zoomed up and down the beach barking.

The slope back up to Loch View made them pant, but soon Daisy was drinking thirstily from her water bowl in the kitchen of Thistledome. Before Thea could grab the humans a drink, too, her door-knocker clattered, and Daisy leapt up in a frenzy of barking.

'Shush, Daisy,' Thea complained, swooping up the frenetic canine as she unlatched the front door and swung it wide, expecting Ezz, as Fraser and Maisie would probably be indoors for the night by now.

When her eyes fell on who stood on her threshold, she gasped.

Fredek Kowski.

He stood awkwardly, as always, braced against his stick. 'Lovely dog,' he said, as Daisy burst into a fresh volley of arf-arfs from Thea's arms. He wore an unusually ingratiating smile. But then his gaze shifted to Thea's left and the smile vanished. 'Deveron,' he snapped. 'Weston hasn't put you on this story again, has he? I *told* him I'd got hold of Thea's home address from someone at the pub.'

Thea's gaze flew to Deveron. '*What*? What story? How does he know you?'

Dev looked as if he'd just been stabbed: mouth slack, eyes huge.

Thea watched the lines of his face shift from horror to chagrin. His eyes slid sidelong to her, those hazel eyes with their flecks of black and ginger. Eyes that had morphed from happy to hunted. 'I can explain,' he muttered.

Dimly, Thea realised Fredek was talking again, urgently, ignoring Deveron now in favour of entreating Thea. 'Did your sister talk to you about the World Marketing Influencer Convention in Glasgow? I'm the keynote speaker. It would be huge for me and my career if you'd be part of my presentation. I'm trying to break into the cruise circuit and there's going to be a scout there. In fact, there's a whole convention on a cruise liner next year . . .'

Slowly, Thea swung shut the door shut.

From the other side came a muffled, 'Bloody charming.'

Deveron's face was set in furrows of misery. 'I kept thinking I should explain,' he said. 'But then it would seem as if everything was blowing over. And when I developed feelings for you . . .' He moved closer, but she stepped back, clutching Daisy like a shield.

From outside came the slam of a door followed by the sound of a car drawing away, engine grumbling as if in disappointment at a wasted trip.

'What was blowing over?' she whispered. 'And what did he mean about someone putting you "on this story"? I'm a story?'

Deveron jammed his hands into his pockets. Miserably, he said, 'I used to provide copy for Everyday Celebs. I was commissioned to interview you and Fredek for the *Where are they now?* page.'

Her stomach knotted. 'Everyday Celebs – that horrible website? And "providing copy" means "writing the stories", right?' Thea remained behind the barrier of Daisy, who kept glancing round as if wondering why she was up in the air.

He nodded. 'Weston, the site owner, focused on your story from the start, even providing a travel budget for an in-person interview, as it was impossible to reach you by phone. It put off sleeping on Mum's sofa for a day to come and see if I could get the interview. When you thought I'd come for a job and to stay on Skye, at Rothach, it seemed like a gift. I immediately told Weston I couldn't write the piece.'

Thea's legs turned to water, and she stumbled blindly

303

backwards to the kitchen and half fell into a wooden chair. Daisy, looking puzzled, settled on Thea's lap. Deveron trailed after them. Thea had to lick her lips before speaking. 'Was saving Daisy staged, to get my attention?'

Horror crossed his face. 'Do you seriously think I'd throw a dog into fast water just so I could "save" her?'

'I don't know.' Thea cuddled Daisy, remembering that day and how she'd thought Deveron a hero, yet still found it weird that his car was stuffed with his possessions.

'Well, I wouldn't.' Deveron edged closer. 'Weston refused to let me kill the story because Fredek's a popular influencer and would bring a shitload of traffic to the site. We argued. But when he said he'd let Fredek write the piece, I couldn't let that happen, so I wrote it, but made it so positive that he complained I'd made you look like an angel.'

He went on, explaining, justifying, muddling her with phrases about ethical journalism and clicks and polls and advertising revenue. 'I was incandescent when Weston used my article as a springboard for the damning *You decide!* post. His readership's always ripe to be incited.'

She cut in. 'Did you arrange for Fredek to turn up with those smartphone filmmakers?'

'No.' His voice turned flat and weary, as if aware she wasn't sympathetic to his explanation. 'I kept trying to disassociate myself from the situation, but it was like trying to get rid of Japanese knotweed. You spray it, pour salt on it, dig it up, but every time you think you've killed it, up it comes again.'

She pictured the six-foot-high canes of knotweed with its heart-shaped leaves. 'Fredek knows no boundaries,' she agreed. 'Will you leave now, please?'

His mouth fell open. 'It might not seem like it, but I was trying to protect you.'

She gave a funny, harsh laugh that hurt her throat. 'I don't need protecting, especially not like that. Really, Deveron, just . . . *go*.' She buried her face in Daisy's fur and closed her eyes.

After several long seconds, she heard the front door opening and closing.

She wasn't sure how long she sat there but finally realised Daisy was restless over being used as a canine comfort blanket and let her jump down. 'Sorry,' she whispered.

Tomorrow, she'd have to talk to Ezz about what Deveron had done, because Ezz was as bound up in the horrible, shitty Fredek Kowski situation as Thea.

Then she buried her face in her arms on the table, howling out her pain that Deveron, the man who'd shared her bed, who she'd laughed with and cried on, had betrayed her. And only this afternoon *she'd* worried about *him* being dragged into the shitty Fredek Kowski situation.

When all along, he'd been part of it, writing the post that had been the beginning of the end of her serenity and security here on Skye. The *bastard*.

Chapter Twenty-Three

Thea was used to sleeping through the late dusks and early dawns of a Skye summer. Tonight though, she couldn't even sleep through the dark hours, but lay staring at nothing through dry, unseeing eyes.

If only she had Maxie's cheerful good sense or Vince's gruff but loving advice. But no matter how much she tried to summon her parents' voices from her memory, she fell frustratingly short.

She had no idea how to deal with Deveron's betrayal. He'd been deceitful. Untrustworthy. The idea of seeing him every day at Rothach Hall was abhorrent.

She had the authority to end his contract. He was a seasonal worker; a zero-hours, disposable, passer-through.

As it turned out, she needn't have worried.

By the time she'd dragged herself to work the next morning, Deveron had gone.

'Gone?' Thea repeated stupidly, when Ezz informed her.

Ezz nodded from behind the big desk Thea had trouble thinking of as Ezz's rather than belonging to Tavish

Macbetha. 'He was waiting for me to arrive, said it would be better for you if he left and gave me the key to his accommodation. Next thing I knew, his SUV was rolling out of the courtyard.'

'Right.' The conversation must have been taking place even as Thea walked up from the village. She sank onto the nearest chair. 'Did he explain what was behind him being here at Rothach?'

Ezz picked up a pen and twiddled it, blue eyes sad. 'I think I got the gist.'

Thea looked out down the empty drive, before facing her sister again. 'He's saved me the job of asking him to leave.'

For an instant, Ezz looked as if she might say something. But then she rounded the desk and pulled Thea into a huge hug. 'I'm always on your side, Thea. You know that.'

Thea snuggled against Ezzie, breathing in the scent of sisterhood. 'I do. Do you fancy dinner, later? We could go over to Plockton.' Anything rather than stay at home, alone but for Daisy, reality pounding on her like a sledgehammer.

'OK. I'll make a reservation and pick you up.' Ezz hugged her harder.

Somehow, numbly, brokenly, Thea struggled through the day.

Ezz must have given Hadley some background to Deveron's abrupt departure because he didn't even breathe Dev's name, but showed silent support by taking Thea to the café for shortbread and coffee. The café was full to bursting, the opposite of Thea's heart, which was as empty as a deflated balloon. As they left, Hadley said gruffly, 'I'll come back for October after my holiday, if you want me.'

The unexpected consideration sent hot tears spurting to Thea's eyes, and she could only nod and squeeze his arm.

As the day wore on, she tried hard not to think about Dev. She chatted to visitors as she worked in the walled garden and gave Daisy a lunchtime run to see Mary Pony and Clive Donkey, whom she'd neglected lately, comforted when they nosed her pockets for treats. Then she reworked the roster with Ezz, which mainly consisted of removing Dev from it with angry stabs of the delete button on Ezz's computer.

After work, she collected Bouncer and Scotty to go out with her and Daisy, choosing a route along Chapel Road to Low Road. She didn't want to visit the beach or Friday Furlong for fear of the memory of Deveron Dowie beside her, taunting her with the realisation that, despite her protestations, she'd harboured hopes that even if his job had been seasonal, their relationship would be full time.

Back home, she hurried through her shower, hair drying, dressing and make-up to be ready in time for Ezz to pick her up for the forty-minute journey to Plockton, over the soaring Skye Bridge, where the sat nav made it look as if they were driving over the sea, and along the coast.

Over dinner, Thea talked about Ynez and the notebook. 'I'm not sure what to make of her giving it to me. I've put it away for now.' She managed not to mention Deveron, which was quite a feat when every memory of Quimper and Ynez was inextricably linked with him.

Ezzie, the best sister in the world – or joint best sister, along with Valentina – played along. 'I can read it to you, if you want. You know, if you ever feel ready.' Her eyes might say she knew Thea was shrivelling up inside, but never once did the word 'Deveron' pass her lips, not even when Thea's phone rang in the car on the way home and she jumped on it with a flame of hope, despite her enormous sense of let-down and anger. Of course she wouldn't talk to Dev! But her heart yearned for him, as if it couldn't face the truth.

The caller wasn't Deveron. It was Valentina, 'Just to say hello while you're both together.' She managed not to mention Deveron either, so Thea knew Ezz had already told her that he'd gone.

They really were the *best* sisters in the world.

On Saturday, Thea set Hadley and Nell to mowing and edging the west lawn while she cut back leggy roses in the family garden – a quiet, isolated job. Deveron still hadn't tried to contact her. Maybe he'd run out of lies. She wondered where he was. Back in Dumfries? Now she'd met Pammie and Cyril and all of Deveron's lovely family, she knew they'd look after him.

Then she jeered at herself for caring what happened to such a horrendous fake.

When her phone rang, she was glad to give those thoughts a rest. 'Hey, Ezzie,' she said, expecting a query about staff hours or equipment servicing.

But Ezz sounded odd. Flat. 'Erm . . . something's come up. Can you come to the mud room door?'

Puzzled, Thea secured her secateurs and tucked them into her side pocket. 'On my way.'

She hurried across the courtyard, refusing to glance over at the patch of garden behind the staff accommodation that Deveron had made his own. It would be all weeds and long grass again soon, hiding his rockery and the evidence that he'd ever been there.

At the back door, Ezzie, her face a mask of compassion,

swept Thea into her arms. 'I'm so sorry. A man's on the landline. He thinks Daisy's his dog.'

Ice seemed to form around Thea's spine. She jerked away. 'What? How do they even know about her?'

'Those stupid-arse women who posted pictures of you on social media for that awful competition – in one of them, Daisy was running with you but glancing back over her shoulder. They think she's the dog that was stolen from their garden in Fort Augustus a while ago.' Ezzie rubbed Thea's arms, as if to warm her.

Thea sucked in a long, steadying breath. 'I'd better talk to him,' she said bleakly.

Ezzie fell into step beside her as they headed into the office. 'His name's Ruairidh Brown and he says their dog was called Beanie.'

It was a nightmare, Thea thought as she spoke to Ruairidh Brown on the phone. He sounded so nice, and so hopeful. 'My little girl's distraught over Beanie. I've no idea how she could have got from Fort Augustus to Skye, but it looks like her,' he explained awkwardly. 'A friend saw those pictures. They'd been around for a couple of weeks, evidently, but you know how things suddenly reappear on social media.'

'Yes.' Thea's voice echoed in her own ears. 'So, you think Daisy and Beanie are the same dog?'

'She is,' a little girl's voice burst out from the background. 'Isn't she, Daddy?'

Ruairidh, sounding embarrassed, murmured, 'Let me deal with this, sweetheart.'

Thea's broken heart wanted to throw as many obstacles as she could in the way of someone else claiming Daisy but the longing in that tearful young voice gave her pause. 'I suppose we'd better find out. Could you send me pictures of Beanie and I'll send you some of Daisy? Then we can compare.'

Eagerly, Ruairidh said, 'Thank you. And for looking after Beanie so well.'

He was *that* sure Daisy was Beanie? Pain tightened like a fist around Thea's heart. 'It wasn't me who saved her from drowning. But that person couldn't take her, and I could.'

'Drowning?' Shock rang in Ruairidh's voice.

Thea recounted the story, light on the Deveron involvement. She hoped that any thickening in her voice would be put down to the memory of Daisy's brush with death six weeks ago, rather than Thea's memory of a determined, curly-haired figure sprinting across the paddock to fling himself into the burn and drag out the bedraggled, malnourished dog.

By the time the call ended on the landline, Thea's mobile phone was pinging with photos of . . . well, a younger version of Daisy in a garden in Fort Augustus, at the south end of Loch Lomond, a couple of hours away.

Ezz, who'd waited quietly, gave Thea another huge hug. 'This is shitty.'

'Yes,' Thea agreed dolefully, as she selected half a dozen recent photos of Daisy to send in exchange. Within seconds, Ruairidh returned: *We think it's a match. Can we come and see her weekend 17th/18th August, please?* And, before Thea could reply, he followed up with: *We realise this is difficult for you. Thank you for making it easy for us.*

With a howl, Thea turned into her sister's arms and cried for the almost certain loss of Daisy, along with the rest of her heart, which had already gone with Deveron. Finally, when she'd regained control, she blew her nose and explained snuffily, 'Animals leave their pawprints in your heart.'

Ezzie answered, 'I know how much you love her,' as if Daisy was the only one Thea had been crying for.

It was hard to continue to work in Rothach's beautiful gardens as if her world wasn't imploding, but Thea had little choice. Nell and Hadley finished the lawn, leaving it smooth and green, and moved on to sweeping paths. Thea weeded the flowerbeds in the family garden. The memory of the day she'd berated Deveron for filming the family side of the hall filtered into her brain, but she booted it out.

She gracefully declined Ezzie's offer to spend another evening together, knowing it came from the bottom of her sister's huge heart. But after Ruairidh Brown's phone call, Thea longed to be alone with dear, darling Daisy who pranced and waggled a welcome when Thea got home, floppy ears pinned back and tail a furious fluffy blur.

Thea collapsed to her knees and gathered Daisy into her arms. 'I think we only have a week left together, so let's enjoy it,' she choked. 'And your first family sound lovely. You'll soon . . . forget me.' Daisy licked up the tears that bled hotly down Thea's cheeks.

After dinner, they went out for an evening ramble, waving to Fraser and Maisie sitting in Fraser's garden with friends. For once she didn't offer to take Bouncer and Scotty. Thea went on down Glen Road to the copse that joined Rothach village to Rothach Hall, steeling her heart to the memories of walking the leafy pathways with Deveron. Her life in Skye would go on, so she might as well get used to treading the routes they'd trodden together, alone. In the grounds of the hall, she even paused at the scrap of land he'd made his garden, where the last of the flowering thyme sprawled from the broken pot atop the rockery.

As they passed the staff accommodation, Daisy glanced at the door and then at Thea, as if wondering why they weren't going in. Finally, they trailed down the drive to visit Mary Pony and Clive Donkey, leaning on the gate and stroking their warm necks as Daisy stood on her hindlegs to exchange breaths, while Thea cried again.

After the return journey, Daisy curled up on her bed, while Thea stood and listened to the silence. Until Deveron left, she hadn't even realised how much she'd been hoping her single days were over.

Her eyes fell on the front door of her home, remembering seeing Fredek standing there, first berating Deveron, then wheedling for Thea to help him out at his stupid conference – World Influencer Crap Shit or whatever it was called. She'd rather read the complete works of Shakespeare.

Deveron's guilty shock at being caught out.

He knows the truth about the accident.

Her heart lurched and she covered her eyes. What if Deveron wrote – or 'provided content' – about it on Everyday Celebs? Supported Fredek's tale of recovered memories? Would he do it for the fee, having lost his income from Rothach Hall? Could she look forward to more visitors attempting to get selfies, or Fredek renewing his demands for an interview?

And the police asking to speak to Ezz and her?

Would she be forced to leave beautiful, wild Skye? Her heart recoiled. She loved this rugged island, with the green landscape disappearing and reappearing in the mist hanging over the silver sea. The sightings of dolphins or orcas, sea eagles or stags. She loved Rothach, both village and hall. Here she was at peace, away from the troubles of the world – or at least, she had been.

How she wished Maxie were alive to hug her. This was one thing she couldn't talk over with Valentina. And Ezz viewed herself as the cause of the whole shitty situation and needed comfort as much as Thea did. Who could she turn to?

A touch drifted into her mind, a touch on her arm that had hit her like a force field.

Her birth mother, Ynez.

There had been no communication between them since Thea ran out of her apartment above the restaurant, but what if Thea had been too quick to judge? It had been twenty-three years since she'd had a mother. In her indignation, had she thrown away a second chance at the special bond between child and mother?

Her mind strayed to the notebook Jean-Jacques had passed to her on . . . had it been only Monday? So much had happened that now, Friday, felt like a different year.

Thea *never* wanted to read books. Ever.

On the other hand . . . that fat little notebook would never come out in audio. And somehow it seemed wrong to accept Ezzie's offer to read it to her, intruding on Ynez's personal writing without permission. For the first time she thought how many hours it must have taken to produce an entire book of handwritten pages, and what it might have cost Ynez to send it to her without knowing whether it would ever be read.

She trailed upstairs to pull her suitcase from the wardrobe and retrieve the notebook she'd discarded so unceremoniously. Then she dropped onto her bed and gazed at the floral cover and remembered the painted flowers on the colourful table outside Côté Rivière. Flowers were always close to Thea's heart. They seemed close to Ynez's too.

Perhaps she'd wade through a page, she determined, turning dubiously to the slanting handwriting and the date early in May 1984. Then the first line jumped out at her.

Oh, Althéa-Dora, I did not realise I had so many tears to shed!

The hair prickled on the back of her neck as Ynez's voice floated into her mind: high, with a rhythm that was neither the Scots she heard every day nor the English of herself and Ezzie.

I have thrown away a good life with my child for another immature boy who used me. I hope he is eaten by worms. I will not use swear words because you are a nice, beautiful, perfect small girl. A 'toddler', Maxie calls you.

Althéa-Dora, I cannot give you a good life. Or I CAN give you a good life . . . but not with me. By giving you to Maxie and Vince, I have given you two good parents and two good sisters and no bad men.

Vince, he is worried to let me see you, or Valentina and Esmerelda, now I am, he says, a criminal. His concern is all for you girls.

I am a criminal. I write that word again, so I have no doubt that I know myself.

Thea blinked at the line, feeling the sorrow and regret in every syllable. For once, she had no need to coax herself to read another paragraph.

Vince and Maxie can give you good things. I love you too much to take you away, but my heart is ripped. We have agreed you will not know your story with the French criminal. I return to France today to find again my

*honourable parents and I will try to be honourable too.
I will try! I promise I will try.*

Then, if we ever meet, you will not need to be ashamed.

Tears began, and Thea had to put down the notebook
to blow her nose. But then she turned straight on to page
two to read of Ynez toiling at college on her return to
France as well as helping her parents at their café, biting
her tongue when her father harked back to her 'disgrace'
– Thea recoiled to realise that he meant Thea, the baby
Ynez had left behind. *And he does not even know his
daughter is a criminal,* Ynez concluded sadly.

Every one of Thea's birthdays had been marked by a
letter from Ynez's heart, declaring that she was *so
respectable now* and speculating about Thea's life with
Vince and Maxie. *I imagine whether you have dancing
lessons or horse riding. I dream of ways to visit you. But
Vince said, 'Better not', and he is right, perhaps. How
should I ever let you go again? You are a little English
girl. Mine, but not mine.*

Thea paused to blot her eyes on her T-shirt, remembering
her own words: *Didn't you even want to visit me?* How
had she not heard the accusation in her question, even
when Deveron had gently hinted that it had been there?

The pages seemed to turn themselves until, around the
time of Thea's tenth birthday:

*Do not ever go to prison, darling. Last night I dreamed
you did, with no freedom and bullies making gangs to
hurt you. I woke up and was sick. Do not EVER do bad
things to go to prison.*

Sweat beaded Thea's brow and she felt as guilty as if
Ynez had had a premonition.

Was her birth mother the one person who would
understand Thea's wrongdoing for Ezzie?

316

Though Thea literally couldn't remember the last time she'd read an entire book since conceiving such a distaste for reading at school, she read on and on, puzzling occasionally over Ynez's handwriting, her crossed sevens and the way she wrote Z, lighting the bedside lamp when the evening turned dark, learning of Ynez and her parents selling the café to start the restaurant, of their deaths – first Phillipe and then Sylvie-Marie – and Ynez feeling alone. Business struggles. Political changes in Quimper. Finally paying off the loans on Côté Rivière. Decorating the interior. Painting the jolly flowered tables where Thea had sat with Dev.

Missing her daughter. Missing her daughter. Missing her daughter. Blaming herself. Letters from Maxie ending and Ynez not understanding why. Should Ynez write? Or would Thea somehow find the letter and know the truth Ynez had agreed she should never know?

Thea's throat ached as she realised how much Ynez had truly loved her little Althéa-Dora.

The tone of the annual entries lightened around the time when Ynez met Jean-Jacques. *For the first time, I have a good man.*

Thea winced at that, thinking of Deveron's perfidy, and how she'd considered him a good man. She read on.

Jean-Jacques is kind and gives me smiles and affection without using it against me. There is an English phrase, that I forget. Ynez must have remembered it later as there was an arrow to a squeezed-in sentence: *He does not use my love for him as a stick to beat me with.* Thea smiled.

A final letter was tucked in the back of the book, dated the day Jean-Jacques had pressed the book into Thea's hand. It was written on pretty notepaper, with a posy of violets printed in the corner.

Monday August 5th

Dear Althéa,
   This is the last letter I will write to you. If we never meet again, I want you to know that it was only as you ran away that I realised my manner had become unpleasant. Angry. Perhaps rude. I was angry with MYSELF, for letting a stupid boy make use of me, which meant that I lost you. If you have read this journal, you will know that I longed and longed and longed to visit England and hold you again.
   Althéa-Dora, I love you. I always will. I am sorry if I could not make you know. I hope one day you can forgive me for leaving, but it was for you. For me? I would have swept you up and run away with you for ever.
   You have my telephone number and address. Any moment of any day, you will be welcome.

Then there was a small word, untidily written, which Thea eventually decided was 'Maman' and a kiss.

She stared at the French equivalent of 'Mum' and knew she *did* have someone to turn to, someone not Ezzie or Valentina, but who might understand. All she had to do was reach out.

She picked up her phone and, with shaking fingers, dialled. The single ringtone buzzed once, twice, then a groggy voice answered sharply, 'Althéa?'

Thea swallowed the lump in her throat. 'I've just read your notebook. And the letter. I'm sorry I ran away.'

Unsteadily, Ynez answered, 'I am sorry I was so bad at expressing the correct emotion. Always, I have been this way. But I am so glad to hear your voice.'

318

Thea sniffed. 'I'm not sure you will be. I called because I'm in a mess and think you might understand it. I'm sorry if that's a crap reason to get in touch but I don't know where to turn.'

'Then turn to me,' Ynez encouraged softly. 'Please.'

So Thea spilled out how she and Ezz were 'criminals', too, and how, if Fredek went to the police, it was possible they'd be in trouble. 'I knew I was breaking the law, but I didn't want Ezz to go to prison.'

'No, no,' Ynez agreed airily. She listened and asked questions. Eventually she said, 'I believe Esmerelda is right. You two have served a sentence that is worse than prison – endless fear of discovery – but the authorities will not agree. And this Fredek, tell me why he visited yesterday. What did he say that you were upset?'

Not wanting to muddy the water by bringing Deveron into it, especially as he was now so thoroughly out of her life, she explained. 'It was more of what he said to Ezzie on the phone – especially as when he called at my house I didn't give him much chance to try to blackmail me with threats of going to the police, this time. He wants me to speak with him at some influencer conference. Can you imagine? He said it was a huge conference, and he wants me to stand on the stage with him in front of everyone. I know I did some road safety talks with him a long time ago, but then he didn't know the truth.'

'What is this "influencer"?' Ynez interrupted, and they paused while she consulted the internet for the French word and found it to be the same. 'I do not like this social media,' she commented with a sniff.

'Me neither.' In fact, Thea hated it with bone-deep revulsion.

'*Bien*,' Ynez said thoughtfully. 'I have the name for this

bad website, and this Fredek. Let me read the internet and think.' Then, sounding suddenly unsure, she added, 'It is permitted that I telephone you back?'

'Of course.' Thea half laughed. 'Sorry that I wouldn't take your calls before.'

'We have too many apologies, Althéa,' Ynez said wistfully. 'Let us not say sorry to each other again. I will telephone you, perhaps tomorrow or Sunday.' Then she said, 'Is Deveron with you?'

'No. He's left Skye,' she said briefly. Then, though she'd meant not to speak of his part in the Everyday Celebs trouble, out it all tumbled, all the hurt and stupefaction at what he'd done.

'*Merde*,' Ynez said, making Thea think of Deveron once more. A hesitation. Then: 'Send to me his telephone number. Perhaps he knows helpful information.'

Thea's shoulders hunched in dismay. 'Oh, I'm not sure—'

'He will help because I will tell him he must,' Ynez said firmly. 'But first we must sleep well. *Bonne nuit*, Althéa-Dora. We will speak again, soon.'

'*Bonne nuit*,' Thea returned. Shyly, she added, 'And thank you. I needed someone tonight.'

And though Thea expected her demons to parade around her bed, she did indeed sleep, cocooned by the maternal love she'd read of in the pages of Ynez's notebook, which had prompted a cautious answering warmth in her own heart.

To some degree, she had a mother again.

Chapter Twenty-Four

All weekend, Deveron lay on his mum's sofa in her small apartment. Once Pammie realised how little he wished to talk, she whisked off on her usual round of social activities – book club with this friend, afternoon tea with that and a Women's Institute outing on Sunday – leaving Dev to wallow in his grief and remorse.

Though he stared at the pre-season footie coverage on TV, he felt no reawakening of the intense interest he used to have for it before his summer idyll on the Isle of Skye.

Over the earnest faces of the pundits, he saw Thea's shocked, hurt expression.

Above their segues to reminders of last season's action, he heard her shaky voice. '"*Providing copy*" means "*writing the stories*", right? . . . Will you leave now, please? . . . Really, Deveron, just . . . go.'

But on Monday, his mum evidently felt his pity party had gone on long enough, as Pammie woke him with an unceremonious shake. 'Get off your bahookie, Deveron. Fair enough if you don't want to tell me what happened with Thea, but you can be miserable *and* useful. Go and do your brother's garden because he and Caro are run off their feet. And take Grandpa with you for an outing.'

He saw his mum's reproachful frown and rolled to his feet, with a sheepish, 'Aye, OK.' Soon he was calling for Grandpa Cyril and then driving the lanes to Leith's family home in Lockerbie, trying not to think that last time he'd done so Thea had been with him.

'This is a rare treat,' Grandpa kept saying as they passed fields dotted with harvesters and tractors. 'A day in a garden, eh lad? Nothing finer.'

'True.' Deveron did feel an infinitesimal lift in his spirits as the summer breeze blew through the open car window.

They gardened together as they had in the years after Deveron's dad died, deadheading roses, trimming creepers, digging weeds, and discussing everything from butterflies to climate change. Anything apart from what had made Deveron exchange wild and craggy Skye for the green rolling countryside of Dumfries and Galloway.

Leith arrived in the afternoon to work from home. When Cyril went indoors to the bathroom, he took the opportunity to cock a knowing eyebrow at his little brother. 'Will you be off back to Skye?'

Deveron focused on the vine he was reshaping. 'I doubt it.'

Leith pulled a sympathetic face. 'Always here if you want to talk.'

But Deveron didn't. Or couldn't. The emptiness of losing Thea was too huge.

It was an hour later, when Leith was indoors shackled to his computer and Cyril was snoozing in a deck chair at the end of the garden, that Deveron's phone rang. His heart skipped, but it subsided into its natural rhythm when 'unknown number' flashed up. 'Yeah?' he answered discouragingly.

But the voice he heard made him straighten his spine. 'Deveron? This is Ynez Bourgault. Althéa told me what happened. I am very upset and astonished because I met you and you're not a bad boy. So, please tell me your side. No bullshit.'

He had to stifle a laugh at Ynez's plain speaking. 'Thea *told* you?' Hard to believe, considering she'd spent almost an entire week in Quimper refusing contact with Ynez.

'Yes, yes,' she said impatiently. 'She does not wish to go to prison, and she and Esmerelda are very worried by this Fredek. Why you wrote about Althéa we can deal with later. Please, describe to me why Fredek desires to be an influencer. Who pays him?'

Deveron brushed back his hair. 'An influencer constructs social media channels to attract followers. And where you get internet traffic, advertisers will pay to advertise. You can make a lot of money.' He flopped onto the grass and propped his back against a raised flowerbed as he went on to explain about measuring 'clicks' and page visits. 'He's working with Weston, who owns Everyday Celebs and has almost identical aims,' he rounded out. 'Two money-hungry click-baiters together.'

'Ah.' A silence drew out, presumably while Ynez considered. Finally, she said, 'I think we have Fredek's weak spot to press on.'

Deveron's stomach shifted. 'We have?'

'We can . . . I cannot think of the English word. Wait. I will look it up.' Ynez muttered in French too rapid for Deveron to catch, then, triumphantly, '*Manipuler*! Manipulate. If he likes to be popular and important, we can manipulate him.'

'Aye?' Deveron watched pearly white clouds stealing the sun, and wondered what Ynez was on about. Then he thought she might not be familiar with 'aye', and added, 'Can we?'

'Of course,' Ynez pronounced. 'But first you must explain why you worked with these people.'

So, he did, being frank about lowering his standards because he needed money and, when he tried to extricate himself, being outgunned by those less principled.

Presently, she said, 'You made wrong choices. I understand that. But you'd like to help Althéa, yes? I think we can.'

And as Deveron listened to her plan, the sun broke through the clouds like warmth returning to his heart. There was something he could do.

Late on Monday afternoon, Thea stared at her phone screen, hardly able to believe the message from Ynez. *I would like to visit you on Isle of Skye. How do you feel about this?*

She paused to gaze over the south lawn from her vibrating perch on the thrumming mower. How *did* she feel? Her sentiments regarding her mother had switched so abruptly from disappointment to acceptance that she barely trusted her heart.

She needed to talk things over with Ezz, whom she'd already updated after her Friday-evening heart-to-heart with Ynez. Abandoning the mower, she hurried into the hall and found her sister putting down the phone in her office. 'It's all very well for Grete to say that she wants more ponies for when the children come at Christmas, but you don't find them easily,' she remarked, waving Thea in.

As Ezz opened her mouth as if to continue, Thea plonked down her phone, exhibiting Ynez's message. Ezz's mouth snapped shut and her eyes grew wide. 'Ooh,' she breathed. 'How *do* you feel?'

'Full of butterflies,' Thea admitted. 'Scared. Cautious. And . . .'

'And?' Ezzie prompted, her blue gaze gentle. 'It's your life. She can't come into it if you don't want her to.'

Heat rushed into Thea's eyes, and she clamped her hands over them. 'I want her to,' she whispered. 'But I'm scared. This summer's been like a set of emotional millwheels, grinding me up. Finding Ynez. Losing Deveron. Threatened by Fredek. About to lose Daisy.'

'Fredek's gone quiet about the conference. And the police haven't turned up,' Ezz said, holding up crossed fingers but with an apprehensive expression that suggested she didn't believe in finger-crossing power.

'A bit odd, since he was trying blackmail not long ago. But we don't know even if his stupid conference has taken place yet,' Thea pointed out. She summoned a smile. 'Anyway, out of the four emotional millwheels, only finding Ynez has the potential to become something good. I'll tell her she can come.' She picked up her phone and replied before she lost her nerve. *I would like you to visit. I have a spare room, but it's small.*

Her phone pinged straight away. *I too am small. I will fly to London tomorrow and take the overnight train to Glasgow. Then I must see. I do not like driving on your side of the road.* Then, a new message. *You live in a remote place!*

Thea found herself smiling as she typed back. *You're setting off tomorrow?? Yes, Skye is remote.* Then her phone rang in her hand, and she answered to hear Ynez's rapid delivery. 'Jean-Jacques, he says it is two or three trains

325

from Glasgow to Kyle of Lochalsh, near Skye. Or there is a bus. When you came to Quimper, I didn't realise the journey was so inconvenient.' She sounded anxious.

Thea found she wanted to reassure her. 'Public transport's not necessarily quick, so why don't I collect you from Glasgow? I can usually borrow Ezz's car.' She raised an eyebrow at her sister, who nodded, making her hair shake around her face.

Still, Ynez hummed and hawed. 'It is a long drive between Skye and Glasgow, especially for twice in one day. I would like to see Glasgow a little. Will you meet me there on Wednesday? I will book two rooms and then we can drive to Skye on Thursday.'

'I can drive there and back in a day,' Thea said hastily, thinking with dismay of two days spent away from Daisy when she was so close to losing her for good.

In a small voice, Ynez answered, 'I would like to see the city.'

Hearing her disappointment, Thea glanced again at Ezzie. 'I think I'm OK to change my rest days to Wednesday and Thursday, aren't I?' When Ezz nodded, Thea said to Ynez, 'OK, but I must be back at work on Friday. And especially on Saturday.' Her heart tripped up. Saturday was the day the Brown family were coming to collect Daisy. At least Ynez being around might distract Thea from the horrible pain of losing the dog she'd fallen in love with. 'And then you'll stay with me for the rest of the week?'

'I need to go now and prepare baggages and tickets,' was Ynez's only answer. 'We will talk on Wednesday when we meet.'

'OK,' Thea agreed, surprised at the speed at which the call was ending and that Ynez had left her plans open-ended.

'Oh,' said Ynez, as if something had just occurred to her. 'I hope you can arrive in Glasgow by lunchtime. I wish to take you somewhere in the afternoon. *Bisous!*'

And Ynez had gone.

Wednesday was only two days away and it felt unreal to Thea that they'd meet again so soon. Somehow, Ynez had seemed fixed among the colourful timbered buildings near the River Steir.

Then her mind returned to the here and now, and she glanced at Ezzie, who stared at her so expectantly that Thea recounted the arrangements so far, ending with: 'I'm not quite sure how I let myself be steamrollered into staying overnight in Glasgow.'

'Because she doesn't want you to drive both ways in one day,' Ezzie said soothingly. 'Just look forward to a lovely, stress-free visit from your mother.'

The thought cheered Thea. 'I will,' she declared. 'The whole finding-her thing's been a whirlwind, so maybe now's the time to relax and get to know her.'

Chapter Twenty-Five

Thea was astonished to learn that Jean-Jacques had arranged for Ynez to 'borrow' a two-bedroomed city-centre apartment in Dunlop Street, Glasgow, with parking. Ynez brushed away Thea's amazement. 'Jean-Jacques knows many people in business. He asked a favour.' Thea remembered that evening in the lobby of their Quimper hotel and the silver-haired man with the gentle smile. Although he'd described himself as a businessman, she hadn't thought of him as someone with far-reaching and useful contacts.

So, late Wednesday morning saw Thea parking Ezz's little yellow car in an underground car park and whizzing to a plush lobby in a near-silent lift, where she found Ynez waiting.

'Althéa!' Ynez beamed and treated Thea to kisses on each cheek. She wore a chic sweater with red trousers – Thea having had the forethought to warn her that Scotland, even in mid-August, would not be as warm as Brittany – and her hair was sleek and stylish.

Thea felt distinctly country mouse in her jeans and was

glad that she had something smarter in her overnight bag. She returned the kisses, though not with the same unselfconscious effusion as Ynez, and found she meant it when she said, 'It's nice to see you again.' Now she understood her mother's early defensiveness, she was able to forgive it and enjoy this opportunity to get to know her better.

There was another lift to the upper floors. Thea glanced at its thick carpet and concealed lighting. 'Jean-Jacques' friend is fantastically kind to lend us an apartment here.'

Ynez looked pleased. 'And so central. We are lucky.'

They arrived at the apartment to enormous windows overlooking the city and décor of contemporary grey and gleaming white. Each of its two bedrooms had its own bathroom. 'Wow.' Thea stroked the quartz island that formed the boundary between lounge and kitchen. 'My little cottage and the village are very different from this.'

'Good,' said Ynez comfortably. 'Big cities make nice visits, but I am looking forward to seeing your home.'

Thea hoped she could take Ynez at her word, because her bathroom here was bigger than the spare bedroom at Thistledome. But Ynez distracted her with: 'Jean-Jacques has booked us somewhere lovely for lunch.'

If Thea hadn't met Jean-Jacques in the flesh, she'd suspect him of being a figment of Ynez's imagination, a fairy godfather to explain away her extravagances. She swung her overnight bag off her shoulder. 'I'd better change.'

Ynez's sleeper train had arrived early this morning and she'd already found time to locate the restaurant in Princes Street. Though it occupied the ground floor of a grand sandstone building in the pedestrianised area, the restaurant itself was as contemporary and upmarket as the apartment, with acres of chrome and white.

It was only when they'd ordered wine – which Ynez considered essential – and salad, that Ynez's smile faltered. 'I hope you will not be angry,' she said, looking suddenly apprehensive.

Alarm bubbled through Thea. She was already getting the impression that her mother could be impulsive and unexpected at times. 'I hope so, too. Why might I be?'

Ynez's dark eyes had become troubled. 'The place I want you to come at two o'clock. It is the conference where this bothersome Fredek Kowski makes his speech.'

'*What?*' Thea couldn't have been more shocked if Ynez had suggested she ride one of the seals in Broadford Bay and she almost knocked over her wineglass. 'But that horrible, shitty article – he's going to talk about it. *Boast* probably. And he might even . . .' She caught herself and glanced around at the occupants of other tables with their white pristine cloths. Nobody was paying them attention, but she lowered her voice. 'He's going to say what really happened.'

Ynez reached for Thea's hands. 'I have studied Fredek online. He brags. Today he is on all his channels boasting about being the keynote speaker at World Influencer Marketing Conference, and talking of "excitement, connectedness, community".' She drew in a long, slow breath. 'His talk is called, "Crash victim to influencer".'

Thea broke out in a sweat. 'So, he *is* going to out me and Ezz as liars and criminals.'

Ynez's grip on her hands tightened. 'If we sit in the audience, under his nose, I do not think he will dare.' Her smile became grim. 'And if he does, you will leap to your feet and snort, like this—' she assumed an exaggeratedly disdainful expression and emitted a dramatic, disbelieving *puh!* '—and discredit, discredit,

330

discredit his story. He has not a single witness. You and Esmerelda have not been contacted by the police, so he cannot have given a statement. Fredek, he is full of air. You will make him look a liar and a fool.' She leant forward, her dark eyes intent. 'But I do not think he will get that far, when we are staring him in the face from the front row.' Then she added with the air of one prepared to be reasonable, 'If you do not wish to leap to your feet and shout, I will do it for you.' Her expression was eager, as if she might enjoy it.

Thea was no longer glad to see Ynez or have the opportunity to know her better. She felt sick and cold with resentment at being coerced. 'That's a rubbish plan. It'll never work. He'll just try and get me up on stage with him. He might even assume that's why I'm there – after he threatened me through Ezz.'

Ynez released Thea's fingers, looking disappointed. 'I understand that worry. I will go alone because if we do nothing, he wins. It does not take the police to make a criminal of you. Social media can do it very well. *Very* well,' she repeated. 'You know this already. You told me.'

'I never read social media,' Thea whispered. But she knew Ynez's reply before it came.

'Everybody else does.' She leant forward, hissing urgently, 'Althéa, he is already doing this to you. I am reading his social media. It is *good* for him that you are ignoring his posts. He talks of the garden television show you were on, and in the same post talks of his appearance at World Influencer Marketing Convention. He is using your name. If we do not challenge him, I fear he will feel confident enough to approach the police, just so he has more to talk of.'

* * *

An hour later, Thea knew she hadn't been so stomach-churningly terrified since the day she'd raced out of the village to find Ezz gazing in horror at Fredek Kowski bleeding on the ground. Gripped by the same dread of running towards danger instead of away from it, she followed Ynez to seats front and centre of the auditorium. Dumb with fear, she didn't even protest when Ynez calmly removed jackets with which people had reserved those seats and deposited them at the end of the row.

Brightly lit above the stage was a big screen, currently displaying an image of Fredek and, beneath it in dramatic red lettering:

CRASH VICTIM TO INFLUENCER
— making a living from almost dying

At the foot of the screen were Fredek's social media handles and:

#WIMCGlasgow #keynote #influencer

The huge image hovered like a threatening cloud, ready to rain down scorn and truth, only fuelling Thea's sweaty fear.

The auditorium began to fill. Two women, the owners of the jackets Ynez had disposed of so cavalierly, turned up to find 'their' seats occupied. Ynez pretended she couldn't speak English. '*Comment? Je ne comprends pas.*' The women retreated, defeated, but hurling daggers with their eyes.

Usually, the scene would have mortified Thea into giving up her seat, but today all her energy was focused on trying not to flee. 'These are crap seats, anyway,' she muttered. The stage was taller than the front row and the view was further inhibited by a row of wedge-shaped black boxes of footlights. Ynez had wasted her time bulldozing them into these supposedly under-the-nose-of-the-speaker seats because in actuality they were out of the natural eyeline of anyone standing centre stage.

Any last drops of faith Thea might have had in Ynez's plan to discredit Fredek drained away. Unable to even look at this stranger who'd given birth to her, she closed her eyes and wished that old-neighbour Lois had never chirped up with Thea's adoption story.

The lighting in the room altered. Conversation sank to whispers. A blast of music heralded a tall, tanned woman with turquoise hair swanning onto the stage as if more used to a red carpet. Thea could just about see her above the footlights, and from that vantage point it looked as if a microphone stand rising from the floor would go up her nose. Magically, it positioned itself to capture her rousing greeting. 'Yo! You're all as glad as me to be here. Let's hear it for WIMC Glasgow!'

Everyone except Thea and Ynez applauded and whooped.

Graciously, the woman accepted the applause, before her voice became softer and more confiding. 'It's my pleasure now to introduce our keynote speaker.' Then she switched back to the enthusiasm of a political leader whipping up her audience, with motivational phrases like: '. . . making lemons from lemonade . . . creating robust income streams . . . a far-ranging, exciting, complex campaign . . .'

Thea decided she would be sick. Right there, in front of the stage. That would bring this nightmare to an end.

Then the woman howled, 'Fred . . . ek . . . *Kowski*!' and the audience applauded.

And there he was, though at the same odd, foreshortened angle above the bank of lights as the MC – on two crutches, rather than his usual stick – nodding and smiling as he took the microphone.

'Thanks for that WIMC welcome,' he began. 'My name's Fredek Kowski. I'd like to invite you back in time to when I was a fitter man who, in an instant's absent-mindedness, paused astride my bicycle . . . and seconds later found myself flying across the bonnet of a moving car.' The introductory backstory was clearly designed to curry audience sympathy and he utilised a ringing delivery interspersed with significant pauses to allow his audience to suck the import out of every single word.

'And in that moment, I became a statistic—' meaningful pause to stare around the audience '—and I lost my health and my ability to work as a mechanic.' He assumed the hushed tone of doom. 'And as I was self-employed, I lost my business.' Another stare.

On and on he went, slides appearing on-screen to step his audience through his cleverness in using 'the most terrible moment of my life' as a springboard to becoming a self-made expert on road safety and cyclist responsibility, and going on to his career as an influencer, growing followers on social media, curating a flow of blog posts, appearances, motivational speaking and videos. Thea supposed the MC had been right in saying he'd made lemonade out of lemons, but her own sour view of him translated it as taking advantage of every opportunity for a publicity-hungry, attention-seeking, self-important arse to get his name out there.

She glanced along her row at a host of avid expressions. There was no doubt that he captivated his audience. She tried to imagine herself leaping to her feet and snorting with derision as Ynez had suggested, but knew her panicked voice would cling to her throat and refuse to emerge.

'So, my podcast, YouTube channel, TikTok and all my other social media began with an accident,' Fredek proclaimed, in case the audience had forgotten. 'And *then*,' he suddenly roared, 'the owner of the car that hit me—' Thea's breath halted. Not *the driver of the car* but *the owner of the car*. 'Thea Wynter was on the telly, on a show called *Garden Gladiators*,' he went on, 'so I got her to help me in my safety campaign. Until she . . . *vanished*.' A long, meaningful pause. Slowly, a publicity shot of Thea from her *Garden Gladiators* days faded in on the screen, a younger Thea with her hair short and, frankly, stripey; studs in her nose and above her top lip glistening. Thea wanted to close her eyes but could only watch, fascinated, as he brought his hand to his mouth as he pantomimed deep thought, the lenses of his glasses reflecting the spotlights.

He paused to settle his arms through his crutches, drawing attention to them. 'And I thought to myself . . . why would that be? Why would a woman used to the camera, used to semi-scripted shows, shun speaking engagements?' Pause. 'My mind returned a lot to that, over the years.' Pause.

He began to speak more briskly, as if moving on. 'A few months ago, I identified a new opportunity, a community news website called Everyday Celebes that has a popular "Where are they now?" feature, dedicated to digging up people who had their five minutes in the limelight. You may have heard of it. I thought, maybe their journalists could find her . . . and give me some answers.'

As Fredek opened his mouth again, a new voice broke in through the sound system, and a man strode onto the stage as if he owned it. 'And that's where I came in,' he boomed, beaming at the audience, tall and good-looking with recently trimmed curly dark hair. 'I'm Deveron Dowie, the journalist commissioned by Everyday Celebs.'

Thea turned to stone.

Ynez nudged her. 'It's Deveron,' she said unnecessarily.

And while Fredek gaped, Deveron, with a black box on his belt and a radio mic close to his mouth, stole his audience. 'We began with a video interview,' he said, as if this was a planned part of the presentation. On-screen, a couple of slides flicked through. The poor AV person in charge of the slideshow was probably searching the brief, trying to identify where they were up to.

While Fredek froze to the stage, Dev expounded joyfully, engagingly, about travelling to Skye at the editor's behest, then shaking his head over the frustration of Thea not wishing to co-operate.

Thea sat stupefied. What the actual fuck?

On and on Dev rolled, admiring how cleverly Fredek and the owner of Everyday Celebs had planned, about Dev writing a positive piece for Fredek to trump with . . . 'An exposé!' Dev brought out with a flourish. 'He wrote an exposé.'

He posed, his hand aloft, with the audience in the palm of it.

Then he turned to Fredek with a matey grin. 'But that's where you went wrong, wasn't it, laddie?' The 'laddie' lent a patronising touch.

Fredek plainly had no answer. None of this was in the script. *His* script, which he'd obviously prepared with painstaking care.

Dev whipped his gaze back to the audience. 'What did he do? Do any of you know? Anybody?'

And Ynez rose to her feet, drew herself up and shouted, 'He told lies!'

Hand swinging towards Ynez like a quiz show host congratulating a successful contestant, Dev boomed, 'He told . . . well, madam, let's not say *lies*.' He waggled his brows and the audience tittered. 'He said something *unbelievable* – let's call it that.' He gave Ynez a conspiratorial wink as she resumed her seat, and the audience outright laughed.

'Hey,' Fredek protested uncertainly.

Thea couldn't have interfered with what was going on before her if her life had depended upon it. For the first time she appreciated what was meant by the phrase 'a train wreck': that powerless, helpless feeling of having to look on as something awful happens.

Dev boomed over Fredek, engaging with the audience, keeping them on his side. He was the better-looking man, the more confident man, the one in control. 'The mistake Fredek made – and in any campaign mistakes are there to be learnt from, which is why it's part of his fantastic keynote speech – is that he wrote something too hard to swallow.'

He glanced at Fredek and grinned. 'Didn't you, laddie? I mean—' he swung back to the rows of listening people '—who believes that Fredek, *nine years after the accident*, suddenly, conveniently, *remembered that Thea Wynter had not been driving the car*?' Nobody in the audience moved. Neither did Fredek, who gazed at Dev in open-mouthed horror. Dev dropped his voice. 'Now, I'm not sure who *was* supposed to be driving the car – whether it was little green men come down to Earth or a ghost

337

– but it was not a believable tale.' He looked around the rapt audience. 'I mean, c'mon. Is there a single person here who believes that nine years after the event, Fredek suddenly regains a lost memory – maybe you had hypnosis or something, eh, Fredek? – and yet he doesn't go straight to the police. Anyone?' Everything about Dev's tone, stance and expression poured scorn on the idea.

Ynez shouted again, 'It was lies.'

And not a single audience member put up their hand. Thea glanced around to check.

Dev grinned at poor Fredek, who was mouthing like a fish. 'See, I was right, laddie. You got a touch carried away. But here's what you could have done instead . . .'

Thea hardly heard a word after that. She stared at this strange, unfamiliar Deveron Dowie who'd just hijacked Fredek's keynote speech and made the truth look false. And, so far as she could remember, without telling a single lie.

Vaguely, she became aware of Dev 'handing back to Fredek' who tried manfully to pick up his script at a point that was, she presumed, after the 'exposé' he'd planned, and Dev interpolating admiring comments and helpful prompts, allowing Fredek to stumble to a conclusion.

Dev called, 'Let's have a massive round of applause for Fredek Kowski, keynote speaker!' and backed off the stage as if to leave the limelight on the sweating, bewildered Fredek.

Ynez seized Thea's elbow. 'Now we leave.'

Thea somehow lurched to her feet. 'Did you know?'

'Hush,' Ynez hissed. 'Not yet.'

Thea followed – appropriately – like a child, as her mother towed her from the auditorium, out of the conference hotel and down a flight of steps to the pavement. Traffic grumbling through the city centre filled the air with fumes and Thea caught a glimpse of the greenish roofs of Glasgow Cathedral, then somehow, they were seated a café.

Ynez ordered espressos.

Thea stared at Ynez.

Though pale, Ynez smiled, albeit a small, wavering example. 'Yes, I knew.'

The coffee arrived, dark and strong. Thea daren't pick up the tiny cup for fear of dropping it. 'How?'

'I telephoned Deveron,' Ynez said composedly, though her eyes were apprehensive. 'Together, we contrived it. He has given many presentations and knew exactly what to do. How to introduce his own microphone to the set-up. How to discredit that horrible man. He called it rearranging the truth. He did this for you.'

'You telephoned him?' Thea tried and failed to imagine herself 'contriving' anything like the circus she'd just witnessed. But . . . he'd done it for her? A storm of butterflies began cartwheels in her stomach. She glanced around. 'Is he meeting us here?'

Ynez's gaze dropped. 'No. He told me to get you out, in case Fredek called security after he left the stage. Deveron didn't want you to be questioned – or maybe be put on social media again. He chose our seats carefully, out of range of cameras and behind the lights. The speaker can never see who's seated behind the lights.' Her gaze lifted again. 'He knows he has done things that hurt you, but he sent a message.'

'What?' Thea's voice emerged as a croak.

Ynez's cup trembled in her hand. 'He said that he hopes he has undone some of the wrong he did you. And—'

339

she put the cup down with a clatter '—I wanted to do the same. Surely, Fredek won't go to the police now Deveron has so publicly ridiculed his chance of being believed?'

Thea's heart galloped so hard she felt woozy. 'You two put me through the wringer, to "make up". But all you said this morning about jumping up and challenging Fredek . . . Why, when you knew what Dev was planning?'

'To persuade you to be there to see it,' Ynez said quaveringly. 'Or you might never believe how hard Deveron had tried to put things right.' In the tiniest voice, she added, 'Was I wrong?'

A hot tear leaked from the corner of Thea's eye. 'It's a relief that Fredek's been discredited,' she allowed. 'A huge relief, of course. But . . .' But she needed longer to think how much she minded that Dev's way of helping had been to manipulate her, using Ynez as his aide, and once again rearrange the truth. Somehow, Thea felt that if he'd done all that, he should be here with his big grin and newly trimmed hair and give her the opportunity to say, 'Well, that was like a nightmare, but thanks'? And then find a way to make her believe his methods were OK.

She burst into tears. Perhaps they were from relief or conversely from disappointment, but she felt unequal to explaining or justifying the complex ball of emotions inside her to Ynez, so choked out, 'I've missed two of my last days with Daisy.'

After a hesitation, Ynez slipped one arm about Thea, softly, gingerly, as if not sure her embrace would be welcome. 'I don't know who is Daisy but soon you will be home.'

Yes, that was what Thea needed – to be home in Thistledome, the heather tinging the landscape purple and the soft waves of Rothach Bay lulling her to sleep. That was where she always found peace.

Chapter Twenty-Six

They left Glasgow early on Thursday, Thea driving, emotions seesawing. On one hand she wanted to believe Fredek to be defeated and enjoy the car journey as an opportunity to chat with her mother; on the other, she'd thought she'd consigned Fredek to the past before and been mistaken. And now she had to deal with the horrible experience of losing Daisy.

For her part, Ynez took photos of the bridges and mountains they passed and had a long telephone conversation with Jean-Jacques, of which Thea understood *mon cher* and *bisous!* It didn't escape her that Ynez's love life was better than Thea's and the man Ynez loved didn't make use of his clever journalist's mind to present the truth any way he chose.

At the very bottom of Thea's heart, there was a tiny, curled-up shred of understanding that she was still processing her feelings about Dev.

She hadn't expressed her appreciation of what he'd done: not through a message via Ynez or even picking up her phone and calling him or texting.

But he hadn't contacted her either.

They ate a late lunch at Kyle of Lochalsh, just before Skye Bridge, then refuelled the car. While they visited a supermarket, the bridge was engulfed in sea mist, only reappearing before their vehicle as they drove, as if a big hand unrolled the bridge before them like a carpet on stilts.

Thea's mood steadied once she was on the island, hugging the misty coast for a few miles before swinging left across the granite-strewn moor towards Rothach. The car burst from the mist at the perfect moment to reveal the village laid out in its scoop of land, a scattering of coloured cottages with the grey turret of Rothach Hall visible above, between the pines.

Ynez clasped her hands. 'How charming.'

Thea smiled. 'It is, but also small. I hope you won't be bored, because I have to work.'

'I will not,' Ynez declared. 'I will walk or catch a taxi and explore.'

At Thistledome – Thea had to explain the 'this'll do me' joke – she found Ezz had left a posy of flowers in the kitchen, along with an invitation for Thea, Ynez and Daisy to join her for supper that evening.

Ynez beamed. 'Esmerelda wishes to meet me again? I should have brought her a gift. Perhaps I shall bake as she enjoyed my *galette bretonne* when she was a child. And do you think Valentina might visit?'

The joy in her voice made Thea smile. 'I'm afraid Edinburgh, where Valentina lives, is even further away than Glasgow.' Then the door knocker banged, and Daisy barked.

Thea hurried to the door, flung it open and, ignoring Fraser on the human end of the lead, scooped the dog into her arms. 'Have you missed me?'

343

The poignancy of Daisy's licking, whining demonstration of having missed Thea very much made tears start, but Thea grinned through them. It would be a poor last couple of days together if she allowed herself to sink into misery. 'Thanks, Fraser. Won't you come in for a cuppa and meet Ynez? Hiya, Scotty,' she added, stooping to pet the black terrier at Fraser's feet. She elected not to refer to Ynez as her mother, mainly because that still felt new and weird, but also because she was tired from the long drive and didn't want to explain.

Instead, she called Maisie and invited her and Bouncer over, too, and the four humans sat together in the garden over tea and biscuits, while the three dogs played a complicated game of tag before flopping down in the shade to pant.

'The Isle of Skye is so beautiful,' Ynez said, endearing herself to Maisie and Frasier immediately.

'Och, aye,' Frasier said. 'Is it anything like where you live?'

'Perhaps the coloured houses, a little,' Ynez allowed. 'But I live beside rivers, not the sea, and I have nothing like this.' She indicated the sheet of rock that formed the end of Thea's garden.

Thea occasionally translated the Hebridean accent for Ynez, and joined in with the chatter, trying to ignore the twin losses of Daisy and Dev while she built up an ever-deepening impression of the interesting character who was Ynez, liking her again now, and wondering if she'd always have mixed feelings about her.

After Maisie and Frasier had gone home for supper, Thea drove Ynez in Ezz's yellow car to Chapel Road, beginning to suffer the spaced-out feeling of one who has slept too little and worried too much.

When they arrived, Ynez laughed at Ezzie's meadow-like garden and said, 'So many lovely wildflowers.'

Ezzie opened the door in time to hear this. 'At last, someone who appreciates my taste in gardens. Hello, Ynez.'

Ynez kissed Ezzie's cheeks. 'You remember me?' she asked.

'I'm afraid not,' Ezzie was forced to admit. 'But welcome anyway.'

Ezzie had cooked a deliciously British roast dinner, which made Ynez clutch her cheeks and breathe, 'Oh no. I have just remembered brussels sprouts.'

Laughing, Ezzie said, 'They're not compulsory.'

'Phew,' said Ynez. 'Now let me see how many likes and dislikes of you and Valentina I remember.' She touched one fingertip to her chin in thought. 'You liked cakes and chips, and hated sardines and beef soup. Valentina liked oranges and chocolate but would not eat baked beans. Valentina was the organiser, choosing your games and making tents from old sheets but you wouldn't always do as she told you. We all liked to picnic in the back garden,' she added reminiscently. 'Thea would crawl off the blanket and try to eat grass.'

Thea was fascinated by this view of the past. 'I know I was there, but it feels as if you're talking about other people.'

Ynez's shoulders rose and fell on a sigh. 'Our much younger selves always feel like other people.'

After supper, Ezzie sat back. 'So what happened in Glasgow?'

Thea's smile faded. 'It was like something from a movie.' She hesitated and glanced at Ynez, not wanting to be too frank and disturb the uneven bond developing between them.

345

Ynez, however, was unafraid to own up. 'I'm afraid I interfered.'

Between them, they filled Ezz in on Ynez and Dev's plan to discredit Fredek, and Deveron's masterful execution of it.

Ezz bit her lip. 'But we don't actually know Fredek won't go to the police. It's not as if he said he won't.'

'He didn't say much at all,' Thea agreed hollowly. Ezz was right. That horrible experience in the auditorium could have been for nothing.

Ynez, though, was more positive. 'But many of his social media followers are speaking out. Some have posted video clips of Deveron making Fredek look a liar. He will want to put it behind him now.'

'Really? I didn't think of his followers turning against him.' Because Thea's phone didn't have a single social media app on it, of course.

'Even if they do not turn against him, they judge, and he will wish to let it die down,' Ynez clarified, the pucker between her eyebrows suggesting it was important to her to convince Thea. Then, to Ezzie she confided, 'Deveron was very good.'

Thea, remembering the shock of him taking the stage, impressively at ease – and annoyingly attractive – said, acerbically, 'That all depends on your interpretation of "good".'

To focus on happier things, after dinner, they FaceTimed Valentina. 'Don't mention anything to her about Fredek,' Thea warned. 'Valentina's a lawyer.'

'I understand.' Ynez even managed to look vaguely surprised that Thea would have to warn her to be careful.

Valentina was dressed to go out when they caught her, hair swept up and pearls at her ears. 'Barnaby's in bed,' she told them. 'We have a sitter as Gary and I have tickets to see an Indian dance company at the Festival Theatre.' Then she smiled. 'I wouldn't have recognised you, Ynez, but it's good to see you.'

'She remembers you,' Thea put in. 'Apparently you hated baked beans and were bossy.'

'Still the same,' Valentina laughed, then she chatted amiably to Ynez until her smartwatch beeped to tell her it was time to leave for the theatre. She was, after all, the only one of them who thought she could dimly remember Ynez, the au pair who came to Suffolk to look after two girls and ended up leaving another behind.

When Thea recognised that as an unproductive thought, she yawned, and, as Valentina had said goodbye, 'I need to go home to bed. Thanks for letting me borrow your car for the last couple of days, Ezz.'

She clipped on Daisy's lead to the dog's jaunty tartan collar, and she and Ynez set off along Chapel Road.

'It isn't properly dark at nearly ten o'clock,' Ynez observed, glancing over at the Jolly Abbot, then stepping around a hydrangea lolling over a wall.

Thea stifled another yawn. 'In June, it's ten-thirty before dusk even starts to fall. In winter, we get very short days but then you do get the Northern Lights.' The sky had turned a steely grey-blue and the gulls had quieted. As they climbed, they caught glimpses of the bay and the sea fading into evening mist, a couple of bobbing lights indicating moored yachts.

'You have chosen to live in a lovely village.' Ynez sidestepped so Daisy could take what she obviously saw as her rightful place between the humans.

Thea felt a tiny spark of pleasure and supposed the desire to please a parent lurked inside everyone, no matter

347

the odd circumstances of parentage. 'Maybe tomorrow evening we could visit the beach. It's a small bay but pretty – natural and completely unspoilt. I love it.'

'Then I will love it too,' Ynez declared. And finally, they reached the path to Thistledome and a completely unobscured view of a beautiful Skye twilight, just fading to lavender. 'In fact, I love it already.'

Friday flew by. Thea arranged things so she could work in the private family garden, to ensure she could take Daisy to work. Each edge and hedge was trimmed to within an inch of its life by the end of the afternoon whilst Daisy happily lolled in the sun.

Ynez had decided to take a bus to Portree, enabling her to see a nice swathe of the island. Thea wouldn't have to worry about her until they ate together that evening. She was beginning to feel easy in Ynez's company, as her birth mother had been a perfect guest since arriving in Skye, exclaiming with joy even over the sloping ceilings of Thistledome.

But then Saturday came.

Thea awoke with a feeling of doom. She found Ynez drinking coffee in the kitchen. 'It's today the man called Ruairidh Brown's coming to the hall to reclaim Daisy.' It broke Thea's heart to think of losing the 'wee dawgie' and, in the safety of the shower, she'd shed hot tears. Daisy scampered over at the sound of her name, and Thea knelt down to pet her fluffy head.

Ynez sighed. 'Fraser and Maisie have invited me to join them and their friends at the Jolly Abbot for lunch, but I can come to work with you, if you want somebody nearby.'

Thea considered for a moment, struck by having the

option of maternal support but also imagining Ynez trying to 'contrive', as she'd 'contrived' with Deveron, to manufacture a favourable result for Thea. 'I think I'll be better on my own. But thanks.'

She brushed Daisy, having some mad thought of having her look gorgeous when the Browns turned up. Half an hour later, they bid Ynez farewell and climbed the steep path from the village and through the copse to the hall. Thea was glad their last walk was alone, when the sun was shining, and Daisy snuffled along happily with no idea that this day was different to any other work day. Thea blinked back tears. Ruairidh Brown and his daughter were due between ten-thirty and eleven, so at least there wasn't long to agonise.

At the hall, Hadley and Sheena were already piling the last of the bedding on the garden cart. Thea said, 'I'll dig out those ash seedlings from the burn before they get a proper hold. They'll be forty feet high in ten years.' It was a task that would allow Thea and Daisy to be alone.

'Aye, good,' said Hadley, clapping Thea on the shoulder, which was his version of a hug.

Thea trailed off to grab two forks from the gardeners' room, intending to use them back to back to lever the more stubborn seedlings from the ground. She couldn't bear to tie Daisy to the fence, so tied the long lead to her belt, which meant Daisy assumed her function was to jump up to lick Thea's face whenever she bent over, even though Thea, wearing rubber boots, was up to her shins in water.

'You daft dog,' she spluttered. 'I don't know why I bothered brushing you. The wet parts of you are rats' tails.'

349

Eventually, Thea just sat and cuddled Daisy on the bank, watching the burn bubble past. 'Don't miss me too much,' Thea whispered, as Daisy licked her cheeks. 'I'm sorry you were never really mine.'

Then Thea's phone rang, making her jump, and Ezz, oozing sympathy, said, 'The Browns are here. Call me back when you're in the courtyard and I'll bring them out.'

'Yeah,' Thea agreed dully. She grasped Daisy's lead in one hand and the forks in the other, and prepared to meet her doom, Daisy dancing inappropriately gaily beside her. Even less appropriately, she remembered one of Dev's 'wee dawgie' jokes. *Why couldn't the wee dawgie dance? She had two left feet.*

Then, as she trudged along the old paving of the courtyard, she became aware of a tall figure on a collision course with hers and Daisy going into her waggly greeting routine, snuffling and whining. Thea stopped. The figure stopped, curls blowing and hazel eyes cautious, clearly uncertain of his welcome.

Thea's stupid, unreasonable heart began to march in double time. 'What are you doing here, Deveron?'

'Arf!' shouted Daisy, who, though straining at her lead, couldn't quite reach the one she obviously wished to hurl herself upon.

Both Thea and Deveron took one step forward, and Dev crouched to rub Daisy's ears and head, while Daisy whined and wagged and licked his hands. He looked up at Thea, squinting against the sun.

'Wanted to see Daisy,' he said gruffly.

Thea realised that Daisy wouldn't be here if not for him. 'Who told you she's going back today? Ynez? Or Ezz?'

'Ynez.' He turned his attention to Daisy, who rubbed her head against him in joy.

'You and she are quite the conspirators,' Thea observed. 'It's fair you have a few minutes with Daisy. You were her heroic rescuer. I'll go in and see the Browns. I want to be sure they'll look after her properly this time.' She tossed the end of the lead in his direction, off-balance, angry and sad, but not completely certain why and at whom.

She marched towards the mud room door, uncaring of his eyes on her back. She arrived in Ezz's office complete with dirty boots and a shitty attitude.

She did clear her frown when she saw a kind-looking man holding the hand of a blonde, frizzy-haired little girl. The man wore a rueful but hopeful expression. The little girl bounced on the spot. The man was saying, 'Calm down, Dulcie,' when Thea arrived.

Ezz looked surprised, raising an eyebrow, clearly questioning why Thea hadn't stuck to the plan to call her from the courtyard, but merely said, 'Here's Thea. Thea, this is Ruairidh and Dulcie.'

'Hello.' Ruairidh smiled tentatively. Thea managed a stiff smile in return, then she looked at little Dulcie and her bad attitude leaked away. The sunny little face held so much hope and joy, and she was about the same age as Barnaby. It certainly wasn't this pixie's fault that Deveron turned up without warning and dangerously rocked Thea's apple cart.

'Hello, Ruairidh and Dulcie,' she managed.

Then she said to Ruairidh, 'I just wanted to check with you about microchipping. Daisy didn't have a chip, or a collar, or we could have got her back to you right at the start.'

Guilt stole over Ruairidh's face. 'She was wearing a collar when she was taken, but that's easily removed. I kept meaning to get her chipped. I'm rubbish with admin and organisation and she was only a few months old.'

'It's the law that she has one, though,' Thea couldn't help pointing out. Then she realised that she hadn't had Daisy chipped either, though she'd meant to within a few weeks of fostering her. 'Bad at admin' was her default, too. 'She was about eight months old when she was found, the vet thought.' With Dulcie listening, she forbore from admitting that poor Daisy had been as thin as a stick.

Ruairidh pulled an agonised face. 'Aye. Maybe she was more than a few months.'

Looking from Ruairidh to Dulcie and back again, Thea wondered if he had a problem like hers. For him to be so uncertain seemed more than just being admin-shy. Obviously, she couldn't ask.

'Where's Beanie?' Dulcie asked shyly.

Thea swallowed. 'Let's go see her,' she said, with a horrible, heart-sinking sensation of bowing to the inevitable. She led the way over the wonderful tiles of the reception area to the door marked 'Staff access only' and out through the mud room.

In the courtyard, Deveron still crouched beside Daisy, smoothing her ears and murmuring, feeding her the tiny bone-shaped dog treats that were her favourite. He must have brought them for her especially. Thea heard Ezz give a quiet, 'Oh!' when she saw him.

He straightened up and glanced at Thea as if looking for a cue, nodding to the others. Heart breaking, Thea took Daisy's lead, careful not to touch Deveron's hand. Daisy went into her waggle dance, and it was impossible to know whether her greeting was for Thea or her first family. Thea turned round and cleared her throat, trying desperately not to cry.

Then she realised Ruairidh and Dulcie had halted.

'Oh dear,' murmured Ruairidh.

Dulcie's beaming smile sagged off her face. 'She's too wee,' she whimpered.

Trying not to let herself hope, Thea looked at Ruairidh. He rubbed his chin. 'Unless you've shrunk her, that's not our Beanie. My goodness, she's like her – except about four inches too small.'

The courtyard seemed to pirouette around Thea as the truth of his words sank in. *It wasn't Beanie. They couldn't take Daisy away.*

Dulcie buried her face in Ruairidh's jacket, and he curled over her, trying to shelter her from hurt with his body while he crooned, 'I'm sorry, darlin', I really am.' He glanced up at Thea. 'And I'm sorry to have put you wrong about Beanie. I suppose the first photo we saw was you running and maybe the dog looked bigger.'

Deveron spoke for the first time, his voice soft with sympathy. 'Thea's not the tallest. Maybe Daisy looked larger in comparison.'

'Ah, well, Deveron knows all about tricks of perspective, so I expect that's it,' she told Ruairidh, refusing to look Deveron's way. 'I'm so sorry, Dulcie. You must be disappointed.'

Dulcie nodded without showing her face, and Ezz and Thea exchanged 'this is sticky' looks. Ruairidh tried simultaneously to comfort Dulcie, apologise to Thea and thank Ezzie. 'I shouldn't have brought Dulcie with me, but there's just us, and I've no one to leave her with.'

Ezz's heart was plainly touched. 'How about we take you to the café for brunch?' It wasn't much of a sop for the disappointment of discovering that Daisy wasn't Beanie, but Dulcie did nod, choking out, 'Can the lady with the doggy come too?'

Thea said, "Course I will. It's warm enough to sit outside. Daisy's not allowed inside, you see.' When she turned to glance at Deveron, she found that he was already walking away, back stiff, his long strides carrying him around the corner of the greenhouse and out of sight.

She bit her lip. Her 'Deveron knows all about tricks of perspective' had been waspish and uncalled for. Wherever he'd been since leaving Rothach, he'd turned up in Glasgow just two days ago, apparently solely to help Thea out of the jam with Fredek, and now he was back here, a drive of several hours north. She should at least invite him to brunch. 'Give me a minute,' she said to Ezzie, and followed him, Daisy trotting alongside.

But when Thea rounded the corner, she couldn't see Deveron, not even in the Project Deveron garden, and she didn't know if he was heading for the car park, or for a walk in the woods, or into the greenhouse to try to find Hadley. He was just gone.

There was nothing for it but to catch up with the café-bound party.

There, Dulcie's eight-year-old heart was soothed by a haggis burger, a milkshake and a brownie. Thea and Ezz drank a quick coffee with her and Ruairidh to be sociable, then excused themselves to return to work.

As they headed back towards the hall, pausing occasionally to let Daisy sniff, Ezz said casually, 'So . . . Deveron?'

Thea shrugged. 'Appeared and disappeared.'

Ezz linked Thea's arm. 'That wasn't a "couldn't care less" voice.'

Thea mumbled, 'I suppose I might have talked to him if he'd stuck around.' Dismay crept up on her. She'd been offish and rude, still upset that he'd pulled that stunt at the World Influencer Marketing Convention and then kept away, after putting her through that.

By now she was so confused that she wasn't sure if she was angrier about his colluding with Everyday Celebs, Fredek or Ynez. Or staying away . . . 'It's nearly lunchtime,' she said. 'I'm going to walk Daisy home and leave her there. I tried to dig seedlings out of the burn this morning and she kept joining in. Didn't you, fluffball?' And when Daisy wagged enthusiastically, swooped her up and cuddled her tightly, hardly able to believe she was still there. 'And my very next day off, I'm going to take you to the vet's for chipping, and then you're mine.'

'Arf,' agreed Daisy.

'You could probably do with an hour on your own, you two,' Ezz said shrewdly. 'See you later, little sis.' She gave Thea a big hug before putting on a spurt and heading for the hall, blonde hair lifting in the breeze and heels tapping on the pavers.

An hour to herself *was* a good idea, Thea realised, heading past the staff accommodation to the footpath. She needed to reset her dials to zero and return to work this afternoon as the competent head gardener, with all the bruises from the implosion of her life masked. This evening, she'd take her mother to the beach, as promised, and continue to get to know her. Ynez had come a long way to show Thea her love.

'C'mon, Daisy,' she cried, trying to feel carefree, and together they careered downhill with gravel and pine needles crunching underfoot.

Chapter Twenty-Seven

She was back at work an hour later, her dog secure and an appointment made at the vet in Armadale for Daisy to be formally microchipped.

After that, a deep breath later, she'd tried to call Dev. He had not picked up.

As she tramped uphill to Rothach Hall, she listened to the birdsong and the breeze soughing through the trees, and acknowledged that summer romances ended for many reasons, and the reasons hers had ended were more complex than most.

But as she drew close to the hall, she heard a distinctive ululating noise nearby. A strimmer.

Her steps slowed as she emerged into full sunlight.

The wail of the strimmer came from her left, closer than the family garden and much closer than the drive where Sheena and Hadley would be working, if they'd even returned from lunch yet. Heart thumping, she turned behind the staff accommodation to Deveron's garden.

And there he was, yellow ear defenders clamped to his

head, green strimmer arcing through the overgrown grass: *ee-ow, ee-ow.*

Though her heart jumped with gladness, it also shrank when it remembered what Deveron had done. The things he'd hidden. The strimmer's yowl died. Gaze on her, he removed his ear defenders. Thea found herself thinking waspishly once more. 'Why did you come? To rescue Daisy again?' she asked.

His expression shuttered. 'No, I knew you'd do what was best for her. I'm guessing from your tone you didn't like what I did in Glasgow?'

She stepped closer. The familiar scent of fresh-cut grass was sharp in her nose from where he'd trimmed the grass around his cute rockery and blue bench and table. 'Ynez said you wanted to make up for what you did.' She kept her voice neutral.

With a sigh, he let the strimmer topple at his feet. 'Aye. That's it, pretty much.' His gaze roved over the patch of ground on which he'd spent his off-duty hours . . . when he hadn't been writing for a sensational website.

'The scales might be balanced, but trust doesn't turn on like a tap,' she said stiltedly.

'Aye.' Wearily, he hooked the ear defenders over his arm and the strimmer over his shoulder. She'd seen him the same way a dozen times, though in green uniform rather than jeans and a rust-coloured T-shirt that brought out the streaks in his eyes. He glanced around, as if bidding Project Deveron goodbye, and turned away.

She heard herself add, 'But maybe it should.' She crossed to the blue bench and flumped down as if her strings had been cut. 'I lied for Ezz. I broke the law. And I'd do it again in a heartbeat.' A pause. He didn't turn, but he'd stopped walking, so she knew he was listening.

Sometimes people do the wrong thing for the right reasons.'

He turned, dropping the equipment to the ground.

Thea's voice wobbled. 'Did you have to put me through the wringer at that freaking conference? I thought everything was going to blow up in my face. Could I trust you not to spill the beans if someone offered you a fee to write about it? Would Fredek back you up? I'd be arrested and Ezz, too . . .' She paused to swallow sudden, helpless tears that welled in her throat. 'I was frightened,' she said. 'And that made me angry with you and Ynez for taking *my* life into *your* hands.'

His brow puckered and he came to sit on the bench, leaving air between them. 'I see that,' he admitted, in his soft accent. 'But we weren't convinced you'd play along, even though Fredek thought nothing of trampling all over the new life you'd made for yourself.' He turned to look at her, his eyes flashing green and black and ginger in the sunlight. 'I'm glad you admit that we all compromise our morals sometimes. I'm sorry I was ever involved with Everyday Celebs, but I was at a low ebb and out of options. But without that connection, I would never have come to Rothach, never had saved Daisy and never had had a fantastic summer on Skye. With you.'

He inched towards her, frowning, his gaze urgent. 'See, Ynez and me, we both love you. We wanted an end to the fear and uncertainty you – and Ezz – have been living under. I'm sorry if you hate our method but, like you, I'd do it again in a heartbeat. It's that old theme – "the things we do for love".'

In the silence, two gulls cried and flapped overhead. Inappropriately, the rhyme about magpies flooded into Thea's head . . . *one for sorrow and two for joy.* Maybe it worked with seagulls too. 'You love me?' she whispered.

His brow cleared and the tiniest of smiles glowed in his eyes. 'Oh, aye. Did I not mention that?' He slid even closer on the bench. 'Or can I just show you?'

Thea must have nodded because then she was in his arms and meeting his mouth with hers, pulling him close and kissing him so thoroughly that her body all but burst into flames. She wanted the kiss never to stop, in case she discovered a fly in what promised to be ointment sweeter than any rose in Rothach's garden.

So the kiss went on and on, hot velvet and what felt like the sparkles from a magic wand.

Until her phone rang.

Against her mouth, Dev groaned a protest.

'Ezz's ringtone,' she mumbled, and broke off to yank the handset from her pocket, fumbling because her hormones were running laps of her heart. 'What?' she demanded impatiently.

Ezz sounded anxious. 'Are you OK? It's like . . . quite a long lunch hour. More like two.'

'Oh.' Thea checked the time and her cheeks flamed. 'I, um . . . I've been talking to Dev. I'll make the time up.' He gave her an 'is that what you call talking?' look.

'Ah. Shall I bugger off?' Suddenly, Ezz sounded as if she was trying not to laugh. 'Say hello to Deveron for me.'

Thea stuffed her phone away. 'Ezz asked if you're staying. You could have your old job back until October, which would give you time to find something else. Or are you going home to Dumfries?' She supposed there were gardens there, but none of them would be a patch on Rothach.

He pulled her into his lap and nuzzled her neck. 'That

wasn't what Ezz said. I could hear her side of the conversation and she said, "Say hello to Deveron for me".'

'Same thing,' Thea said, letting her head tilt back with a sigh.

His hands slid up inside the back of her top and ran lightly over her bare skin. 'Well,' he said equably. 'If *you're* asking if I'll stay, the answer's a great big yes. I love Skye. I love you even more.'

Thea felt tears start in her eyes as she gazed into his dear, smiling face, his lips moist from her kisses, his eyes crinkling at the corners. She choked out, 'I don't think it's possible to be happier than I am now.'

He brushed a wisp of her hair from her face. 'Aye, it is,' he predicted confidently. 'What about if I told you I fixed Fredek so he never bothers you in any way, ever again? Would you mind me taking your life into my hands that wee bit?' He demonstrated the size of a 'wee bit' by showing her a millimetre gap between his thumb and finger.

Shock jolted through her. 'Well . . . I suppose it would depend on how,' she said cautiously.

'I did him a favour.' He threw back his head and laughed when she gave him a disbelieving look. 'I did,' he insisted. 'In the morning, before his moment in the spotlight, I asked around until I found the scout for the cruise circuit he wants to get onto. I bigged Fredek up as a special-interest lecturer – creative, educational, contemporary and all that crap – and gave her the nod that his keynote speech would be unexpected and have the audience riveted. I set up a meeting between them for after. Then . . .' He twinkled at her wickedly, pausing to drop several kisses on her lips.

'I told Fredek he had to promise to forget you ever existed – both on social media and in real life – before I let him in on the secret of who she was and made the introduction. He almost wet his pants in eagerness to agree.'

'Wow,' Thea breathed. 'You're crafty.'

He shrugged modestly. 'I prefer the term "thorough". I researched what she was likely to want and showed him in that light.' He sobered, gazing deep into her eyes. 'I don't think he'll go back on it. He'd probably been embarrassed into giving you a wide berth anyway. I just gave him cause to. He's all over social media this morning boasting that he's about to sign up to the cruise circuit.'

She lifted her hands to cup his face, feeling his stubble prickle. 'I'd normally say I don't need anyone to fight my battles for me, but thank you for making the most of an opportunity. You could sell snow to penguins.'

He didn't return her smile. 'All I want is to sell myself to you.'

Slowly, she slid her fingers up into his hair and pulled his head down to hers. 'Sold.'

Chapter Twenty-Eight

One week later

Thea's joy in living peacefully amongst the wild scenery of Skye was entirely restored – not least because Deveron was spending every night in her bed, and every evening with her and Daisy. Perhaps she should have felt her style cramped by the continued presence of Ynez, who had stretched her visit and was still occupying Thistledome's spare room, but instead she felt only content. It was a long time since she'd come home to find a mother with a nourishing meal ready for her.

That this was a different mother didn't matter. That she was enjoying Ynez's company didn't make her love Maxie any less.

Deveron was enjoying Ynez taking charge of the evening meal, too. 'Smells good,' he said now, taking the lid off a large iron pan to sniff mightily.

Ynez looked at him severely. 'Close it, please. We need the steam to make the lamb tender.' Ynez, hair styled casually and without make-up, looked lovely and natural.

Thea could imagine looking something like that in twenty-odd years.

Before Thea could do more than laugh at Dev's pretended chagrin, Daisy scampered up the hall. 'Arf, arf.'

A second later, the door knocker clattered. 'Her hearing's amazing,' Thea observed, following up the hall but pausing, hand on the door, to say gently, 'Quiet, Daisy. Not every visitor needs to be challenged.' Thea opened the door to find in the porch a man in dark trousers and a pale yellow short-sleeved shirt, looking like a businessman on holiday. A playful breeze swept up from the sound and ruffled his silver hair.

With a shock, Thea recognised him from their brief meeting in the hotel in Quimper, when he'd passed on Ynez's notebook, which Thea had taken reluctantly. 'Jean-Jacques?' she breathed.

'Arf,' said Daisy experimentally, as if ready in case Thea wanted her to see him off.

'Althéa,' Jean-Jacques answered with a cheerful wave, as if there was nothing odd about him turning up on the Isle of Skye.

Thea felt wrong-footed as she surveyed the man Ynez referred to as 'my lover' and with whom she had long, daily phone conversations. 'Have you come to take Ynez home?'

Jean-Jacques smiled, but there was a hesitant light in his eye. 'Do you wish it?'

'Not yet,' Thea countered swiftly. Thea wasn't ready for Ynez to return to her own life. They were still discovering their similarities and differences. Enjoying each other, after four decades of thinking they'd never meet again.

'I missed her, and I had business in Glasgow, so I hired a car,' Jean-Jacques explained, when Thea made no move to invite him in.

363

Then Ynez emerged from the kitchen, one of Thea's tea towels tucked in the waistband of her shorts as an apron. 'Deveron is stealing my hummus,' she complained. Then her hands flew to her cheeks. '*Jean-Jacques.*' Her face was a picture of astonishment. 'Oh, Jean-Jacques.' There followed a stream of French, high-pitched and glad on the part of Ynez and rumbling, but just as glad, from Jean-Jacques, as he enfolded Ynez's short figure in his arms. Thea, realising her presence was not required, took Daisy into the kitchen.

'It's Jean-Jacques,' she told Deveron. 'I've come in here to give them privacy.'

'Which gives us privacy, too.' Deveron slipped his arms about Thea. 'I've been wanting to kiss you all day.' So, when her mother and Jean-Jacques entered, it was to find Thea pink in the face from receiving a whole day's kisses in half a minute.

Ynez looked just as pink and pleased. 'Luckily, I have prepared salad along with lamb ragout, which is easily shared four ways instead of three. Jean-Jacques has arrived by surprise.'

'So, I see,' Thea murmured. 'Well, he looks relaxed and happy, so I don't think he can be bringing bad news about the restaurant burning down while you're away.'

'He is just happy to see me,' Ynez said, and Thea wondered whether she and Deveron would still be happy to see each other when they were in their sixties.

Deciding that this might be a good opportunity to learn more about Jean-Jacques, who she realised would be her stepfather if he and Ynez ever married, she said, 'It's lovely to see you again, Jean-Jacques. Tell me what brought you to Scotland.'

Jean-Jacques waved his hand vaguely, as if it wasn't

364

an interesting subject. 'I have a little property – mainly commercial.'

Dev chimed in, sounding surprised. 'In Glasgow?'

Ynez began setting out plates. 'He has developed shopping malls in several European countries.'

'Blimey,' said Thea, trying to imagine that kind of career. It seemed a long way from gardening on a Scottish island – and even from Ynez's ownership of what appeared to be a successful restaurant in a good area of Brittany. 'But you're not building one of your malls on Skye?' The very idea of a vast box of a building amongst the gorse and heather sent her cold. And what would he make of a simple supper in her thistle-purple cottage in a far-from-manicured village clinging to the hillside above the sound?

Jean-Jacques grinned as he let Ynez usher him to a place at the table. 'No. We do need big spaces, but those that are close to many people.'

Relieved, she filled a water jug and added a basket of bread to the table before taking her own seat. Deveron immediately rested his knee against hers while Ynez ladled ragout onto each plate.

The conversation ranged from Ynez enjoying exploring Skye and being with 'Althéa', to Jean-Jacques' journey, to Thea and Deveron's work at Rothach Hall. At length, Jean-Jacques helped himself to a piece of bread. 'Your cottage is delightful, Thea.' He turned to Ynez. 'I thought I might buy a Scottish cottage. Would you like one?' He waved the bread. 'Like this one?'

Thea spilled salad from her side plate. 'Here in Rothach?'

Jean-Jacques dipped his bread in the ragout sauce as if a Frenchman buying a cottage in Scotland was unremarkable. 'Perhaps on the mainland. Close enough to visit you,

Althéa, but nearer to an airport.' He turned his gentle smile on Ynez. 'I am ready to take longer breaks from work, now, to have a second home for long holidays. And perhaps you? Virginie looks after Côté Rivière very well.'

Then Ynez was wreathed in smiles. '*Mais, oui.* And Thea and Deveron, they can help us look for the cottage.' Then her face fell. She turned and grasped Thea's shoulder, hand warm and face wrinkled apprehensively. 'But will you like me to be nearer, sometimes? I intended to ask you to return to Quimper in a few months, and stay in my apartment, but I do not want to make you feel obliged.'

Thea's heart, a poor pummelled thing lately, went all soft and fuzzy. *Her mother wanted her.* 'I'd love it,' she choked. 'Either. Both.'

Ynez's eyes grew misty. 'I am so glad,' she said huskily, and yanked Thea into a long, hard hug. 'And where will we buy our cottage?'

She looked expectant that Thea would have the answer to this question but Thea only managed, 'Um . . .'

Dev, with his broader familiarity with Scotland, rescued her. 'Maybe you'd like to look at the Fort William, Lochyside, Banavie area. It's en route from Glasgow Airport to Skye, and very pretty.'

And then Thea, filling up with tears at the thought, found she couldn't speak.

Deveron and Ynez each put one arm around her, making a Thea sandwich, while Jean-Jacques topped up her water and pressed the glass into her hand. Finally, Thea managed a husky, 'I'm so happy.'

It was a couple of hours later when Jean-Jacques, smothering a yawn, addressed Thea. 'I hope you do not mind that I have booked a hotel room for us. I will not enjoy two people in a small bed.'

366

'Of course,' Thea murmured, but conscious of a sinking sensation. Just when she was getting to know Ynez.

Ynez pouted. 'I am not ready to leave my daughter.'

Jean-Jacques patted her hand. 'Only to sleep, sweetness. The hotel is nearby, in Broadford. You will see Althéa tomorrow, in the evening, perhaps. During the day, we will look online at Scottish cottages.'

Instantly, Ynez cheered up. 'Althéa, will you help me pack?'

Later, it was as the Skye twilight was falling and a faint moon rising over the bay that Jean-Jacques drove the silver car out of Loch View, vanishing down the slope of Balgown.

Thea slipped her arms around Deveron. 'After being so uncertain I wanted to find her, now I'm going to miss her when she's back in France. It's great that she and Jean-Jacque plan to make nice long visits to Scotland.'

Dev's stubble brushed her forehead as he kissed her. 'And also great that we have Thistledome to ourselves tonight?'

She grinned. 'Definitely.' She lifted her hand to caress his cheek, his soft but prickly stubble and the warm smooth skin beneath. 'I'm so happy, Dev. All the rubbish stuff's in the past and I like the mother I've found. And most of all, I love you. It's as if my heart's not big enough for everything I feel.'

Seriously, he replied, 'Your heart's big enough for anything. And I want to fill up all the parts that don't belong to Ynez, Esmerelda, Valentina and your nephew Barnaby. Or Daisy,' he added, as Daisy gave a little bark into the gathering gloom as if to remind them that she deserved a mention.

Happiness bubbled in Thea's chest, as if her heart was, indeed, rearranging its contents to get as much of Deveron in there as possible. 'When I went up to help Ynez pack what she has here, she wrote me a note. Well, more of one last page for her journal.' She giggled. 'I think she might write "one last page" whenever she has advice to impart.' She felt in her pocket and brought out the folded sheet of thin pink paper, remembering Ynez's expression, half joking, half fierce, as she'd written it and pushed it into Thea's hand.

She settled more closely into the circle of Dev's arms, as the moon sailed higher and the stars began to peep at the Isle of Skye.

'*Dear Althéa,*' she read aloud, not even stumbling over the words.

'*Deveron is a very, very good man. KEEP HIM. Never swap him for a bad man, no matter how exciting a bad man might seem. Don't break any more laws (learn from my mistakes) and you will be very, very happy.*'

Dev burst out laughing, his breath hot on her skin. 'Your mother's wise.' Then, apologetically: 'I'm not sure I lived up to the title of "very, very good man" before, but I will in future.'

She pressed her lips to the skin of his neck. 'I haven't been an entirely good woman. But I'll be law-abiding from now on.'

'Aye, that sounds good,' he said contentedly.

It might not yet be clear what Deveron would do when winter came and his time as a seasonal gardener was up, but it wouldn't take him away from Thea. She knew that he, like her, was now tied to the Isle of Skye, and Rothach.

And, anyway, they still had the last of summer to enjoy.

She took his hand, and they turned their backs on the bobbing lights from boats moored on the sheltered waters of the Sound of Sleat, beckoned Daisy, and stepped into the welcoming interior of Thistledome together.

Loved

Under a Summer Skye?

Then get ready for the next two books in the Skye Sisters trilogy.

A Skye Filled with Stars – **October 2024**
Over the Sea to Skye – **May 2025**

Available to pre-order now

Grab your sun hat, a cool glass of wine, and escape with these gloriously uplifting summer reads . . .

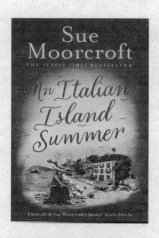
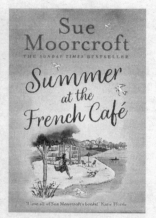
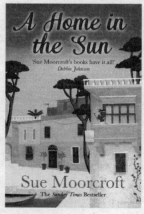

Dive into the summer holiday that you'll never want to end . . .

Curl up with these feel-good
festive romances . . .

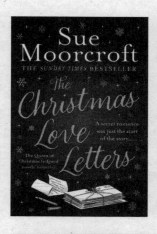

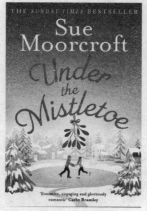

More heartwarming stories of love, friendship and Christmas magic!